LIBRARY OF SOVIET LITERATURE

Alexei Tolstoi

THE GARIN DEATH RAY

University Press of the Pacific
Honolulu, Hawaii

The Garin Death Ray

by
Alexei Tolstoi

ISBN 0-89875-271-X

Translated from the Russian by George Hanna
Designed by Yevgeny Rakuzin

Reprinted from the Original edition

University Press of the Pacific
Honolulu, Hawaii
http://www.universitypressofthepacific.com

1

That season the entire Paris business world assembled
for lunch at the Hotel Majestic. Men of all nations were to
be met there, with the exception of the French. Business
talks were conducted between courses and contracts were
signed to the accompaniment of orchestral music, the popping of corks and the chattering of women.

A tall, grey-headed, clean-shaven man, a relic of France's heroic past, paced the priceless carpets of the hotel's magnificent hall with its gleaming plate-glass revolving doors. He was dressed in a loose-fitting, black frock-coat, silk stockings and patent-leather shoes with buckles, and wore a silver chain of office on his chest. This was the chief commissionaire, the personification of the company that operated the Majestic.

His rheumatic hands clasped behind his back, he came to a halt in front of the glass partition behind which the guests were lunching amidst palms and blossoming trees in green tubs. He looked for all the world like a biologist studying plant and insect life through the glass wall of an aquarium.

The women looked lovely, there was no denying it. The young ones were seductive in their youth, in the flash of their eyes—the Anglo-Saxon blue, the French dark violet, the South American black as night. The elder women wore toilets that served as a piquant sauce to their fading beauty.

As far as women were concerned all was well. The chief commissionaire, however, could not say the same about the men seated in the restaurant.

From what weed-bed had these fellows emerged in the post-war years—fat, short of stature, with beringed hairy fingers and flushed cheeks that defied the razor?

From morning to night they busied themselves with the consumption of all manner of drinks. Their hairy fingers spun money out of the air, money, money, money.... In the majority of cases they came from America, that accursed country where people waded up to their knees in gold and were going to buy up the good old world at a bargain price.

A long, suave Rolls Royce with a mahogany-panelled body glided noiselessly up to the hotel entrance. The commissionaire, his chain rattling, hurried to the revolving doors.

The first to enter was a man of medium stature with a pale, sallow face, a short, trimmed black beard, and a fleshy nose with distended nostrils. He wore a long, sack-like coat and a bowler hat tilted over his eyes.

The man stood still, disdainfully awaiting his companion; she had stopped to talk to a young man who had darted out to meet their car from behind a column of the hotel portico. With a nod of her head she passed through the revolving doors. This was the famous Zoë Montrose, one of the smartest women in Paris. She wore a white woollen costume, the sleeves trimmed with black monkey fur from wrist to elbow. Her diminutive felt hat was the creation of the great Collot. Her movements were confident and negligent. She was tall, svelte, handsome, with a long neck, a somewhat large mouth and a nose very slightly turned-up. Her bluish-grey eyes gave the impression of both coldness and passion.

"Are we going to lunch, Rolling?" she asked the man in the bowler hat.

"Not yet. I'll talk to him before lunch."

Zoë Montrose smiled, condescendingly excusing the sharp tone in which he answered her. The young man who had spoken to Zoë at the car slipped through the revolving doors. His old, worn overcoat was unbuttoned and he carried a stick and soft felt hat in his hand. His excited face was sprinkled with freckles and the thin, stiff moustache looked as if it were glued in place. He apparently intended shaking hands but Rolling, keeping his in his overcoat pockets, spoke to him in still sharper tones.

"You are a quarter of an hour late, Semyonov."

"I was detained.... On our business.... I'm terribly sorry.... Everything has been arranged.... They agree.... Tomorrow they can leave for Warsaw...."

"If you shout at the top of your voice like that you'll be thrown out of the hotel," said Rolling, staring at him with dull eyes that boded no good.

"Excuse me, I'll whisper.... Everything is ready in Warsaw, passports, clothing, weapons, and so on. Early in April they will cross the frontier...."

"Mademoiselle Montrose and I are going to lunch now," said Rolling. "You will go to these gentlemen and tell them that I wish to see them today a little after four. And tell them that if they think they can double-cross me, I'll hand them over to the police...."

This conversation took place at the beginning of March in the year 192....

3

At dawn a rowing-boat pulled into the bank near the landing-stage of the rowing school on the River Krestovka in Leningrad.

Two men got out and there at the water's edge talked for a few minutes—actually only one of them spoke, brusquely and imperatively, while the other gazed at the swollen waters of the calm, dark river. The spring dawn broke through the blue of night away beyond the thickets on Krestovsky Island.

Then the two of them bent over the boat and the flame of a match lit up their faces. They lifted some bundles from the bottom and the one who had not spoken took them and disappeared into the forest while the one who had done the talking jumped into the boat, pushed off from the bank and rowed away with a creak of rowlocks. The silhouette of the rower passed through a streak of dawn-lighted water and disappeared into the shadow of the opposite bank. A tiny wave splashed against the landing-stage.

Tarashkin, stroke oar of the Spartak racing gig, was on duty that night at the club's boathouse. Tarashkin was young and it was spring, so he did not thoughtlessly waste the swift-flying hours of his life in sleep, but sat on the landing-stage over the dreamy water, his arms clasping his knees.

There was plenty to think about in the silence of the night. For two years in succession those damned Muscovites, who did not know even the smell of real water, had defeated the Leningrad Rowing School in the singles, fours, and eights. And that was humiliating.

A sportsman, however, knows that defeat leads to victory. That was one thing and then there was the fascination of the spring sunrise filled with the pungent odour of grass and wet wood that gave Tarashkin the confidence essential to successful training in preparation for the grand regatta in June.

Sitting on the landing-stage, Tarashkin had seen the boat draw up and, later, leave the river-bank. In general, Tarashkin had an imperturbable kind of mind, but on this occasion there was something that struck him as strange: the two men who came in the boat were as like each other as two peas in a pod. They were the same height, were dressed in similar wide overcoats and soft felt hats worn low on the forehead, and both had pointed beards.

But then, after all, it wasn't his headache, there was nothing in the laws of the Republic forbidding a man to go about with his double, by day or by night, on land or on water. Tarashkin would probably have forgotten all about the men with the pointed beards if it had not been for what occurred that same morning in a half-ruined, boarded-up country cottage standing in a birch grove near the rowing school.

11

When the sun appeared out of the rosy dawn over the wooded islands, Tarashkin flexed his muscles and set out to tidy up the boathouse yard. It had just turned five when the wicket-gate opened and Vasily Vitalyevich Shelga appeared wheeling his bicycle down the damp path.

Shelga was a well-trained athlete, muscular and light, of average height, with a strong neck, swift, calm and cautious. He served in the C.I.D. and rowing was part of his general training.

"Hallo, Tarashkin. How's things? Everything all right?" he asked, leaning his bicycle against the porch. "I've come to give you a hand.... There's an awful lot of rubbish here."

He pulled off his uniform blouse, rolled up the sleeves on wiry, muscular arms and set about clearing up the wood chips and other rubbish left over from the repair of the landing-stage.

"The fellows from the factory are coming today, we'll fix things in one evening," said Tarashkin. "By the way, are you going to put your name down for the sixer team?"

"I really don't know," answered Shelga, rolling a barrel of tar. "On the one hand I'd like to help beat the Muscovites but on the other hand I'm afraid I shan't be attending training very punctually. There's a funny sort of a job cropped up."

"What is it, gangsters again?"

"Look a bit higher. Crime on an international scale."

"That's a pity. You'd have had a good time with us."

Shelga went out on to the landing-stage, watched for a moment the patches of sunlight dancing on the water, knocked on the boom with his broom handle and called to Tarashkin in a low voice:

"Do you know all the people who live in the summer bungalows around here?"

"There are a few who live here all the winter."

"Did anybody come to one of them in the middle of March?"

Tarashkin squinted at the sunny river and with the toes of one foot scratched the other.

"There's a boarded-up cottage in that grove over there," he said. "About four weeks ago I remember seeing smoke coming from the chimney. We thought at the time that either some homeless kids or some bandit gang had got in there."

"Have you seen anybody from that house?"

"Just a minute, Vasily Vitalyevich. Why, I must have seen them today."

Tarashkin told him then about the two men whose boat had visited the swampy river-bank at dawn.

Shelga kept nodding and muttering, "Yes, yes," and his sharp eyes narrowed to tiny slits.

"Come and show me that house," he said, touching the revolver holster that hung at his side.

5

The house hidden amongst the stunted birch-trees seemed uninhabited—the wooden porch had rotted and the windows were fastened with boards nailed across the shutters. The attic windows were broken, the walls were moss-grown below the remnants of the gutter spouts and under the windows there was a growth of goosefoot.

"You're right. There's somebody living there," said Shelga, examining the house from the cover of the trees. Then he walked cautiously round the house. "Somebody has been here today.... But why the hell did they have to climb in through the window? Tarashkin, come here, something looks fishy here."

He ran over to the porch; here there were footprints.

To the left of the porch a shutter hung down, one of its hinges freshly broken. The window had been opened inwards. There were more footprints in the damp sand under the window, big marks made, apparently, by a heavy man, and others, small and narrow, with the toes turned inwards.

"The footprints on the porch were made by different boots," said Shelga.

He looked in at the window, whistled softly and called out, "Hi, you in there, your window's open, something may be stolen." There was no answer. An unpleasant, sweetish odour drifted out of the half-dark room.

Shelga called again in a louder voice, climbed on to the window-sill, drew his revolver, and jumped lightly into the room. Tarashkin jumped in after him.

The first room was empty, the floor littered with broken brick, plaster, and scraps of newspaper. A half-open door led to the kitchen. On the kitchen stove, under a rusty cowl, on tables and stools stood a number of primus-stoves, porcelain crucibles, glass and metal retorts, jars and zinc boxes. One of the primus-stoves was still hissing as the last of the kerosene burned out.

Shelga again shouted, "Hi, mister!" He shook his head and cautiously opened the door leading into a room whose semi-darkness was cut by narrow strips of bright sunlight penetrating through cracks in the shutters.

"Here he is," said Shelga.

At the other end of the room a fully-dressed man lay on his back on an iron bed. His arms were pulled over his head and tied by the wrists to the bed rails. His legs were bound with a rope. His jacket and shirt were torn across the breast. The head was thrown back in an unnatural pose, the pointed beard sticking up.

"So that's what they did to him," said Shelga examining the dagger that had been driven in to the hilt under the left nipple. "They tortured him.... Look at this...."

"Vasily Vitalyevich, that's the man that came in the boat. It can't be more than an hour and a half since they killed him."

"You stay here on guard, don't touch anything and don't let anybody in, d'you get that, Tarashkin?"

A few minutes later Shelga was speaking from the club telephone.

"Send men to the station.... Check up on all passengers.... Send others to all the hotels and check up on everybody who returned between six and eight this morning. And send a man with a dog to me."

6

While he was waiting for the police-dog to arrive Shelga made a careful examination of the cottage, beginning with the attic.

The whole place was littered with rubbish, broken glass, scraps of wall-paper, and rusty tins. The windows were covered with cobwebs, in the corners there were mildew and toadstools. Apparently, the cottage had not been inhabited since 1918. Only the kitchen and the room with the iron bedstead showed signs of habitation. There was not even a suggestion of any sort of comfort and no remains of food with the exception of a roll and a piece of breakfast sausage in the pocket of the murdered man.

People did not live here, they came to the house in order to do something that had to be kept secret. This was the first conclusion that Shelga came to after his inspection of the building. The state of the kitchen showed that somebody had been working here with chemicals. An examination of the piles of ashes on the stove under the cowl and of some booklets with turned up corners revealed that the dead man had been engaged in nothing more serious than ordinary pyrotechnics.

Such a conclusion brought Shelga to a dead end. He made another search of the dead man's clothing but found nothing new. Then he approached the problem from another angle.

The footprints under the window showed that there had been two murderers, that they had entered through the window at the almost certain risk of meeting with resistance since the man inside could not help hearing the noise made by their breaking open the shutters.

This could only mean that the murderers were determined either to obtain something important at all costs or kill the man in the house.

Further: if they had merely wanted to kill him they could have done it much more easily, by waylaying him on his way to the house, for example; secondly, the position of the body on the bed showed that he had been tortured before he had been stabbed. The murderers had been trying to find out something that the dead man had refused to tell them.

What could they have been trying to get out of him by torture? Money? It was hardly likely that a man who went to an abandoned house at night to indulge in exercises in pyrotechnics would have taken a large sum of money with him. It was more probable that the murderers wanted him to reveal some secret connected with his nocturnal work.

In this way Shelga's deductions led him to a fresh search of the kitchen. He moved some boxes away from the wall and discovered the trap-door of a cellar such as are often built directly under the kitchen in suburban summer bungalows. Tarashkin lit a candle end and, lying on his stomach, provided light for Shelga who made his way carefully down a slimy, half-rotten ladder into the damp cellar.

"Come down here with the candle," called Shelga out of the darkness, "this is where he had his real laboratory."

The cellar occupied the whole area under the house: along the brick walls stood rough plank tables on trestles, cylinders of gas, a small engine and dynamo, glass baths such as are used for electrolysis, mechanic's tools and everywhere, on all the tables, little heaps of ash....

"This is what he was doing here," muttered Shelga in some perplexity, examining the thick wooden beams and sheets of iron that stood leaning against the wall. The beams and the sheets of metal were all drilled through in many places, some of them were cut in two and the places where they were drilled or cut showed signs of burning or molten metal.

In an oak board standing on end the holes were no more than a tenth of a millimetre in diameter as though they had been made with a needle. In the middle of the board, in big letters, was the name, P. P. Garin. Shelga turned the board round and on the other side he saw the same letters in reverse; by some unknown means the inscription had been burnt through a three-inch oak board.

"What the hell!..." exclaimed Shelga. "That P. P. Garin wasn't engaged in pyrotechnics here."

"Vasily Vitalyevich, what's this?" asked Tarashkin, showing him a pyramid about an inch and a half high on a base of about an inch made of some compressed grey substance.

"Where did you find it?"

"There's a whole box full of them over there."

Shelga turned the pyramid this way and that, smelled it, placed it on the edge of the table, jabbed a burning match into the side of it and moved away to the far corner of the cellar. The match burned down, the pyramid burst into flame, giving off a blinding, bluish-white light. It burned for five minutes and some seconds, without smoke and almost odourless.

"It probably wouldn't be advisable to try a trick like that a second time," said Shelga. "That pyramid might have been a gas candle and we wouldn't have got out of here if it had been. But what have we found out? Let's go over the evidence. Firstly, the murder was not committed for revenge or robbery. Secondly, we know the name of the murdered man, P. P. Garin. And so far, that's all. Of course you would say it was Garin who went away in the boat. I don't think so. Garin himself wrote his name on that board. It's a matter of psychology. If I, for instance, were to invent such a tricky gadget I'd be so pleased with myself that I'd write my own name and not somebody else's. We know that the dead man worked in the laboratory; that can only mean one thing, he is the inventor, that is, Garin."

Shelga and Tarashkin climbed out of the cellar and smoked cigarettes on the porch while they waited for the detective to arrive with the dog.

7

A fat, reddish hand appeared over one of the counters of the Central Post-Office where foreign telegrams were accepted, a hand with a telegraph form held between trembling fingers.

The reception clerk looked at the hand for some seconds and at last realized what was wrong: "There's a finger missing, the little finger." Then he took the form.

"Semyonov, Marszalkowska, Warszawa. Mission half fulfilled. Engineer gone, documents not obtained. Awaiting instructions. Stas."

The clerk underlined the word "Warszawa" with a red pencil. Then he stood up and looked over the grille at the sender of the telegram. The latter proved to be a massive, middle-aged man with a yellow-grey, unhealthy-looking, puffed face and drooping yellow moustaches that covered his mouth. His eyes were hidden behind the narrow slits formed by his swollen eyelids. His shaven head was surmounted by a brown velvet cap.

18

"What's the matter?" he asked gruffly. "Take the telegram."

"The telegram is in code," said the clerk.

"What d'you mean, in code? Don't talk nonsense. It's a commercial telegram and you must accept it. I'll show you my papers, I belong to the Polish Consulate and shall hold you responsible for a minute's delay."

Four-Fingers grew angry, his cheeks shook, he barked rather than spoke, but the hand which lay on the counter was still trembling.

"You see," said the clerk, "although you assure me that your telegram is commercial, I'm equally sure that it's political and in code."

The clerk smiled. The yellow-faced gentleman fumed and raised his voice but did not notice a girl take his telegram to a table where sat Vasily Vitalyevich Shelga examining all outgoing telegrams dispatched that day.

He glanced at the form: "Marszalkowska, Warszawa," and then went round the partition into the public room, stood behind the infuriated sender and made a sign to the clerk. The latter sniffed, muttered something disparaging about the *panowe* and sat down to write out a receipt. The Pole snorted irascibly, shifting his weight from one foot to another so that his patent-leather shoes squeaked. Shelga looked closely at his big feet. Going to the door he indicated the Pole to the detective on duty.

"Follow him."

The morning before the dog had led them from the cottage in the birch grove to the River Krestovka where the murderers had apparently got into a boat. The day had brought nothing new. It seemed obvious that the criminals had gone to ground in Leningrad. The examination of telegrams had also been fruitless. Only that last telegram, addressed to Semyonov in Warsaw, might possess a certain interest.

The reception clerk gave the Pole his receipt and the

latter fumbled in his vest pocket for small change. At that moment a handsome, dark-eyed man with a pointed beard came up to the counter with a telegraph form in his hand and, waiting his turn, gazed with calm hostility at the expansive stomach of the bad-tempered Pole.

Then Shelga saw the man with the pointed beard suddenly straighten up: he had noticed the four-fingered hand and glanced at the Pole's face.

Their eyes met. The Pole's jaw dropped. His puffy eyelids opened wide. Terror filled his dull eyes. His face, like the skin of a monstrous chameleon, changed to a leaden hue.

It was only then that Shelga recognized the bearded man who confronted the Pole: it was the double of the man who had been murdered in the house in the birch grove on Krestovsky Island. . . .

The Pole gasped and made for the door with unbelievable speed. As the detective on duty there had only been ordered to follow him, he allowed him to pass through the door and slipped out after him.

The murdered man's double remained standing at the counter. His cold, dark-ringed eyes expressed nothing but surprise. He shrugged his shoulders and when the Pole had disappeared handed a telegram to the clerk.

"Poste Restante No. 555, Boulevard Batignolles, Paris. Begin analysis immediately, improve quality by fifty per cent, shall expect first consignment middle May. P. P."

"The telegram concerns scientific research on which my companion is engaged in Paris where he was sent by the Institute of Inorganic Chemistry," he said to the clerk. Leisurely he pulled a box of cigarettes out of his pocket, took one out, tapped it on the box and lit it with great care. Shelga spoke to him courteously.

"Might I have a couple of words with you."

The bearded man glanced at him, lowered his eyelids and answered with utmost politeness:

"Certainly."

"I am an agent of the Criminal Investigation Department," said Shelga, showing his card. "Perhaps we can find a more convenient place for a talk."

"Do you want to arrest me?"

"Not the slightest intention. I want to warn you that the Pole who just ran away wants to kill you, just as he killed Engineer Garin on Krestovsky Island yesterday."

The bearded man thought for a moment. He did not lose either his calm demeanour or his politeness.

"All right, then," he said, "let's go, I have a quarter of an hour to spare."

8

Out in the street the detective from the Post-Office came running up to Shelga, his face flushed and patchy.

"Comrade Shelga, he got away."

"Why did you let him go?"

"He had a car waiting, Comrade Shelga."

"Where's your motor-bike?"

"It's over there," said the detective pointing to his motor-cycle, some hundred steps from the Post-Office, "he ripped a tyre with a knife. I blew my whistle and he jumped into a car and drove off."

"Did you get the number of the car?"

"No."

"I'll report you for this."

"But I couldn't . . . the number had been plastered with mud."

"All right, go back to headquarters, I'll be there in twenty minutes."

Shelga caught up with the bearded man. For some minutes they walked side by side in silence. They turned into the Trade-Union Boulevard.

"You're astonishingly like the dead man," began Shelga.

"I've heard that many times already," the other answered readily. "My name is Pyankov-Pitkevich. I read about the murder in yesterday evening's paper. It's an awful business. I knew him very well, a competent fellow, excellent chemist. I've often been in his laboratory on Krestovsky Island. He was developing an important discovery connected with chemical warfare. Do you know anything about smoke candles?"

Shelga glanced sideways at him; instead of answering he asked a further question.

"Do you think Garin's murder is connected with Polish interests?"

"I don't think so. There are much deeper reasons for his murder. Information concerning Garin's work has found its way into the American press. Poland could be nothing more than an intermediary."

On the boulevard Shelga suggested sitting down. There was nobody about. Shelga took a number of Soviet and foreign newspaper cuttings from his briefcase and smoothed them out on his knee.

"You say that Garin was working on some chemical discovery and information concerning it had reached the foreign press. Some of the things here support your statement, but some things are not quite clear to me. Read this."

"In America some interest has been aroused by a report from Leningrad concerning the work of a Russian inventor. It is believed that his apparatus has greater destructive power than anything yet known."

Pitkevich read it and laughed.

"That's funny," he said. "I don't know. . . . I've never heard of anything like that. It can't be about Garin."

Shelga offered him another cutting.

"In connection with the U.S. Navy's forthcoming grand manoeuvres in Pacific waters the War Department has been asked whether information is available concerning weapons of great destructive power being manufactured in Soviet Russia."

Pitkevich shrugged his shoulders: "Nonsense!" and took a third cutting.

"Rolling, the multimillionaire chemical king, has left for Europe His trip is connected with cartelizing factories processing coal tar and salt products. In an interview given in Paris Rolling said that his monster chemical concern will bring peace to the countries of the Old World that are shaken by the forces of revolution. Rolling spoke very aggressively about the Soviet Union, where, it is rumoured, mysterious experiments are being made to transmit heat energy over long distances."

Pitkevich read it attentively. He sat for some time wrapped in thought, a frown on his face.

"Yes," he said at last, "it is quite possible that Garin's murder is in some way connected with this newspaper story."

"Do you go in for sport?" asked Shelga suddenly. He took Pitkevich's hand and turned it palm upwards. "I'm awfully keen on sport."

"Are you looking for blisters from rowing, Comrade Shelga? You see these two, that's proof that I'm a rotten oarsman and that two days ago I had to row a boat for about an hour and a half when I took Garin to Krestovsky Island.... Does that satisfy you?"

Shelga dropped his hand and laughed.

"You're pretty smart, Comrade Pitkevich. I wouldn't mind having a real tussle with you."

"I'm not the one to avoid it."

"Listen, Pitkevich, did you know that four-fingered Pole before?"

"You want to know why I was astonished when I saw his hand with a finger missing? You're very observant, Comrade Shelga. Yes, I was astonished, more than that, I was scared."

23

"Why?"

"That's what I'm not going to tell you."

Shelga glanced indifferently along the empty boulevard.

"He not only has a finger missing," continued Pitkevich, "he also has a ghastly scar across his chest. Garin did that in 1919. The man's name is Stas Tyklinski...."

"Did Garin disfigure him in the same way as he cut through three-inch boards?" asked Shelga.

Pitkevich turned his head sharply towards his interlocutor and for a brief space of time they gazed into each other's eyes: one of them calm and impenetrable, the other frank and merry.

"So you do intend to arrest me, Comrade Shelga?"

"No.... There's plenty of time for that."

"You're right. I know a lot. But you must understand that no sort of coercion will force me to tell you what I don't want to. I was not mixed up in the crime, you know that yourself. If you like we can play an open hand. The conditions are: after a good blow has been struck we meet for an open discussion. It will be like a game of chess. We're not allowed to kill one another. Incidentally, all the while we have been talking you have been in grave danger of your life—believe me, I'm not joking. If Stas Tyklinski had been sitting in your place, I'd have looked round, nobody in sight ... and would have walked away calmly to, let us say, Senate Square, and he would have been found stone dead on this bench with horrible patches all over his body. Once again, however, those tricks are not for you. Do you accept?"

"All right. I agree," said Shelga, his eyes flashing. "I'll make the first move, eh?"

"Naturally, if you had not caught me at the post-office I would never have suggested the match. As far as Four-Fingers is concerned I promise to help in your search for him. Wherever I chance to meet him I will immediately inform you by telephone or telegraph."

"Good. Now, Pitkevich, show me that gadget that you threatened me with. . . ."

Pitkevich shook his head and then smiled. "Have it your way, we're playing an open hand." And he cautiously pulled a flat box out of his side pocket. Inside the box lay a metal tube about the thickness of a finger.

"That is all there is, only if you press one end a glass capsule inside will be broken. . . ."

9

On his way back to the Criminal Investigation Department Shelga suddenly stopped as though he had run into a telegraph pole. "Huh!" he snorted and stamped his foot madly, "huh, what an actor! He's as smart as they make 'em."

Shelga realized that he had been completely fooled. He had stood within two paces of the murderer (of that he no longer had any doubt) and had not arrested him; he had spoken with a man who apparently knew all the ins and outs of the affair and that man had managed to tell him exactly nothing. That Pyankov-Pitkevich was in possession of some secret. . . . Shelga suddenly realized that this was a secret of state, even international importance. And he had had Pyankov-Pitkevich by the tail. . . . "One twist, damn him, and he slipped away!"

Shelga ran up the stairs to his office on the third floor. On his table lay a package wrapped in newspaper. In the deep window niche sat a fat, humble-looking individual in heavy jackboots. Pressing his cap to his stomach he bowed to Shelga.

"Babichev's the name, house superintendent," he said, breathing out the fumes of home-made vodka, "from house number 24 on Pushkarskaya Street, cooperative house."

"Did you bring this package?"

"Yes, I brought it. From apartment No. 13.... That's not in the main building, it's in the annexe. The occupant hasn't been seen for two days. Today I called the police, forced open the door, and made out an affidavit in accordance with the law." The house superintendent covered his mouth with his hand, his cheeks flushed red, his eyes rolled and filled with tears and the room was inundated with the odour of cheap spirit. "That packet I found extra, in the stove."

"What was the occupant's name?"

"Ivan Alexeyevich Savelyev."

Shelga opened the packet. Inside he found a photograph of Pyankov-Pitkevich, a comb, a pair of scissors and a bottle containing a dark liquid, hair dye, apparently.

"What was Savelyev's business?"

"Something scientific. When something went wrong with the ventilator the house committee asked him to fix it. 'I'd be glad to,' he said, 'only I'm a chemist!' "

"Was he often away from home at night?"

"At night? No, not as far as I know." The house superintendent covered his mouth again. "But he always left the house at daybreak, that's true. But night, no, I never noticed it and I never saw him drunk."

"Did he have visitors?"

"I never saw any."

Shelga phoned the police division in the Petrograd District and was informed that in the annexe of house No. 24 on Pushkarskaya Street, there lived Ivan Alexeyevich Savelyev, thirty-six years of age, chemical engineer. He had taken up residence on Pushkarskaya Street in February and had presented identification papers issued by the Tambov police.

Shelga sent a telegram to Tambov for further information and then went with the house superintendent to the

Fontanka Police Department where the body of the man murdered on Krestovsky Island lay on ice in the morgue. The house superintendent immediately identified him as the occupant of apartment No. 13.

10

At approximately the same time, the man who had called himself Pyankov-Pitkevich drove in a closed cab to an empty lot in the Petrograd District, paid off the cabby and continued his way on foot. He opened the gate in a fence, crossed the yard to the back entrance of a house and mounted the narrow staircase to the fifth floor. He opened the door with two keys, hung up his hat and coat on the only hook in the entrance hall, entered a room where the four windows were whitewashed half-way up, sat on a shabby sofa, and covered his face with his hands.

It was only here, in this solitary room (furnished with bookcases and physical apparatus), that he could at last give vent to that terrific nervous excitement, almost despair, that had held him in its grip for the last two days.

The hands pressed against his face trembled. He realized that he was still in mortal danger. He was surrounded on all sides. There was just one chance in his favour, ninety-nine against. "How careless, ach, how careless," he whispered.

By the exercise of great will power he got his nerves under control, jabbed his fist in the dirty pillow, lay down on his back, and closed his eyes.

He allowed his overburdened mind to rest from the terrible strain. A few minutes of deathlike stillness revived him. He got up, poured out a glass of Madeira, and drank it in one gulp. As the wave of warmth spread through his body he bagan walking up and down, calmly and unhurriedly, seeking the slightest possibility of salvation.

With great care he pulled up the old wall-paper where it had parted company with the wall near the wainscotting and drew out from behind it a number of drawings that he rolled up carefully into a tube. He took a few books out of the bookcase and together with the drawings and parts of some physical apparatus packed them in a suitcase. Listening carefully as he went, he took the suitcase down to one of the cellars used for storing firewood and hid it under a pile of rubbish. Returning to his own room, he took a revolver from the drawer of his desk, examined it, and stuffed it into his hip pocket.

It was a quarter to five. He lay down again and smoked one cigarette after another, throwing the butts into a corner of the room. "Of course they haven't found it!" he almost screamed, threw his legs off the sofa and again began pacing the room diagonally from corner to corner.

At dusk he drew on heavy, clumsy top-boots, donned a sail-cloth coat and went out.

11

The police officer on night duty in the 16th Division was called to the telephone at midnight. Somebody speaking in a great hurry said:

"Send a squad car immediately to Krestovsky Island, to the house where the man was murdered the day before yesterday."

The voice broke off suddenly. The police officer swore into the mouthpiece, checked up on the call, found that it came from the rowing school, and rang through there. The bell rang for a long time before a sleepy voice answered:

"What do you want?"

"Did somebody just ring up from there?"

"Yes," answered the voice with a yawn.

"Who rang up? Did you see him?"

"No, I didn't, there's something wrong with the electricity here. He said he had instructions from Comrade Shelga."

Half an hour later four policemen jumped out of a squad car outside the boarded-up cottage. The last glow of the setting sun made a crimson patch beyond the birch grove. Faint groans broke the silence. A man in a sheepskin coat lay face downwards near the back door of the house. They turned him over—it was the watchman. Beside him lay a handful of cotton-wool saturated with chloroform.

The back door was wide open, the lock smashed. When the police entered the house they heard a voice calling faintly from under the floor:

"The trap-door, clear the trap-door in the kitchen. . . ."

Tables, boxes, and heavy bags were piled up against the wall. They threw them aside and opened the cellar flap.

Out of the cellar scrambled Shelga, with wild staring eyes, all covered in dust and cobwebs.

"This way, quick!" he shouted, disappearing through a door. "Bring a light, quick!"

In the room with the iron bedstead, by the light of the policemen's flash-lights, they saw two revolvers (both had been fired) and a velvet cap lying on the floor; everywhere there were disgusting traces of vomit that gave off an acrid smell.

"Careful!" shouted Shelga. "Don't breathe, get out of here, that's deadly. . . ."

Backing out and pushing the policemen towards the door he looked with horror and repugnance at a little metal tube, no bigger than a man's finger, that lay on the floor.

Like all big businessmen, Chemical King Rolling engaged a special office in which to receive business visitors, where they were filtered by his secretary who established their degree of importance, read their thoughts, and answered all questions with exaggerated politeness. A typist converted into pearls of human speech all Rolling's ideas, which (if we take the arithmetical average for the year and multiply it by a financial equivalent) were valued at about fifty thousand dollars for each fraction of an idea expounded by the king of inorganic chemistry in the course of one second. The almond finger-nails of four typists hovered incessantly over the keys of four Underwoods. The messenger-boy appeared the instant he was called like the coagulated material of Rolling's will.

Rolling's office on the Boulevard Malesherbes was a gloomy establishment of serious aspect. The walls were hung with dark material, there was a thick dark carpet on the floor and the furniture was upholstered in dark leather. On the dark glass-topped tables lay collections of advertisements, reference books in brown morocco and the prospectuses of chemical plants. A few rusty gas shells and a trench mortar brought from the field of battle decorated the mantelpiece.

Behind the high, dark walnut doors Chemical King Rolling sat in his sanctuary amidst diagrams, cartograms and photographs. Filtered visitors passed softly across the thick carpet of the anteroom, took their seats on leather chairs and glanced nervously at the walnut portals. There, behind those doors, the very air in the king's office was of unbelievable value for it was saturated with thoughts that cost fifty thousand dollars a second.

What human heart could beat calmly when, amidst the reverent silence of the anteroom, the massive bronze door handle in the form of a claw holding a ball suddenly moved and through the walnut doors appeared a little man in a dark-grey jacket, with the world-famous beard covering his cheeks, a man agonizingly ungracious, almost a superman, with a yellow, unhealthy face that was reminiscent of his wold-renowned trade-mark: a yellow circle with four black bars. . . . Opening the door slightly the king would fix his eyes on the visitor and say with a strong American accent, *"Entrez."*

13

Holding his gold pencil with two fingers the secretary asked (with excessive politeness):

"Won't you be so good as to tell me your name?"

"General Subbotin, Russian émigré."

The general angrily straightened his shoulders and wiped his grey moustache with a crumpled handkerchief.

The secretary, smiling as though the conversation touched on the most pleasant and most friendly matters, made a rapid note on his pad and then asked with extreme caution:

"May I ask, Monsieur Subbotin, the object of the talk you wish to have with Mr. Rolling?"

"Something of extraordinary importance."

"Maybe if you were to tell me I could put it briefly to Mr. Rolling?"

"You see, my object is a very simple one, so to say . . . a plan. . . . Mutual advantage. . . ."

"The plan concerns chemical warfare against the Bolsheviks, I presume?" asked the secretary.

"Absolutely right. . . . I intend to propose to Mr. Rolling. . . ."

"I'm afraid," the secretary interjected with charming politeness and his pleasant face even registered pain, "I'm afraid that Mr. Rolling is somewhat overloaded with such plans. This week we have received a hundred

31

and twenty-four proposals for chemical warfare against the Bolsheviks from Russians alone. In our portfolio we have an excellent plan for a simultaneous chemical air attack on Kharkov, Moscow, and Petrograd. The author of the plan very cleverly places his forces on the territories of the buffer states—very, very interesting. The author even provides a precise estimate of the cost: six thousand eight hundred and fifty tons of mustard gas for the annihilation of the inhabitants of those three cities."

General Subbotin turned a deep red from a rush of blood to his head.

"Then what's the matter, mister what's your name," he interrupted the secretary. "My plan's just as good, but that's brilliant, too. You must act! You must go over from words to deeds.... What's the hold-up?"

"My dear general, the trouble is that Mr. Rolling does not yet see any return for his outlay."

"What d'you mean—return?"

"It would be no trouble at all for Mr. Rolling to drop six thousand eight hundred and fifty tons of mustard gas from aircraft, but a certain expenditure would be involved. War costs money, doesn't it? In the plans that have been presented to Mr. Rolling he finds nothing but expenditure. Unfortunately no equivalent, that is no profit, from acts of sabotage against the Bolsheviks is indicated."

"Why, it's as clear as daylight ... profits, colossal profits for anybody who will give Russia back her lawful rulers, a lawful, normal social system—mountains of gold are in store for such a man!" The general, like an eagle, peered from under his brows fixedly at the secretary. "Then I must also show the profit?"

"Yes, give the exact figures, credit on the left, debit on the right, a line and a balance with a plus sign that might interest Mr. Rolling."

"I see," the general snorted, pulled his dusty hat over his eyes and walked determinedly to the door.

The general had no sooner left than the voice of the errand-boy rose in protest at the door, followed by another voice expressing the desire that the devil might take the boy; Semyonov appeared in front of the secretary, his coat unbuttoned, his hat and stick in his hand, and a chewed cigar in the corner of his mouth.

"Good morning, old boy," he said hastily to the secretary, throwing his hat and stick on to the table, "let me straight in to the king, will you?"

The secretary's gold pencil hovered in the air.

"But Mr. Rolling is very busy today."

"Nonsense, old boy.... I've got a fellow waiting in my car who's just arrived from Warsaw.... Tell Rolling we've come about the Garin business."

The secretary's brows flew up and he immediately vanished behind the walnut doors. A moment later his head appeared round the door. "Monsieur Semyonov, come in please," he hissed in a caressing whisper. And he himself pressed the claw and ball door handle.

When Semyonov confronted the Chemical King he was not particularly flustered, firstly, because he was a boor by nature, and secondly, because at the present moment the king needed him more than he the king.

Rolling's green eyes pierced him through and through. Unperturbed, Semyonov sat down opposite him on the other side of the desk.

"Well?" asked Rolling.

"We've done the job."

"The drawings?"

"You see, Mr. Rolling, there has been a slight hitch...."

"I asked where the drawings are. I don't see them," said Rolling viciously, slapping the table lightly with his hand.

"Listen, Rolling, we agreed that I should not only bring you the drawings but also the apparatus itself.... I've done an awful lot.... I found people.... I sent them to Petrograd. They got into Garin's laboratory. They saw the work of the apparatus.... And then, the devil alone knows what happened.... In the first place there were two Garins."

"I assumed that from the very beginning," said Rolling contemptuously.

"One of them we managed to remove."

"You killed him?"

"If you like, something of that sort. In any case he died. That should not worry you; he was liquidated in Petrograd and was a Soviet subject, so it doesn't matter. But then his double appeared. We made a tremendous effort...."

"In a word," Rolling interrupted him, "the double or Garin himself is still alive and you haven't brought me either the drawings or the apparatus itself, despite the money I have spent."

"If you like I'll call Stas Tyklinski, he's sitting in the car outside; he took part in the whole business and can give you the details."

"I don't want to see any Tyklinski, I want the drawings and the apparatus.... I'm surprised at your boldness, to come here empty-handed...."

Rolling was convinced that the coldness of those words and the killing look he gave Semyonov when he stopped speaking would shrivel up that lousy Russian émigré, but Semyonov, nothing daunted, stuck his well-chewed cigar into his mouth and continued in his glib tones:

"If you don't want to see Tyklinski you needn't—it's no pleasure, anyway. There's another thing, Rolling, I need money—some twenty thousand francs. Will you give me a cheque or cash?"

34

For all his tremendous experience and his knowledge of people, Rolling had never before in his life come up against such insolence. Something like perspiration appeared on his fleshy nose, so great was the effort he made to keep his temper and not hurl the ink-pot in Semyonov's freckled face.... (And how many valuable seconds had been lost through this useless conversation.) Controlling himself he reached out towards the bell.

Semyonov followed the movement of his hand.

"The fact of the matter is, Mr. Rolling," he said, "Engineer Garin is at the moment in Paris."

15

Rolling jumped up—his nostrils dilated and a vein stood out sharply between his brows. He ran to the door and locked it, then came close up to Semyonov, took hold of the back of the chair with one hand and grasped the edge of the table with the other.

"You're lying," he said, bending close to Semyonov's face.

"Why should I lie to you.... This is how it was: Stas Tyklinski saw that double in the Petrograd post-office when he was handing in a telegram and noted the address: Paris, Boulevard Batignolles.... Yesterday Tyklinski arrived from Warsaw and we went straight to Boulevard Batignolles—there in a cafe, we ran into Garin—or maybe his double, the devil knows which."

Rolling's eyes examined Semyonov's freckled face closely. Then he straightened up, his breath coming in short gasps.

"You know quite well that we're not in Soviet Russia but in Paris—if you commit a crime here I shall not save you from the guillotine. But if you try to hoodwink me I'll crush you."

He went back to his place and with a look of aversion opened his cheque-book. "I won't give you twenty thousand, five's enough for you. ...." He wrote out the cheque, flicked it across the table to Semyonov with his fingernail and then—not for more than a second—placed his elbows on the desk and pressed his face into his hands.

16

It stands to reason that Zoë Montrose did not become the Chemical King's mistress by accident. It is only idiots and those who do not know the meaning of struggle and victory that put everything down to luck. "Lucky fellow," they say enviously and regard the successful one as something of a miracle. If he falls a thousand fools will tread him underfoot in ecstasy—the great goddess Fortune has rejected him.

There was not even a suggestion of chance—it was wits and will that brought Zoë into Rolling's bed. Her will had been tempered like steel by the events of 1919. Her wits were so sharp that she quite consciously maintained amongst her acquaintances the belief that she was under the special protection of the great goddess Fortune.

In the district where she lived (Rue de la Seine on the left bank of that river) the owners and customers of the general shops, grocer's, wine, coal, and other shops almost worshipped Zoë Montrose.

Her daytime car—a 24 h.p. black limousine, her touring car—a quasi-divine 80 h.p. Rolls Royce, her evening electric car—upholstered in silk, with silver handles and vases for flowers inside and especially her winning of a million and a half francs in the casino at Deauville, all served to arouse the adoration of the arrondissement.

Exercising great care and an excellent knowledge of the business, Zoë "invested" half of her winnings in the press.

From October (the opening of the Paris season) onwards the press kept the beautiful Montrose well to the fore. At first a petty-bourgeois newspaper published a scurrilous account of Zoë Montrose's ruined lovers. "This beautiful lady costs us too much!" exclaimed the newspaper. After that an influential radical newspaper made use of the story to rage about the *petit bourgeois* who sent to parliament shopkeepers and wine-sellers with an outlook that did not extend beyond their own parish. "What if Zoë Montrose has ruined a dozen foreigners," exclaimed this newspaper, "their money is in circulation in Paris, it increases our vital energy. Zoë Montrose is to us merely a symbol of healthy relations in life, a symbol of eternal movement where one falls and another rises."

Zoë Montrose's portrait and her biography were published in all the papers.

"Her late father sang in the Imperial Opera of St. Petersburg. At the age of eight charming little Zoë entered a ballet school. Just before the war she graduated the school and her début created a furore such as the Northern Metropolis had never before known. Then came the war and Zoë Montrose, her young heart filled with loving kindness, donned a grey uniform with a Red Cross on her breast and hurried to the battle line. She was to be found in the places of greatest danger, calmly bending over a wounded soldier amidst a hurricane of enemy shells. She was wounded, but the grace of her beautiful young body was not affected; she was taken to St. Petersburg where she made the acquaintance of a captain of the French Army. Revolutionary Russia betrayed the allies. Zoë Montrose's heart was broken by the Peace of Brest-Litovsk. Together with her friend, the French captain, she fled to the south and there, mounted on horseback, rifle in hand, she fought against the Bolsheviks like one of the angered Graces. Her friend died of typhus. French sailors brought her to Marseilles on a destroyer. Arriving in Paris she threw herself at the feet of the French President and begged him to allow her to become a French subject. She danced for the benefit of the unfortunate inhabitants of war-wrecked Champagne. She is to be found at all charity fêtes. She is a radiant star that has fallen on to the streets of Paris. . . ."

In essence the biography was true enough. In Paris she took a quick look round and plunged into life—always forward, always battling, always striving towards the most difficult and most valuable. She actually had ruined a dozen of the *nouveaux riches*, those stumpy young men with hairy, beringed fingers and flushed cheeks. Zoë was an expensive woman and they were broken.

She soon realized that young men of this class would not give her a reputation for chic in Paris. She took as her lover a fashionable journalist, betrayed him for a parliamentary deputy representing the bigger industrialists and then discovered that in the twenties of the twentieth century chemistry was the thing.

She engaged a secretary who made her daily reports of the progress of the chemical industry and kept her supplied with the necessary information. In this way she learned of the expected visit to Europe of Chemical King Rolling.

She immediately left for New York and there she purchased, body and soul, a reporter from one of the bigger newspapers; this resulted in the appearance of press reports of the arrival in New York of Europe's cleverest and most beautiful woman, a ballerina who showed a deep interest in the most fashionable of modern sciences, chemistry, and who had even abandoned such vulgar jewellery as diamonds for a necklace composed of little globes of fluorescent gas. These globes captured the imagination of the Americans.

When Rolling boarded a steamer leaving for France, on the tennis court on the upper deck there sat Zoë Montrose in a wicker chair placed between a broad-leafed

palm that rustled in the sea breeze and a flowering al-
mond-tree.

Rolling knew that she was the most fashionable woman
in Europe and, apart from that, he really liked her. He
proposed that she become his mistress. Zoë Montrose made
one condition—a written contract, a breach of which
would cost Rolling a million dollars.

Wireless messages from mid-ocean informed the world
of Rolling's new liaison and of the extraordinary contract.
The sensational news was received by the Eiffel Tower and
next day all Paris was talking of Zoë Montrose and the
Chemical King.

17

Rolling made no mistake in his selection of a mistress.

"My dear," said Zoë, while they were still on the
steamer, "it would be foolish for me to poke my nose into
your business. You'll soon see that I'm even more useful
as a secretary than a mistress. I'm not greatly interested
in women's nonsense. I'm ambitious. You're a great man
and I believe in you. You must win. Don't forget that I
have lived through a revolution, I've had typhus, I've
fought like a soldier and have done a thousand-mile trek
on horseback. All that cannot be forgotten. My heart has
been seared by hatred."

Rolling found her icy passion amusing. He touched
the tip of her nose with his finger.

"Baby," he said, "you've got too much temperament
for a businessman's secretary; you're crazy and in politics or in business you will always be a dilettante."

In Paris he began his negotiations for the cartelizing
of chemical plants. America was making big capital invest-
ments in the industries of the Old World. Rolling's agents
carefully bought up shares. In Paris he was known as the
"American Buffalo." And really he was a giant amongst

39

the European industrialists. He went straight ahead, smashing his way forward. His field of vision was narrow: he saw only one aim before him—the concentration of the chemical industries of the whole world in his own hands.

Zoë quickly studied his character and his fighting methods. She found out his strength and his weakness. He had a poor knowledge of politics and often talked nonsense about revolution and the Bolsheviks. Without his knowing it she gradually surrounded him with necessary and useful people. She connected him up with the newspaper world and herself guided his talks. She bought up little newspaper-men to whom he did not pay any attention, but they did him greater service than the big newspaper-men since they penetrated into every hole and corner, like mosquitoes.

When she "arranged" for one of the Right deputies to make a little speech in Parliament on the "necessity of maintaining close contact with the American chemical industry in the interests of the chemical defence of France," Rolling for the first time shook hands with her as he would have done with a man friend.

"O.K., I'll take you as my secretary on a salary of twenty-seven dollars a week."

Rolling believed in Zoë's usefulness and from then on began to tell her all his business secrets.

18

Zoë Montrose kept in touch with a number of Russian émigrés. One of them, Semyonov, was on her regular payroll. He was a chemical engineer who graduated during the war, was appointed ensign in the Russian Army, later became an officer of the White Army and in exile had performed all manner of petty commissions and finally sank as low as the sale of second-hand clothing to street women.

On Zoë's staff he headed her counter-intelligence department. He brought her Soviet newspapers and magazines and kept her up to date on everything, including gossip and rumour. He was punctual, quick-witted and not a bit fastidious.

One day Zoë showed Rolling a cutting from a Revel newspaper containing a report of an apparatus of tremendous destructive power now being built in Petrograd. Rolling smiled.

"Nonsense, that won't scare anybody. . . . You've got a much too vivid imagination. The Bolsheviks aren't capable of building anything."

Then Zoë invited Semyonov to lunch and he told them a strange story connected with that newspaper report.

". . . In 1919, in Petrograd, shortly before I got away, I met a friend in the street, a Pole by the name of Stas Tyklinski, we graduated the Technological Institute together. He had a sack on his back, his feet were bound up in pieces of carpet, and the figures chalked on his back showed that he had been standing in queues. In other words, everything as it should be. But he looked very cheerful and winked at me. I wondered what the matter was. 'I've got on the track of big money, oh, la-la, millions!' he said. 'No, not millions, hundreds of millions, gold, of course.' I naturally did not let him go but kept trying to get him to tell me about it, but he only laughed. With that we parted. A couple of weeks later I was on Vasilyevsky Island, where Tyklinski lived. I remembered his talk about millions and thought it would be a good idea to ask the millionaire for half a pound of sugar. So I went to his house. Tyklinski was lying in bed, feeling pretty bad. His chest and his hand were in bandages.

" 'Who did this to you?' I asked.

" 'Wait a bit,' he answered, 'with the Holy Virgin's help I'll get better—I'll kill him!'

" 'Who?'

" 'Garin.'

"Then he told me, hazily and rambling, of course, because he didn't want me to know the details, about an old acquaintance of his, Engineer Garin, who had proposed to Tyklinski that he prepare carbon candles for him for some apparatus of unusual destructive power. He offered Tyklinski a share in the profits to get him interested. He proposed that on the conclusion of their experiments they should fly to Sweden, patent the apparatus and then exploit it themselves.

"Tyklinski got busy making carbon pyramids. The problem was to get the maximum heat effect with the minimum volume. Garin kept the principle of the apparatus a secret but said it was so extraordinarily simple that any sort of hint would give away the secret. Tyklinski supplied him with his carbon pyramids but could not persuade Garin to show him the apparatus.

"Such mistrust infuriated Tyklinski and they often quarrelled. One day Tyklinski followed Garin to the place where he was making his experiments—a half-ruined house in one of the back streets of the Petersburg District. Tyklinski followed Garin into the house and for a long time wandered up and down staircases, through empty rooms with broken windows and at last heard a loud hissing noise, like that of escaping steam, coming from the cellar and at the same time noticed the familiar smell of burning pyramids.

"He made his way carefully into the cellar but stumbled over some broken bricks, fell noisily and, some thirty paces away, through an archway saw Garin's distorted face lit up by a smoky oil-lamp. 'Who's there, who's there?' Garin shouted wildly and at the same time a blinding ray of light, no thicker than a knitting needle, ran across the wall and cut across Tyklinski's chest and hand.

"Tyklinski regained consciousness at dawn, for a long time called for help and then crawled out of the cellar on all fours, bleeding profusely. Some passers-by picked him up and brought him home on a hand-cart. By the time he had recovered the war with Poland had begun and he had to get out of Petrograd."

This story made a tremendous impression on Zoë Montrose. Rolling smiled disparagingly: he believed only in the power of asphyxiating gases. Ironclads, fortresses, guns, huge armies—all these were, in his opinion, remnants of barbarism. Aeroplanes and chemicals were the only powerful weapons of war. As to some crazy apparatus from Petrograd—utter nonsense!

But Zoë was not to be put off. She sent Semyonov to Finland to collect more precise information concerning Garin. A White-guard officer engaged by Semyonov crossed the Russian frontier on skis, found Garin in Petrograd, talked with him and even proposed their working together. Garin behaved very warily. Apparently he knew that people abroad were watching him. As far as his apparatus was concerned he said that whoever owned it would be possessed of miraculous power. Experiments with a model had given brilliant results. He was only awaiting the completion of the work on the pyramidal candles.

It was a rainy Sunday evening in early spring and the lights from the windows and from countless street-lamps were reflected in the pavements of the Paris streets.

Wet motor-cars seemed to be running along black canals over an abyss of lights, wet umbrellas whirled and twisted, buffeting against each other. The rainy darkness was saturated with the musty damp of the boulevards, the smells of vegetable shops, the odour of petrol and of rich perfumes.

The rain poured down the slate roofs, the grilles of balconies and down the huge striped awnings over the cafés. The flaming advertisements of all manner of amusements flashed on and oft, whirled and flickered dully through the haze.

The little people, men and women from the shops and offices, amused themselves as best they could on Sundays. The big people, the serious businessmen, sat at home by the fireside. Sunday was the day of the mob, thrown to them to be devoured for their pleasure.

Zoë sat amidst numerous cushions on a wide divan, her feet tucked up under her. She was smoking and staring at the fire in the grate. Rolling, in evening dress, occupied a deep armchair, his feet on a footstool; like Zoë he was also smoking and studying the coals.

The firelight gave a fiery-red hue to the fleshy nose, bearded cheeks, half-closed eyelids and the slightly inflamed eyes of the master of the universe. He had abandoned himself to that period of inactivity so essential once a week to rest his brain and nerves.

Zoë stretched her beautiful bare arms out in front of her.

"Rolling," she said, "it is two hours since we lunched."

"Yes," he answered, "I also presume that the process of digestion is over."

Her limpid, almost dreamy eyes ran over his face. Softly and in serious tones she called him by his Christian name. He answered without stirring in his warm armchair:

"Yes, I'm listening to you, baby."

Permission to talk had been given. Zoë moved to the edge of the divan and clasped her knee.

"Tell me, Rolling, is there a very great danger of an explosion at a chemical works?"

"There is. The fourth derivative from coal, trotyl, is a very powerful explosive. The eighth derivate from coal, picric acid, is used to fill the armour-piercing shells of naval guns. There is a still more powerful explosive, tetryl."

"What is tetryl, Rolling?"

"The same coal. Benzene (C_6H_6) mixed with nitric acid (HNO_3) at a temperature of 80^0 C. gives us nitrobenzene which has the formula of $C_6H_5NO_2$. If we substitute 2 parts of hydrogen (H_2) for two parts of oxygen (O_2), that is if we begin slowly mixing iron filings with nitrobenzene at 80^0 C. and add a small amount of hydrochloric acid we get aniline ($C_6H_5NH_2$). Aniline, mixed with wood alcohol under a pressure of fifty atmospheres, will give dimethylaniline. Then we will dig a big hole, build an earth rampart round it, put a shed in the middle and there treat dimethylaniline with nitric acid. During the reaction we shall watch the thermometers through a telescope. The reaction of nitric acid with dimethylaniline will give us tetryl. That tetryl is the very devil himself: for some unknown reason it sometimes explodes during the reaction and reduces huge buildings to dust. Unfortunately we have to deal with this stuff; when it is treated with phosgene it gives a blue dyestuff—crystal violet. That stuff brings in good money. You asked me an amusing question.... Hm-m.... I thought you were better acquainted with chemistry. Hm-m.... In order to make, say, a tablet of pyramidon from coal tar so as to cure your headache we have to go through a number of stages.... On the way from coal to pyramidon or a bottle of perfume or some ordinary photographic chemical there are such devilish substances as trotyl and picric acid, such wonderful little things as brombenzylcyanide, chlorpicrin, diphenylchlorarsine and so on, that is, those very war gases that make men sneeze, weep, tear off their gas-masks, choke, vomit blood, break out in sores all over the body, rot away alive...."

Rolling was bored on that rainy Sunday evening and gladly plunged into a contemplation of the great future of chemistry.

"I believe (he waved his half-smoked cigar near his nose), I believe that the Lord God of Sabaoth created heaven and earth and all that therein is using only coal tar and kitchen salt. The Bible doesn't exactly say so but it is to be deduced. Whoever owns coal and salt is master of the world. The Germans started the war in 1914 only because nine-tenths of the chemical plants in the world belonged to Germany. The Germans understood the secret of coal and salt: they were the only enlightened nation of the day. They did not, however, foresee that we Americans could build Edgewood Arsenal in nine months. The Germans opened our eyes and we realized where we had to invest our money and now we, and not they, are going to dominate the world, because since the war we have the money and we have the chemicals. We'll turn Germany and other countries that know how to work (those who don't will die a natural death and we'll help them die) into a single gigantic factory.... The American flag will encircle the world round the equator and from pole to pole like the ribbon on a chocolate box...."

"Rolling, you're just asking for trouble," Zoë interrupted him, "*they'll* all turn communist.... The day will come when *they'll* say that *they* don't need you any longer, that *they* prefer to work for themselves.... Oh, I've already been through that horror.... They won't give you your millions back...."

"In that case I'll drown Europe in mustard gas, baby."

"It'll be too late, Rolling!" Zoë hugged her knees and leant forward. "Rolling, believe me, I've never given you bad advice.... I asked you whether there was a danger of explosion at a chemical works.... In the hands of the workers, revolutionaries, communists, in the hands of our enemies, there will be a weapon of tremendous power.... The workers will be able to blow up chemical plants, powder magazines, set fire to squadrons of aircraft, destroy supplies of gas—they will be able to destroy from a great distance everything that will explode or burn."

Rolling took his feet off the footstool, his reddish eyelids flickered and for a while he looked at the young woman.

"As far as I can understand you're again referring to. . . ."

"Yes, Rolling, yes, to Garin's apparatus. . . . Everything that has been said about it has escaped your attention. But I know how serious it is. . . . Semyonov has brought me a strange thing. He got it from Russia."

Zoë rang the bell. A footman entered. She ordered him to bring in a little pinewood box; in it lay a strip of steel about half an inch thick. Zoë took it out of the box and held it in the firelight. Slots, whorls, and holes were cut through the whole thickness of the steel with some very fine instrument and across it the words "Trial of strength . . . trial . . . Garin" were scribbled as though with a fine pen. Pieces of metal that formed the interior of some of the letters had fallen out. Rolling looked long at that strip of steel.

"It looks like a 'trial of the pen,' " he said softly, "it might have been written in soft dough with a needle."

"This was done during the test of a model of Garin's apparatus at a distance of thirty paces," said Zoë. "Semyonov maintains that Garin expects to build an apparatus that can easily cut through a dreadnought at a distance of twenty cable's lengths. . . . Excuse me, Rolling, but I insist, you must get hold of this terrible apparatus."

Not for nothing had Rolling passed through the school of life in America. To the last ounce he was trained for the fight.

Training, as everybody knows, evenly distributes work amongst the muscles and permits of the greatest possible strain. It was the same with Rolling when he started a fight; his fantasy began working first—it plunged into a dense thicket of enterprise and discovered there something worthy of attention. Stop. The work of his fantasy ceased and the brain took over. Common-sense came into its own, evaluated, compared, weighed, and reported: useful. Stop. The practical mind came into its own, calculated, considered, and struck a balance: credit balance. Stop. Will power came into its own, that terrific Rolling's will power, as strong as high-grade steel, and he, like a buffalo, with bloodshot eyes, smashed his way to the goal and attained it whatever it may have cost him and others.

This is approximately what was happening today. Rolling cast a glance into the unknown jungle and common-sense told him: Zoë is right. His practical mind told him the most profitable way would be to steal the drawings and the apparatus and liquidate Garin. And that would end it. Garin's fate was determined, credit was opened and will power took over. Rolling rose from his chair, stood with his back to the fire, and thrust out his chin.

"I shall expect Semyonov tomorrow at the Boulevard Malesherbes."

20

Since that evening seven weeks had passed. Garin's double had been murdered on Krestovsky Island. Semyonov had reappeared on the Boulevard Malesherbes without either drawings or apparatus. Rolling had almost smashed his head with an ink-pot. Garin, or his double, had been seen the day before in Paris.

The following day at one o'clock Zoë picked up Rolling at the Boulevard Malesherbes as usual. Rolling sat beside her in a closed limousine resting his chin on his walking-stick.

"Garin's in Paris," he muttered between his teeth.

Zoë sank back on the cushions and Rolling looked gloomily at her.

"Semyonov should long ago have been led to the guillotine," said Rolling. "He's slipshod, a common murderer, he's an insolent fool. I trusted him and found myself in a ridiculous situation. I suppose he'll drag me into some nasty business now...."

Rolling told Zoë about his conversation with Semyonov. They hadn't managed to steal the drawings and the apparatus because the hoodlums Semyonov had hired had not killed Garin but his double. The appearance of the double worried Rolling more than anything. He realized that his opponent was no fool. Either Garin had had warning of the attempt to be made on his life or he assumed that such an attempt was unavoidable and had covered his tracks leaving them a dummy. All this was very vague. The most incomprehensible thing of all was—what the hell was Garin doing in Paris?

The limousine moved slowly amongst many other cars along the Champs Elysées. The day was warm and damp, a delicate blue haze wreathed the winged horses and glass dome of the Grand Salon, the round roofs of the tall houses, the awnings over the windows, and the luxuriant crowns of the chestnuts.

Those occupying the cars—some lolling back, some with one foot on the other knee, some sucking the knobs of their canes—were in the majority of cases *nouveaux riches*, young men, not very tall, in soft spring hats and gaudy ties. They were on their way to lunch in the Bois de Boulogne accompanied by those pretty girls that Paris gladly supplies for the amusement of foreigners.

On the Place de l'Étoile a hired car in which sat Semyonov and a man with a fat, yellow face and dusty moustaches overtook Zoë Montrose's limousine. They were both leaning forward in something resembling frenzy, watching a little green car that wound its way across the Place to the entrance of the underground railway.

Semyonov pointed out the car to his chauffeur but it was difficult to penetrate the throng of traffic. At last they got through and at full speed tried to cut across in front of the little green car. The latter, however, had already stopped at the Metropolitaine entrance. A man of medium height, in a voluminous coat, jumped out of the car and disappeared below ground.

All this occurred in two or three minutes before the eyes of Rolling and Zoë. She called to her chauffeur to turn towards the Metropolitaine. They stopped almost simultaneously with Semyonov. Waving his cane, Semyonov ran to the limousine, pulled open the plate-glass door, and spoke in terrific excitement.

"That was Garin. Got away. Doesn't matter, though. I'll go to him at Rue Batignolles and propose an agreement. Rolling, we must come to an understanding: how much will you give to acquire the apparatus? And you needn't worry, I'll keep within the law. Incidentally allow me to introduce Stas Tyklinski. He's a very decent chap."

Without waiting for permission he called Tyklinski. The latter ran up to the luxurious limousine, pulled off his hat, bowed and kissed *Pani* Montrose's hand.

Rolling did not offer his hand to either of them but glared out of the depths of the limousine like a puma in a cage. To remain there in full view of all passers-by on the Place de l'Étoile was not wise. Zoë proposed driving to the left bank for lunch in the Restaurant Laperouse which would not be overcrowded at this time of the year.

21

Every minute Tyklinski kept bowing, smoothed his pendant moustaches, stared at Zoë Montrose with moist eyes, and ate with suppressed voracity. Rolling sat gloomily with his back to the window. Semyonov chattered away at his ease. Zoë seemed calm, she smiled charmingly and with her eyes indicated to the *maître d'hôtel* that he fill the guests' glasses more frequently. When the champagne was brought in she asked Tyklinski to tell his story.

He pulled his napkin from his collar.

"We did not even grudge our lives for *Pan* Rolling. We crossed the Soviet border near Sestroretsk."

"Who do you mean—we?" asked Rolling.

"I and my assistant, sir, a Russian from Warsaw, an officer of Balakhovich's army. A very cruel man. Damn him and all Russians, he gave me more trouble than help. My task was to find out where Garin was conducting his experiments. I went to the ruined house—the lady and gentleman, of course, know how the damned swine almost cut me in two with his apparatus. It was there in the cellar that I found the steel strip; Madame Zoë has got it and has evidence of the effort I made. Garin moved his experiments to another place. I did not sleep day or night, I wanted to justify the trust placed in me by Madame Zoë and Mr. Rolling. I chilled my lungs in the swamps of Krestovsky Island but I achieved my goal. I traced Garin. On the night of the 27th April my assistant and I got into his cottage, bound Garin to an iron bedstead and searched the place thoroughly. Not a thing. It was enough to drive you mad, there was no sign of the apparatus. And all the time I knew he had hidden it in that cottage. Then my assistant got a bit rough with Garin.... The lady and gentleman will understand that we were excited. I do not say that we acted on the instructions of Mr. Rolling. No, my assistant forgot himself...."

Rolling looked into his plate. Zoë's long fingers tapped rapidly on the table-cloth flashing their polished nails, emeralds, diamonds, and sapphires. Tyklinski was inspired as he gazed at that priceless hand.

"The lady and gentleman know how I met Garin at the post-office a day later. Mother of God, who would not be scared out of his wits coming face to face with a living corpse? And then the police came chasing after me. We were the victims of a trick, that accursed Garin had foisted another man on to us instead of himself. I decided to make another search of the cottage. There must have been a cellar there. That night I went there alone and put the watchman to sleep. I got in through the window. Let Mr. Rolling not misunderstand me. When Tyklinski risks his life, he risks it for an idea. I could very well have jumped back through the window when I heard such a banging and crashing that would make anybody's hair stand on end. Yes, Mr. Rolling, I realized then that the Lord guided you when you sent me to wrest that awful instrument out of the hands of the Russians, a weapon they could turn against the whole civilized world. That was an historical moment, *Pani* Zoë, I swear on the honour of a Polish nobleman. I threw myself like a wild beast into the kitchen, where the noise was going on. I saw Garin. He was piling up tables, sacks and boxes against the wall. When he saw me he seized the leather suitcase that I knew so well, the one in which he carried the model of his apparatus, and slipped into the next room. I drew my revolver and chased after him. He was already opening the window to jump out. I fired. With his suitcase in one hand and his revolver in the other he ran to the other end of the room, took cover behind the bed, and opened fire. It was a real duel, Madame Zoë. A bullet holed my cap. Suddenly he covered his nose and mouth with a rag of some sort and held out a little metal tube towards me—there was a shot, no louder than the popping of a champagne cork, and at that moment a thousand little claws clutched at my nose, eyes, throat, and chest, I began to sneeze and cough, my insides were turned inside out, and, excuse me, *Pani* Zoë, I vomited so badly that I rolled on the floor."

"Diphenylchlorarsine mixed with phosgene half and half—that's cheap enough, we use it in the bombs our police are armed with," said Rolling.

"You are right, sir, it was a gas bomb. Fortunately the draught drove the gas away quickly. I soon regained consciousness and managed to make my way home half-alive. I was poisoned, half-dead, detectives were seeking me all over the town, there was nothing left to do but run away from Leningrad, which I did with great difficulty and in great danger."

Tyklinski spread his arms and bowed his head, giving himself up to the mercy of his employer.

"Are you sure that Garin also fled from Russia?" asked Zoë.

"He had to get away. After that business he would have been obliged to give an explanation to the Criminal Investigation Department."

"Why did he choose Paris?"

"He needs carbon pyramids. Without them his apparatus is like an unloaded gun. Garin is a physicist. He knows nothing about chemistry. On his instructions I worked on the production of those pyramids, after me the man who paid with his life on Krestovsky Island. But Garin has another companion here in Paris, he sent him a telegram to an address on the Boulevard Batignolles. Garin has come here to watch the experiments with the pyramids."

"What do you know about Garin's companion?" asked Rolling.

"He lives in a cheap hotel on the Boulevard Batignolles. We were there yesterday and learned a few things from the concierge," answered Semyonov. "He comes home only to sleep and is away all day. He has no luggage. He leaves the house in a sail-cloth smock, the sort medical students and laboratory workers in Paris wear. He must be working somewhere near by."

"What does he look like? What the hell do I care about his sail-cloth smock! Did the concierge tell you what he looks like?" shouted Rolling.

Semyonov and Tyklinski exchanged glances.

"If the gentleman wishes we will find out what the man looks like today," answered Tyklinski, placing his hand on his heart.

Rolling did not speak at once, but sat frowning.

"How can you be sure that the man you saw yesterday in a café on the Boulevard Batignolles and the man who went underground on the Place de l'Étoile was one and the same person and that he is Engineer Garin? You were mistaken once already in Leningrad. Well?"

Semyonov and Tyklinski again exchanged glances. Tyklinski smiled with extreme politeness.

"Mr. Rolling surely cannot believe that Garin has doubles in every city."

Rolling stubbornly nodded his head. Zoë sat with her hands wrapped in ermine, looking out of the window as though she were not interested.

"Tyklinski knows Garin too well to make such a mistake," said Semyonov. "At the moment we have something more important to decide. Are you going to let us do this job alone and one fine morning bring the drawings and the apparatus to your office on the Boulevard Malesherbes, or are you going to work with us?"

"Under no circumstances!" said Zoë suddenly, still looking out of the window. "Mr. Rolling is very interested in Engineer Garin's experiments, Mr. Rolling would very much like to acquire the rights for this invention; Mr. Rolling always keeps strictly within the law; if Mr. Rolling were to believe even one word of what Tyklinski has said it stands to reason that he would not hesitate to call the police commissioner and hand over such a scoundrel and criminal to the authorities. As Mr. Rolling understands perfectly well that Tyklinski invented the whole story in order to get more money out of him he will be kind enough to allow him to continue to perform some small services."

For the first time during that lunch Rolling smiled,

took a gold toothpick out of his waistcoat pocket, and poked it between his teeth. Beads of sweat stood out on the bald patches on Tyklinski's red forehead, his cheeks hung flabbily.

"Your job will be to give me precise and complete information, point by point, in accordance with detailed instructions which you will receive at three o'clock today at my office on the Boulevard Malesherbes," said Rolling. "You are required to work as decent detectives and nothing more. Not one step, not one word without my orders."

22

The gleaming, white, plate-glass-sided train of the Nord-Sud underground line sped with a soft rumble through dark, winding tunnels under Paris, past tangled networks of cables, past niches in which workers crouched lit up by the passing train, past yellow letters on a black background: "Dubonnet. Dubonnet. Dubonnet," a drink that the advertisements hammered into the minds of Parisians.

A momentary stop. A station flooded with underground light. Square, coloured advertisements: *Wonder Soap, The World's Strongest Braces, Lion Head Shoe Polish, Red Devil Rubber Tyres*, sales at the Louvre, La Belle Fleuriste, and Gallerie Lafayette department stores.

The noisy, smiling crowd of pretty women, midinettes, messenger-boys, foreigners, young men in tight-fitting jackets, workers in sweat-stained shirts tucked under red sashes, milling and swarming, stormed the train. The glass doors slide open.... "Oo-oo-oo ..." came like a huge sigh from the whirlpool of hats, staring eyes, gaping mouths, flushed, happy, angry faces that swirled into the train. Conductors in brick-red jackets, hanging on to the handrails, forced the passengers into the train with their stomachs. The doors close with a crash; a short whistle and the train disappears like a ribbon of fire into the black tunnel.

Semyonov and Tyklinski were sitting on a side seat of the Nord-Sud train with their backs to the door. *Pan* Tyklinski was fuming.

"I ask you to bear in mind that it was only propriety that kept me from making a scene. I could have lost my temper a hundred times. As though I've never eaten lunch with a multimillionaire! To hell with them and their lunches. I can give as good a lunch myself at the Laperouse and won't have to listen to the insults of a street woman.... Proposing that Tyklinski play the detective! The bitch, the hussy!"

"Oh, cut it out, *Pan* Tyklinski, you don't know Zoë, she's a wonderful woman, an excellent comrade. Perhaps she was a bit too hard on you...."

"Apparently Madame Zoë is used to having dealings with the dregs of society, with your émigrés.... But I'm a Pole, I'd ask you to remember that." Tyklinski blew out his moustaches in a terrifying manner. "I will not permit people to talk to me in that tone...."

"All right, Stas, you've shaken your moustaches and let off steam," said Semyonov after a short pause. "Now listen carefully to me: we're getting good pay for nothing much. The work is safe, even pleasant: just hang around pubs and cafés.... Personally, I'm very pleased with today's talk. You talk about tecs.... Nonsense! I'm telling you, we're offered a splendid job in the secret service."

Near the door behind the seat occupied by Semyonov and Tyklinski a man stood leaning his elbow against the brass upright of the car—the man who had called himself Pyankov-Pitkevich during his conversation with Shelga on the Trade-Union Boulevard in Leningrad. His overcoat collar was turned up, concealing the lower part of his face, and his hat was pulled down over his eyes. He stood there in a careless attitude, sucking the bone handle of a walking-stick; he listened to the whole conversation between Semyonov and Tyklinski, politely made way for them when they hurried out of the carriage, got out himself two stations farther on at Montmartre. At the nearest post-office he handed in a telegram:

"Shelga. C.I.D. Leningrad. Four-Fingers here. Menacing developments."

23

Leaving the post-office he walked up the Boulevard Clichy, keeping on the shady side.

From every doorway, from the basement windows, from under the striped awnings stretched over marble-topped tables and cane chairs, drifted the sour smell of night drinking dens. Pasty-faced *garçons* in short dinner jackets and white aprons, hair plastered on either side of an immaculate parting, were sprinkling the tiled floors and sidewalks between the tables with damp sawdust, setting out armfuls of flowers, turning bronze handles, to raise the awnings.

In the daytime the Boulevard Clichy looked dowdy, like the decorations after a carnival. Tall, ugly old houses were all occupied by restaurants, bars, cafés, overnight hotels and little shops selling tawdry rubbish. The frames and tin-plate structures of the advertisements, the be-draggled sails of the famous Moulin-Rouge, the cinema posters on the pavements, the two rows of anaemic trees in the middle of the boulevard, the *pissoirs* covered with unprintable scribble, the stone-paved roadway over which the centuries had rolled noisily by, the rows of stalls and roundabouts in their canvas coverings—all this awaited the night when the idlers and merrymakers would come up from the bourgeois quarters of Paris.

And when night comes the lights flash on, the *garçons* flit busily to and fro, the roundabouts turn to the screaming music of the steam organs; on golden pigs, on bulls with golden horns, in boats, saucepans and pots, reflected in a thousand mirrors, girls with skirts above their knees, bourgeois with astonishment written on their faces, thieves with magnificent moustaches, Japanese students with smiling mask-like faces, *gamins,* homosexuals and morose Russian émigrés awaiting the downfall of the Bolsheviks—all race round and round and round.

The fiery sails of the Moulin-Rouge begin to turn. Broken fiery arrows dart across the façades of the buildings. The names of world-famous night bars flash out in letters of fire, the raucous trumpeting and wild drumming of jazz bands stream through the open windows on to the hot boulevard.

The crowd is noisy with its cardboard whistles and wooden rattles. The underground railways disgorge more crowds of people on to the boulevards. This is Montmartre, the Hill of Martre, its night lights gleaming high above the city of Paris—the most care-free spot in the world. Here there are places to leave your money and plenty of opportunities to spend a merry night with a laughing girl.

Merry Montmartre—the Boulevard Clichy between the two round Places, the Place Pigalle and the Place Blanche, two centres of ultimate pleasure. To the left of the Place Pigalle stretches the wide, quiet Boulevard Batignolles. To the right, beyond the Place Blanche, begins the Faubourg Saint-Antoine, the quarter of the Parisian poor and the working class. From here, from the Boulevard Batignolles, from the heights of Montmartre and Saint-Antoine, armed workers have descended on many occasions to seize Paris. On four occasions they were driven back to their heights by cannon fire. And the lower city, spread along both banks of the Seine, the banks, offices, luxurious shops, hotels for millionaires and barracks for the thirty thousand police, on four occasions launched a counter-

offensive and the blazing lights of world-notorious dens of
infamy branded the very heart of the workers' city—Place
Pigalle, Boulevard Clichy, Place Blanche—with the sexual
seal of the lower city.

24

When the man in the loose overcoat reached the middle
of the boulevard he turned into a narrow side street
whose worn steps led to the summit of Montmartre; glancing carefully round he entered a dark bar whose habitués
were prostitutes, taxi-drivers, half-starved writers of cou-
plets and would-be artists who from force of habit still
wore baggy trousers and wide-brimmed hats.

He asked for a glass of porto and a newspaper and
settled down to read it. The red-faced, moustached, sev-
enteen-stone Frenchman who owned the bar, his shirt-
sleeves rolled up above the elbows of his hairy arms,
was washing glasses under a tap behind his zinc-covered
counter and talking—listen if you like, if not, don't.

"Say what you like, Russia's given us plenty of trouble
(he knew that his visitor was a Russian, Monsieur Pierre).
Russian émigrés don't bring an income any more. Played
out, oh, la-la.... But we're still rich enough to be able to
afford the luxury of harbouring a few thousand unfortu-
nates. (He was sure that his visitor was a Montmartre
street trader.) There must be an end to everything, of
course. The émigrés must go home. *Hélas!* We'll reconcile
you with your big country, we'll recognize the Soviets and
Paris will be good old Paris again. I'm fed up with war,
I can tell you. Ten years of that indigestion. The Soviets
agree to pay small holders of Russian stock. Clever, very
clever on their part. *Vive les Soviets!* Their politics aren't
at all bad. They're Bolshevizing Germany. Excellent! I
applaud! Germany will become Soviet and will disarm
herself. We shan't get belly-aches any more at the thought

59

of her chemical industry. The idiots in this district call me a Bolshevik. Oh, la-la. . . . I've thought it all out. We've got nothing to fear from Bolshevization. Just count up how many good bourgeois there are in Paris and how many workers. Oho! We, the bourgeois, we can look after our savings. . . . I'm quite calm when our workers shout 'Vive Lénine!' and wave red flags. The worker is a barrel of fermenting wine, you mustn't keep him sealed up. Let him shout, 'Vive les Soviets!' I shouted it myself last week. I have Russian bonds for eight thousand francs. No, you have to come to terms with your government. Enough nonsense. The franc's falling. The damned speculators, the parasites that feed on every nation whenever currency begins to fall, that whole tribe of inflators has again moved back from Germany to Paris."

A thin man with an uncovered head of fair hair, dressed in a sail-cloth smock, came hurriedly into the bar.

"Good evening, Garin," he said to the man reading the newspaper. "You may congratulate me on my success."

Garin jumped up and squeezed his hand.

"Victor. . . ."

"Yes, yes. I'm awfully glad. I insist that we take out a patent."

"Under no circumstances. Let's go."

They left the bar, climbed up the steps, turned to the right, and continued their way for a long time between the dirty houses of the Faubourg, past empty lots fenced off with barbed wire where shabby linen hung on lines, past tiny factories and workshops.

The day was drawing to a close. On their way they met groups of tired workers. It seemed that a different race of people lived up here on the hill, they had different faces—firm-set, gaunt, and strong. It seemed as though the French nation had climbed to the heights above Paris to save itself from degeneration and was here calmly and grimly awaiting the hour when it would be possible to

clean out the lower city and turn the golden ship of Lutèce*
into the ocean of sunshine.

"This way," said Victor, opening the door of a low brick
shed with a Yale key.

25

Garin and Victor Lenoir went to a small brick furnace
under a cowl. The little pyramids stood in rows on a
near-by table and on the furnace there was a bronze ring
with twelve porcelain cups arranged around its circumference. Lenoir lit a candle and looked at Garin with a
strange smile.

"Pyotr Petrovich, we've known each other for about
fifteen years, haven't we? Surely that's long enough for
you to know whether I'm honest or not. When I fled from
Soviet Russia you helped me. From that I gather that
you don't think badly of me, so tell me straight out—why
the hell are you keeping your apparatus hidden from me?
I know that without me, without those pyramids, you're
helpless. Let's act like friends."

Garin kept his eyes fixed on the bronze ring and the
porcelain cups.

"You want me to disclose my secret?" he asked.

"Yes."

"You want to participate in my business?"

"Yes."

"If necessary, and I think it will be necessary in the
future, you must be prepared to go to any lengths for
success."

Keeping his eyes on Garin, Lenoir sat on the edge of
the furnace, the corners of his mouth trembling.

"Yes," he said firmly, "I agree."

* The coat of arms of Paris (the ancient Lutèce, Lat. Lutetia)
is a golden ship. — *Author's note.*

He pulled a rag out of his smock pocket and wiped his forehead.

"I'm not trying to force your hand, Pyotr Petrovich. I started this conversation because you're the closest friend I have, strange as it may seem.... I was a first-year student when you were in your second year. Ever since then I've, well, how should I put it ... I've sort of worshipped you.... You're terribly gifted ... brilliant. And you're terribly bold. Your mind is analytical, daring, terrible. You're a terrible man. You're hard, Pyotr Petrovich, and like every man of great talent you're no judge of people. You asked me whether I was prepared to go to any length to work with you.... Of course I am. Of course. How can you doubt it? I've nothing to lose. Without you there is nothing for me but humdrum work to the very end of my life. With you it's either a merry life or death.... Do I agree to everything, you ask? ... You're funny. What does that everything mean? Steal? Kill?"

He stopped. Garin's eyes said "yes." Lenoir smiled.

"I know the French criminal laws.... You ask me whether I'm prepared to run the risk of having them applied to me? Yes, I am. Incidentally, I saw the famous German gas attack on 22nd April, 1915. A thick cloud arose out of the ground and crawled towards us in yellow-green waves, it was like a mirage, something worse than you ever saw in a nightmare. Thousands of men abandoned their arms and fled across the fields in unbearable horror. The cloud overtook them. Those who managed to get out of it had dark, blood-red faces, their tongues hanging out and their eyes seered.... What nonsense 'moral concepts' are.... Oh no, since the war we're no longer children."

"In a word," said Garin, mockingly, "you've come to the conclusion that bourgeois morality is one of the smartest of all juggling acts and only fools would swallow green gas in its defence. To tell you the truth I haven't thought much about such problems.... All right ... I voluntarily accept you as my partner. You will obey my instructions implicitly. There is only one condition. ..."

"All right, I agree to any conditions."

"You know, Victor, that I came to Paris on a false passport, every night I go to a different hotel. Sometimes I have to take a girl from the streets in order to avoid suspicion. Yesterday I found out that I was being followed. Some Russians have been entrusted with the job of tracking me. Apparently I'm mistaken for a Bolshevik agent. I must put the detectives on to a false scent."

"What do you want me to do?"

"Make up to resemble me. If you are caught you can show your papers. I want you to be my double. We're of the same height. You can dye your hair, glue on a false beard and we can buy similar clothes. Then tonight you will leave your hotel and go to another part of the town where you are not known—the Quartier Latin, for example. Is it a deal?"

Lenoir jumped down from the furnace and took a firm grasp of Garin's hand. Then he started explaining how he had succeeded in making the pyramids from a mixture of aluminium and ferric oxide (thermite) with heavy oil and yellow phosphorus.

He placed twelve of the little pyramids in the porcelain cups and lit them with the aid of a fuse cord. A pillar of blinding flame rose above the furnace. They had to retreat to the other end of the shed, to get away from the unbearable heat and light.

"Superb," exclaimed Garin. "I hope there is no smoke?"

"There is complete combustion at that terrific temperature. The materials are chemically pure."

"Good. In a day or two you will see miracles performed," said Garin. "Let's get some dinner. We'll send a messenger to the hotel for your things. Tonight we'll stay on the left bank. Tomorrow there'll be two Garins in Paris. ... Have you got a second key to this shed?"

26

In this city there was no stream of gleaming cars, there were no idle people twisting their necks to see everything displayed in the shop-windows, no dizzy women, and no industrial monarchs.

Here there were piles of freshly sawn timber, heaps of paving-stones, mounds of blue clay thrown up in the middle of the street, and sections of drain-pipe lying along the gutter like a huge worm cut into pieces.

Tarashkin of the Spartak Sports Club was making his way slowly to the club-house on the island. He was in the best possible spirits. Had you met him you might have thought him a bit glum-looking, for Tarashkin was serious and well-balanced, outwardly showing nothing of his mood, however good it might have been, with the possible exception of his soft whistling and care-free gait.

He was still about a hundred yards from the tram stop when he heard scuffling and squeaking between the piles of wooden blocks. Everything that went on in the city was, of course, Tarashkin's own personal concern.

He glanced over the pile and saw three small boys in bell-bottomed trousers and thick, short jackets; snorting angrily they were all three pounding away at a fourth boy, smaller than any of them, barefooted, bare-headed and wearing a wadded jacket torn and ragged to such a degree that one could only wonder how it held together. He was defending himself in silence. His thin face was scratched, his lips firmly set, and his hazel eyes glittering like those of a wolf-cub.

Tarashkin immediately picked up two of the boys by the scruff of their necks, gave the third one a kick in a soft spot so that he squealed and disappeared behind a pile of wooden blocks.

The other two, suspended in the air, began threatening

him with awful things. Tarashkin just gave them a shake and they quietened down.

"Bullying again, you young hooligans," said Tarashkin, glancing at their dirty faces. "I'll teach you to hit kids smaller than yourselves! Don't let me catch you again. Get it?"

The boys were compelled to give him a positive answer to his question and muttered morosely:

"All right."

He let them go and they made off, hands in their pockets, telling the other boy what would happen if he fell into their hands again.

The boy they had been beating would also have run away but he was too weak, he just shifted from one foot to another and then with a faint moan sat down on the ground, his head disappearing in his ragged jacket.

Tarashkin bent over him. The boy was crying.

"Hi, you, where do you live?"

"Nowhere," answered the boy from under his jacket.

"What do you mean, nowhere? Have you got a mother?"

"No."

"And no father? I see."

Tarashkin stood there for a short time, wrinkling his nose. The boy buzzed under his jacket like a fly.

"D'you want something to eat?" asked Tarashkin gruffly.

"Yes."

"All right, come along to the club with me."

The boy tried to stand up but his legs would not support him. Tarashkin picked him up in his arms—the boy didn't weigh more than forty pounds—and carried him to the tram. They had a long way to go and when they changed trams Tarashkin bought a roll; the boy bit into it hungrily. The last bit of the journey they walked. As Tarashkin opened the gate of the club-house and let the boy in he said to him:

"See that you don't steal anything here."

"I won't, I only steal bread."

The boy looked sleepily at the sunbeams playing on the water and on the varnished sides of the boats, at the green and silver willow whose beauty was reflected in the river, at the two- and four-oared gigs and their muscular occupants. His thin face was tired and listless. Tarashkin had no sooner turned his back than he dived under the boardwalk that ran from the club-house to the landing-stage, curled up in a ball and, apparently, immediately dropped off to sleep.

In the evening Tarashkin pulled him out from under the boards, told him to wash his hands and face in the river, and took him in to supper. He sat the boy at the supper table with the club members.

"We can keep this boy at the club," Tarashkin told his fellow-clubmen. "He won't eat much and we can get him used to the water; in any case, we need a smart boy about the place."

The others agreed to let him stay. The boy listened calmly to this conversation and ate with dignity. After supper he left the table without speaking. Nothing astonished him— he had seen stranger things.

Tarashkin led him out to the landing-stage, sat down beside him, and began to talk.

"What's your name?"

"Ivan."

"Where did you come from?"

"From Siberia. From the Amur, from the upper reaches."

"Long since you left there?"

"I arrived yesterday."

"How did you get here?"

"Part of the way I walked, part of it I rode on the brake-beams of trains."

"What did you want to get to Leningrad for?"

"That's my business," answered the boy and turned away, "I've come here because I had to."

"Tell me, I won't hurt you."

The boy did not answer and again hunched his shoulders so that his head disappeared in his jacket. That evening Tarashkin could not get anything out of him.

27

The polished wooden racing gig, as slim and elegant as a violin, was gliding softly over the mirror-like water, its two pair of oars sliding gently over the surface. Shelga and Tarashkin, in white shorts and naked to the waist, their shoulders and backs burned by the sun, were sitting motionless with their knees drawn up.

The cox, a serious-looking youth in a naval cap and a scarf wound round his neck, was studying a stop-watch.

"There's going to be a storm," said Shelga.

It was hot on the river and not a leaf stirred on the densely wooded bank. The trees stood as straight and still as if they were on parade. The sky was so saturated with sunshine that its bluish-white light seemed to be tumbling down in showers of crystals. It hurt the eyes and one's temples ached.

"Ready!" ordered the cox.

The oarsmen bent forward over their knees and their oars flew back, the blades dipping into the water; at a command from the cox they began to pull, leaning back and straightening their legs until they almost lay across the thwarts.

"One, two! . . ."

The oars bent under the strain and the gig cut through the water like a razor.

Regularly, rapidly, in time with the beating of their hearts—breathe in, breathe out—the oarsmen bent double, hanging over their own knees, and then straightened out like steel springs. Their muscles worked rhythmically, intensely, keeping time with the circulation of the blood.

The gig flew past pleasure boats in which men in braces were helplessly catching crabs. As they rowed Shelga and Tarashkin looked straight ahead, keeping their eyes fixed on the bridge of the coxswain's nose to maintain their balance. The people in the pleasure boats only had time to shout a word or two after them as they flashed past.

"That's something like!"

They reached the seacoast. Again for one minute their gig lay motionless on the water. They wiped the perspiration from their faces. "One, two!" They turned back past the Yacht Club, where the sails of the Leningrad Trade-Union Club's racing yachts hung limp in the crystal heat. A band was playing on the Yacht Club verandah. The brightly coloured flags and signs along the bank also hung motionless. Raising a shower of spray, brown bodies plunged into the water from boats out in the middle of the river.

The gig made its way through the bathers along the River Nevka, flew under the bridge, for a few seconds hung on the rudder of an outrigger four from the Arrow Club, overtook it (the cox asked politely over his shoulder, "Shall we take you in tow?"), turned into the narrow, densely wooded River Krestovka where, under the shadow of the silvery willows, flashed the red kerchiefs and bare knees of the women's training team, and drew up alongside the landing-stage of the rowing school.

Shelga and Tarashkin leaped ashore, carefully placed their oars on the sloping board-walk, bent over the gig, lifted it on to their shoulders in response to the coxswain's command, and carried it through wide doors into the boathouse. After that they went into the shower-bath. They rubbed themselves red and, following the usual custom, each drank a glass of tea with lemon. After this they felt that they had only just been born into this wonderful world which was so good to look at that it was worth while making it fit to live in.

28

On the open verandah, a storey above the ground, where they drank their tea, Tarashkin told Shelga about the boy he had found the previous day.

"A smart kid, just as clever as they make 'em." He leaned over the railing and called to the boy, "Ivan, come up here."

He was immediately answered by the patter of bare feet on the steps. Ivan appeared on the verandah. His ragged jacket had gone (for hygienic reasons it had been burned in the kitchen stove). He was wearing rowing shorts and on his bare body a waistcoat of unbelievable age, tied in a dozen places with string.

"Here he is," said Tarashkin, pointing to the boy. "No matter how much you talk to him he won't take that waistcoat off. How are you going to bathe in that thing? It isn't as if the waistcoat were any good, it's just a mass of dirt."

"I can't bathe," said Ivan.

"We'll have to wash you in the bath-house, you're black and dirty."

"I can't wash in the bath. Up to here I can," and he pointed to his navel, cowered, and backed towards the door.

Tarashkin, scratching his calf where the sunburnt skin had peeled off, groaned in despair.

"There, you see, what can you do with him?"

"Are you scared of water?" asked Shelga.

The boy looked at him without a ghost of a smile.

"No, I'm not."

"Then why don't you want to bathe in the river?"

The boy lowered his head, his lips stubbornly pressed together.

"Why are you afraid to take off your waistcoat, are you afraid it'll be stolen?"

Ivan shrugged his shoulders and grinned.

"All right, Ivan, if you don't want to bathe you needn't, that's your business. But we're not going to let you keep that waistcoat. Here, you can have mine. Take that off."

Shelga began unbuttoning his own waistcoat. Ivan drew back. The pupils of his eyes began darting from side to side. Once he looked beseechingly at Tarashkin but kept edging towards the glass doors that opened on to a dark staircase.

"Oh no, that's not in the rules." Shelga got up, locked the door, put the key in his pocket and sat down right opposite the door. "Come on, take it off."

The boy looked round like a wild animal. He was now standing close up to the door, his back to the glass. He knitted his brows and suddenly, with a determined movement, threw off his rags and held them out to Shelga.

"Here, give me yours."

Shelga, however, with great astonishment was looking past the boy, over his shoulder, peering at the glass door.

"Give it to me," said Ivan, angrily, "why are you making fun of me, you're not children."

"What a dope!" Shelga laughed uproariously. "Turn round!" The boy fell back as though he had been pushed, and banged his head against the glass. "Turn round. I can see what's written on your back, anyway."

Tarashkin jumped up. The boy bounded across the verandah like a ball and sprang over the railing. Tarashkin just managed to catch him before he dropped. Ivan's sharp teeth bit into his hand.

"You fool! Stop biting!"

Tarashkin held the boy tightly. He stroked his greyish, shaven head.

"The kid's quite wild. He's trembling like a mouse. Stop being a fool, we shan't hurt you."

The boy calmed down in his arms, only his heart beat fast. Suddenly he whispered in Tarashkin's ear:

"Tell him he mustn't read what's on my back. Nobody must. They'll kill me for that."

"We won't read it, we're not interested," repeated Tarashkin, his eyes filled with the tears of laughter. Shelga still stood at the other end of the verandah; he was biting his nails and frowning like a man trying to solve some riddle. Suddenly he sprang forward and, notwithstanding Tarashkin's resistance, turned the boy round to look at his back. Amazement, almost horror, was registered on his face. Under the boy's shoulder blades, partially obliterated by perspiration, were words written with an indelible pencil:

"To Pyotr Gari.... Resul... very comforti... depth... olivine believe five kilome... continu... search ... need help ... hunger ... hasten expedi...."

"Garin, that's for Garin!" shouted Shelga. At that moment a motor-cyclist from the Criminal Investigation Department clattered into the club yard.

"Comrade Shelga, an urgent telegram."

That was Garin's telegram from Paris.

29

The gold pencil hovered over the writing-pad.

"Your name, sir?"

"Pyankov-Pitkevich."

"The object of your visit?"

"Tell Mr. Rolling that I am authorized to negotiate concerning Engineer Garin's apparatus; he knows all about it."

The secretary immediately disappeared. A minute later Garin passed through the walnut doors into the Chemical King's room. Rolling was writing. Without raising his eyes he offered his visitor a seat. Then, still without raising his eyes:

"Petty financial operations are conducted by my secretary." With a weak hand he picked up the blotter and jabbed it on what he had written. "Nevertheless I'm ready to listen to you. I give you two minutes. What's new about Garin?"

Garin crossed his legs and placed his hands on his knee.

"Engineer Garin wants to know whether you are aware of the exact purpose for which his apparatus is designed," he said.

"Yes," answered Rolling, "as far as I know the apparatus may be of some interest in industry. I have spoken with some of the members of the board of our concern. they agree to buy the patent."

"The apparatus is not intended for use in industry," said Garin, brusquely. "It is a machine of destruction. It is true it may be used in the iron and steel and mining industries, but at the present moment Engineer Garin has different ideas."

"Political?"

"Hardly. Engineer Garin isn't very interested in politics. He hopes to establish the particular social system he finds to his liking. Politics—a mere bagatelle, a function."

"Where does he want to establish his system?"

"Everywhere, naturally, on all five continents."

"Oho!" exclaimed Rolling.

"Engineer Garin is not a Communist, don't worry. Neither is he fully on your side. I repeat, he has very extensive plans. Engineer Garin's apparatus will enable him to put into effect the whims of the wildest fantasy. The apparatus has already been built and can be demonstrated even today."

"Hm-m!" said Rolling.

"Garin has been watching your activities, Mr. Rolling, and finds that you have scope but lack a great idea. This business of the chemical concern, and the chemical warfare in the air, and the conversion of Europe into an American market.... That's all petty, there's no central idea. Engineer Garin is offering you a partnership."

"Are you, or is he, mad?" asked Rolling.

Garin laughed and rubbed the side of his nose energetically with a finger.

"You see, it's already a good sign that you have listened to me not two minutes, but nine and a half."

"I'm prepared to offer Engineer Garin fifty thousand francs for his invention," said Rolling, again beginning to write.

"I understand your offer this way: you intend, either by cunning or by force, to get hold of the apparatus and then deal with Garin in the same way as you dealt with his assistant on Krestovsky Island. Am I right?"

Rolling put down his pen. Only two red patches on his face betrayed his excitement. He took a smoking cigar from the ash-tray, leaned back in his chair and stared at Garin with dull, expressionless eyes.

"If we assume that that is just what I am going to do with Engineer Garin, then what?"

"Then, it seems, Engineer Garin is mistaken."

"In what?"

"In assuming that you were a crook on a larger scale," Garin said slowly, syllable by syllable, smiling and looking impudently at Rolling. The latter merely blew out a cloud of smoke and waved his cigar in front of his nose.

"It would be foolish to share profits with Engineer Garin when I can take the whole hundred per cent myself," he said. "Well, in order to put an end to this, I offer a hundred thousand francs and not a single centime more."

"You're not at all consistent, Mr. Rolling. You're

not risking anything. Your agents Semyonov and Tyklinski have discovered where Garin lives. Report to the police and they'll arrest him as a Bolshevik spy. Then Semyonov and Tyklinski can steal the apparatus and the drawings. All that won't cost you more than five thousand. And so that Garin can't try to remake the drawings you can send him back to Russia through Poland under escort and have him killed at the frontier. Simple and cheap. Why do you want to waste a hundred thousand francs?"

Rolling got up, glanced at Garin out of the corner of his eye and began walking up and down, his patent-leather shoes sinking into the silver carpet. Suddenly he pulled his hand out of his pocket and snapped his fingers.

"A cheap game," he said, "you're bluffing. I've thought out all possible combinations five moves ahead. There's no danger. You're just a cheap swindler. Garin is check-mated. He knows that and has sent you to bargain. I won't give two louis d'ors for his patent. Garin has been followed home and he's in my hands. (Rapidly he glanced at his watch and just as rapidly thrust it back into his waistcoat pocket.) Get to hell out of here!"

At that moment Garin also got up and stood beside the desk with his head bowed. When Rolling sent him to hell he passed his hand over his hair and said in a hollow voice, like a man who had unexpectedly fallen into a trap:

"All right, Mr. Rolling, I agree to your terms. You spoke about a hundred thousand. . . ."

"Not a centime!" shouted Rolling. "Get out of here before you are thrown out."

Garin pulled at his collar with his fingers and his eyes began to roll. He staggered.

"Don't try any tricks," roared Rolling. "Get out!"

Garin groaned and fell sideways on the desk. His right hand dropped on to the papers Rolling had been writing and grabbed them spasmodically. Rolling jumped to the electric bell. In an instant the secretary appeared.

"Throw that thing out of here. . . ."

The secretary crouched like a leopard, his elegant moustache bristled and his steel muscles flexed under his thin jacket. Garin, however, was already edging away from the desk and bowing to Rolling. He ran down the marble staircase on to the Boulevard Malesherbes, jumped into a taxi with a raised top, shouted an address, closed both windows, pulled down the green blinds, and laughed a short, sharp laugh.

He pulled a crumpled sheet of paper out of his pocket and carefully spread it out on his knees. On that crumpled paper (it was torn from a big writing-pad) there were business notes for the day in Rolling's scrawling hand. Apparently, when Garin entered his office, Rolling had been on the alert and his hand had begun to write mechanically, betraying his secret thoughts. Three times, one after the other, was written an address: "Rue des Gobelins, 63. Engineer Garin." (This was Victor Lenoir's new address that Semyonov had just reported over the phone.) Then: "Semyonov—five thousand francs."

"Luck! What devilish luck!" whispered Garin, carefully straightening out the paper on his knee.

30

Ten minutes later Garin left his car on the Boulevard Saint-Michel. The plate-glass windows of the Café Pantheon were raised. At a table at the back of the café sat Victor Lenoir. When he saw Garin he raised his hand and snapped his fingers.

Garin hurriedly sat down at his table, back to the light. It seemed as though he were sitting opposite a mirror: Victor Lenoir's pointed beard, soft hat, bow tie, and striped jacket were exactly the same.

75

"Congratulate me on my success! Quite phenomenal!" said Garin, with a smile in his eyes. "Rolling agrees to everything. He will meet all the expenses himself. When we begin to exploit the machine fifty per cent gross to him and fifty to us."

"Have you signed a contract?"

"We'll sign it in three or four days. We must put off the demonstration of the apparatus. Rolling's terms are— he'll sign the contract only after he's seen the machine at work."

"Will you stand a bottle of champagne?"

"Two, three, a dozen."

"Still, it's a pity that shark's going to swallow half the profits," said Lenoir, calling a waiter. "A bottle of Irroise, the driest there is. . . ."

"Without capital we can't move. I'll tell you one thing, Victor, if my Kamchatka enterprise turned out all right, I'd send a dozen Rollings to the devil."

"What Kamchatka enterprise?"

The waiter brought a bottle and glasses, Garin lit a cigar, leaned back in the cane chair, rocking it on its back legs, and, frowning, began to tell his story.

"Do you remember Nikolai Khristoforovich Mantsev, the geologist? In 1915 he found me out in Petrograd. He'd just returned from the Far East, was scared of mobilization and asked my help so that he would not be drafted into the army."

"Mantsev worked for the British gold company, I believe?"

"He prospected on the Lena, on the Aldan, and then on the Kolyma. He had a wonderful tale to tell. They found thirty-pound nuggets just lying around. It was then that I first got my idea, the great idea of my life. It is more than bold, it is even mad, but still I believe in it. And if I believe in anything, then Old Nick himself won't stop me. You see, my friend, the one thing on earth that I value with all my heart and soul is power. Not just regal or imperial power—that's petty, vulgar, and boring. No, I mean absolute power. Some time I'll tell you about my plans in detail. In order to get power I must have gold. In order to rule in the way I intend to, I must have more gold than all the industrial, banking, and other kings taken together."

"Your plans are certainly bold enough," said Lenoir, laughing merrily.

"But I'm on the right track. The whole world will be in my hands—like this!" And Garin clenched his fist. "The milestones on my road are the genius Nikolai Khristoforovich Mantsev, then Rolling, or rather his billions, and thirdly my death ray...."

"What about Mantsev, then?"

"In 1915 I mustered all the money I could, and more by sheer impudence than by bribery I freed Mantsev from military service and sent him with a small expedition to Kamchatka, to the backwoods.... Up to 1917 he kept writing to me: the work was hard, terribly laborious, the conditions under which he worked not fit for a dog.... Since 1918 I've lost track of him, well, you know why.... Everything depends on his prospecting."

"What is he looking for?"

"He isn't looking for anything. Mantsev merely has to confirm my theoretical assumptions. The Pacific seaboards, both Asiatic and American, are the edges of an ancient continent that has sunk to the bottom of the sea. Such a gigantic weight must have had some effect on the distribution of the rock strata that were in a state of flux.... The chains of active volcanoes in South America, in the Andes and the Cordilleras, the volcanoes of Japan and of Kamchatka confirm the fact that the molten mass of the Olivine Belt—gold, mercury, olivine and so on—is nearer to the surface of the earth around the edges of the

Pacific Ocean than anywhere else in the world.* Do you understand so far?"

"I don't know what you want with that Olivine Belt."

"In order to conquer the world, old man. . . . Let's drink to our success."

31

Zoë Montrose, heavily powdered, with mascara-treated eyes, wearing the black silk blouse of a midinette and a short skirt, got off the bus at the Porte de Saint-Denis, ran across the busy street and entered the Café Globe, a huge corner establishment with entrances on two streets, the refuge of singers from Montmartre, second-rate actors and actresses, thieves, prostitutes, and anarchically-minded young men of the type that roam the streets with ten sous in their pockets, licking their dried, feverish lips in their lust for women, shoes, silk underwear, and everything else in the world. . . .

Zoë found a vacant table. She lit a cigarette, sat down, and crossed her legs. Immediately an old man brushed past, muttering huskily, "Why the angry look, *ma petite*?" She turned away. Another, squinting at her from his table, stuck out his tongue. A third came running up as though by mistake, "Kiki, at last. . . ." Zoë dispatched him briefly to the devil.

Apparently she was the titbit here although she had tried to get herself up like a street girl. The habitués of the Café Globe had a nose for women. She ordered the *garçon* to bring her a litre of red wine, poured out a glass, and sat with her head in her cupped hands. "That's bad, *ma petite*, taking to drink," said an elderly actor, patting her on the back as he passed.

---

* There exists a theory that between the earth's crust and a solid core in the centre there is a layer of molten metals, the so-called Olivine Belt.—*Author's note.*

She had already smoked three cigarettes when the man she was waiting for at last strolled leisurely into the café, a morose, thickset individual with a low, hairy forehead and cold eyes. He wore his moustache with the ends upturned and his strong neck was tightly encircled by a coloured collar. He was excellently dressed, without extravagance. He sat down and greeted Zoë curtly. As he looked round the room some people lowered their eyes when they met his. This was Gaston Bec de Canard, formerly a thief and later a bandit in the notorious Boneaut gang. During the war he was promoted to the rank of sergeant and since demobilization had been quietly pimping on a large scale.

At the moment he was with the well-known Susanne Bourge. That lady, however, was fading. She had descended to a level that Zoë had long since left behind her.

"Susanne is good material," Gaston Bec de Canard would say, "but she doesn't know how to make the best of herself. Susanne has no sense of modernity. What is so marvellous in lace knickers and milk baths? That's all old stuff that only gets the provincials. No, I swear by the mustard gas that burned my back at the ferryman's house on the Ysère that if the modern courtesan wants to be *élégante* she must have a wireless set in her bedroom, she must learn to box, she must be as prickly as barbed wire, as well-trained as an eighteen-year-old boy, must learn to walk on her hands and dive twenty metres into the water. She must attend fascist meetings, must be able to talk about poison gas, and must change her lovers once a week so that they won't learn any swinishness. But my lady, if you please, lies in a milk bath like a Norwegian salmon and dreams of owning a ten-acre farm. She's a vulgar fool, she can't rise above the brothel level."

He treated Zoë with the greatest respect. When he met her in night restaurants he asked her politely for a dance and kissed her hand, something he did to no other woman in Paris. Zoë would no more than nod her head to the well-known Susanne Bourge but she kept up her friendship with Gaston and from time to time he carried out some of her more delicate operations.

Today she had given Gaston a hurried call to the Café Globe and had herself appeared in the seductive guise of a midinette. Gaston merely clenched his teeth and behaved in the approved manner.

Sipping his sour wine and screwing up his eyes in the smoke from his pipe he listened gloomily to what Zoë had to say. When she had finished she pulled her fingers till they cracked.

"But that's . . . dangerous," he said.

"Gaston, if it comes off you're made for life."

"Not for all the money in the world will I get mixed up in anything in the stealing and killing line: things aren't what they used to be. Today the apaches prefer a job in the police and professional thieves publish newspapers and go in for politics. It's only beginners that kill and rob, provincials, you know, and boys with V.D. And what can we do about it? We grown-ups have to look for a quiet haven. If you want to hire me for money—I refuse. It is different if I do it for you. For you I might risk my neck."

Zoë blew the smoke out of the corner of her reddened lips, smiled tenderly, and placed her beautiful hand on Bec de Canard's sleeve.

"I think we can come to terms."

Gaston's nostrils quivered, his moustache twitched. He lowered his bluish eyelids, hiding the intolerable brilliance of his protruding eyes.

"Do you mean to say that I can now relieve Susanne of my services?"

"Yes, Gaston."

He bent over the table and squeezed his glass tightly between his fingers.

"Will my moustache smell of your skin?"

"I imagine that's unavoidable, Gaston."

"All right." He leaned back. "All right. It shall be as you wish."

32

Dinner was over. Coffee with hundred-year-old cognac had been drunk. The Corona-Corona—at two dollars a cigar—had been smoked half-way through and the ash had not yet fallen. The critical moment had come: what next? With what Satanic bow to play some jolly tune on jaded nerves?

Rolling demanded the programmes of all the Paris amusements.

"Do you want to dance?"

"No," answered Zoë, covering half her face with her fur.

"Theatre, theatre, theatre," read Rolling. They were all boring: a three-act dialogue comedy in which the actors were so bored and disgusted that they did not even bother to make up and actresses in toilettes from famous dressmakers stared at the audience with vacant eyes.

"Revue, Revue. Here: *Olympia*. A hundred and fifty nude girls wearing only slippers and a technical miracle, a wooden curtain designed as a chess-board on which nude women stand as it is raised and lowered. Shall we go there?"

"My dear, they're all bandy-legged, girls from the boulevards."

"*Apollo*. . . . We haven't been there. Two hundred girls wearing only. . . . We'll give that a miss. *Le Rouleau*. More women. Aha! What about the 'World-Famous Musical Clowns Pim and Jack'?"

"They are talked about," said Zoë, "let's go there."

They took a stage box. When they entered the Revue was under way.

A volatile young man in immaculate evening dress and a mature woman in red with a broad-brimmed hat and a long staff were exchanging good-natured impertinences about the government and innocent witticisms at the expense of the Prefect of Police, were charmingly mocking in respect of high-currency foreigners, but not enough to make them want to leave Paris immediately and advise their friends not to come to that city of joy.

After some more chatter on politics during which they kept their legs moving all the time, the young man and the lady with the staff exclaimed, "Houp-la." Girls with extremely white bodies, as naked as the day they were born, wearing only their powder, ran on to the stage and arranged themselves in a *tableau vivant* depicting an army in attack. The orchestra played a brave fanfare and there was a blare of bugles.

"That ought to affect the young men," said Rolling.

"It doesn't work when there are so many women," answered Zoë.

The curtain was lowered and raised again. A property grand piano placed near the footlights occupied half the stage. With a clatter of percussion instruments Pim and Jack appeared. Pim was in the conventionally ridiculous evening jacket, a vest that reached his knees and trousers that would not keep up, boots a yard long that ran away ahead of him (applause), and with the face of a kindly idiot. Jack was covered in flour, a high felt cap on his head and a bat hanging from his backside.

To begin with they did everything to create roars of laughter; Jack smacked Pim's face and Pim blew out a cloud of dust from behind, then Jack hit Pit on the head and raised a big rubber blister.

Said Jack, "Listen, d'you want me to play on that piano?" Pim laughed terrifically and said, "All right, play on that piano," and went away and sat down. Jack banged at the keys with all his might and the tail fell off the piano.

Pim again burst into a terrific laugh. Jack banged the keys a second time and the side fell off the piano. "That's nothing," said Jack and slapped Pim's face. Pim staggered all the way across the stage and fell. (Boom! went the big drum.) Pim got up. "That's nothing," he said and spat out a handful of teeth, took a brush and shovel (of the sort used for picking up horse-dung in the streets) out of his pocket and set about brushing his clothes. Jack banged the keys for a third time and the piano fell to pieces; underneath was an ordinary concert piano. Pushing his felt cap down over his nose, Jack, with incomparable mastery, gave an inspired performance of Liszt's "Campanella."

Zoë's hands went cold. Turning to Rolling she whispered: "What an artist!"

"That's nothing," said Pim when Jack had finished. "Now listen to me."

He began pulling out of his various pockets ladies' knickers, an old shoe, a clyster-tube, a live kitten (applause), and at last a violin; with the sad face of a kindly idiot he turned to the public and played an immortal étude by Paganini.

Zoë got up, threw her furs round her neck, her diamonds sparkled.

"Let's go, this is sickening. Unfortunately I also was once an artiste."

"Where can we go, baby! It's half past ten."

"Let's drink."

33

A few minutes later their limousine pulled up in a narrow street in Montmartre that was lit up by the ten windows of the den known as the Souper de Roi. In the low, hot, smoky hall, draped in scarlet silk, mirrors on walls and ceiling, amidst streamers, celluloid balls and confetti, half-naked women were dancing, entangled in the paper ribbons, while men, red-faced or pale, drunken and excited, pressed their faces to the rouged cheeks of their partners. A piano rattled. Violins wailed and three perspiring Negroes banged on wash-bowls, pumped motor horns, beat wooden boards, rang bells, clattered plates, and bashed a kettle-drum. Somebody's wet face pushed close up to Zoë. A woman's arms wound round Rolling's neck.

"Make way for the Chemical King, *mes enfants*," shouted the maître d'hôtel, with the greatest of difficulty finding them places behind a narrow table placed along a silk-hung wall. As Zoë and Rolling sat down, celluloid balls, confetti, and streamers flew at them.

"You're attracting attention," said Rolling.

Zoë, her eyes half closed, was drinking champagne. She felt hot and damp under the light silk that scarcely covered her bosom. A celluloid ball hit her in the cheek.

Slowly she turned her head—a man's dark eyes, so dark that they seemed to be outlined in charcoal, were peering at her in sullen admiration. She leaned forward, lay her bare arms on the table and drank in that look as though it were wine: did it really matter what she got drunk on?

The face of the man who was staring at her seemed to shrink in those few seconds. Zoë rested her chin on her interlocked fingers and met the man's stare through half-open eyes.... She had seen him somewhere before. Who could he be? He was neither English nor French. His dark beard was dotted with confetti. He had a fine mouth. "I wonder whether Rolling is jealous?" she asked herself.

A waiter forced his way through the dancing crowd and handed her a note. In her astonishment she fell back in her seat and before she read it glanced sideways at Rolling who sat sucking his cigar.

"Zoë, that man you are looking at so tenderly is Garin.... I kiss your hand. Semyonov."

She must have turned terribly pale for a voice near by said above the noise, "Look, that lady's ill." Then she held out her empty glass and the waiter filled it with champagne.

"What did Semyonov write?" asked Rolling.

"I'll tell you afterwards."

"Was it something about that fresh guy who's staring at you? That's the one who came to see me yesterday. I had him thrown out."

"Rolling, don't you know him? Don't you remember the Place de l'Étoile? That's Garin!"

Rolling only sniffed. He took his cigar out of his mouth. "Aha." His face suddenly changed: he looked the same as he did when he walked up and down the silver carpet of his office thinking out every possible combination in the game five moves ahead. That time he had snapped his fingers energetically. But now, on this occasion, he turned to Zoë, his mouth distorted.

"Let's go. We've got some serious things to talk over."

In the doorway Zoë looked back. Through the smoke and the tangle of streamers she again saw Garin's burning eyes. Then, incredibly, dizzily, his face doubled: somebody sitting with his back to the dancers got up and stood beside him; both of them looked at Zoë. Or was it an illusion worked by the mirrors?

For a second Zoë shut her eyes and then ran down the worn carpet to her car. Rolling was waiting for her. When he had shut the door he touched her hand.

"I didn't tell you everything about my talk with that guy who called himself Pyankov-Pitkevich.... There are things I can't understand. Why the fake hysterics? Surely he couldn't expect to get any sympathy out of me? Altogether his behaviour was suspicious. And why did he come to me, anyway? Why did he flop on the table?..."

"Rolling, you didn't tell me that."

"Yes, yes. He knocked over the clock. Crumpled my papers. . . ."

"Did he try to steal your papers?"

"What? Steal?" Rolling pondered over that. "No, I don't think he did. He lost his balance and fell with his hand on my writing-pad. There were several sheets of paper lying there."

"Are you sure nothing is missing?"

"They were just notes of no importance. He crumpled them and I threw them into the wastepaper-basket."

"I beg you, try to remember every detail of the conversation."

The limousine drew up on the Rue de la Seine. Rolling and Zoë went straight to the bedroom. Zoë disrobed rapidly and got into the wide, carved four-poster standing on eagle's claws—one of the genuine beds that had belonged to the Emperor Napoleon I. Rolling undressed slowly, walking up and down the carpet as he did so and leaving articles of wearing apparel on the gilded chairs, the little tables and the mantelshelf; while he was undressing he gave Zoë full details of everything that had occurred during Garin's visit the day before.

She listened to him, leaning on her elbow. Hopping on one leg to pull off his trousers, Rolling looked like anything but a king. With the words: "That is absolutely everything," he got into bed and pulled the satin quilt up to his nose. A bluish night-light illuminated the luxurious bedroom, the scattered clothing, the golden cupids on the bedposts, and Rolling's fleshy nose stuck into the quilt. His head was sunk deep in the pillow, his mouth half-open—the Chemical King was asleep.

That snorting nose did more than anything to disturb Zoë's thoughts. It brought back undesirable memories of other events. She shook her head to get rid of them and imagined another head on the pillow in place of Rolling's.

Growing tired of struggling against her own thoughts, she closed her eyes and smiled. Garin's face, pale from excitement, floated before her.... "Perhaps I should ring up Gaston Bec de Canard and tell him to wait?" Suddenly a thought pierced her like a needle: "He had a double sitting with him, just as he did in Leningrad...."

She slipped out of bed and began pulling on her stockings. Rolling mumbled in his sleep but only turned over on his side.

Zoë ran into the dressing-room. She put on some clothes, and a mackintosh which she belted tightly, then went back to the bedroom for her bag with the money in it.

"Rolling," she called softly, "Rolling.... We're done for...."

Again he mumbled in his sleep. She ran down to the vestibule and with an effort opened the heavy street doors. The Rue de la Seine was empty. A dull yellow moon peeped through a gap between the mansards. Zoë's heart sank. She glanced up at the disc of the moon that hung over the sleeping city. "Oh, my God, how terrifying, how gloomy." With both her hands she pulled her hat down over her forehead and ran to the embankment.

34

The old, three-storeyed house, number sixty-three on the Rue des Gobelins, had one wall facing an empty lot. On this side the only windows were in the mansard. Another, a blank wall faced a park. On the side facing the street the ground floor was occupied by a café catering for carters and lorry-drivers. The first floor was an overnight hotel and the top floor, the mansard, was let out in single rooms to permanent lodgers. The entrance to the upper floors was through gates and a long tunnel.

It was past one o'clock, and not a single lighted window on the whole of the Rue des Gobelins. The café was closed, the chairs were up-ended on the tables. Zoë stopped in the gateway for a moment, staring at the number sixty-three. A shiver ran down her back. She plucked up courage and rang the bell. There was the rustle of a rope and the gates opened. She slipped into the dark entrance and the voice of the concierge growled, "Night's the time to sleep, you ought to get home earlier," but did not ask who it was.

The place was a real den of infamy and Zoë was genuinely frightened. Before her stretched a low, dark tunnel. A gas jet burned on the rough wall, the colour of ox blood. Semyonov's instructions were: at the end of the tunnel turn left, up a spiral staircase to the top floor, turn left, to number eleven.

Half-way down the tunnel Zoë stopped. She fancied she saw someone peep out at the far end and then disappear again. Perhaps she ought to turn back? She listened but did not hear a sound. She ran to a bend in the tunnel where there was a sort of a smelly hallway out of which led a narrow spiral staircase faintly lit from above. On tiptoe Zoë climbed the stairs, afraid to put her hand on the clammy rail.

The whole house was asleep. On the first-floor landing an arch with flaking plaster led into a dark corridor. As she continued up the stairs Zoë looked back and again she fancied that somebody peeped out of the arch and then disappeared. Only it wasn't Gaston Bec de Canard. "No, no, Gaston hasn't been here, he can't have been, he hasn't had time to. . . ."

On the top-floor landing a gas jet was burning, throwing its light on a brown wall covered with inscriptions and drawings that told a tale of unsatisfied desires. If Garin were not at home she would wait for him here until morning. If he were at home and asleep, she would not leave until she had got what he took from the desk in the office on the Boulevard Malesherbes.

Zoë took off her gloves, pushed back her hair under her hat, and went along the corridor that took a sharp turn to the left. On the fifth door the number 11 was painted in big white figures. Zoë turned the handle and the door opened easily.

The moonlight fell through the open window of a small room. On the floor lay an open suitcase. Scattered papers showed up white in the moonlight. Between the washstand and a chest-of-drawers, a man wearing nothing but a shirt was sitting on the floor by the wall with his bare knees drawn up; his feet looked enormous. . . . The moon lit up one half of the face, showing a bright, wide-open eye and gleaming white teeth in a grinning mouth. Zoë gasped, she could not get her breath as she stood staring at that face with its ghastly grin—it was Garin.

That morning in the Café Globe she had told Gaston Bec de Canard to steal the apparatus and the drawings and, if possible, to kill Garin. But in the evening she had seen Garin's eyes through the smoke over a glass of champagne and felt that if such a man wanted her she would abandon and forget everything in order to follow him. At night, when she realized the danger and had set out to intercept Gaston, she had not known what it was that drove her in such alarm through the Paris night, from bar to bar, into gambling houses and other places where Gaston might have been and had finally brought her to the house in the Rue des Gobelins. What was it that urged the clever, cold, cruel woman to enter the room of the man she had condemned to death?

She stared at Garin's white teeth and protruding eye. With a hoarse half-suppressed cry she ran and bent down over him. He was dead. His face was blue and his neck swollen with bruises. It was the same face—haggard, attractive, with excited eyes, with confetti in the silken beard. . . . Zoë grasped the ice-cold marble of the washstand and pulled herself up with difficulty. She had forgotten what she came for. Bitter saliva filled her mouth. "That's all I need, to fall in a faint." With a final effort she tore off the button on the collar that was strangling her, and turned towards the door. In the doorway stood Garin.

His teeth gleamed white, his face was frozen in a grin, the very counterpart of the man on the floor. He lifted a warning finger. Zoë understood and covered her mouth with her hand to smother a scream. Her heart was beating madly as though she had just come up out of the water. "He's alive. . . . He's alive. . . ."

"You didn't kill me," said Garin in a whisper, continuing to shake his finger at her, "you killed Victor Lenoir, my assistant. . . . Rolling will go to the guillotine. . . ."

"Alive, alive . . ." she said hoarsely.

He took her by the elbows. She immediately threw back her head in complete surrender, offering no resistance. He pulled her towards him and feeling that her legs were giving way under her, put his arm round her shoulders.

"Why are you here?"

"I was looking for Gaston."

"What Gaston?"

"The man I sent to kill you."

"I foresaw that," he said, looking into her eyes.

She answered as though in a dream:

"If Gaston had killed you I would have killed myself."

"I don't understand."

She repeated his words as though in a trance, in a soft, falling voice:

"I don't understand myself."

This strange conversation took place in the doorway. The moon, sinking behind the slate roofs, shone through the window. Against the wall Lenoir grinned.

Garin spoke in a low voice.

"You've come for Rolling's autograph?"

"Yes. Have mercy."

"On whom? On Rolling?"

"No. On me. Have mercy on me," she repeated.

"I've sacrificed my friend in order to ruin your Rolling. I'm as much a murderer as you are. Mercy? . . . No . . . no. . . ."

Suddenly he grew tense and listened. With a brusque movement he pulled Zoë out of the door. Still squeezing her elbow he looked through the arch on to the staircase.

"Come along. I'll take you out of here through the park. Listen, you're an unusual woman." His eyes flashed with mad humour. "Our paths have crossed. D'you feel it, too?"

Taking Zoë with him he ran down the spiral staircase. She did not resist, overcome by a strange sensation that surged up inside her like turbid wine just beginning to ferment.

On the lower landing Garin turned away into the darkness, stopped, lit a wax vesta, and with an effort opened a rusty lock that had obviously not been opened for years.

"You see I've thought of everything."

They went out under the dark, damp trees of the park. At that same moment a police squad, called for by Garin a quarter of an hour earlier on the telephone, entered the gateway from the street.

35

Shelga well remembered how he had lost a pawn at the house on Krestovsky Island. During their talk on the Trade-Union Boulevard he had realized that Pyankov-Pitkevich was certain to be back for what was hidden in the cellar of the cottage. That same day, at dusk, Shelga had gone back to the island, had entered the cottage without disturbing the watchman and descended into the cellar with a dark lantern. The pawn was lost right away: Garin stood two paces away from the trap-door in the kitchen. Just a second before Shelga arrived he had climbed out of the cellar with a suitcase in his hand and had flattened himself against the wall behind the door. With a crash he closed the trap-door over Shelga's head and piled sacks of coal on it. Shelga raised his lantern and smiled ironically as dust poured down through the cracks in the trap-door. He intended to start peace negotiations. Suddenly, however, there was silence in the kitchen. Shelga heard running footsteps, revolver shots, and a wild scream. This was the tussle with Four-Fingers. An hour later the police arrived.

Having lost his pawn Shelga made a clever move. In the squad car he drove straight from the cottage to the Yacht Club, woke up the hoarse-voiced, tousled old sailor who served as caretaker and without more ado demanded:

"In what quarter is the wind?"

The old salt responded unhesitatingly:

"South-west."

"Strength?"

"Fresh to strong."

"Are you sure all the yachts are at their moorings?"

"I'm sure they are."

"Is there a night watchman there?"

"Yes, Petka."

"Let me take a look at the moorings."

"Aye, aye," answered the sailor, still half-asleep, fumbling to get his arms into the sleeves of his jacket.

"Petka!" he called in a hoarse voice that told of quantities of consumed spirit as they went out on to the club verandah. There was no answer. "He must be asleep somewhere, sink him," said the sailor, turning up his coat collar against the wind.

They found the night watchman near by in the bushes, snoring heartily with his head covered by the big collar of his sheepskin coat. The sailor let out a stream of profanity. The night watchman groaned and got up. They went out along the landing-stage where a forest of masts swayed above the steel-grey water, tinged blue by the approaching dawn. Waves broke against the landing-stage, there was a fresh wind blowing, with squalls.

"Are you sure all the yachts are in place?" asked Shelga again.

"The *Orion* isn't here, she's at Peterhof. And two boats were driven into Strelna by the wind."

Shelga walked along the spray-splashed landing-stage and picked up the end of a painter fastened to a ring—the rope had obviously been cut. The sailor slowly examined the end of the painter. He pushed his sou'wester forward on to his nose but said nothing. He walked along counting the yachts with his finger. Then he slashed at the air with his hand. Club discipline forbade the use of curses belonging to the imperialist past and so he confined himself to a number of vivid extraneous expressions.

"The so and so," he shouted with unbelievable vigour. "A marlinespike in his liver! He's taken the *Bibigonda*, the crack yacht in the fleet, the son of a bitch, a rope's end where he wouldn't like it.... Petka, may you be thirty times drowned in stinking water, where were your eyes, you parasite, you lousy swede-basher? The *Bibigonda*'s gone, damn your soul."

The night watchman Petka groaned, expressed astonishment, and beat his thighs with the long sleeves of his sheepskin coat. The sailor raced on before the wind into unfathomed depths of the Russian language. There being nothing left for him to do Shelga went off to the port.

At least three hours had passed before he reached the open sea in a swift motor-boat. There was a heavy swell running and the boat took a bad tossing. Spray dimmed the glass of his binoculars. When the sun came up a sail was sighted in Finnish waters far beyond the lighthouse and close offshore; it was the unfortunate *Bibigonda* tossing about amidst submarine crags. Her deck was deserted. They fired a few shots from the motor-boat just for the sake of doing something and returned with empty hands.

And so that night Garin had fled across the frontier, winning yet another pawn. Only he and Shelga knew of the part played by Four-Fingers in that game. Shelga's general train of thought on his way back to the port was somewhat as follows:

"Garin will either sell his mysterious apparatus or exploit it himself abroad. For the time being the invention is lost to the Soviet Union and who can tell but that it may play a decisive part in future events. Garin, however, is in danger abroad—Four-Fingers. Until he's disposed of, Garin won't dare bring his apparatus out into the open. If I take Garin's side in the fight I might win in the long run. In any case I couldn't do anything more foolish than arrest Four-Fingers in Leningrad, which is just what Garin wants." The conclusion to be drawn from this line of thought was simple enough. From the port Shelga went straight back to his own apartment, changed into dry clothes, rang up his office to inform them that the "case had petered out," cut off the telephone, and went to bed smiling at the thought of Four-Fingers, poisoned by gas and perhaps wounded, at that very moment, clearing out of Leningrad as fast as his legs would carry him. This was Shelga's answer to the "lost pawn."

Then came the telegram from Paris: "Four-Fingers here. Menacing developments." This was a cry for help.

The more Shelga thought of it the more obvious it became—he must leave for Paris immediately. He telephoned for the time of departure of passenger planes and went back on to the verandah where Tarashkin and Ivan were sitting in the white twilight of the northern summer night. Ever since Shelga had read the message on the waif's back the boy had calmed down and had not left Tarashkin's side.

Voices, women's laughter, and the splashing of oars came drifting to them from the orange-coloured water visible through the branches of the trees. The oldest game in the world was being played under the dark foliage of the wooded islands where birds called to each other in alarm and nightingales were singing. All living things, having emerged from the rains and blizzards of winter, were now in a hurry to live and were hungrily drinking in the inebriating beauty of the night. Tarashkin was standing perfectly still, leaning on the verandah railing, with one arm round the boy's shoulders and gazing through the trees at the water where boats slid noiselessly past.

"Well, Ivan, how goes it?" asked Shelga, drawing up a chair and bending down to look into the boy's face. "D'you like it better in Leningrad or out in the Far East? You probably went hungry most of the time out there, didn't you?"

Ivan stared at Shelga without batting an eyelid. In the twilight his eyes had a sad look, like those of an old man. Shelga took a sweet out of his waistcoat pocket and tapped it against Ivan's teeth until he opened them and the sweet slid into his mouth.

"We're kind to little boys, Ivan. We don't make them work, we don't write letters on their backs and don't send them five thousand miles under railway coaches. It's nice here on the islands, isn't it? And do you know whose it is, all of it? We've given it to the children for keeps. The river, the islands, the boats, bread and sausage—eat as much as you like—it's all yours."

"You'll get the boy all mixed up," said Tarashkin.

"Oh, no, he's smart, he'll understand. Where are you from, Ivan?"

"We're from the Amur. Mother died and father was killed in the war."

"How did you live?"

"I worked for all sorts of people."

"A kid like you?"

"Yes. I went out with horses to graze."

"And then what?"

"Then they took me."

"Who did?"

"Some people. They needed a boy to climb trees, gather mushrooms and nuts, catch squirrels for food, and run all sorts of errands."

"So you were taken on some expedition? (Ivan blinked but did not answer.) Did you go far? Don't be afraid, tell me all about it. We won't give you away, you're one of us now."

"We went eight days by steamer. We thought we wouldn't live through it. Then we went eight days on foot, until we came to a fire mountain."

"Huh, huh, so the expedition went to Kamchatka."

"Yes, to Kamchatka. We lived there in a hut. We didn't know anything about the revolution for a long time. When we did hear about it three of them went away and then two others went. There was nothing left to eat. I stayed there with him."

"With whom? Who's the 'he'? What's his name?"

Ivan turned sulky again and wouldn't answer. Shelga soothed him for a long time, stroking his bowed cropped head.

"He'll kill me if I tell you. He promised to kill me."

"Who?"

"Nikolai Khristoforovich Mantsev. He said, 'I've written a letter on your back, don't you wash, or take off your shirt and waistcoat, not even if it is a year, or two years, until you get to Petrograd and find Pyotr Petrovich Garin; show him what's written on your back and he'll pay you well.'"

"Why didn't Mantsev come to Petrograd himself if he wanted to see Garin?"

"He was afraid of the Bolsheviks. He said, 'They're worse than devils. They'll kill me. They've ruined the whole country,' he said. 'Trains don't run, there's no post, there's nothing to eat, people have all run away from the towns. . . .' How could he know, he's been sitting on his mountain six years."

"What's he doing there? What's he looking for?"

"D'you think he'd tell me? But all the same I know. (Ivan's eyes flashed merrily and with cunning.) He's looking for gold under the earth."

"Did he find any?"

"He? Of course he did."

"Could you find the way to that mountain where Mantsev is sitting if you had to?"

"Of course I could. Only don't you give me away, he'll get awful mad at me."

In rapt attention Shelga and Tarashkin listened to the boy's story. Shelga again studied the inscription on the boy's back and then photographed it.

"Now go downstairs, Tarashkin will give you a good wash with soap and you can go to bed," said Shelga. "When you came here you had nothing, no father, no mother, nothing but an empty belly. Now you've got everything you need, you can live, learn, and grow up well. Tarashkin will teach you what you have to know and you do what he tells you. Good-bye. I'll be seeing Garin in a couple of days and I'll give him your message."

Shelga laughed and soon the light of his bicycle lamp went jumping away behind the dark bushes.

36

Aluminium wings swept across the green carpet of the aerodrome and the six-seater passenger plane disappeared behind the snow-white clouds. The small group of people who had come to see their friends off craned their necks to look into the radiant blue sky where a hawk was lazily circling and swallows darted through the air, but the dur-alumin bird had disappeared the devil alone knew where.

The six passengers, sitting in their creaking wicker chairs, looked down at the receding bluish-green earth. Roads ran across it like threads. Groups of buildings, belfries, all slightly leaning, looked like toys. Far away to the right stretched an expanse of blue water.

The shadow of a cloud slipped over the surface of the earth hiding its irregularities. Soon the cloud itself was below them.

Glued to the windows all six passengers smiled with that somewhat strained smile of people who know how to control themselves. Air travel was still something new. Despite the comfortable cabin, the magazines and catalogues littering the tables, despite the appearance of cosiness and safety, the passengers still had to convince themselves that air travel was far less dangerous than, say, crossing the street. There are no obstacles in the air—if you meet a cloud you dive into it and all that happens is that the windows get moist, or hail rattles on the metal wings, or the machine jumps as though it were going over ruts in the road—you hold on tight to the arms of your wicker chair and open your eyes wide but your neighbour just winks and laughs—nice little rut, that! ... If the metal bird is struck by one of those squalls that break the masts of sailing-boats, smash the rudder and sweep the lifeboats and crew into the raging sea, it just doesn't care; strong and agile, it tips over on to one wing, the engines roar and it is well away, three thousand feet above the centre of the storm.

In short, before an hour had passed the passengers were getting used to the tossing of the aircraft and to the idea of space underfoot. Some of them put on headsets with earphones and microphones and conversation began. Opposite Shelga sat a thin man of about thirty-five in a rather shabby overcoat and a check cap he had probably bought for his trip abroad.

He had a pale face with thin skin, a clever, frowning but handsome profile, a light beard and a calm and firm mouth. He sat hunched up with his hands on his knees. With a smile Shelga made a sign to him. The man put on his earphones.

"Didn't you attend the technical school in Yaroslavl?" asked Shelga. The man nodded his head. "I remember you. You're Alexei Semyonovich Khlinov aren't you? (A nod.) Where are you working now?"

"In the Physical Laboratory of the Polytechnical Institute," came Khlinov's faint voice, drowned by the roar of the engines.

"Business trip?"

"To Reicher in Berlin."

"Secret?"

"No. Last March we heard that Reicher's laboratory had effected the nuclear disintegration of mercury."

Khlinov turned to face Shelga and peered straight at him, his eyes betraying his excitement.

"That's beyond me, I'm not a specialist," said Shelga.

"So far the work has been confined to the laboratory. It has still a long way to go before it can be applied in industry. Although," Khlinov glanced down at rolling snow-white clouds far below that hid the earth from view, "from the scientist's study to the factory is not a very far cry. The principle by which the atom can be forcibly disintegrated ought to be very simple. You know, of course, what an atom is?"

"Something very small." Shelga indicated the size with his fingers.

"An atom compared with a grain of sand is as a grain of sand compared with the earth. Nevertheless we can measure the atom, the velocity of the electrons that circulate around the nucleus and the strength of their electric charge. We are getting close to the very heart of the atom, to its nucleus. In that nucleus lies the whole secret of power over matter. The future of mankind depends on whether or not we can master the atomic nucleus, a tiny fragment of material energy one hundred billionth of a centimetre in size."

At a height of six thousand feet above the earth Shelga heard a story more wonderful than any told by Scheherazade, but this was no fairy-tale. At a time when the dialectics of history had led one class to a destructive war and another class to insurrection, when cities were burning, when clouds of dust and ashes and poison gas hid ploughlands and orchards, when the very earth shuddered at the wrathful shrieks of suppressed revolutions and, as in days of old, torturers were busy in prison dungeons with rack and pincers, when at night monstrous fruits with their tongues hanging out grew on the trees in the parks, when the cloak of idealism that mankind had so lovingly painted fell off—in that monstrous and titanic decade the amazing minds of scientists gleamed here and there like torches.

37

The aeroplane circled low over Kovno. The green fields, wetted by the rain, rushed to meet it. The aircraft taxied along the runway and came to a standstill. The pilot jumped out on to the grass and the passengers got out to stretch their legs and smoke a cigarette. Shelga lay down on the grass, placed his hands behind his head, and looked up wonderingly at the distant blue-lined clouds. He had just come from there, he had been flying amongst those light, snow-like mountains and azure valleys.

His recent companion, the slightly round-shouldered Khlinov, was standing beside him, in his shabby overcoat, near the wing of the plane. He looked very ordinary, even his cap came from a Leningrad factory.

Shelga laughed.

"It's good to be alive, anyway. It's devilish good."

When they took off from Kovno Aerodrome Shelga sat beside Khlinov and, without naming any names, told him what he knew of Garin's extraordinary experiments; he told him that very great interest had been displayed in these experiments abroad.

Khlinov asked whether Shelga had seen Garin's machine.

"No, nobody has seen the machine."

"So it's all a matter of guesswork and assumptions, to say nothing of a vivid imagination, eh?"

Then Shelga told him about the cellar under the ruined cottage, about the pieces of steel that had been cut, about the boxes of carbon pyramids. Khlinov nodded.

"I see." He nodded. "Pyramids. Very good. I understand. Tell me, if it isn't too much of a secret, are you by any chance talking about Engineer Garin?"

For a moment Shelga did not answer but looked Khlinov straight in the eyes.

"Yes," he answered, "about Garin. D'you know him?"

"A very, very capable man." Khlinov pulled a face as though he had something sour in his mouth. "An extraordinary man. But he's no scientist. He's ambitious. An absolutely isolated individual. An adventurer, a cynic with the makings of a genius. Too much temperament. A monstrous imagination. But that wonderful mind of his is always motivated by the lowest desires. He will go a long way but will finish up either as a hopeless drunkard or by trying to 'horrify mankind.' A genius needs discipline more than anybody else, he has too much responsibility to bear."

Again reddish patches blazed on Khlinov's cheeks.

"An enlightened, disciplined mind is the holy of holies, the miracle of miracles. The earth is like a grain of sand in the universe and man on that earth is no more than a billionth part of the smallest measure. That speculative particle, living on an average some sixty revolutions of the earth around the sun, has a mind that grasps the whole universe. In order to understand this we should use the language of higher mathematics. What would you say, for example, if somebody took the most valuable microscope from your laboratory and used it to hammer in nails? That's exactly the way Garin uses his genius. I know that he has made an important discovery concerning the transmission of infra-red rays over a distance. You've heard, of course, of the Rindel-Matthews Death Ray? That death ray proved to be a fake although he had the right principles. Heat waves at a temperature of a thousand degrees centigrade transmitted parallel to each other constitute a monstrous weapon of destruction and defence in time of war. The whole secret lies in the transmission of a ray that does not disperse. So far nobody has been able to do this. Judging by your story Garin has constructed a machine that will do it. If it is so it is an extremely important discovery."

"I've been thinking for a long time that this invention smells of higher politics," said Shelga.

For some time Khlinov sat silent, then flushed so that even his ears turned red.

"Find Garin, take him by the scruff of the neck, and bring him back to the Soviet Union together with his machine. Our enemies mustn't get it. Ask Garin whether he knows what his duty is, or whether he's just a Philistine.

If he is, give him money, as much as he wants. Let him have expensive women, yachts, racing cars. Or kill him."

Shelga raised his brows. Khlinov placed the microphone on the table, leaned back, and closed his eyes. The aeroplane was flying over level, green chequer-board fields and roads as straight as an arrow. From their altitude they could see in the distance the brown outlines of Berlin amidst the bluish patches of the lakes.

38

As usual, at half past seven in the morning, Rolling awoke in the Emperor Napoleon's bed on the Rue de la Seine. Without opening his eyes he took a handkerchief from under his pillow and blew his nose with determination, chasing away the left-overs of yesterday evening's amusement together with sleep.

Not quite refreshed, it is true, but in full possession of his faculties, he threw the handkerchief on to the carpet, sat up amongst the silk pillows, and glanced round. The bed was empty, the room—also empty. Zoë's pillow was cold.

Rolling pressed the bell push and Zoë's maid appeared. Looking past her he asked, "Madame?" The maid raised her shoulders and turned her head this way and that like an owl. She went on tiptoes into the lavatory, from there, in a hurry now, to the dressing-room, slammed the door of the bathroom, and returned to the bedroom, her fingers tremblingly pulling at the lace of her apron. "Madame is nowhere here."

"Coffee," said Rolling. He filled the bath himself, dressed himself, and poured out his own coffee. Meanwhile the household was in a state of a quiet panic, everybody walking on tiptoes and talking in whispers. As Rolling went out of the house he jabbed the porter with his elbow when the latter, terrified, rushed to open the door. He was twenty minutes late at the office.

There were fireworks that morning on the Boulevard Malesherbes. The secretary's face expressed absolute non-resistance to evil. Visitors came out of the walnut doors with distorted faces. "Mr. Rolling is in a bad mood today," they reported in a whisper. Exactly at one o'clock Mr. Rolling glanced at the clock and broke a pencil. It was clear that Zoë Montrose would not call for him to go to lunch. He waited until a quarter past one. During that terrible quarter of an hour two grey hairs appeared on the secretary's impeccable parting. Rolling went to lunch at Griffon's, alone.

The restaurateur, M'sieur Griffon, a tall, stoutish man, formerly a cook and owner of a bar, now chief consultant on the Grand Degustatory and Digestive Arts, met Rolling with an heroic wave of the hand. In a dark-grey frock-coat, with an immaculate Assyrian beard and a noble forehead, M'sieur Griffon stood in the middle of the small hall of his restaurant, resting one hand on what was almost an altar, the silver pedestal of special design on which his famous roast—saddle of mutton with haricot beans—was braising under a domed dish-cover.

The habitués of the restaurant sat on red leather couches placed along the four walls behind long narrow tables; they were mostly businessmen from the Grands Boulevards, and a few women. Except for the altar, the middle of the room was empty. Turning his head, the restaurateur could observe the process of degustation in each of his clients. Not the slightest grimace of dissatisfaction escaped him. Furthermore—he anticipated much: the mysterious process of the secretion of juices, the helical workings of the stomach and the whole psychology of eating based on memories of something eaten some time before and on the flow of blood to various parts of the body—all this was an open book to Monsieur Griffon.

With a severe and at the same time fatherly expression he would walk over to a client and say to him with charmingly gruff tenderness, "Your temperament today, M'sieur, demands a glass of Madeira and a little *Pouilly, très sec*— you may send me to the guillotine but I won't give you a single drop of *vin rouge*. Oysters, a little boiled turbot, the wing of a chicken and a few stalks of asparagus. That collation will give you back your strength." Only a Patagonian, used to a diet of water rats, could object under such circumstances.

M'sieur Griffon did not run with servile haste to the Chemical King's table as might have been expected. Here, in the Academy of Degustation, the multimillionaire and the bookkeeper, the man who thrust his wet umbrella to the porter and the man who stepped importantly out of a Rolls Royce smelling of Havana cigars—all paid the same bill. M'sieur Griffon was a republican and a philosopher. With a benign smile he handed Rolling the menu and advised him to begin with honey-dew melon, and follow it by lobster baked with truffles and saddle of mutton. Mr. Rolling did not drink wine during the day, he knew that.

"Give me a whiskey and soda and put a bottle of champagne in ice," said Rolling through his clenched teeth.

M'sieur Griffon stepped back and for a moment astonishment, fear, and disgust flashed up in his eyes: a client was beginning with whiskey, that dulled the palate, and wanted to continue with champagne, that bloated the stomach. M'sieur Griffon's eyes grew dull, he bowed his head respectfully: his client was lost for today, he could only reconcile himself to that undoubted fact.

After his third whiskey Mr. Rolling began to crush his napkin. A man with such a temperament but standing at the other end of the social ladder, Gaston Bec de Canard, for example, would have found Zoë Montrose before sundown—the bitch, the filthy hussy picked up out of the gutter—and would have sunk the blade of a clasp-knife deep into her side. Different methods were more becoming to Rolling. As he looked at the plate on which the lobster was growing cold he was not thinking of battering the nose of the harlot who had fled from his bed during the night.

The most refined and morbid ideas of revenge emerged from the yellow whiskey fumes, blended and grew in Rolling's brain. It was only now that he realized what beautiful Zoë had meant to him. In his torment he dug his finger-nails into the napkin.

The waiter removed the untouched food and poured out champagne. Rolling seized the glass and drank down the contents thirstily, his gold teeth chattering against the edge of the glass. At that moment Semyonov rushed into the restaurant from the street. Seeing Rolling he pulled off his hat, leaned across the table, and whispered to him:

"Have you seen the newspapers? I've just come from the morgue. It's him. We know nothing about it. I could swear it under oath. We have an alibi. We spent the whole night on Montmartre with the girls. It has been established that the murder took place between three and four in the morning, I got it from the newspapers, the newspapers...."

An earthy, twisted face jumped up and down before Rolling's eyes. His neighbours turned to look at them. A waiter approached with a chair for Semyonov.

"Go to hell," said Rolling through a curtain of whiskey, "you're disturbing my lunch."

"All right, excuse me, I'll wait for you in the car at the corner."

39

All those days there had been nothing of importance in the Paris newspapers, everything was as calm as a forest lake. The bourgeois yawned as they read leading articles on literary subjects, feuilletons about theatre shows, and stories from the lives of artistes.

This untrammelled calm of the press was preparing the way for a hurricane attack on the purse of the *petit bourgeois*. Chemical King Rolling's organization had been set up, petty competitors had been crushed, and he was about to launch a campaign to raise prices. The press had been bought, the journalists had been armed with the necessary information on the chemical industry. Really staggering documents had been prepared for leading articles on political themes. A couple of faces slapped and a couple of duels had got rid of the fools who had said something that ran counter to the general line of the cartel.

Peace and repose reigned in Paris, the sales of the dailies had dropped so that the murder at number sixty-three Rue des Gobelins came as a real godsend.

The next morning all the seventy-five newspapers came out with heavy headlines featuring "the mysterious, nightmare crime." The identity of the murdered man had not been established, his papers had been stolen, at the hotel he had registered under an obviously false name. The murder was apparently not committed for the sake of robbery, gold articles and money in the dead man's pockets had not been touched. It could not possibly have been a crime of revenge since room number eleven bore very obvious signs of a thorough search. Mystery, baffling mystery.

The two o'clock editions reported an astounding detail: a lady's tortoise-shell comb decorated with five large diamonds had been found in the fatal room. On the dusty floor there were traces of a woman's shoes. Paris shuddered at the story of the comb. The murder had been committed by a woman of elegance. A society woman? A bourgeois? A courtesan of the upper ten? Mystery.... Mystery....

The four o'clock editions filled their columns with interviews given by the most famous women of Paris. In one voice they all exclaimed, "No! No!" It could not be a Frenchwoman, this was the work of a German, a Boche. A few voices hinted at Moscow, but that was not a success. The well-known Mimi, from the Olympia Theatre, pronounced an historic phrase, "I am prepared to give myself to whoever solves the mystery for me." That statement was an undoubted success.

In short, Rolling, as he sat at Griffon's, was the only man in the whole of Paris who knew nothing of the murder on the Rue des Gobelins. He was in a very bad temper and deliberately made Semyonov wait in the taxi. Appearing at the corner of the street at last, he got into the taxi and ordered the driver to take them to the morgue. On the way Semyonov, in his most ingratiating manner, told Rolling everything that was in the papers.

At the mention of a tortoise-shell comb with five diamonds Rolling's hands trembled on the knob of his walking-stick. As they neared the morgue he suddenly leaned towards the driver with a gesture to stop, but thought better of it and only gave a snort of fury.

There was a crush at the doors of the morgue. Women in expensive furs, snub-nosed midinettes, suspicious characters from the faubourgs, curious concierges in knitted capes, reporters with perspiring noses and limp collars, actresses hanging on to the arms of fleshy actors—all were trying to get a glimpse of the murdered man on the marble slab, his shirt torn, his feet bare, and his head towards the semi-basement window.

These bare feet made a ghastly impression—they were big and bluish, with untrimmed nails. The deadly pale face was "convulsed in horror." The beard jutted upwards. The women surged eagerly around that grinning mask, they stared with dilated pupils, uttered soft cries and twitters. There he lay, the lover of the lady with the diamond-studded comb.

Semyonov wriggled through the crowd like an eel, making way for Rolling. Rolling looked fixedly into the face of the dead man. He scrutinized him for a second. His eyes screwed up, his fleshy nose wrinkled, his gold teeth flashed.

"Well, it's him, isn't it?" whispered Semyonov.

This time Rolling answered him:

"Another double."

These two words had scarcely been pronounced when a blond head appeared from behind Rolling's shoulder, looked him in the face as though photographing him, and then disappeared in the crowd.

The head belonged to Shelga.

40

Leaving Semyonov in the morgue Rolling drove to the Rue de la Seine. Everything was as he left it, the same quiet panic. Zoë had not been in the house and had not phoned.

Rolling locked himself in the bedroom and walked up and down staring at the tips of his shoes. He stopped on his own side of the bed. He rubbed his chin. He closed his eyes. At last he remembered something forgotten that had been troubling him all day.

"Rolling, Rolling, we're done for...."

It had been said in a soft, hopeless voice, Zoë's voice. It had happened last night—he had suddenly fallen asleep half-way through their conversation. Zoë's voice had not awakened him, had not reached his brain. Now, however, those despairing words rang in his ears.

Rolling jumped as though motivated by a spring. He remembered—Garin's strange fit on the Boulevard Malesherbes; Zoë's excitement at the Souper de Roi night bar; her insistence on knowing what papers Garin might have stolen from the office. And then that "Rolling, Rolling, we're done for . . ." followed by her disappearance; the corpse of the double at the morgue; the comb with the diamonds . . . he remembered that the night before those five diamonds had sparkled in her luxuriant hair.

In the whole chain of events one thing was quite obvious: Garin had employed his old method of diverting the blow from himself to a double. He had stolen papers in Rolling's handwriting to leave on the scene of the murder and bring the police to his office on the Boulevard Malesherbes.

For all his habitual composure Rolling felt a cold shiver run down his back. "Rolling, Rolling, we're done for. . . ." She must have anticipated, must have known of the murder. It took place between three and four in the morning. (The police had arrived at half past four.) Rolling remembered that the last sound to which his brain had been receptive as he fell asleep was the clock striking a quarter to two. After this Zoë had disappeared. Obviously she had hurried to the Rue des Gobelins to destroy anything in his handwriting.

How could Zoë have known exactly when the murder was to take place unless she had planned it herself? Rolling went over to the fireplace, put his elbows on the marble mantleshelf, and covered his face with his hands. Then why had she whispered in such terrified tones, "Rolling, Rolling, we're done for"? . . . Something must have happened yesterday to upset her plans. But what? At what particular moment? In the theatre, in the bar, at home? . . .

Suppose she wanted to correct some error she had made. Had she done it? Garin was alive, Rolling's handwriting had not yet been discovered, and the double had been killed. Did this mean salvation or ruin? Who was the murderer, an accomplice of Zoë's or Garin himself?

And why had Zoë disappeared, why, why, why? In his memory he sought for the moment when the change had come over Zoë—he tried to recall every word, every gesture she had made during the previous day, racking a brain that was accustomed to work of a different kind until his head ached.

As he stood there by the fire he felt that if he could not remember every detail of what happened the game would be lost, he would be defeated, ruined. In three days he was to launch his grand offensive on the stock market and the mere mention of his name in connection with the murder would mean an uproar on the stock exchange and consequent collapse. . . . A blow struck at Rolling would mean a blow at huge sums of money moving thousands of enterprises in America, China, India, Europe, and the African colonies. It would disturb the precision working of the whole mechanism. . . . Railways, steamship lines, mines, factories, banks, hundreds of thousands of clerks, millions of workers, tens of millions of shareholders—the whole thing would wobble, stop dead and then—panic.

Rolling was in the position of a man who did not know from which side the blow would fall. He was in mortal danger. His brain was working as furiously as if he had been paid a million dollars per thought-second. That quarter of an hour by the fireside might have gone down in history as a parallel of Napoleon's famous presence of mind on the Pont d'Arcole.

But then at this most decisive moment (and for the first time in his life) Rolling, the collector of billions, the almost symbolical figure, suddenly abandoned himself to a most absurd occupation as he stood with dilated nostrils before a mirror without seeing his own reflection: instead of analyzing Zoë's actions he began to imagine her person, her delicate, pale face, her icy eyes, her passionate mouth. He sensed the warm smell of her chestnut hair, the touch of her hand. He began to imagine that he, Rolling, with all his desires, tastes, ambitions, thirst for power, with all his bad moods born of indigestion, and his bitter thoughts of death—that all of him had transmigrated to a new shell, into that of a clever, young, and attractive woman. She was not there. It was as if he had been thrown out on a slushy night. He was no longer necessary to himself. She was not there. He was homeless. What use were his global enterprises without her? Heartache, the heartache of a naked, pitiful mannikin!

The Chemical King was startled out of this state of mind by the sound of two feet landing on the carpet. The bedroom window (it was on the ground floor), leading to the park, was open. Rolling trembled all over. In the mirror appeared the reflection of a thickset man with a big moustache and a wrinkled forehead. He bowed his head and stared at Rolling with unblinking eyes.

41

"What do you want?" squealed Rolling, fumbling for the Browning in his hip pocket. The thickset man had apparently anticipated this move and jumped back behind the curtain. From that point of vantage he poked out his head.

"Keep quiet. And don't shout. I don't intend to kill you or steal anything," he raised his hands, "I've come on business."

"This is no place for business. Take your business to 48b Boulevard Malesherbes, from eleven a.m. You came in by the window like a thief."

"I beg your pardon," answered the man, politely. "My name is Gaston Leclaire. I have the rank of sergeant and a war medal. I never go in for petty business and have never been a thief. I advise you to apologize to me immediately, Mr. Rolling, otherwise our conversation cannot continue."

"Go to hell!" said Rolling, already calmer.

"If I go to that address then Mademoiselle Montrose, a lady not unknown to you, will die."

Rolling's face changed. He went straight to Gaston. The latter spoke with the respect due to the owner of many millions and at the same time there was a suggestion of that rough friendliness a man uses when speaking to the husband of his mistress.

"And so, monsieur, you apologize?"

"Do you know where Mademoiselle Montrose is hiding?"

"And so, monsieur, before we continue our conversation am I to understand that you apologize to me?"

"I apologize," roared Rolling.

"I accept!" Gaston came away from the window, smoothed his moustache with an accustomed gesture, coughed, and continued, "Zoë Montrose is in the hands of the murderer of whom all Paris is talking."

"Where is she?" Rolling's lips trembled.

"At Ville d'Avray, near the Parc Saint Cloud, at an overnight hotel close to the Musée Gambetta. Last night I followed them in a car to Ville d'Avray, today I found out the exact address."

"Did she go with him voluntarily?"

"That's what I'd like to know more than anything else," answered Gaston so maliciously that Rolling looked at him in astonishment.

"Excuse me, Monsieur Gaston, but I don't quite understand where you fit into this story. What have you got to do with Mademoiselle Montrose? How comes it that you follow her at night and establish her whereabouts?"

"Enough!" Gaston held out his hand with a noble gesture. "I understand you. You had to ask me that question. And I answer: I am in love and I am jealous."

"Aha!" exclaimed Rolling.

"You want the details? Here they are: last night as I came out of a café where I had drunk a glass of grog I saw Mademoiselle Montrose. She was driving at great speed in a hired car. Her face was ghastly. It was a matter of a second to jump into a taxi and follow her. She stopped her car on Rue des Gobelins and went into the gateway of house number sixty-three. (Rolling blinked as though he had been stung.) Beside myself with jealousy I strode up and down the pavement in front of that house. Exactly at a quarter past four Mademoiselle Montrose came out of the house, not through the street door as I had expected but through a gateway leading into an adjacent park. A man with a black beard, dressed in a cloth coat and a grey hat, held her by the shoulders. The rest you know."

Rolling sank on to a chair (a period piece from the time of the Crusades) and for a long time sat silent, his fingers clutching the carved arms. Here was the missing information. The murderer was Garin. Zoë—his accomplice. The criminal plan was obvious. They had killed the double on the Rue des Gobelins in order to involve him, Rolling, in crooked business and then browbeat him into giving them money to build the machine. The honest sergeant and classical idiot, Gaston, had accidentally discovered the crime. It was all so clear. He must act resolutely and without mercy.

There was an evil gleam in Rolling's eyes. He stood up and kicked the chair aside with his foot.

"I'll ring for the police. You will come with me to Ville d'Avray."

An evil grin spread over Gaston's bewhiskered face.

"Mr. Rolling, I don't think it would be advisable to have the police mixed up in this business. We can manage on our own."

"I want to have the murderer and his accomplice arrested and handed over to justice." Rolling straightened himself up and his voice was as hard as steel.

Gaston made a vague gesture.

"That may be so. But I've got a fine bunch of reliable boys who've seen a thing or two. I could bring them to Ville d'Avray in two cars in an hour's time. I assure you it isn't worth while getting mixed up with the police."

Rolling only snorted at this and snatched at the telephone on the mantelshelf. Gaston, however, was quicker in grasping his hand.

"Don't phone the police!"

"Why not?"

"Because you couldn't think of anything more foolish. (Rolling again reached for the telephone.) You're a man of great intelligence, Mr. Rolling, surely you must understand, there are things one doesn't speak plainly about. I implore you, don't phone. Oh, hell! If you must know, it's because your call for the police will bring us both to the guillotine. (Rolling pushed him in the chest and snatched up the receiver. Gaston looked hastily round and then whispered right into Rolling's ear.) There's a certain Russian engineer living on the Rue des Gobelins and on your instructions Mademoiselle Zoë hired me to send him posthaste to his forefathers. Last night the mission was fulfilled. Now I need ten thousand francs as an advance to my boys. Have you got the money with you?"

A quarter of an hour later a touring car with the hood raised drew up on the Rue de la Seine. Rolling ran from the house and jumped into it. While the car was turning in the narrow street Shelga emerged from behind a corner of the house and jumped on to the back.

The touring car drove along the embankment. On the Champ de Mars, on that spot where Robespierre once stood with ears of corn in his hand and swore before the Altar of the Supreme Being that he would compel all mankind to sign a great collective agreement on eternal peace and eternal justice, there now stood the Eiffel Tower; two and a half million electric candles winked and blinked from its iron carcase, fiery arrows drew pictures and wrote the whole night through for all Paris to read: "Buy Citroën cars— cheap and practical. . . ."

42

It was a warm, damp night. The window, stretching from floor to ceiling, was open, and through it came the occasional rustling of unseen leaves. The room on the first floor of the Hotel A la Grive Noire was dark and quiet. The damp odour of the park mingled with that of perfume. The ancient drapings on the walls, the worn carpets, and the huge wooden bed that had in the course of years given refuge to a whole procession of lovers—all were permeated with these odours. It was a good old place for love in solitude. The trees rustled outside the windows, the breeze brought sad, earthy odours from the park, and a warm bed nurtured the short happiness of lovers. It was also said that Béranger had written his songs in that room. Times had changed, of course. Hurrying lovers, escaping from seething Paris to get away for an hour from the blinding, howling lights of the Eiffel Tower, had no time for the rustling of leaves, no time for love. In our days who could stroll dreamily along the boulevards with a volume of Musset in his pocket? Today everything was speeded up, everything was done at a speed dictated by petrol. "Hallo, *ma petite*, we have an hour and twenty minutes at our disposal! In that time we must see a movie, eat dinner, and get in a spot of love. There's nothing to be done about it, Mimi, that's civilization."

However, the dark crowns of the lime-trees and the gentle chattering of the tree-frogs outside the windows of the Hotel A la Grive Noire did not fit in with the general flow of European civilization. All was quiet and peaceful. Inside the room a door squeaked and steps could be heard on the carpet. The vague outline of a man halted in the middle of the room. He spoke softly and in Russian.

"You must decide. In thirty or forty minutes the car will arrive. What is it to be—yes or no?"

There was movement in the bed but no answer. He drew nearer.

"Zoë, be sensible."

The only answer was a mirthless laugh.

Garin bent over Zoë's face, peered at her, and then sat at her feet on the bed.

"Yesterday's adventure can be regarded as not having occurred. It began somewhat unusually and ended in this bed—I suppose you would call that banality? I agree. Regard it as expunged. Listen, I don't want any other woman but you—how can I help it!"

"Vulgar and stupid," said Zoë.

"I agree with you completely. I am just a vulgar Philistine, I'm primitive. Today I discovered what I need money, power, and fame for—to possess you. Later on, when you woke up I explained my viewpoint to you: I don't want to part with you and don't intend to."

"Oho!" said Zoë.

"'Oho!' means nothing. I understand that you are a clever and proud woman and that you are very indignant at the idea of somebody forcing your hand. What else can I do? We have the nexus of blood holding us together. If you go back to Rolling I shall fight. And as I am a vulgar Philistine I will send us all to the guillotine, Rolling, you, and myself."

"You've said that before. Don't repeat yourself."

"Aren't you convinced?"

"What have you to offer in exchange for Rolling? I'm an expensive woman."

"The Olivine Belt."

"What?"

"The Olivine Belt. H-m-m, it would take too long to explain what that is. We'd need a free evening and reference books. In twenty minutes we have to leave. The Olivine Belt is power over the whole world. I'll hire your Rolling as my door-porter, that's what the Olivine Belt is. It'll be in my hands in two years. You will not be just a rich woman, or even the richest in the world—that's insipid. But power! The inebriation of power never before known on earth. We have means to achieve this more perfect than those of Genghis Khan. You want to be worshipped as a goddess? We'll order temples to be built to you on all five continents and in each of them your statue will be crowned with wreaths of vine leaves."

"How terribly bourgeois!"

"All right. I'm not joking now. If you wish it you may be the vicar of God or the Devil on earth, whichever is the more to your liking. If you feel a desire to kill—sometimes one feels such an urge—you will have power over all mankind. A woman like you, Zoë, will find plenty of use for the wealth of the Olivine Belt. I am making you a good offer. Two years of struggle and I'll reach the Olivine Belt. Don't you believe me?"

For some time Zoë did not answer and then said in a low voice:

"Why should I take the risk alone? Show some courage yourself."

Garin, it seemed, was endeavouring to see her eyes in the darkness, then, almost sadly, almost tenderly, he said:

"If not, you may go. I shall not follow you. Make your choice voluntarily."

Zoë heaved a short sigh. She sat up in bed and lifted her hands to adjust her hair (this was a good sign).

"In the future we have the Olivine Belt. What have you got now?" she asked, holding hairpins between her teeth.

"At the moment I have my apparatus and carbon pyramids. Get up. Come to my room and I'll show you the apparatus."

"It's not much. All right, I'll look at it. Let's go."

43

In Garin's room the balcony window was closed and curtained. Against the wall stood two suitcases. (He had been at the Hotel A la Grive Noire over a week.) Garin locked the door. Zoë sat down, put her elbows on the table, and shaded her eyes from the ceiling lamp. Her grass-green silk mackintosh was crumpled, her hair was put up carelessly, and her face wore a tired expression—all of which made her more attractive than ever. Garin, as he opened a suitcase, kept glancing at her with burning eyes framed in blue rings.

"This is my apparatus," he said, putting two metal boxes on the table: one of them was narrow, like a piece cut from a pipe, the other was a flat, twelve-sided affair three times the diameter of the first.

He placed the two boxes together and fastened them with bolts. The pipe he pointed towards the fire-grate and then took the round lid off the twelve-sided box. Inside this housing a bronze ring stood on edge with twelve porcelain cups attached to it.

"This is a model," he said, taking a box of pyramids out of the other suitcase. "It won't stand up to more than an hour's work. The machine must be built from exceptionally durable materials and ten times stronger than this. It would be very heavy to carry and I am constantly on the move. (He placed twelve pyramids in the twelve cups.) From the outside you can't see or understand anything. Here is a diagram, the long cross-section." He leaned over Zoë's chair, inhaling the perfume of her hair, and opened out a drawing about half the size of a sheet of newspaper. "You want me to risk everything in this game as you do, Zoë. Look here. This is the general scheme.

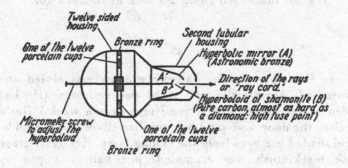

"It's as simple as ABC. It's the purest accident that nobody discovered it before me. The whole secret is in this hyperbolic mirror (A), shaped like the reflector in an ordinary searchlight, and this piece of shamonite (B), also made in the form of a hyperbolic sphere. The hyperbolic mirror functions in this way:

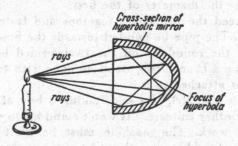

"Rays of light falling on the inner surface of the hyperbolic mirror meet at one point, at the focus of the hyperbola. This is common knowledge. Here is something new: in the focus of the hyperbolic mirror I place a second hyperbola (B) in reverse, as it were, in relation to the other—this is the revolving hyperboloid, turned from shamonite, a mineral that polishes well and has a very high fuse point—there are inexhaustible deposits of it in the north of Russia. What happens to the rays?

"The rays concentrated at the focus of the mirror (A) are directed on to the surface of the hyperboloid (B) and are reflected from it geometrically parallel—in other words the hyperboloid (B) concentrates all the rays into one ray, or into a ray cord of any thickness. By turning the micrometer screw I adjust the hyperboloid (B) and can produce a ray of any thickness.

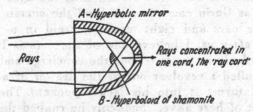

"The energy lost by transmission through the atmosphere is negligible. In actual practice I can reduce the 'ray cord' to the thickness of an ordinary needle."

Hearing this Zoë got up, pulled and cracked her fingers, and sat down again, clasping her knee.

"For my first experiments I used ordinary tallow-candles as the source of light. By adjusting the hyperboloid (B) I reduced the ray to the thickness of a knitting needle and easily cut through an inch board with it. Then I realized that the whole secret lay in the discovery of sufficiently powerful but compact sources of radiant energy. Three years of work which have cost the lives of two of my assistants have produced these carbon pyramids. There is so much energy in these pyramids that if I place them in the apparatus and light them (they burn for about five minutes), they give me a 'ray cord' powerful enough to cut through a railway bridge in a few seconds.... Do

121

you realize what possibilities this offers? There is nothing in the whole world that can stand up against the power of the ray. . . . Buildings, fortresses, dreadnoughts, airships, rocks, mountains, the earth's crust . . . my ray will pierce, and cut through and destroy everything."

Garin stopped suddenly and raised his head, listening. He heard the crunching of gravel, and the dying sound of motor-car engines as they were shut off came drifting into the room. He leaped to the window and slipped behind the curtain. Zoë watched Garin's motionless figure outlined behind the dusty red velvet; then the figure seemed to waver as Garin came from behind the curtain.

"Three cars and eight men," he said in a whisper. "They're after us. I believe one of the cars is Rolling's. There's nobody in the hotel but the concierge and us. (He quickly pulled a revolver out of the drawer of a bedside table and thrust it into his jacket pocket.) They won't let me out of here alive." Suddenly he rubbed the side of his nose gleefully. "Well, Zoë, make up your mind: yes or no? There'll never be another moment like this."

"You're mad." Zoë's face flushed and she looked younger. "Get away while you can."

Garin stuck his beard out defiantly.

"Eight men. . . . That's nothing!" He lifted the apparatus and turned it with the muzzle towards the door. He slapped his pockets. His face suddenly changed colour.

"Matches," he whispered, "I've no matches."

Perhaps he said that in order to test Zoë. Perhaps he really had no matches in his pocket—and his life depended on matches. He looked at Zoë dumbly, like an animal awaiting death. As though moving in her sleep, she took her bag from a chair, opened it, took out a box of wax vestas, and gave them to him slowly, with difficulty. As he took them he felt the icy coldness of her thin hand.

From the spiral staircase came the sound of wary footsteps.

44

A number of men stopped outside their door. They could hear the sound of their breathing.

"Who's that?" asked Garin loudly in French.

"A telegram," answered a gruff voice. "Open the door."

Zoë, without a word, grasped Garin by the shoulders and shook her head. He drew her towards the corner of the room and forcefully sat her down on the carpet. Then he went straight back to the apparatus and shouted:

"Push the telegram under the door."

"Open the door when you're told," growled the same voice.

Another voice asked cautiously:

"Is the woman there with you?"

"Yes, she's here."

"Give her to us and we'll leave you in peace."

"I'm warning you," said Garin viciously, "if you don't get to hell out of here not one of you will be alive in a minute's time."

"Oh, la-la! . . . Oh-ho-ho! . . . Hi-hi! . . ." voices whined and brayed; bodies were hurled against the door, the china door handle turned, plaster fell from around the door frame. Zoë did not take her eyes off Garin. His face was pale, his movements were swift and confident. He squatted on his heels and turned the micrometer screw of his apparatus. He took out a few vestas and placed them on the table beside the box. Then he took out his revolver, straightened up, and stood waiting. The door was giving way. Suddenly glass fell from the window with a crash and the curtains bulged. Garin fired into the window. He squatted down, lit a match, pushed it into the apparatus, and shut the round lid.

After the shot came a few seconds' silence, then came an attack at the door and window simultaneously. They banged on the door with some heavy object and the panels were splintered. The curtain covering the window was twisted and fell together with the curtain rod.

"Gaston!" screamed Zoë. Bec de Canard came crawling over the window grille with an apache-knife in his mouth. The door still held. Garin, as white as a sheet, turned the micrometer screw of his apparatus and the revolver danced in his left hand. A flame jumped and roared inside the machine. The circle of light on the wall (opposite the muzzle of the machine) grew smaller, the wallpaper began to smoke. Gaston, his eye on the revolver, was creeping along the wall, crouched for a spring. He now held the knife in his hand, Spanish fashion, point towards his own body. The circle of light became an incandescent spot. Bewhiskered faces peered through the broken panels of the door. Garin seized the apparatus in both hands and turned the muzzle towards Bec de Canard.

Zoë saw it all: Gaston opened his mouth, either to scream or to gasp for air. A strip of smoke passed across his chest and the hands that he tried to raise fell. He fell backward on to the carpet. His head together with his shoulders fell from the lower part of his body like a piece of bread cut off a loaf.

Garin turned the machine towards the door. On the way the ray from the apparatus cut through the electric lighting wires and the lamp on the ceiling went out. The dazzling, dead straight ray, as thin as a needle, played above the door and pieces of wood fell down. The ray crawled lower down. There came a short howl, as though a cat had been trodden on. Somebody stumbled in the dark. A body fell softly. The ray danced about two feet from the floor. There was an odour of burning flesh. Suddenly there was silence broken only by the flame roaring in the apparatus.

Garin coughed and said in a hoarse voice that almost refused to obey him:

"They're all finished with."

Outside the broken window the breeze played in the invisible lime-trees and they rustled sleepily. Out of the darkness below, where the cars were standing motionless, a voice called out in Russian:

"Pyotr Petrovich, are you alive?" Garin appeared at the window. "Careful. It is I, Shelga. Remember our agreement? I've got Rolling's car. You must get away. Save the apparatus. I'm waiting."

45

Following his usual Sunday evening custom Professor Reicher was playing chess on the little balcony of his third-floor flat. On this occasion his opponent was Heinrich Wolf, his favourite pupil. They smoked in silence, their eyes fixed on the chess-board. The last glow of evening had long since died away at the end of the long street, the night air was heavy, there was not a movement amongst the leaves of the ivy that covered the balcony. Below them the asphalted square lay deserted under the starry sky.

Grunting and snorting the professor was thinking out his move. His hand with its yellow finger-nails hovered over the board but did not touch any of the chessmen. He removed the cigarette end from his mouth.

"I must think about this."

"As you please," answered Wolf. His handsome face with its high forehead, clean-cut chin and short, straight nose gave one the impression of a mighty machine at rest. The professor was more temperamental (he belonged to the older generation)—his steel-grey beard was dishevelled and there were red patches on his wrinkled forehead.

A tall lamp under a wide, coloured shade threw its light on their faces. A few consumptive, green creatures fluttered around the lamp or sat on the freshly ironed table-cloth twitching their whiskers, staring with their

125

tiny dots of eyes, little dreaming that they were watching the gods at play. Inside the room a clock struck ten.

Frau Reicher, the professor's mother, a neat-looking old lady, sat motionless; she could no longer read or knit by artificial light. In the distance, where the lights of a high house showed bright through the darkness of the night, the huge stone expanse of Berlin could be faintly discerned. If it had not been for her son at the chess-board, the soft light of the lampshade, the green creatures on the table-cloth, the horror that had long since filled her soul would have risen up again as it had done so often in the years that had drained the blood from her dried-up face—the horror of the millions that were advancing on the city, advancing towards that stone balcony. These millions were not called Fritz, Johannes, Heinrich or Otto, they were called "masses." They were all alike, badly shaven, with paper shirt-fronts, grimy with iron and lead dust—and from time to time they filled the streets. They thrust out their chins and made many demands.

Frau Reicher remembered those happy days when her fiancé, Otto Reicher, had returned from Sedan after the victory over the Emperor of France. He smelled of leather, like a real soldier, wore a beard, and talked in a loud voice. She went to meet him outside the town, in a blue dress with ribbons and flowers. Germany raced on from victory to victory, to happiness, together with Otto's beard, together with pride and hope. Soon the whole world would be conquered. . . .

Frau Reicher's life was over. A second war had come and gone. Somehow they had managed to drag their feet out of a morass in which millions of human bodies were rotting. And then came the masses. Look anyone of them in the eyes under the peak of his cap. They were not German eyes. Their expression was stubborn, morose, and incomprehensible. There was no way of approach to those eyes. Frau Reicher was filled with horror.

Alexei Semyonovich Khlinov appeared on the balcony. He was neatly dressed in his grey Sunday suit.

Khlinov bowed to Frau Reicher, wished her good evening, and sat down beside the professor who frowned good-humouredly and winked jokingly at the chess-board. Magazines and foreign newspapers lay on the table. The professor, like all other intellectuals in Germany, was poor. His hospitality was confined to the soft light of the lamp on the freshly ironed cloth, the offer of a twenty-pfennig cigar, and to conversation that was probably worth more than a supper with champagne and other superfluities.

From seven in the morning till seven at night, on working days, the professor was business-like, severe, and uncommunicative. On Sundays he willingly accompanied his friends on an "excursion into the realms of fantasy." He liked talking from "one end of the cigar to the other."

"Yes, I have to think this over," repeated the professor through a cloud of smoke.

"As you please," answered Wolf, coldly polite.

Khlinov opened the Paris newspaper *L'Intransigeant* and under the headline "Mysterious Crime at Ville d'Avray" saw a picture showing seven men cut to pieces. "Oh, well," thought Khlinov. But what he read farther made him sit up and think.

"... It is assumed that the crime was committed with some weapon hitherto unknown, either a hot wire or heat ray working at extremely high tension. We have succeeded in establishing the nationality and appearance of the criminal: he is, as could be expected, a Russian. (Here followed a description given by the proprietress of the hotel.) On the night of the crime he had a woman with him. All else is wrapped in mystery. It may be that the bloody find in the forest at Fontainebleau, where an unknown man was found unconscious some thirty yards from the road, will throw some light on it. Four bullet wounds were found on the body. Papers and everything else that might have established the identity of the man had been stolen. The victim had apparently been thrown from a car. Up to time of going to press he was still unconscious. . . ."

46

"Check!" exclaimed the professor. "Check and mate. Wolf, you're defeated, your territory is occupied, you're on your knees, you'll have to pay reparations for sixty-six years. Such is the law of higher imperialist politics."

"Revenge?" asked Wolf.

"Oh, no. We're going to enjoy all the advantages of the conqueror."

The professor tapped Khlinov on the knee.

"What was that you were reading in the paper, my young and irreconcilable Bolshevik? About the seven dissected Frenchmen? What else can you expect? Victors are always inclined to excesses. History always strives to establish an equilibrium. The victors carry pessimism home with them together with their booty. They start eating too richly. Their stomachs cannot handle the fat and their blood is tainted with poison. They cut people to pieces, hang themselves on their braces, and jump over bridges. They lose their love of life. Optimism is all that is left to the conquered in place of what they have lost. It is a superb quality of the human will to believe that everything is for the best in this best of worlds. Pessimism must be uprooted. The morose and bloody mysticism of the East, the hopeless sorrow of the Hellenic civilization, the unbridled passions of Rome amidst the smoking ruins of conquered cities, the fanaticism of the Middle Ages when people awaited the end of the world and the Day of Judgement at any moment and, lastly, our own age that is building card houses of well-being and swallows the intolerable twaddle of the cinema—on what foundation, I ask you, is the feeble psyche of the Lord of Nature built? The foundation is pessimism. Damned pessimism. I've read your Lenin, my friend. He's a great optimist. I admire him."

"You're in excellent form today, professor," said Wolf, darkly.

"Do you know why?" The professor leaned back in his wicker chair, his chin folded up into wrinkles, his eyes were merry and youthful under his heavy brows. "I've made the most curious discovery. I have received a number of reports and in comparing certain data I suddenly came to a remarkable conclusion. If the German government were not a gang of adventurers, if I were sure that my discovery would not fall into the hands of adventurers and scoundrels, I would most probably publish it. As it is, it is better to keep quiet."

"But you can share your secret with us, can't you?" said Wolf.

The professor winked at him slily.

"What would you say, for example, my friend, if I were to offer an honest German government ... you hear me, I stress the word 'honest,' I give it a specific meaning ... if I were to offer them unlimited quantities of gold?"

"Where from?" asked Wolf.

"Out of the earth, of course."

"Where is that earth?"

"Anywhere. At any point on the earth's surface. In the centre of Berlin if you like. But I won't make that offer. I don't believe that gold would enrich us, all the Fritzes, Michels. ... We would probably be only the poorer for it. ... Only one man," he turned his grey head with its lion's mane towards Khlinov, "your compatriot, proposed a proper use for gold. You understand?"

Khlinov smiled and nodded his head.

"Professor, I'm accustomed to take you seriously," said Wolf.

"I'll try to be serious. In Moscow the frosts go down to thirty degrees below zero centigrade in winter. If you splash water out of a third-storey window it falls to the ground in little balls of ice. The earth has been revolving in interplanetary space for ten thousand, fifteen thousand million years. It should have grown cold in that time, shouldn't it? I maintain that the earth has long since grown cold, that it has irradiated all its heat into interplanetary space. You will naturally ask: what about the volcanoes, the molten lava, the hot geysers? Between the hard crust of the earth, slightly warmed by the sun, and the basic nuclear mass there is a belt of molten metals, the so-called Olivine Belt. It owes its existence to the constant atomic disintegration of the central mass. This central mass is a sphere with the temperature of interplanetary space, that is two hundred and seventy-three degrees below zero centigrade. The products of this disintegration —the Olivine Belt—are nothing more than metals in a state of flux: olivine, mercury, and gold. According to numerous data the Belt does not lie very deep in the earth—from ten to fifty thousand feet. It is possible to sink a shaft in the centre of Berlin and molten gold will pour out spontaneously, like oil, from the Olivine Belt."

"Logical, tempting, but impracticable," said Wolf after a short silence. "With the appliances we have at present it is impossible to sink a shaft that depth."

47

Khlinov placed his hand on the outspread pages of *L'Intransigeant.*

"Professor, that picture reminds me of a conversation that I had on board the plane when I was on my way to

Berlin. The task of boring as far as the disintegrating elements of the earth's centre is not quite so impossible."

"What has that got to do with chopped up Frenchmen?" asked the professor, lighting another cigar.

"The murders at Ville d'Avray were committed with a heat ray."

Hearing these words Wolf moved to the table, an expression of caution on his cold face.

"Ach, those rays again." The professor screwed up his face with a sour look. "Nonsense, bluff, a *canard* spread by the British War Office."

"The apparatus was designed by a Russian, I know him," answered Khlinov. "He is a talented inventor and a ruthless criminal."

Khlinov told them all that he knew of Engineer Garin: about his work at the Polytechnical Institute, the crime on Krestovsky Island, the strange finds in the cellar of the cottage, about his calling Shelga to Paris, and the mad hunt after Garin's apparatus that was apparently going on at the moment.

"Here is the evidence." Khlinov pointed to the photograph in the paper. "That's Garin's work."

Wolf frowned as he examined the picture. The professor continued absent-mindedly:

"You think that heat rays could be used to bore through the earth? Although . . . yes, clay and granite melt at three thousand degrees centigrade. Very, very interesting. Couldn't we get hold of that Garin by telegraph? H-m-m. If we were to combine the drilling with artificial refrigeration and use electric lifts to remove the rocks as they are dug out we could dig pretty deep. My friend, I'm devilishly interested in what you have said."

Contrary to his custom the professor walked up and down the balcony until two o'clock in the morning, puffing at his cigar and evolving plans each more astounding than its predecessor.

48

When they left the professor's house, Wolf and Khlinov usually parted company on the square. On this occasion, however, Wolf walked on beside Khlinov, his head bowed; he tapped the ground moodily with his walking-stick as they went along.

"So you think that Garin disappeared with his machine after that business at Ville d'Avray?" he asked.

"Yes."

"And what about the 'bloody find in the forest at Fontainebleau'? Couldn't that be Garin?"

"Do you mean that Shelga might have got the apparatus?"

"I do."

"I hadn't thought of that. Yes, that wouldn't be at all bad."

"I suppose not," said Wolf, mockingly, and raised his head.

Khlinov cast a swift glance at his companion. They both stopped. A distant street-lamp lit up Wolf's face, his malicious sneer, his cold eyes, his stubborn chin.

"In any case it's all guesswork, so far we've nothing to quarrel about," said Khlinov.

"Yes, I know."

"Wolf, I'm not trying to be smart with you, but I tell you in all seriousness that Garin's apparatus must be in the U.S.S.R. That one desire of mine is enough to make me your enemy. On my word of honour, my dear Wolf, you have a very vague idea of what is good and bad for your country."

"Are you trying to insult me?"

"Oh, hell. Although . . . yes." Khlinov, in true Russian style, which Wolf immediately noticed, pushed his hat over one ear and scratched behind the other. "After we've killed about seven million men between us is there any sense in getting insulted at a word? ... You're a German from head to foot—armoured infantry, a maker of machines, I suppose your nerves are made of different stuff from mine. Listen, Wolf, if Garin's apparatus fell into the hands of somebody like you, the devil alone knows what you would do with it."

"Germany will never become reconciled to her abasement."

When they reached the house where Khlinov rented a room on the ground floor they parted in silence. Khlinov went in and Wolf stood outside for some time slowly rolling his extinguished cigar between his teeth. Suddenly a ground window burst open and Khlinov leaned out excitedly.

"Ah. You're still here. Thank God. Wolf, I've got a telegram from Shelga in Paris. Listen. 'Criminal escaped. Am wounded, shall be inactive long time. Danger of world calamity. Your presence essential.' "

"I'm coming with you," said Wolf.

49

Shadows of leaves flitted across the white window-curtains beyond which could be heard the constant gurgle of water. Portable sprays on the hospital lawns set up fine showers of water that turned to rainbows in the sunshine and dripped from the leaves of a plane-tree under the window.

In a high, white room Shelga lay dozing in the soft light penetrating through the curtain.

The noises of Paris came drifting in from a distance. Nearer sounds were the rustling of the trees, the voices of the birds, and the monotonous splashing of the water.

Whenever a car hooted near by or there were footsteps in the corridor Shelga swiftly opened his eyes and glanced sharply at the door in alarm. He could not move. Both his arms were rendered immobile by plaster casts, his chest and head were bandaged. His only defence were his eyes. And again the sweet sounds from the garden lulled him to sleep.

A Sister of the Carmelite Order, in white from head to foot, woke Shelga: with her plump hands she carefully raised a porcelain gravy bowl filled with tea to his lips. After she had gone the fragrance of lavender remained.

The day passed in sleep alternating with alarm. This was the seventh day since Shelga, bleeding and unconscious, had been picked up in the forest at Fontainebleau.

A *juge d'instruction* had twice questioned him already. Shelga's deposition was the following:

"At twelve o'clock, midnight, I was attacked by two men. I defended myself with my stick and my fists. I was four times wounded and remember nothing more."

"Did you see the faces of your attackers?"

"The lower parts of their faces were covered with handkerchiefs."

"And so you defended yourself with a walking-stick?"

"Actually it was a branch I had picked up in the forest."

"How did you come to be in the forest at Fontainbleau so late at night?"

"I had been for a walk, had had a look at the palace, wanted to come back through the forest, and lost my way."

"How do you account for the fact that fresh traces of a car were found near the place where you were attacked?"

"The criminals must have used a car."

"To kill or rob you?"

"Neither the one nor the other, I think. Nobody knows me in Paris. I do not work at the Embassy. I have no political mission to fulfil. I had very little money with me."

"Then it could not have been you the criminals were waiting for when they stood under the double oak in the glade where one of them smoked and the other lost a cuff-link with a valuable pearl in it."

In all probability they were young society scapegraces who had lost a lot of money at the races or in the casino. They were probably looking for an opportunity to retrieve their fortunes. A man with his pocket-book full of thousand-franc notes might very well come their way in the Fontainebleau Forest.

At the second interrogation, when the *juge d'instruction* confronted him with the telegram he had sent to Khlinov in Berlin (given to the *juge d'instruction* by the Carmelite Sister) Shelga said:

"That's in code. It concerns the arrest of an important criminal who escaped from Russia."

"Can't you be a little more frank with me?"

"No, it's not my secret."

Shelga answered all questions precisely and clearly, looking straight into his interlocutor's eyes honestly and even a little foolishly. There was nothing left for the *juge d'instruction* to do but believe in his sincerity.

The danger, however, was not past. There was danger in the columns of the newspapers that were filled with details of the "nightmare crime at Ville d'Avray," there was danger behind the door, behind the white curtains that quivered in the breeze, there was danger in the gravy bowl lifted to his lips by the plump hands of the Carmelite Sister.

There was only one way out: to get the plaster casts and the bandages off as quickly as possible. Shelga lay motionless, half asleep.

50

...Dozing, he remembered.

The headlamps were shut off. The car slowed down. Garin leaned forward and whispered loudly through the window of the car.

"Shelga, turn here. There's a glade. There it is."

The car lumbered heavily across the ditch, passed between the trees, and came to a standstill.

In the starlight lay a winding glade. Rocks loomed vaguely in the shadow of the trees.

The engine was switched off. There was a strong smell of grass. A stream babbled sleepily, a haze hanging over it merged like a vague shroud into the depths of the glade.

Garin jumped out on to the wet grass and gave his hand to Zoë. Her hat pulled down over her eyes, she got out of the car and lifted her face to the stars. She shrugged her shoulders.

"Get out, will you?" snapped Garin.

Then Rolling crawled out of the car, head first. His gold teeth gleamed brightly in the shadow cast by his bowler hat.

The stream splashed and gurgled amongst the stones. Rolling pulled a hand out of his pocket, a hand that had apparently been clenched for a long time.

"If you're preparing my execution here," he began in a husky voice, "I protest. In the name of justice. In the name of humanity. I protest as an American. As a Christian. I offer you any ransom you like for my life."

Zoë stood with her back towards him. Garin spoke contemptuously.

"I could have killed you there, if I'd wanted to."

"Ransom?" asked Rolling promptly.

"No."

"Participation in your . . ." Rolling blew out his cheeks, ". . . in your strange enterprises?"

"Yes. You ought to remember.... On the Boulevard Malesherbes I told you...."

"Good," answered Rolling, "tomorrow I'll receive you. I must think over your proposal again."

Zoë said in a low voice:

"Rolling, don't talk nonsense."

"Mademoiselle!" Rolling jumped and his bowler hat fell on to his nose. "Mademoiselle.... Your conduct is unheard of. You've deceived me.... You whore...."

Zoë answered him in the same low voice:

"Go to hell! You can talk to Garin."

Rolling and Garin moved over to the double oak. Over there an electric torch was switched on and two heads bent close together. For a few seconds nothing could be heard except the splashing of the water amongst the stones.

"...But there aren't three of us ... there's a fourth here ... there's a witness," Rolling's sharp voice reached Shelga's ears.

"Who's there, who's there?" muttered Shelga, shuddering and still half-asleep. His pupils distended in alarm.

Before him on the white chair sat Khlinov with his hat on his knees.

51

"I had no time to think out their move," Shelga told him, "I acted like a fool, that's all."

"It was a mistake to take Rolling with you in the car," answered Khlinov.

"Like hell I took him! When the shooting and killing began in the hotel Rolling crouched in his car like a rat in its hole, with a couple of Colts ready for action. I had no weapon with me. I climbed on to the balcony and saw how Garin dealt with the gangsters. I told Rolling about it. He got scared, hissed something at me but refused to get out of the car. Then he tried to shoot at Zoë Montrose but Garin and I twisted his hands behind his back. There was no time to spare so I jumped into the driver's seat and made off."

"When they went into a huddle under the oak-tree surely you must have realized what was going on?"

"I knew they meant to finish me off. What could I do? Run for it? You know, I'm a sportsman, after all.... Apart from that, I had a plan worked out. I had a fake passport for Garin with half a dozen visas on it. His machine was within reach ... in the car.... Under those circumstances how could I think of my own skin?"

"I suppose you couldn't. And so they came to an agreement...."

"Rolling signed some paper, there under the tree, I saw that quite clearly. After that I heard what he said about the fourth witness, about me, that is. In a whisper I said to Zoë, 'Listen, we just passed a policeman and he noted the number of the car. If I'm found dead you'll all three be in handcuffs tomorrow.' D'you know what she answered me? What a woman! ... She didn't look back but over her shoulder she said, 'All right, I'll bear that in mind.' And how lovely she is! ... A real she-devil. But never mind. Garin and Rolling came back to the car. I acted as though nothing had happened. Zoë got in first and then leaned out and said something in English. Garin said to me, 'Comrade Shelga, now get going, full speed westwards.' I stooped down in front of the radiator.... That was where I blundered. And that was the one chance they had. Once the car was moving at speed they would have been afraid to do anything. And so I started the engine. ... Suddenly on the top of my head, in my brain ... it was like a house falling on me, bones cracked, something hit me, light seared my eyes, and I went out. The only thing I noticed was Rolling's distorted mug. The

son of a bitch. He put four bullets into me. When I
opened my eyes I was in this room."

Shelga had grown tired from talking. He lay silent for
a long time.

"Where can Rolling be now?" asked Khlinov.

"Where? Why, in Paris of course. He's handling the
press. He's making a grand offensive on the chemical front.
He's simply shovelling in the money. The point is that at
any moment I'm expecting a bullet through the window
or poison in that gravy bowl they feed me from. He'll
finish me off, of course."

"Then why do you keep quiet? ... You must communicate with the Prefect of Police at once."

"My dear comrade, you're out of your mind! I'm only
alive because I keep quiet."

52

"And so you actually saw the machine at work, Shelga?"

"I saw it and now I know—guns, gas, aeroplanes, and
all that are just toys for babies. Don't forget that Garin
isn't alone. Garin plus Rolling. A death-dealing machine
and Rolling's billions. We can expect anything from that
combination."

Khlinov raised the blind and stood for a long time
at the window staring out at the emerald green lawn, at
the old gardener who was having difficulty in dragging the
metal pipes of the sprinkler over to the shady side of the
garden, at the black thrushes that were busy hunting earth-
worms under the verbena bushes. The sky, delightfully
blue, gave the garden an air of eternal peace.

"Suppose we leave them to themselves, let Rolling
and Garin unfold their scheme in all its magnificence,"
began Khlinov, "and it will soon be over. The world must
inevitably perish. Here only the thrushes live sensibly."

Khlinov turned away from the window. "Stone-age man was undoubtedly greater. He decorated the interiors of his caves because he felt an artistic urge and not for pay; sitting by his fire he thought about mammoths and thunderstorms, about the strange cycle of life and death and about himself. The devil knows that was really dignified! His brain was still small, his skull thick, but spiritual energy radiated from his head. What the hell do people of today want with flying machines? I'd like to take some dandy from the boulevards and confront him with a paleolithic man in his cave. That hairy gentleman would ask him, 'What has your brain been doing these hundred thousand years, you son of a sick bitch?' And that dandy would twist and turn: 'Ah, d'you know I don't go in much for brainwork, I prefer to enjoy the fruits of civilization. Monsieur Ancestor.... If it were not for the danger of the *hoi polloi* revolting our world would be truly beautiful. Women, restaurants, a little excitement over cards in the casino, a little sport.... But the real trouble is these constant crises and revolutions—they make one tired....' And the ancestor would fix his burning eyes on the dandy and would say, 'As for me, I like to think, I sit here and admire the genius of my mind. I would like it to penetrate into the universe.'"

Khlinov stopped talking. He smiled, staring into the half-light of a paleolithic cave. He shook his head.

"What do Garin and Rolling want? They want to be tickled. Let them call it power over the whole world, if they like, all the same it's nothing more than just tickling. Thirty million people perished in the last war. This time they want to kill three hundred million. Spiritual energy is in a state of coma. Professor Reicher only dines on Sundays. All the week he eats two pieces of bread with margarine and jam for lunch and boiled potatoes with salt for dinner. Such is the reward for brainwork.... And that's how it will be until we have blown up all that 'civilization' of theirs. We'll put Garin in a lunatic asylum and send Rolling away to use his administrative ability on some Wrangel Island.... You're right. We must fight. I'm ready. Garin's machine must belong to the U.S.S.R."

"We shall have that machine," said Shelga, closing his eyes.

"Where do we begin?"

"With a spot of intelligence work."

"In what direction?"

"Garin is most likely building machines at top speed now. That was only a model he had at Ville d'Avray. If he manages to build a full-size machine it will be difficult to get it away from him. The first thing we want to know is—where is he building his machines?"

"That will take money."

"Go today to Rue Grenelle and talk with our ambassador. I've already told him a little. He'll give you money. The second thing: we must find Zoë Montrose. That's very important. She's a clever woman, cruel and with a tremendous imagination. She has brought Garin and Rolling together to the death. She is the spring that works their whole mechanism."

"Excuse me, but I'm not going to fight women."

"Alexei Semyonovich, she's stronger than you and I together. She'll spill plenty of blood yet."

53

Zoë got out of the low round bath and offered her back—the maid placed a bath-robe of Turkish towelling on her shoulders. Zoë, still covered with little bubbles of sea foam, sat down on a marble bench.

Flickering sun-rays slanted through the portholes, a greenish light played on the marble walls, the bathroom swayed slightly. The maid wiped Zoë's legs cautiously, like something very precious, and drew on stockings and white shoes.

"Your lingerie, madame."

Zoë got up lazily and the maid dressed her in cobwebby underwear. She glanced past the mirror and frowned. The maid dressed her in a white skirt and a white jacket with gold buttons, cut sailor fashion, all proper and fitting for the owner of a three-hundred-ton yacht in the Mediterranean Sea.

"Make up, madame?"

"You're crazy," answered Zoë, looked slowly at the maid and went up on deck where breakfast was laid on a low wicker table on the shady side.

Zoë sat down at the table. She broke a piece of bread in her fingers absent-mindedly and looked over the side. The narrow white hull of the yacht slid over the mirror-like surface of the water—the sea was a clear blue, a little darker than the cloudless sky. An odour of freshly-washed decks pervaded the air and a warm breeze caressed her legs under her skirt.

On both sides of the slightly curved deck of narrow yellowish planks stood wicker armchairs and in the centre a silver Anatolian carpet was spread, on which a number of brocade cushions lay scattered. From bridge to stern stretched a blue silken awning with fringe and tassels.

Zoë sighed and began her breakfast.

Stepping softly, Captain Jansen came smilingly up to her —he was a Norwegian, clean-shaven, rosy-cheeked, like a grown-up boy. He slowly raised two fingers to a cap worn over one ear.

"Good morning, Madame Lamolle." (Zoë sailed under that name and under the French flag.)

The captain was all in white, well-groomed and elegant in a clumsy, sailor fashion. Zoë looked him over from the gold oak-leaves on his cap to his white, rope-soled shoes. She was satisfied.

"Good morning, Jansen."

"Permit me to report: course, north-west by west, latitude and longitude (such and such), Vesuvius is visible on the horizon. We shall see Naples in less than an hour."

"Sit down, Jansen."

With a movement of her hand she invited him to participate in her breakfast. Jansen sat down on a wicker stool that creaked under the weight of his strong body. He refused breakfast, he had eaten at nine o'clock. Out of politeness he took a cup of coffee.

Zoë examined his sun-tanned face with its blond eyebrows—it gradually was suffused with colour. Without even tasting his coffee he placed the cup back on the table.

"We must take in fresh water and oil for the engines," he said without raising his eyes.

"What? Put into Naples? How boring. If you must have water and oil, we can stand in the outer roads."

"Aye, aye, madame," answered the captain softly.

"Jansen, weren't your ancestors pirates?"

"Yes, madame."

"That must have been thrilling! Adventure, danger, revelry, the rape of beautiful women. . . . Aren't you sorry you're not a buccaneer?"

Jansen did not answer. His reddish eyelashes flickered. There were wrinkles on his forehead.

"Well?"

"I was well brought up, madame."

"I don't doubt it."

"Is there anything about me that leads you to suppose that I am capable of illegal or disloyal acts?"

"Huh," said Zoë, "a big, strong man, the descendant of pirates, and all he can do is cart a capricious female about on a hot and boring pond. Huh!"

"But, madame. . . ."

"Do something silly, Jansen, I'm fed up. . . ."

"Aye, aye, madame, I will."

143

"When there's a big storm run the yacht on to the rocks."

"Aye, aye, madame, I'll run the yacht on to the rocks...."

"Do you mean to do that, seriously?..."

"If you order it."

He looked at Zoë. The hurt that showed in his eyes was mingled with admiration. Zoë reached over and placed her hand on his white sleeve.

"I'm not joking, Jansen. I've only known you for three weeks but it seems to me that you're the sort that can be loyal (he clenched his teeth). It seems to me that you are capable of actions that go beyond the bounds of loyalty, if...if...."

At that moment running feet appeared on the lacquer and bronze companion-way leading from the bridge.

"It's time, madame..." interjected Jansen.

The first mate descended to the deck. He saluted.

"Madame Lamolle, it's three minutes to twelve. There will be a wireless call now...."

54

Her white skirt bellied out in the breeze as Zoë went towards the radio cabin on the upper deck. She screwed up her eyes and breathed deeply of the salt air. From that height, from the captain's bridge, the sun-filled expanse of ruffled, glassy sea seemed boundless.

Zoë looked around and was lost in admiration as she stood at the rail. The narrow hull of the yacht with its raised bowsprit flew along amidst the breezes on that sparkling sea.

Her heart beat faster from sheer joy. It seemed that if she took her hands off the rail she would fly away. Man is a wonderful being—what measure can be used to gauge the unexpectedness of his transformations? Evil radiations of will power, the venomous fluid of lust, a soul that seemed to have been shattered—all Zoë's tormenting and dubious past had been pushed aside, dissolving in that bright sunshine....

"I'm young ... I'm young ..." it seemed to her on the deck of a vessel with its bowsprit raised to the sun, "I'm beautiful, I'm kind...."

The breeze caressed her neck and face. Enraptured, Zoë desired happiness. Scarcely able to drag herself away from the light, the sky, the sea, she turned the cold door handle and entered a glass cabin in which the blinds were drawn on the sunny side. She took up the earphones. She rested her elbows on the table and covered her eyes with her fingers—her heart was still beating fast. Zoë turned to the first mate.

"You may go."

He went out of the cabin with a side-glance at Madame Lamolle. She was not only devilishly beautiful, graceful, svelte, elegant—some inexplicable excitement radiated from her.

55

The double strokes of the chronometer, like a ship's bell, marked the hour of twelve. Zoë smiled, only three minutes had elapsed since she rose from her chair under the awning.

"I must learn to feel, to turn every minute into an eternity," she thought. "I must know that ahead of me are millions of minutes, millions of eternities."

She pushed the switch over to the left and tuned the apparatus in on a wavelength of a hundred and thirty-seven point five metres. From the black emptiness of the earphones came Rolling's slow, harsh voice:

"Madame Lamolle, Madame Lamolle, Madame Lamolle.... Are you listening, are you listening, are you...."

"Hallo, yes, I'm listening, calm yourself...."

" ... Is everything all right? Have you any trouble? Do you need anything? Today, at the same hour as usual I shall be happy to hear your voice.... Use the same wavelength as usual.... Madame Lamolle, do not go too far from fourteen degrees east longitude, forty degrees north latitude. It is quite possible that we shall meet soon. Everything here is all right. Things are fine. The man who has to keep his mouth shut, does so. Don't worry, good luck and pleasant sailing...."

Zoë took off the earphones. A frown marred her forehead. Glancing at the hands of the chronometer, she muttered between her teeth, "I'm fed up!" These daily vows of love by wireless were getting on her nerves. Rolling could not and would not leave her in peace. He was prepared to commit any crime as long as she permitted him to croak into the microphone every day, "Don't worry, good luck and pleasant sailing."

56

Zoë and Rolling had not met since the murderous incidents at Ville d'Avray and Fontainebleau and a mad ride with Garin along the empty, moonlit road to Havre. He had fired at her that evening, had insulted her and then calmed down. Zoë imagined he was weeping in silence as he sat hunched up in the car.

In Havre she boarded Rolling's yacht *Arizona* and at dawn put out into the Bay of Biscay. In Lisbon, Zoë was handed papers in the name of Madame Lamolle and became the owner of one of the most luxurious yachts in the west. Leaving Lisbon, the *Arizona* entered the Medi-

terranean and had since been cruising in the vicinity of
14⁰ E. long. and 40⁰ N. lat., keeping within reach of the
Italian seaboard.

Rolling immediately established contact with the yacht
through his private wireless station at Mendon near Paris.
Captain Jansen reported all details of the trip to Rolling.
Rolling called Zoë every day. Every evening she reported
to him on her "moods". Ten days had passed in this mo-
notony when the *Arizona's* wireless operator heard short-
wave signals in an unknown language. Zoë was informed
and she heard a voice that caused her heart to miss a beat.

"Zoë, Zoë, Zoë...."

Garin's voice buzzed in her earphones like a blue-
bottle buzzing against a window-pane. He repeated her
name and then after a short pause said, "Answer me between one and three tonight."

Then again: "Zoë, Zoë, Zoë.... Be careful. Be careful...."

That same night, over the dark sea, over sleeping
Europe, over the ancient ash-heaps of Asia Minor, over
the dust-covered thorns of the sun-dried vegetation of
Africa's plains, radio waves carried the voice of a woman:

"I am calling to him who asked for an answer between
one and three...."

Zoë repeated this call several times and then said:

"I want to see you. Call it madness if you like. Name
any port in Italy.... Don't call me by name, I'll recognize
your voice...."

While Zoë was persistently repeating her call in the
hope that Garin—be he in Europe, Asia or Africa—would
pick up the electro-magnetic waves emitted by the *Arizona*,
more than a thousand miles away in Paris a telephone bell
rang on the little table beside the double bed where Rolling
slept alone, his nose tucked into the blankets.

Rolling jumped up and snatched up the receiver. Semyonov's voice told him in a hurry:

"Rolling, she's talking."

"With whom?"

"I can't hear, she doesn't mention him by name."

"O.K. Continue listening. Report tomorrow."

Rolling put down the receiver, got back into bed, but sleep had already left him.

Semyonov's task was no easy one: he had to pick out Zoë's weak voice amongst the dance music, advertisements, church choirs, bulletins on international affairs, operas, symphonies, stock exchange reports, and jokes of famous comedians that raged hurricane-like over Europe.

Day and night Semyonov sat in the wireless station at Mendon. He managed to pick up a few phrases in Zoë's voice and that was enough to arouse Rolling's jealousy.

Rolling felt very bad after the night in Fontainebleau. As long as Shelga was alive a terrible threat hung over Rolling's head. He had been forced to sign an agreement with Garin, whom he would willingly have lynched like a Negro. Perhaps Rolling would have held out even then—better death, the scaffold, anything rather than this alliance—but Zoë had broken his will power. By coming to an agreement with Garin he was gaining time: perhaps that crazy woman would think better of it, repent and return to him.... Rolling actually had wept in the car, wept silently in his corner.... The devil alone knew why.... On account of a wanton, mercenary harlot.... But the tears were, nevertheless, bitter and tormenting.... One of the terms of the agreement had been that Zoë should take a long trip on his yacht. (This was essential to cover up all traces.) He hoped to persuade her, to appeal to her conscience, to attract her to him by daily talks over the wireless. His hopes were, if possible, even more foolish than the tears in the car.

In accordance with his agreement with Garin, Rolling immediately launched a "general offensive on the chemical front." On the day when Zoë had boarded the *Arizona* at Havre, Rolling had returned to Paris by train. He informed the police that he had been in Havre and on the way back had been attacked by bandits at night (three of them, their faces covered with handkerchiefs). They had robbed him of his money and his car. (Garin in the meantime had driven Rolling's car across France from west to east, had crossed the Luxembourg border and sunk the car in the first canal he came across.)

"The offensive on the chemical front" had begun. The Paris newspapers set up a tremendous hullabaloo. "The Riddle of the Ville d'Avray Tragedy," "Mysterious Attack on Russian in Fontainebleau Park," "Audacious Robbery of Chemical King," "American Billions in Europe," "Twilight of German National Industry," "Rolling or Moscow?"—all these taken together made a lump that stuck in the throat of the man in the street, especially if he happened to be a shareholder. The stock exchange was shaken to the very foundations. A horde of madmen, with eyes ready to pop out of their heads, shouted and milled around the blackboards between its grey columns, where feverish hands wrote, rubbed out, and rewrote the prices of falling stock.

This, however, was nothing, only the small fry gasping for air. The bigger fish, the industrialists and the bankers, clenched their teeth and sat tight. Even Rolling's buffalo horns found it hard to throw them. It was for that serious operation Garin was making his preparations.

As Shelga had rightly guessed, Garin was in Germany, "feverishly" building a full-sized machine from his model. He travelled from town to town ordering parts in different factories. He kept in touch with Paris through the advertisement columns of a Cologne newspaper while Rolling inserted brief announcements in one of the cheaper Paris dailies: "Concentrate all attention on aniline...", "Every day of value, don't begrudge money...", etc.

Garin replied: "Finishing earlier than expected...."

"Place found...." "Beginning...." "Unexpected delay...."

Rolling: "Worried. Name the day...."

Garin: "Count thirty-five days from signing of contract...."

The last communication coincided with Semyonov's night telephone call to Rolling. Rolling was furious—he was being fooled. Apart from everything else, secret communications with the *Arizona* were dangerous. Not by a single word, however, did Rolling betray himself when he talked to Madame Lamolle the following day.

In the hours of insomnia that were now Rolling's usual lot he pondered over the "game" he was playing with his mortal enemy. He discovered blunders. Garin's defence was not as strong as it seemed to be. He had made a mistake when he agreed to Zoë's voyage on the *Arizona*—the end of the game was predetermined. Rolling would checkmate him on board the *Arizona*.

57

On board the *Arizona*, however, things were not quite what Rolling imagined. He remembered Zoë as a clever, calmly calculating, cold, and loyal woman. He knew her disdain for all women's foibles. He could not believe that her infatuation for that penniless tramp, the bandit Garin, would last long. A good trip in the Mediterranean should clear her mind.

Zoë really had been in a sort of delirium when she had boarded the yacht at Havre. A few days of loneliness on the ocean calmed her down. She awoke, lived through the day and fell asleep amidst blue light, bright, lucid water, and the lapping of waves as tranquil as eternity. Shuddering in disgust she recalled the filthy room and the grinning, glassy-eyed body of Lenoir, the bubbling, smoky streak across Bec de Canard's chest, the damp glade at Fontainebleau, and Rolling's frenzied shots, just as though he were shooting a mad dog....

Nevertheless her brain did not clear in the way Rolling hoped. In her sleeping and waking hours she dreamed of delightful islands and marble palaces with staircases leading down to the sea.... Crowds of beautiful people, music, waving flags.... And she—the mistress of this fantastic world....

Her dreams and her visions in the chair under the blue awning were a continuation of her talk with Garin at Ville d'Avray (an hour before the murders). Only one man on Earth, Garin, would have understood her at that moment. With him, however, were connected the glassy eyes of Lenoir and the horrible, gaping mouth of Bec de Canard.

This explains why Zoë's heart stood still when Garin's voice suddenly muttered to her in the earphones.... Since then she had been calling him daily, imploring and threatening him. She wanted to see him but feared the meeting. She visualized him as a black spot in the azure purity of the sea and sky.... She longed to relate her daydreams to him. She wanted to ask him where that Olivine Belt was. Zoë wandered restlessly about the yacht, robbing Captain Jansen and his first mate of their peace of mind.

"Wait," came Garin's answer. "Everything will be as you wish. You must only wish hard enough. Desire! Go out of your mind—that's good. That is just the way I need you. Without you my enterprise means nothing to me."

That was his last radio message, also intercepted by Rolling. Today Zoë awaited an answer to her question—precisely on what day was she to expect him on the yacht? She went up on deck and leaned on the rail. The yacht was scarcely moving. The wind had died down. In the east there lay a haze over the still invisible land and a column of ashy smoke hung over Vesuvius.

On the bridge Captain Jansen lowered the hand holding his binoculars and Zoë felt that he was looking at her enthralled. How could he do other than gaze at her when all the marvels of heaven and sea were created only to be admired by Madame Lamolle standing at the rail above that milky-blue abyss.

How improbable, how ridiculous seemed those times when, for a dozen pairs of silk stockings, for a dress from a famous house, or simply for a thousand francs, she had permitted those bounders with pudgy fingers and florid cheeks to slobber over her!... Phew!... Paris, drinking dens, foolish street girls, swinish men, the stink of the streets, money, money, money—what squalor!... Restless activity in a cesspool!...

That night Garin had said to her, "If you wish it you may be the vicar of God or the Devil on earth, whichever is the more to your liking. If you feel a desire to kill— sometimes one feels such an urge—you will have power over all mankind. A woman like you, Zoë, will find plenty of use for the wealth of the Olivine Belt...."

Zoë thought:

"Roman Emperors deified themselves. It must have given them pleasure. It ought to be quite amusing nowadays, too. All these miserable little beings ought to be useful for something. The incarnation of God, a living goddess surrounded by fantastic magnificence.... Why not? The press could prepare the way for my deification quickly and easily. The world ruled by a marvellously beautiful woman. That would have undoubted success. Somewhere in the islands I could build a beautiful city for selected youths, the predestined lovers of the goddess. It would be something new in the way of sensations to appear as a goddess amongst those sex-starved boys."

Zoë shrugged her shoulders and again looked towards the captain.

"Come over here, Jansen."

He came, walking with big, soft strides over the hot deck.

"Jansen, don't you think I'm mad?"

"I don't think so, and shall not think so, no matter what you may order me to do."

"Thank you. I appoint you Grand Master of the Order of the Divine Zoë."

Jansen's blond eyelashes blinked. Then he raised his hand and saluted, lowered it, and blinked again. Zoë laughed and his lips also formed a smile.

"Jansen, there is a possibility of the wildest dreams coming true.... Everything that a woman could think of on a hot afternoon like this. But it means struggle...."

"Aye, aye..." answered Jansen, shortly.

"How many knots can the *Arizona* do?"

"Up to forty."

"What vessels could overtake her in the open sea?"

"Very few."

"We might have to hold out through a long chase."

"Do you want me to take on board a full reserve of fuel?"

"Yes. And canned goods, fresh water, champagne.... Captain Jansen, we're going on a very dangerous enterprise."

"Yes, madame."

"But, I'm sure of victory, do you hear?"

The ship's bell rang once. Zoë went to the wireless cabin. She sat down at the table and turned the switch of the receiver. At first she picked up a few bars of a fox-trot from somewhere.

She glanced at the chronometer and frowned. Garin was silent. She again turned the switch, trying to control her trembling fingers.

... An unknown, slow voice spoke into her ear in Russian:

"... If you value the life of ... on Friday land in

Naples...await news at the Hotel Splendide until Saturday noon...."

That was the end of a message sent out on a wavelength of four hundred and twenty-one metres, that is, the wavelength Garin had been using all the time.

58

For the third night in succession the Carmelite Sister had forgotten to close the shutters of Shelga's room. Every evening he pointed out this oversight to her. He watched carefully to make sure that the catch fastening the two halves of the shutters was snapped into place.

In the course of these three weeks Shelga had so far convalesced that he could get up and sit by the window, where he could see the luxuriant foliage of the plane-tree, the black thrushes, and the rainbows playing in the spray in the centre of the lawn.

From his vantage-point the hospital garden, surrounded by a solid brick wall, lay open before him. In the eighteenth century the building had belonged to a monastery destroyed by the revolution. Monks do not approve of curious eyes and so the wall was high and was topped by a fringe of broken glass.

It was only possible to climb over the wall by placing a ladder on the outer side. The narrow streets around the hospital were quiet and empty, nevertheless the street-lamps shone so brightly and the steps of the policeman so often broke the silence that the use of a ladder was out of the question.

It goes without saying that an active man could easily have scaled the wall without a ladder if it had not been for the broken glass. Every morning Shelga examined every brick of the wall from behind the curtain. Danger threatened from that direction alone; Rolling's man would hardly risk entering through the hospital. Shelga had no doubt, however, that sooner or later, one way or another, assassins would come.

He was now awaiting an examination in order to get discharged from the hospital. The doctor usually came five times a week. But now it seemed that he was ill. Shelga was informed that he would not be allowed to leave without the sanction of the head doctor. He did not even try to protest. He got a message to the Soviet Embassy asking them to send him food; the hospital soup he poured down the sink and the bread he fed to the thrushes.

Shelga knew that Rolling had to get rid of the only witness. He was so tensed that he hardly slept any more. The Carmelite Sister brought him newspapers and he worked all day with his scissors and studied the cuttings he made. He had forbidden Khlinov to come to the hospital. (Wolf was in Germany, in the Rhineland, where he was collecting information on Rolling's battle with the German Aniline Company.)

The next morning, going to the window as usual, Shelga glanced round the garden and immediately stepped back behind the curtain. He even felt glad about what he saw. At last! On the northern side of the garden, half hidden behind a lime-tree, a gardener's ladder had been placed against the wall so that its upper end extended nearly a yard above the row of broken glass.

"The swine are clever!" exclaimed Shelga.

There was nothing left to do but wait. He had thought everything out. His right arm, although it was no longer in bandages, was still weak. His left arm was still in a plaster cast and the nurse had bound it tightly to his body. That left arm with its plaster cast weighed about fifteen pounds and was the only weapon of defence left to him.

On the fourth night the Carmelite Sister again forgot to close the shutters. On this occasion Shelga did not protest and by nine o'clock he pretended to be asleep. He

155

heard shutters closing on both storeys of the hospital but his window again remained wide open. When the lights were put out he jumped out of bed and with the aid of his teeth and his weak right hand began to unfasten the bandage holding his left arm.

He stood still and listened, holding his breath. At last the arm hung free. He could unbend it half-way. He looked out into the garden and there, in the light of the street-lamp, saw the ladder still standing against the wall behind the lime-tree. He rolled up his blanket and pushed it under the sheet so that in the semi-darkness it would look like a man lying there.

It was quiet outside, the only sound coming from water dripping from the leaves. Reflected in the clouds above Paris was a faint bluish glow. The noises of the boulevards did not reach him. The black branches of the plane-tree hung motionless.

A motor-car engine growled near by. Shelga strained his ears—it seemed to him that he could hear the beating hearts of the birds asleep in the plane-tree. A long time must have passed. From the garden came a scraping and grating sound as though some wooden object were being rubbed over plaster.

Shelga pressed himself against the wall behind the curtains. He lowered his arm in its plaster cast. "Who? Who is it? Surely not Rolling himself?" he wondered.

Leaves rustled and the thrushes were disturbed. Shelga watched the patch of moonlit parquet floor where the intruder's shadow should fall.

"He won't shoot, of course," thought Shelga. "I must expect some sort of filth like phosgene...." The outline of a head with a hat pulled down hard began creeping across the moonlit floor. Shelga drew back his arm to give greater force to the blow. The shadow increased to include the shoulders, and a hand was lifted up with the fingers outstretched....

"Shelga, Comrade Shelga," the shadow whispered in Russian, "it's me, don't be afraid...."

Shelga had expected almost anything with the possible exception of those words and that voice. He let out an involuntary gasp. He had given himself away and the man immediately leaped into the room, clearing the window-sill with a single spring. He held out both hands in front as though to defend himself. It was Garin.

"You were expecting an attack. I thought so," he said in a hurry. "They were planning to kill you tonight. That wouldn't suit me. The devil alone knows what I am risking, but I must save you. Come along, I have a car."

Shelga moved away from the wall.

Garin's teeth flashed in a smile as he saw Shelga's raised arm in its plaster cast.

"Listen, Shelga, it's not my fault, by God, it's not. Do you remember our agreement in Leningrad? I play fair. The unpleasantness at Fontainebleau you owe entirely to that swine Rolling. You may trust me—come along, every second is precious...."

At last Shelga spoke.

"All right, you'll take me away and then what?"

"I'll hide you. It's only for a short time, don't worry. Until I get a half from Rolling.... Do you read the newspapers? Rolling's having the luck of the devil but he can't play fair. How much do you want, Shelga? Name any figure you like! Ten, twenty, fifty million? I'll give you a note of hand...."

Garin spoke softly but hurriedly as though in a delirium; his face was twitching all the time.

"Don't be a fool, Shelga. Are you trying to play the man of principle or what? I'm offering you an opportunity to work with me against Rolling. Well? Come along."

Shelga stubbornly shook his head.

"I don't want to go with you."

"If you don't they'll kill you."

157

"We'll see about that."

"The nurses, nightwatchman, the administration have all been bought by Rolling. They'll strangle you. I know.... You won't live till morning.... You've warned your embassy, haven't you? Good, very good. The ambassador will demand an explanation. At the very most the French government will apologize. But that won't do you any good. Rolling must get rid of the witness. He'll not allow you to cross the threshold of the Soviet Embassy."

"I've told you I won't go. I don't want to...."

Garin breathed heavily and looked out of the window.

"All right then, if you won't go I'll take you."

He stepped back and thrust his hand into his overcoat pocket.

"Oh, you will, will you...."

"Yes, like this...."

Garin pulled a gas-mask out of his pocket and hurriedly covered his face with it; before Shelga had time to cry out, a stream of some oily liquid hit him in the face. All he saw was Garin's hand squeezing a rubber bulb. Shelga swallowed some sweet asphyxiating narcotic....

59

"Any news?"

"Yes. Good morning, Wolf."

"I've come straight from the station as hungry as I was in 1918."

"You look happy, Wolf. Have found out anything?"

"I've found out a few things. Are we going to talk here?"

"If you like, only quickly."

Wolf sat down beside Khlinov on a stone seat under the equestrian statue of Henri IV, their backs to the black towers of the Conciergerie. Below them, where the lle de Cité ended in a sharp point, a weeping willow hung over the water. Here, centuries ago, the Knights Templars had been burned at the stake. In the distance, beyond the dozens of bridges reflected in the river, the sun sank in a cloud of orange-coloured dust. Along the embankment and on steel barges loaded with sand sat Frenchmen with their fishing-rods, good bourgeois who had been ruined by the inflation, Rolling and the world war. On the granite parapets of the left bank, as far as the Quai d'Orsay, sellers of second-hand books lounged listlessly in the evening sun beside wares that were no longer needed by anybody in that city.

This was the Old Paris that was fast coming to an end. Elderly gentlemen with sclerotic eyes and moustaches that covered their mouths, in long dust-coats and old straw hats, still hovered around the bookstalls, the cages of birds on the quays and the despondent anglers. . . . There had been a time when this had been their bailiwick. Over there in the Conciergerie, *sacrebleu*, Danton had roared like an ox being led to the slaughter. And over there on the right, beyond the slate roofs of the Louvre, where the Jardins des Tuilleries lay in the dusk, there had been great doings when General de Galliffet's grape-shot had whistled down the Rue de Rivoli. And how much gold there had been in France! Every stone here had a story to tell to those who were able to listen, a story of the great past. But now, *mille diables*, a foreign monster by the name of Rolling had become master of the city and the good bourgeois had nothing left to do but throw his line into the Seine and sit there with bowed head. . . . Eh-he-he! Oh, la-la! . . .

Wolf lit a pipe loaded with strong tobacco.

"This is the way things are," he began. "The German Aniline Company is the only one that will not enter into any agreement with the Americans. The company has been given a government subsidy of twenty-eight million

159

marks. All Rolling's efforts are now concentrated on over-throwing the German Aniline Company."

"Is he speculating on a fall in prices?" asked Khlinov.

"He's selling huge quantities of Aniline stock for de-livery on the 28th of this month."

"That's very important information, Wolf."

"Yes, I think we're on the track. Rolling is appar-ently sure of his game although the shares haven't dropped a single pfennig yet and today is already the twentieth. . . . Do you know what he must be relying on?"

"They must have everything ready, then?"

"I believe the apparatus has already been erected."

"Where are the Aniline Company's factories?"

"On the Rhine, near K. If Rolling brings about the collapse of the company he will be master of the entire European chemical industry. We mustn't allow a catas-trophe. We must save German Aniline. (Khlinov shrugged his shoulders but he did not say anything.) I understand: what is to be will be. You and I alone cannot stop the onslaught of America. All the same history sometimes plays some strange tricks."

"Like revolution, for example."

"May be even that."

Khlinov looked at him with something like astonish-ment. Wolf's eyes were round, yellow, and malicious.

"Wolf, the bourgeois won't lift a finger to save Europe."

"I know."

"Do you?"

"During this trip I've taken a good look round. The bourgeois, be he French, German, English or Italian, is blindly, criminally, and cynically selling up the old world. This is where this culture of ours ends, at the auction, under the hammer." Wolf's face grew red.

"I have applied to the authorities, I have hinted at the danger, I've asked for help in the search for Garin. I've spoken about the most terrible things to them. They laughed in my face. To hell with them! I'm not the sort that gives up."

"Wolf, what did you learn on the Rhine?"

"I learned.... The Aniline Company has been given big war orders by the German Government. Production at the Aniline factories has reached the most dangerous stage. They have almost five hundred tons of tetryl being processed at the moment."

Khlinov jumped up from his seat, the walking-stick on which he leaned bent under his weight. He sat down again.

"There has been an article in a newspaper on the necessity of shifting the workers' housing estates farther from those damned factories. There are more than fifty thousand workers employed at the Aniline factories.... The newspaper that published that article was fined. The hand of Rolling."

"Wolf, we mustn't lose a single day."

"I've ordered tickets for the eleven o'clock train today."

"We're going to K.?"

"I think that's the only place where we can get on Garin's tracks."

"Now take a look at what I've managed to find out." Khlinov pulled a bundle of newspaper cuttings out of his pocket. "A couple of days ago I went to see Shelga.... He told me the whole course of his deductions: Rolling and Garin have to keep in touch with each other...."

"That goes without saying—every day."

"By post or telegraph? What do you think?"

"Under no circumstances. Nothing in writing."

"Wireless then?"

"For all Europe to hear? No."

"Through a third person?"

"No. I get what you mean. That Shelga of yours is a smart fellow. Let's have a look at the cuttings."

He spread them out on his knees and began to read what was underlined in red:

"Concentrate all attention on Aniline." "Beginning." "Place found."

" 'Place found,' " whispered Wolf, "that's a newspaper from E., a little town near K. . . ." 'Worried. Name the day.' 'Count thirty-five days from signing of contract. . . .' That could only be from them. The night the agreement was signed in Fontainebleau was the twenty-third of last month. Add to that thirty-five days and that will be the twenty-eighth, the day the stock has been sold for. . . ."

"Further, Wolf, read further. 'What measures have you taken?' That's from K. Garin asking the question. The next day we have Rolling's answer in a Paris newspaper: 'Yacht ready. Arriving day after tomorrow. Information by wireless.' And then, four days ago, Rolling asks: 'Won't there be any light?' and Garin answers: 'District deserted. Distance three miles.' "

"In other words the machine has been erected in the hills: to send a ray over a distance of three miles height is required. Listen, Khlinov, we have very little time. If we take a radius of three miles with the factories as the centre we'll have to examine an area within a circumference of over twenty miles. Are there any other indicants?"

"No. I was just going to phone Shelga. He should have cuttings from yesterday's and today's papers."

Wolf stood up. His muscles swelled visibly under his shirt.

Khlinov suggested phoning from the nearest café on the left bank. Wolf dashed across the bridge in such a hurry that an old man with a chicken neck, wearing a stained jacket, saturated, perhaps, with lonely tears for those who had been lost in the war, shook his head and gazed for a long time after the hurrying foreigners.

"Oh, those foreigners. . . . When they have money in their pockets they push and shove as though they were at home. Ah, the savages! . . ."

Standing at the zinc counter in the café Wolf drank a glass of soda water. Through the glass door of the telephone booth he could see Khlinov's back: he saw him sag over the telephone. Khlinov straightened up and left the call-box, his face was calm but as white as a mask.

"They tell me at the hospital that Shelga disappeared during the night. Everything is being done to trace him. I imagine he's been killed."

60

The twigs crackled on a hearth that was stained with two centuries of smoke; above it hung huge rusty hooks for sausages and hams and two stone saints guarded it on either side; on one of the saints hung Garin's hat and on the other an officer's greasy cap. Four men were sitting at a table lit only by the light from the fire. In front of them stood a straw-covered bottle and glasses of wine.

Two of the men were dressed in town clothes—one of them, a husky fellow, had high cheek-bones and short-cropped stiff hair; the other had a long and evil face. The third, the owner of the farm in whose kitchen the conference was being held, was General Subbotin; he sat there in a dirty linen shirt with his sleeves rolled up. The closely-shaven skin of his scalp twitched and his fat face with a dishevelled moustache was red from the wine he had drunk.

The fourth, Garin, was dressed as a tourist; he was speaking and passing his finger negligently round the edge of his glass.

"All that's quite all right.... Nevertheless I insist that my prisoner, even if he is a Bolshevik, should not suffer any injury. Food three times a day, wine, vegetables, and fruit. In a week's time I'll take him away. How far to the Belgian frontier?"

"Three quarters of an hour by car," said the man with the long face, leaning forward.

"The whole thing will be kept quiet. I understand, general, and you gentlemen, that as officers and aristocrats (Garin smiled) who are selflessly loyal to the memory of the martyred emperor, you are acting from higher, purely ideological motives. Otherwise I should not have turned to you for help."

"We are all gentlemen, is there any need to say more?" said the general in a hoarse voice, wrinkling the skin on his bald pate.

"The terms as I've said are a thousand francs a day for the full board and lodging of my prisoner. Do you agree?"

The general turned his bloodshot eyes in the direction of his companions. The man with the high cheek-bones showed his white teeth, the long-faced man lowered his eyes.

"Oh, yes," said Garin, "excuse me, I almost forgot... the deposit...."

He pulled a bundle of thousand-franc notes from his revolver pocket and threw them on the table into a pool of wine.

"Take them, please."

The general gave a snort of satisfaction pulled the notes across the table, wiped them on his belly and began to count them, sniffing with his hairy nostrils as he did so. His companions edged towards him, their eyes gleaming.

Garin rose to his feet.

"Bring in the prisoner."

61

Shelga's eyes were blindfolded with a handkerchief. A leather motoring coat was thrown over his shoulders. He felt the warmth coming from the fireplace and his legs trembled under him. Garin immediately pushed a stool towards him and Shelga sat down, dropping his plaster-bound arm on to his knees.

The general and the two officers glared at him with such hatred that it was obvious that at the slightest sign, a mere wink, they would have pounced on him and torn him to pieces. Garin, however, did not make a sign. Tapping Shelga on the knee he said in cheerful tones:

"You'll not want for anything here. You are in the hands of decent people and they have been well paid. I will set you free in a few days. Comrade Shelga, give me your word of honour that you will not attempt to escape, cause trouble or attract the attention of the police."

Shelga shook his bowed head in refusal. Garin bent over him.

"If you don't it will be difficult for me to guarantee you a comfortable stay here. Will you give me your word?"

Shelga spoke slowly, in soft tones.

"I give you my word of a Communist. . . ." The skin on the general's shaven pate immediately wrinkled into waves that travelled towards his ears, the officers glanced at each other and smiled malignantly. "I give you my word of a Communist to kill you at the first oppurtunity, Garin. I give you my word to take the machine away from you and bring it to Moscow. I give my word that on the 28th. . . ."

Garin did not let him finish, but seized him by the throat. "Stop! Idiot. . . . Lunatic. . . ."

He turned round and said imperiously:

"Gentlemen, I warn you, this man is dangerous, he has an *idée fixe*."

"I told you the best place to keep him is in the wine-cellar," said the general's bass voice. "Take the prisoner away."

Garin made a motion with his beard, the two officers grabbed Shelga and dragged him through a side door towards the wine-cellar. Garin drew on his motoring gauntlets.

"I shall be here on the night of the twenty-ninth. On the thirtieth Your Excellency may put an end to his experiments in rabbit-breeding, book a first-class berth on a transatlantic liner, and live a life of luxury in New York, on Fifth Avenue if you like."

"You must leave some sort of document to identify that son of a bitch," said the general.

"Here you have the choice of any passport you'd like."

Garin pulled out a bundle of papers tied together with string—the documents he had taken from Shelga's pocket in Fontainebleau but which he had not yet found time to examine.

"These look like passports prepared for me. What excellent forethought. Here, take this, Your Excellency."

Garin threw a passport on to the table and continued examining the contents of Shelga's wallet—something interested him and he moved nearer the lamp. His eyebrows knitted.

"Hell!" He rushed towards the side door through which Shelga had been dragged.

62

Shelga lay on a mattress on the stone floor. A tiny oil-lamp lit up the vaulted cellar and the empty barrels draped with cobwebs. Garin's glance travelled round the cellar, seeking Shelga; then he went and stood over him, biting his lip.

"I lost my temper, Shelga, don't be angry with me. I

still think we may find a common language. We can come to terms. If you want to, that is."

"Try."

Garin spoke ingratiatingly, quite differently from the way he had spoken ten minutes before. This put Shelga on his guard but the excitement he had experienced that night, the after-effects of the gas still ringing in his ears, and the pain in his injured arm made him less alert. Garin sat down on the mattress and lit a cigarette. His face bore a thoughtful look and his whole appearance was one of combined elegance and benevolence.

"What's the swine getting at? What's he want?" thought Shelga, his face wrinkled from the pain in his head.

Clasping his knee and puffing clouds of smoke, Garin looked up at the vaulted ceiling.

"It's like this, Shelga, first of all you have to believe that I never lie. Perhaps it's only because I despise people but that's not what matters. I need Rolling and his billions for a short time only. He needs me just as long. I believe he realizes this in spite of his stupidity. Rolling came here to colonize Europe. If he doesn't succeed in that he will crack up in America together with all his millions. Rolling is a brute beast—his one idea is to push forward, butt, and trample everything underfoot. He hasn't a ha'p'orth of imagination. The only wall against which he may crack his skull is the Soviet Russia. He knows this and all his fury is directed against your beloved country. I don't consider myself a Russian (he added hurriedly), I'm an internationalist."

"That goes without saying," said Shelga with a smile of contempt.

"Our present relations are—up to a certain point we work together...."

"Until the 28th...."

167

Garin cast a rapid glance at Shelga, humour in his flashing eyes.

"So you worked it out, did you? From the newspapers?"

"May be."

"All right. Let's say until the 28th. After that we're bound to get at each other's throats. If Rolling wins it will be doubly dangerous for Soviet Russia: he'll have my apparatus and it will be very hard for you to fight against him. To leave you here for a week to keep the spiders company will give me a better chance of victory."

Shelga closed his eyes. Garin sat at his feet and puffed furiously at his cigarette.

"What the devil do you need my consent for?" asked Shelga. "You can keep me here as long as you like without it. Tell me straight out what you want."

"That's what you should have said long ago. You, and your 'word of a Communist'.... My God, you certainly got under my skin just now ... still, it seems to me that you're beginning to understand at last. It's true we're enemies. Nevertheless we have to work together. From your point of view I'm just a degenerate, I'm individualist number one.... I, Pyotr Petrovich Garin, by the grace of the powers that made me what I am, with the brain of a genius—don't laugh, Shelga—with unsuppressed passions, that both torment and scare me, with my greed and lack of principle, pit myself, literally, against all mankind."

"A thorough-paced scoundrel," said Shelga.

"Quite right: a thorough-paced scoundrel, now you understand me. I'm a voluptuary by nature and I strive to devote every second of my life to pleasure. I'm in mad haste to get rid of Rolling because I am losing valuable seconds. You people there in Russia, you are just a militant, materialized idea. I have no ideology, I consciously, religiously shun everything in the nature of an idea. I have set myself a goal: I intend to create such conditions (I will not give you the details, they would only tire you), to surround myself with such superabundance that the Hanging Gardens of Semiramis and all that other oriental nonsense will be just an anaemic dream compared to my paradise. I will muster all science, all industry, all the arts to serve me. Shelga, you understand that for you I am a distant and fantastic danger, while Rolling is a close, concrete, and terrifying danger. For this reason you and I travel together up to a certain point, until such times as Rolling is crushed. That is all I ask of you."

"What form do you expect my help to take?" asked Shelga between his teeth.

"I want you to take a short trip by sea."

"In other words you want to keep me a prisoner."

"Yes."

"What do you offer in return for my not calling out to the first policeman for help when you take me to the seacoast?"

"Any sum you like."

"I don't want money."

"Clever," said Garin, fidgeting uneasily on the mattress. "Will you do it for a model of my apparatus? (Shelga snorted.) You don't believe me? You think I'd swindle you, that I won't give it to you? Think it over—whether I'm likely to swindle you or not. (Shelga shrugged his shoulders.) I mean it. The idea of the apparatus is so simple as to be almost ridiculous. I couldn't possibly keep it secret for long. Such is the fate of all great inventions. After the 28th all the newspapers will describe the action of infra-red rays and the Germans, most certainly the Germans, will build just such an apparatus within six months. I'm not risking anything. Take the model to Russia with you. Incidentally I have your passports and other papers. Take them, I don't need them any longer. Excuse me for having rummaged in them, I'm terribly curious. What's that photo of a tattooed boy you have?"

"Just a waif we picked up," answered Shelga, realizing

through the pain in his head that Garin was now coming to the real reason for his visit to the wine-cellar.

"On the back of the photo there is a date, the twelfth of last month, which means you photographed the boy on the eve of your departure, eh? And you took the photograph with you in order to show it to me? Did you show it to anybody in Leningrad?"

"No," muttered Shelga through clenched teeth.

"What did you do with the boy? Aha, I didn't notice it before, the name's here as well—Ivan Gusev. You took the photo on the verandah of the Rowing Club, didn't you? That much I recognize, I know those parts. What did the boy tell you? Is Mantsev alive?"

"Yes."

"Has he found what he was looking for?"

"I think so."

"There you are. You see, I always believed in Mantsev."

Garin's calculations had been correct. Shelga's mind was so constructed that he could not lie, firstly, because he had nothing but contempt for lying and secondly, because he considered it cheap both in play and in struggle. In a minute Garin knew the whole story of Ivan at the Rowing Club and all that he had said about Mantsev's work.

"All right." Garin stood up rubbing his hands gleefully. "When we make our car trip on the night of the twenty-ninth we shall have the model of the apparatus with us. I will hide it in any place you point out to me until you want it. That ought to be sufficient guarantee for you. Do you agree?"

"Yes, I agree."

"You won't attempt to kill me?"

"In the immediate future, no."

"I'll order them to take you upstairs, it's too damp here; hurry up and get better, eat and drink whatever you want."

Garin winked to him and went out.

63

"Your name and Christian name?"

"Captain Alexander Ivanovich Volshin of the Kulnev-sky Regiment," answered the officer with high cheek-bones, standing to attention in front of Garin.

"On what income do you live?"

"I assist General Subbotin in the breeding of rabbits at twenty sous a day and food. I was a taxi-driver, earned decent money, but my fellow-officers persuaded me to go as a delegate to a royalist congress. At the first session I bashed the face of Colonel Sherstobitov, one of Kirill's followers. I lost my credentials and my job."

"I'm offering you dangerous work with excellent pay. Do you agree?"

"I agree."

"You will go to Paris. You will receive a recommendation and will be enrolled on the staff. You will go to Leningrad with papers and credentials.... Using this photograph you will search for a boy ..."

64

Five days passed. Nothing had disturbed the tranquillity of the little Rhineside town of K. hidden in a green, humid valley in the vicinity of the famous factories owned by the Aniline Company.

From early morning the winding streets with their narrow pavements resounded to the clatter of school children's clogs and the heavy tread of the workers; women trundled their prams along in the shade of the lime-trees on the road leading to the river. A barber in a canvas waistcoat came out of his shop and placed a step-ladder on the pavement. His lather boy climbed on to the ladder to polish an already glittering trade sign—a brass bowl and a white horse's tail. The plate-glass windows of the café were being cleaned. A high-wheeled brewer's dray loaded with empty barrels rumbled past.

It was a neat, cleanly-swept old town, quiet in the daytime when the sun warmed the curved stone-paved streets and coming to life in the evening when, at sundown, the working men and women returned from the factories and filled the air with their drawling voices, when the lights went up in the cafés and the lamplighter, in a short cape God alone knew how many years old, shuffled along the streets in his clogs.

Women with shopping baskets, the wives of workers and burghers, came out of the market gates. In former days the baskets contained poultry, vegetables, and fruit worthy of Frans Snyders' still lifes. Today they contained a few potatoes, a bunch of onions, some swedes, and a lump of grey bread.

How strange! Germany had become the devil alone knows how rich in the past four centuries. What glory her sons had tasted. What hopes had brought sparkle to blue German eyes! How much beer had trickled down upturned blond beards! How many billions of kilowatts of human energy had been liberated!

And all in vain. In the kitchens—a bunch of spring onions on the table and long-standing yearning in the women's hungry eyes.

Wolf and Khlinov, their boots dusty, their jackets thrown over their arms, their brows damp with perspiration, crossed a humped bridge and plodded up the lime-shaded highway towards K.

The sun was sinking behind the low hills. In the golden light of evening the chimneys of the Aniline works were still smoking. Factory buildings, chimneys, railway lines, and the tiled roofs of warehouses ranged down the hillside to the very edge of the town.

"I'm sure that's the place, over there," said Wolf,

pointing with his hand to cliffs that loomed red in the sunset. "If I had to select the best point for gunfire on the factory that's the only place I'd consider."

"That's right enough, Wolf, but there are only three days left."

"Well, what about it? There can be no danger from the southern side, it's too far away. We've scoured the northern and eastern sectors till we know every stone. Three days will be enough."

Khlinov turned to the blue wooded hills with deep shadows between them. During the past five days and nights Wolf and Khlinov had searched every hollow where some structure—a cottage or a shed with windows facing the factories—might be hidden.

For the fifth day in succession they had not undressed and during the darkest hours of the night had dropped down to sleep wherever they happened to be. Their feet were so numb that they had even ceased to hurt. Along stony roads and paths, cutting straight across ravines and over fences, they had covered almost sixty-five miles around the town. Nowhere, however, had they found the slightest trace of Garin. Peasants, farmers, servants from country bungalows, foresters, caretakers only shrugged their shoulders in answer to their questions.

"There are no newcomers in the district, we know everybody who lives here."

Only the western sector, the hardest, was left. According to the map there was a footpath there leading to the rocky plateau on which was situated a famous ruined castle, *Schloß des gefesselten Gerippes*, and beside it, as was fitting and proper under such circumstances, a beer garden, *Zum gefesselten Gerippe*.

In the ruined castle visitors were actually shown the

remains of a dungeon and behind the iron grille a gigantic skeleton sitting in rusty chains. The same skeleton was depicted on picture postcards, on paper knives, and on beer mugs. For twenty pfennigs visitors could also be photographed beside the skeleton and send the picture to relatives or to a girl friend. On Sundays plenty of holiday-makers came to see the ruins and the beer garden did a good trade. At times there were foreign visitors.

Since the war, however, interest in the famous skeleton had declined. The townspeople were undernourished and had not the energy to climb that steep hill on holidays—they preferred their sandwiches and half-bottles of beer far from historic reminiscences under the lime-trees on the river-bank. Mine host of *Zum gefesselten Gerippe* was no longer able to keep the ruins in good condition. For weeks on end now the famous medieval skeleton would sit undisturbed by anybody's presence, gazing through empty eye sockets down the green valley where, on one fatal day, the owner of the castle had knocked him out of his saddle; he gazed at churches with spires and weathercocks, at the chimneys of factories where poison gas, tetryl and other hellish products were being manufactured on a world-wide scale, products that deprived the local people of all zest for historic reminiscences, postcards of the skeleton and, probably, for life itself.

It was in this direction that Wolf and Khlinov now set off. They first dropped into a café on the town square for a bite and there they examined a map of the locality and questioned the waiter. It seemed that in the western environs of the town the sights worth seeing included, in addition to the ruins and the beer garden, a villa belonging to a typewriter manufacturer who had recently lost his money. Standing on the western slope of the hills, the villa was not visible from the town. The manufacturer lived there alone, never leaving the place.

A full moon rose just before dawn. The vague and seemingly shapeless heaps of rocks and stones now loomed clear-cut in the moonlight, casting velvet shadows into the ravine from the still standing arches and the remains of the castle walls overgrown with stunted, twisted trees and a tangle of blackberry bushes; a square Norman tower, the oldest part of the castle, the Torture Tower, as it was called on the postcards, came to life.

Brick arches clung to the eastern wall belonging, apparently, to a gallery that had connected the ancient tower with the living quarters in the castle. All that now remained were the foundations, heaps of rubble and capitals from sandstone columns. The skeleton sat in his fetters under the cross-vault of a dungeon below the tower.

Wolf took a long look at the skeleton, resting his elbows on the grille, then he turned to Khlinov and said: "Now look over here."

Deep down below them in the moonlight lay a hollow wrapped in haze. Silver scales glittered on the river in those places where the water appeared from under the tree-tops. The town looked like a group of toy houses. Not a single window showed a light. Away to the left behind the town glowed hundreds of lights of the Aniline factories. Clouds of white smoke welled up where chimneys belched pinkish flames. Engine whistles and rumbling sounds came drifting across the valley.

"I was right," said Wolf. "The ray can only be used from this plateau. Look, there are the raw material stockyards and there, behind that earth rampart, are the stocks of half-finished products—they are quite open—and those long buildings are where sulphuric acid is produced by the Russian method, from iron pyrites. Over there, on the other side, under those round roofs they produce aniline and all those devilish substances that sometimes explode spontaneously."

"All right, Wolf. Even if we assume that Garin will not erect his apparatus until the night of the 28th he would have to make some preparations beforehand and there ought to be signs of them."

"We must examine the ruins. I'll take the tower and you take the walls and arches. . . . Still I don't think you could find a better place than where that skeleton thing is sitting."

"We meet at the beer garden at 7 o'clock."

"All right."

Shortly after seven in the morning Wolf and Khlinov were drinking milk on the verandah of the *Zum gefesselten Gerippe.* Their nocturnal search had been fruitless. They sat in silence, their chins resting in their cupped hands. They had got to know each other so well during the last few days that they could read each other's thoughts. Khlinov, more impressionable and less prone to trust himself, kept going over the whole course of deduction that had brought him and Wolf from Paris to this apparently harmless spot. What were these convictions based on? On two or three lines in a newspaper.

"Don't you think we might be making fools of ourselves, Wolf?"

"The human mind has limitations," answered Wolf. "It is always better, however, to rely on that mind rather than doubt it. Apart from that, if we don't find anything and Garin's fiendish plan proves to be a figment of our imaginations we can only thank God for it. We shall have done our duty."

A waiter brought them omelettes and two mugs of beer. Mine host appeared, red-cheeked and fat.

"Good morning, gentlemen!" Wheezing from shortness of breath he waited with a worried air until his guests had broken their fast. Then he waved his hand towards the valley, still bluish and glistening with dew. "I've been watching it for twenty years. Things are coming to an end, that's what I say, *meine Herren.* I saw the mobilization. The troops marched off along that road there. They were fine German columns." The host's fat forefinger shot over his head like an opening spring. "They were the Siegfrieds, those of whom Tacitus wrote: powerful, sowing terror, in winged helmets. *Ober,* two more mugs of beer for the gentlemen. .... In 1914 the Siegfrieds marched off to conquer the world. Only the shields were missing—do you remember the old Germanic custom of holding the shield to the mouth when shouting the war-cry to make the warriors' voices more terrifying? Yes, I saw the cavalrymen's behinds firmly planted in their saddles.... What has happened, I would like to know? Have we forgotten how to die on the battle-field? I saw the troops come back. The cavalrymen, damn them, still sat firmly in their saddles.... The Germans were not beaten on the battle-field. They were pierced with swords in their own beds, at their own hearths...."

Mine host studied the guests with his protruding eyes and turned towards the ruins, his face the colour of red brick. Slowly he pulled a packet of postcards out of his pocket and slapped his hand with them.

"You've been in the town; I ask you, did you see a single German more than five foot six in height? And when those proletarians come home from the factories do you hear one of them who had the courage to say the word 'Deutschland!' in a loud voice? Those proletarians squawk about nothing but socialism over their beer mugs."

He threw the postcards deftly on to the table so that they spread out fanwise. They were pictures of the skeleton—the skeleton with a German in a winged helmet and the skeleton with a warrior of 1914 in full field equipment.

"Twenty-five pfennigs each or two marks fifty a dozen," said mine host with contemptuous pride. "They can't be sold cheaper, they're good pre-war work, coloured photographs with tin foil in the eyes—that produces an indelible impression. D'you think those cowardly bourgeois or those five-and-half-foot proletarians buy my postcards? Pfui! ... They want me to photograph Karl Liebknecht with the skeleton...."

His face again flushed as the blood rushed to it and he suddenly burst out laughing.

"They'll have to wait! *Ober,* put a dozen postcards in our own original envelopes for the gentleman.... Yes, I have to eke out a living.... I'll show you my patent, the Hotel *Zum gefesselten Gerippe* will sell them by hundreds. Here I keep pace with the times and don't depart from my principles."

The landlord went into the house and returned with a small object, like a cigar box. The inevitable skeleton was burned in the lid.

"You want to try it? It works as well as a regular receiver with valves." He quickly arranged the leads and the earphones, and put a plug into a jack built under the table. "It costs three marks seventy-five pfennigs, without earphones, of course." He offered the earphones to Khlinov. "You can listen to Berlin, Hamburg, and Paris, if you like. I'll tune you in to Cologne Cathedral, there's a service on there now, you'll hear the organ. *Kolossal!* ... Turn that switch to the left. What's the matter? Is it that damned Stuffer interfering again? No?"

"Who's that interfering?" asked Wolf, bending over the receiver.

"A ruined typewriter manufacturer by the name of Stuffer, a drunkard and a madman. He built a radio sta-

tion at his villa two years ago. Then he lost all his money.
The station began working again recently."

Khlinov, his eyes shining excitedly, dropped the earphones.

"Wolf, pay up and let's go."

A few minutes later, when they had got rid of the
garrulous landlord, they passed through the gates of the
beer garden and Khlinov squeezed Wolf's arm with all
the strength of his fingers.

"I heard Garin's voice, I could recognize it...."

68

An hour earlier that same morning, in the semi-darkness of the dining-room at his villa on the western slope
of the same hills Herr Stuffer had been sitting at the
table talking with an invisible companion. The talk consisted mainly of snatches of phrases and curses. Empty
bottles, cigar ends, and Stuffer's collar and tie lay in dis-
order on the ash-bespattered table. He sat there in his
underclothes scratching his flabby chest and staring at the
single electric bulb that burned in a huge iron chandelier;
trying his best not to belch he cursed in the foulest terms
all those people whose pictures flashed through his be-
fuddled brain.

In a solemn bass the dining-room clock struck seven.
Almost simultaneously a car stopped outside. Garin, fresh-
ened by the morning breeze, entered the dining-room, a
leather cap on the back of his head and a mocking grin
on his face.

"Been drinking all night again?"

Stuffer turned his bloodshot eyes on him. He liked
Garin. He paid well for everything. He had rented the
villa for the summer months without any bargaining, the
rent including the wine-cellar, but he allowed Stuffer to

do as he wished with the old Rhine wines, the French champagne and the liqueurs. The devil alone knew what he did for a living, some sort of speculation, apparently, but he cursed the Americans roundly, and they had ruined Stuffer two years ago, he despised the government and in general called all people swine—that was also to his credit. The foods he brought in his car were such as Stuffer, even in his most prosperous years, would never have dreamed of—precious Strasbourg *pâtés*, Russian caviare and Camembert cheeses covered with a mass of white maggots, the Camemberts of a connoisseur. One might even imagine that keeping Stuffer in a state of permanent intoxication was part of his plan.

"And what have you been doing? Saying your prayers all night?" asked Stuffer in a hoarse voice.

"I had a very nice time with the girls in Cologne and, as you see, I'm quite fresh and am not sitting around in my underpants. You're going downhill, Stuffer. Incidentally, I've been warned about something not very pleasant. It seems your villa stands too close to the chemical factories. It's like a powder magazine."

"Nonsense!" roared Stuffer. "Again some swine is trying to ruin me. You're in absolute safety at my villa!"

"So much the better. Give me the key to the shed."

Swinging the key by its chain, Garin went out into the garden where there was a small glazed pavilion standing under aerial masts. Here and there in the neglected flower-beds stood terracotta dwarfs befouled by the birds. Garin unlocked the glass door, entered, and threw open the windows. He leaned on the window-sill and stood there for some time breathing in the morning freshness. He had spent almost twenty hours in the car finishing off his business with banks and factories. Everything was now ready for the twenty-eighth.

He did not remember how long he stood at the window. He stretched himself, lit a cigar, started up the dynamo.

examined the wireless equipment, and tuned in. Then he stood before the microphone and spoke loudly and distinctly:

"Zoë, Zoë, Zoë, Zoë.... Can you hear me? Can you hear me? Everything will be as you wish. You must only wish hard enough. I need you. Without you my enterprise means nothing to me. In a day or two I'll be in Naples. I'll tell you exactly when tomorrow. Don't worry about anything. Everything is going well...."

He stopped for a moment, puffed at his cigar and began again, "Zoë, Zoë, Zoë...." He closed his eyes. The dynamo hummed softly and invisible magnetic waves left the aerial one after another.

If a whole regiment of artillery had passed at that moment it is doubtful whether Garin would have heard it. Nor did he hear stones rattling down the slope at the end of the glade. Some five paces from the pavilion the bushes parted and the blue muzzle of a Colt revolver appeared at the level of a man's eyes.

Rolling took up the telephone receiver.

"Yes."

"This is Semyonov speaking. I've just intercepted a wireless message from Garin. Shall I read it to you?"

"Yes."

"Everything will be as you wish, you must only wish hard enough," began Semyonov making a rough translation from Russian into French. Rolling listened without a sound.

"Is that all?"

"Yes, sir."

"Take this down." Rolling began to dictate: "Immediately tune the transmitter to a wavelength of 421 metres. Tomorrow ten minutes earlier than the time at which you

intercepted today's message begin sending this one: 'Zoë...
Zoë... Zoë... An unexpected misfortune has occurred.
We must act. If you value the life of your friend land at
Naples on Friday, stay at the Hotel Splendide and await
news until Saturday noon.' You will repeat this continuously, do you hear me, continuously in a loud and convincing voice. That's all."

Rolling rang the bell.

"Find Tyklinski and bring him to me immediately," he
said to the secretary who appeared at the door. "Go
straight to the aerodrome, hire or buy—it makes no dif-
ference which—a covered passenger aircraft. Hire a pilot
and mechanic. Have everything ready to take off by the
twenty-eighth."

70

Wolf and Khlinov spent the remainder of the day in K.
They wandered about the streets, chatted idly with the
local inhabitants as though they were tourists. When the
town grew quiet Wolf and Khlinov made their way to the
hills. By midnight they were climbing the slope leading to
Stuffer's villa. If the police paid any attention to them they
had decided to be tourists who had lost their way. If they
were detained by the police their arrest would not lead to
any further trouble, the whole town could confirm their alibi.
Less than forty minutes after the shot from the bushes,
when they had seen chips fly from Garin's skull, they had
been back in the town.

Now they climbed over the low fence, crept round the
open glade with great caution and, keeping to the bushes,
approached the house. They stopped, looked at each other
in surprise. All was calm and quiet in the house and in
the garden. Some of the windows were lit up. The main
door leading to the garden was wide open. A peaceful
light fell on the stone steps and on the dwarfs in the

thick grass. On the top step of the porch a fat man sat
playing softly on a flute. Beside him stood a straw-covered
bottle. It was the man that had appeared that morning on the garden path leading to the pavilion and on
hearing the shot had turned about and run back to the
house at an unsteady trot. Now he was in a happy mood
as though nothing untoward had happened.

"Come on," said Khlinov. "We must find out."

"I couldn't have missed," muttered Wolf.

They approached the porch. Half-way up the path
Khlinov said softly:

"Excuse us for disturbing you. Are there any dogs
here?"

Stuffer put his flute down, turned round on the step
where he sat and stretched out his neck to peer at the two
vague figures.

"Yes," he said slowly, "there are savage dogs here."

Khlinov explained the situation:

"We've lost our way. We wanted to visit the castle
ruins. . . . May we take a rest here?"

Stuffer answered with an indefinite grunt. Wolf and
Khlinov bowed to him and sat down on the bottom step,
both were on their guard and excited. Stuffer looked
down on them from his seat.

"By the way," he began, "when I was rich I used to
let dogs loose in the garden. I don't like uninvited midnight visitors. (Khlinov quickly squeezed Wolf's arm—keep
quiet.) The Americans have ruined me and my garden has
been turned into a thoroughfare for loafers although there
are boards everywhere with a warning that trespassers will
be fined a thousand marks. But in Germany people no longer show respect for law or property. I told the man who
rented my villa: put barbed wire round the place and hire
a night watchman. He wouldn't listen to me and he's only
got himself to blame. . . ."

Wolf picked up a pebble and threw it into the darkness.

"Why? Has there been some unpleasantness with these visitors?" he asked.

" 'Unpleasant' is too strong a word, 'funny' would be more like it. No longer ago than this morning. In any case my economic interests have not been affected and I'll devote myself to my own amusements."

He placed the flute to his lips and played a few piercing notes.

"What's it got to do with me, anyway, whether he lives here or goes boozing with the girls in Cologne? He paid me up to the last pfennig.... Nobody can reproach him on that score. But it seems that the gentleman is rather nervous. He ought to have got used to revolver shots during the war. He packed up all his traps and—good-bye.... Well, good luck to him."

"Has he gone for good?" Khlinov asked suddenly in a loud voice.

Stuffer got up but immediately sat down again. They could see that the cheek on which the light from the room fell was flushed, smirking and oily. His fat belly shook.

"So that's what it was, he warned me that two gentlemen would be asking me about his departure. He's gone, he's gone, *meine Herren*. If you don't believe come inside and I'll show you his rooms. If you're friends of his come in and make sure.... It's your right, the rooms have been paid for."

Stuffer tried to get up again but his legs would not hold him. Nothing else of any value was to be got out of him. Wolf and Khlinov returned to the town. Not a word passed between them all the way back. On the bridge over the black water, where a street-lamp was reflected, Wolf suddenly stopped, clenched his fists, and exclaimed:

"What the devil! I saw myself that chips flew off his skull...."

A short, solidly-built man with greying hair carefully parted, his ailing eyes protected by blue spectacles, stood beside a tiled stove listening to Khlinov's story.

At first Khlinov had sat on the sofa, then he had moved to the window-sill, and at last had begun to stride up and down the little reception-room at the Soviet Embassy.

He told what he knew of Garin and Rolling. His story was precise and consistent, but Khlinov himself realized the improbability of that mass of events.

"Suppose that Wolf and I are mistaken.... So much the better, we shall be very glad if we have drawn the wrong conclusions. The chances are fifty-fifty that there will be a catastrophe. We must consider only the other fifty per cent. You, as ambassador, can convince people, influence them, open their eyes. The whole business is an extremely serious one. The apparatus really exists. Shelga has actually touched it. Action must be taken immediately, this very minute. We haven't more than twenty-four hours at our disposal. Tomorrow night things are going to happen. Wolf has remained in K. He is doing what he can to warn the workers, the trade unions, the town population and the factory administration. It goes without saying that nobody believes him. Why, even you...."

The ambassador did not speak or raise his eyes.

"At the offices of the local newspaper they laughed until they cried. At the best we're considered mad...."

Khlinov clutched at his head—tufts of uncombed hair stuck out between his dirty fingers. His face was drawn and covered with dust. His eyes stared fixedly as though he were gazing at some horror. The ambassador looked at him cautiously over his glasses.

"Why didn't you come to me before?"

"We had no facts. Assumptions, conclusions, everything was on the verge of the fantastic, it was mad.... Even now at times I imagine I shall wake up and sigh in relief. . . . I assure you that I'm in my right mind. Wolf and I haven't undressed or lain in a bed for eight days."

After a short silence the ambassador spoke in serious tones.

"I'm sure this is no hoax, Comrade Khlinov. You are probably the victim of an *idée fixe*." He raised his hand to check Khlinov's gesture of despair. "But your fifty per cent sounds convincing to me. I will go and do whatever I can."

Since early morning of the twenty-eighth, groups of citizens had clustered on the town square of K., some in perplexity, others with a certain amount of fear, discussing the proclamation that had been stuck to the walls of corner houses with masticated bread.

"Neither the authorities, nor the factory administration, nor the trade unions want to listen to our desperate appeal. Today, we are absolutely convinced, the factories, the town, and the whole population are threatened with destruction. We have tried to prevent it but were unable to catch the scoundrels in the pay of American bankers. Save yourselves, leave the town for the plains. Believe us for the sake of life itself, for the sake of your children, in the name of God."

The police guessed who had written the proclamation and set out to find Wolf. But Wolf was gone. By midday the town authorities issued a poster warning the people that under no circumstances must they abandon the town and create a panic as apparently a gang of bandits intended to wreak their will in deserted homes that night.

"Citizens of K.! You are being hoaxed. Show your common-sense. The criminals will be discovered and arrested today and will be dealt with in accordance with the law."

The authorities had struck the nail right on the head: their explanation was extremely simple and the citizens calmed down, they even laughed at themselves. "That was a smart trick, they'd have had the run of the shops and houses all night. And we would be the laughing-stock of the country trembling in fear out there on the plains all night."

Evening came the same as thousands of other evenings with the glow of the setting sun reflected in the windows of the houses. Bird in their trees grew quiet. Frogs croaked on the damp banks of the river. The clock on the red-brick church played *Die Wacht am Rhein* to scare the lousy French as it struck eight. Light streamed peacefully from the windows of the bars where visitors methodically wetted their moustaches in foaming beer. Even the land-lord of the out-of-town beer garden *Zum gefesselten Ge-rippe* had calmed down; he walked up and down the deserted verandah of his establishment, for a time cursed the government, the socialists, and the Jews, ordered the shutters to be closed and set out on his bicycle to see his girl friend in the town.

It was at this time that a motor-car, without lights and almost without a sound, moved swiftly along a little-used road on the western slope. The sun had set but the stars were not yet bright and a cold bluish light came from be-yond the hills where the moon was rising. Lights flashed up here and there on the plain. Only in the factories life went on as usual.

Wolf and Khlinov sat on the edge of the cliff surmounted by the castle ruins. Again they had examined every nook and cranny of the ruins, had climbed all over the square tower but had not found any trace of Garin's preparations. There was a moment when they thought they heard a car in the distance. They listened and peered into the dark-ness. It was a quiet evening redolent of the ancient tranquillity of earth. Occasionally some movement of air currents brought a dampish smell of flowers from below.

"I looked at the map," said Khlinov, "and if we descend the western slope we'll cross the railway at a wayside station where the mail-train stops at five-thirty. I don't suppose the police will be watching there."

"The end is foolish, ridiculous," answered Wolf. "Man's adoption of the upright position after moving so long on all fours is far too recent, he is still overburdened by the millions of years of unenlightened brutedom. A mass of humans that is not guided by a great idea is a terrible thing. People must not be left without leaders. The urge to get back on all fours is too strong for them."

"Why be so hard on them, Wolf?"

"I'm tired," said Wolf. He sat on a heap of stones, his strong chin resting on his clenched fists. "Did you for a moment imagine that on the twenty-eighth we'd be hunted like a couple of thieves and scoundrels? If you could have seen the glances exchanged by those representatives of authority when I persisted. What a fool I was! And they're right, that's the trouble. They'll never know the danger that threatened them."

"If it hadn't been for your shooting, Wolf...."

"Hell!... If I hadn't missed! I'd willingly take ten years penal servitude to show those idiots...."

Wolf's voice was dully echoed by the ruins. Some thirty paces away from the two men Garin was creeping along the shadow of a half-ruined wall like a hunter stalking his prey. He had a clear view of the silhouettes of the two men sitting on the cliff edge and could hear every word they said. The open space between the end of the wall and the tower he crossed at a crawl. At the point where the foot of the tower adjoined the vaulted cave in which the shackled skeleton sat, lay a piece of a sandstone column. Garin crouched behind it. The crunching of stones and the rasping of iron brought Wolf to his feet.

"Did you hear that?"

Khlinov looked at the heap of stones behind which Garin had disappeared into the earth. They ran there and then walked right round the tower.

"There are foxes here," said Wolf.

"No, it was probably some night bird's call."

"Let's get away from here. You and I are beginning to have hallucinations."

When they reached the steep path leading from the ruins to the main road they heard a second noise, like that of something falling and rolling along the ground. Wolf trembled all over. Holding their breath they listened for a long time. It seemed that the very silence was ringing in their ears. "Whip-whip-whip," an unseen nightjar called here and there as it flew low overhead.

"Let's go."

"Yes, it's silly to stay here."

This time they walked resolutely down the path without once turning back. This saved the life of one of them.

73

Wolf had not been entirely wrong when he said that he had seen the chips fly off Garin's skull. When Garin had leaned over to pick up a burning cigar from the table during his moment's pause before the microphone, the ebonite earphone that he held pressed to his ear to keep check of his own voice suddenly flew to pieces. At the same time he heard the crack of a revolver shot and felt a blow on the left side of his skull. He fell on his side, rolled over on his face, and lay still. He heard Stuffer squeal and then the footsteps of people running.

"Who was it, Rolling or Shelga?" He was racking his brains over this problem when, two hours later, he raced off in his car to Cologne. It was only when he listened to the conversation of those two men on the cliff that he found the answer. Clever chap, that Shelga. Still, he wasn't playing fair.

He pushed aside the piece of sandstone that covered a rusty manhole, dropped down under the earth, and by the light of an electric flash-light climbed up the crumbling stairs to the "stone box," a solitary cell in the thickness of the wall of the Norman tower. It was a windowless cell two and a half paces square, with the remains of bronze rings and chains cemented into the wall. Garin's apparatus stood to one side on crudely fashioned scaffolding. Opposite the muzzle of the machine a hole had been cut through the wall and was concealed by the bones of the fettered skeleton.

Garin extinguished his flash-light, pushed the muzzle of the machine aside, plunged his arm through the hole in the wall, and threw the bones away from the aperture. The skull fell off the skeleton and rolled along the ground. Through the opening the lights of the factories could be seen. Garin had very keen eyesight and he could even distinguish tiny human figures moving about between the buildings. He trembled from head to foot. His teeth were clenched. He had never thought that it would be so difficult when the time came. Again he directed the muzzle of the apparatus through the aperture and adjusted it. He opened the lid at the back and examined the pyrotechnic pyramids. Everything had been prepared a week before. A second machine and the old model were safe down below in his car.

He closed the lid and placed his hand on the handle of a magneto that would automatically set fire to the pyramids in the machine. The trembling continued. It was not a matter of conscience (as if there were any conscience left after the World War), nor fear (he was too thoughtless), nor pity for the doomed (they were too far away) that raised his temperature and gave him the shiv-

ers by turns. With terrifying clarity he realized that a
single turn of that handle would make him the enemy of
all mankind. This was a purely aesthetic sensation of the
importance of the moment.

He even took his hand off the magneto to get a cigarette from his pocket but his excited brain checked the
movement: "Why do you hesitate, why do you waste time
enjoying the moment, this is madness. . . ."

Garin turned the handle. Flames burst out and hissed
inside the machine. Slowly he began adjusting the micrometer screw.

74

Khlinov was the first to call attention to a strange
patch of light in the sky.

"There's another," he said softly. They were standing half-way down the road over the cliff throwing
their heads back to look up to the sky. Lower than the
first a second ball of fire appeared just above the trees
and, shedding sparks like a dying rocket, began to fall.

"Those are birds burning," whispered Wolf, "look."
Across a bright patch of sky over the forest a bird was
flying hesitantly, apparently the nightjar that had cried
its "whip-whip-whip . . ." It burst into flame, turned over
and fell.

"They're caught on some wire."

"What wire?"

"Can't you see it, Wolf?"

Khlinov pointed to a thin incandescent thread as
straight as a needle that ran overhead from the ruins
towards the Aniline Company's factories.

Its path was marked by leaves bursting into flame
and the burning bodies of birds. Now it was shining
brightly, a long section of it stood out against the black
wall of pines.

191

"It's dropping . . ." exclaimed Wolf but did not finish. They both realized what that thread was. They stood rooted to the ground and could only follow the direction of the ray. Its first blow struck a factory chimney that swayed, broke in the middle, and collapsed. The distance was too great for them to hear the sound of its fall.

Almost immediately to the left of the chimney a cloud of steam appeared over the roof of a long building, turned red, and mingled with the black smoke. Still farther to the left stood a five-storey building. Suddenly its lights went out. From top to bottom a fiery line zigzagged across the façade of the building, then again and again. . . .

Khlinov screamed like a wounded hare. The building seemed to shrink and then collapsed, in a cloud of black smoke.

Only then did Wolf and Khlinov dash back up the hill to the castle ruins. They cut across the bends in the winding road and climbed straight uphill, tearing through the hazel bushes and young growth of trees, falling at times and slipping back downhill. They groaned and cursed, one in Russian, the other in German. Then a dull roar reached them as though the very earth had heaved a deep sigh.

They turned to look back. From their point of vantage they could see the whole group of factory buildings covering many acres. Half of them were burning like paper houses. Down below, on the outskirts of the town, rose a mushroom of greyish-yellow smoke. The ray of the hyperboloid was dancing madly amongst those ruins seeking the most important spot of all, the stock-pile of half-finished explosives. Half the sky was lit up by the glow. Clouds of smoke and huge showers of yellow, brownish and silver-white sparks rose up higher than the hills.

"We're too late!" screamed Wolf.

They could see a living mass pouring out of the town along the chalk-white ribbons of roads. The river, brightly illuminated by the conflagration, was covered in black spots. People were rushing towards the plains, the population was seeking safety.

"Too late, too late!" screamed Wolf, blood and foam pouring down his chin.

It was already too late for the population to get away. The grass field between the town and the factories on which stood rows of tile-capped little houses suddenly heaved up. That was the first thing the eye saw. Through cracks in the earth savage tongues of fire burst out; at the same moment a blinding column of white fire and incandescent gas, of a brilliance never before seen by man, rose up from the flames. The sky seemed to have been lifted higher over the whole plain and all space was filled with a greenish-rosy light. It had the effect of an eclipse of the sun and every branch, every bunch of grass, every stone and two white, petrified human faces stood out clearly.

Then came the sound of the explosion. The earth was torn with a rending roar. The hills trembled. A hurricane shook the trees and bowed them to the ground. Stones and burning brands flew through the air. Clouds of smoke spread right across the plain.

It grew dark and in the darkness came the second, still more awe-inspiring explosion. The whole smoky air was saturated with a dull, reddish-brown, festering light.

The blast knocked Khlinov and Wolf off their feet and carried them down the hillside together with branches of trees and stones.

75

"Captain Jansen, I want to go ashore."

"Yes, madame."

"And I want you to go with me."

Jansen flushed with pleasure. A minute later a varnished boat dropped lightly into the transparent water by the side of the *Arizona*. Three sun-tanned sailors slid down ropes and took their places on the boat's thwarts, slipped the oars into the rowlocks, and waited.

Jansen waited by the gangway. Zoë was in no hurry—she stood with a distracted air looking at Naples rising from the sea in terraces that flickered in the hot haze, at the terracotta walls and turrets of the ancient fortress and at the lazily smoking summit of Vesuvius. There was not a breath of wind and the surface of the sea was as smooth as a mirror.

Large numbers of boats moved lazily across the bay. In one of them stood an old man rowing with a single stern oar—just like a Michelangelo drawing. His grey beard fell on a torn, patched cloak of dark material, his tousled grey curls formed a crown for his head. Slung across his shoulder was a canvas bag.

This was Peppo, a beggar known to all the world.

He was pulling out in his own boat to seek alms. The day before Zoë had thrown him a hundred-dollar bill over the side of her yacht. Today he was again rowing his boat to the *Arizona*. Peppo was old Italy's last romantic, beloved of the gods and the muses. All romanticism was irrevocably lost. Today nobody wept as he looked with joy-filled eyes on those old stones. Rotting on the battlefields were those artists who used to give a gold coin for the privilege of drawing Peppo amid the ruins of the house of Cecilius Jucundus in Pompeii. The world had grown dull.

Plying his oar slowly Peppo floated along the side of the *Arizona*, green-hued from the reflected water; he raised a wrinkled face with bushy eyebrows majestic as an engraving, and held out his hand. He was a god demanding sacrifice. Zoë leaned over the rail and spoke to him in Italian.

"Guess, Peppo, odd or even?"

"Even, Signora."

Zoë threw a bundle of new notes into his boat.

"*Grazie, bella signora,*" was Peppo's regal response.

There was nothing else to wait for. Zoë had used Peppo to allay her doubts: if the old man would come in his boat and guess "even" everything would be all right.

Nevertheless she was tormented by some premonition: suppose there was a posse of police waiting for her at the Splendide? That compelling voice still resounded in her ears: "If you value the life of your friend. . . ." She had no choice.

Zoë went down into the boat. Jansen took his place at the tiller, the oars flashed in the water and towards them rushed the Santa Lucia quay houses with outside staircases and ragged washing on the lines, narrow streets with steps that crept up the hillside, half-naked children, women standing at the doors, rusty-red goats, oyster stalls at the edge of the water, and fishing-nets spread to dry on the granite embankment.

The boat had scarcely touched the green piles of the quay before a crowd of ragamuffins stormed down the steps to meet it—vendors of corals and brooches, hotel agents. Drivers of two-horse cabs cracked their whips, half-naked boys turned somersaults under their feet, howling and asking for soldi from the beautiful foreigner.

"Splendide," said Zoë, entering a carriage together with Jansen.

76

Zoë enquired at the hotel whether any correspondence had arrived for Madame Lamolle. She was handed an unsigned radiotelephone message: "Wait until Saturday evening." Zoë shrugged her shoulders, ordered rooms and went out with Jansen to see the town. Jansen suggested the museum.

Zoë's bored glance swept over the Renaissance beauties immortalized on the canvases—they draped themselves in stiff brocades, did not cut their hair, obviously did not take a bath every day, and were proud of such mighty shoulders and hips as would have been a source of shame to any Paris market-woman. She was still more bored by the marble heads of emperors and the faces of verdigris-covered bronzes—they might well have stayed in the earth. Boring again was the puerile pornography of the Pompeiian frescoes—no, ancient Rome and the Renaissance displayed poor taste. The Romans did not understand the bite of cynicism. They were satisfied with diluted wine, unhurriedly kissed florid and moral women and were proud of their muscles and their courage. They dragged along with them centuries of a revered past. They did not know what it meant to drive at one hundred and thirty miles an hour in a racing car. Nor did they know that with the aid of automobiles, aeroplanes, electricity, telephones, radio, lifts, fashionable dressmakers, and a cheque-book it is possible to squeeze the last drop of enjoyment out of every minute of life.

"Jansen," said Zoë (the captain walked half a pace behind her, dressed all in white, well-groomed, and ready to do anything silly), "Jansen, we're wasting time and I'm bored."

They drove to a restaurant. Between dishes Zoë threw a beautiful bare arm round Jansen's shoulders and danced with him, her eyes half closed, her face expressionless. Men stared at her hungrily. The dances whetted the appetite and raised a thirst. The captain's nostrils twitched, he stared into his plate afraid to betray the glitter in his eyes. He now knew what sort of mistress a multimillionaire would have. Never before had he danced with his hand on such a tender, long, and nervous back, never before had his nostrils breathed such fragrance of skin

and perfume. And her voice . . . singsong and mocking. . . .
And she was clever. . . . And chic. . . .

As they left the restaurant Jansen asked:

"Where do you wish me to be tonight, on board the yacht or at the hotel?"

Zoë cast a swift and strange glance at him, turned her head away immediately, and did not answer.

77

Zoë was intoxicated with wine and dance. "Oh, la-la, as though I have to give an account of everything." As they entered the hotel she leaned on Jansen's granite arm. As the clerk gave her the key to the room his dark, Neapolitan face spread into a smirking smile. Zoë was immediately on the alert.

"Any news?"

"None whatever, signora."

Said Zoë to Jansen:

"Go into the smoking-room, smoke a cigarette, and if you are not fed up with my chatter—I'll ring."

She walked lightly up the red-carpeted stairs. Jansen stood below. At the landing she turned and gave a faint smile. Like a drunken man he went into the smoking-room and sat down beside the telephone. He lit a cigarette, just as she had ordered. Leaning back be pictured her to himself: She enters her room. . . . She takes off her hat, her white cloth cloak. . . . Slowly, languidly, somewhat awkwardly, like an adolescent, she begins to disrobe. . . . Her clothes fall to the floor and she steps out of them. She stands before the mirror. . . . Seductive, staring with big round eyes at her own reflection. . . . She is in no hurry. such is the way of women. . . . Captain Jansen knew how to wait. . . . Her telephone—on the bedside table. . . . He

197

would, of course, find her in bed.... Leaning on one elbow, she stretches out towards the telephone....

The telephone, however, did not ring. Jansen closed his eyes so as not to see the damned instrument. Phew, how could he allow himself to fall in love like a silly kid.... And suppose she changed her mind? Jansen jumped up. Before him stood Rolling. The blood rushed to the captain's head, his face flushed.

"Captain Jansen," croaked Rolling, "thank you for taking care of Madame Lamolle, she has no further need of your services today. I suggest you return to your duties...."

"Aye, aye, sir," muttered Jansen with his lips alone.

Rolling had changed greatly during the past month— his face had grown darker, his eyes were sunken, his beard had spread over his cheeks in a reddish-black scrub. He was wearing a warm jacket and his breast pockets were stuffed with banknotes and cheque-books.... "A straight left to the temple, a right hook straight to the jaw, and all the breath would be knocked out of the swine...." Captain Jansen's iron fists were itching with animosity. One glance from Zoë, if she had been there at that moment, and nothing would have been left of Rolling but a bag of bones.

"I'll be on board the *Arizona* in an hour," said Rolling in an imperious voice and with a deep frown.

Jansen picked up his cap from the table, jammed it down deep over his eyes, and walked out. He jumped into a cab: "To the quay!" He imagined that every passer-by was grinning at him—"the man who had had his face slapped!" Jansen thrust a handful of small change into the cab-driver's hand, ran across the quay, and jumped into the boat: "Row, you sons of bitches." He ran up the gangway on to the deck, shouted at the first mate, "The deck's like a pigsty!" locked himself in his cabin, and without even removing his cap flopped down on his bunk. He growled softly.

Exactly an hour later he heard the voice of the man on watch and a faint voice answering from the sea. The gangway creaked. In a loud and jolly voice the first mate shouted an order, "Pipe all hands on deck!"

The owner had arrived. He could only rescue the remnants of his self-respect by receiving Rolling as though nothing had happened ashore. Jansen went on to the bridge with calm dignity. Rolling mounted the bridge, heard a report on the excellent condition of the vessel, and shook hands with him. The official ceremony was over. Rolling lit a cigar—he looked small and entirely out of place in a warm, dark suit that insulted the elegance of the *Arizona* and the Naples sky.

It was already midnight. The stars twinkled between the masts and the rigging. The lights of the city and of the shipping in the bay were reflected in water as black as basalt. The siren of a tugboat howled and died away.

Rolling appeared to be fully engrossed in his cigar— he kept smelling it and emitting clouds of smoke in the captain's direction. Jansen stood before him in an official pose, his hands by his sides.

"Madame Lamolle wishes to stay ashore," said Rolling. "That is sheer caprice, but we Americans always respect the wishes of a lady, even when they are obviously only a foolish whim."

The captain could do nothing but nod his head in agreement with the owner. Rolling raised his left hand to his lips and sucked the skin on the back of it.

"I shall remain on board until morning, perhaps all day tomorrow.... In order that my presence on board should not be misinterpreted.... (He held up the hand he had been sucking and examined it in the light of the open cabin door.) As I was saying—misinterpreted.... (Jansen looked at the hand and saw traces of finger-nails on it.) I will satisfy your curiosity by telling you that I am expecting somebody to visit the yacht but he doesn't expect to find me here. He may arrive at any time now. Give an order for me to be immediately informed when he comes on board. Good night."

Jansen's head was on fire. He was making a great effort to understand what was going on. Madame Lamolle had remained on shore. Why? Caprice? Or was she awaiting him? No—but the fresh scratches on Rolling's hand. . . . What had happened? Suppose she were lying on her bed with her throat cut? Or in a bag at the bottom of the bay? Multimillionaires are not very particular as to their methods.

At supper in the saloon Jansen asked for a glass of neat whiskey to bring some sort of clarity to his brain. The first mate was relating the latest newspaper sensation—the terrible explosion at the German factories of the Aniline Company that had wrecked a near-by town and caused the death of over two thousand people.

"Our owner has all the luck," said the mate. "The wreck of the Aniline Company's works will bring him in enough profit to buy up the whole of Germany with all the trimmings, Hohenzollerns and Social-Democrats thrown in. I drink to the owner."

Jansen took the newspapers to the cabin with him. He read with great care the description of the explosion and the various explanations, each more improbable than the others, as to the cause of it. Rolling's name occurred time and again in all the newspaper columns. The fashion section of the papers said that next season bearded cheeks would be in fashion and high bowler hats would be worn instead of soft felts. The *Excelsior* had a picture of the *Arizona* on the front page with Madame Lamolle's pretty head in an oval inset. As he looked at her Jansen lost his presence of mind. His alarm grew greater.

At two in the morning he came out of his cabin and saw Rolling seated in an armchair on the upper deck. Jansen returned to his cabin. He stripped off his clothes,

donned a thin suit of finest wool on his bare body and
tied his cap, shoes, and pocket wallet in a rubber bag. Six
bells sounded—three o'clock. Rolling was still sitting
in his armchair. At four o'clock he was still sitting there
but his silhouette, with the head sunk into the shoulders,
showed no life, he was asleep. In a minute Jansen had
slipped noiselessly down the anchor chain into the water
and set out to swim for the quay.

78

"Madame Zoë, don't bother yourself unnecessarily, the
telephone and bell-wires have been cut."

Zoë again sat down on the edge of her bed. A smile
of anger distorted her lips. Stas Tyklinski was lolling in
an armchair in the middle of the room; he curled his
moustaches and studied his patent-leather shoes. He did
not dare smoke, for Zoë had forbidden it with great
determination and Rolling had given strict orders that he
was to be polite with the lady.

He had tried to pass the time by relating stories of his
amours in Warsaw and Paris but Zoë looked at him with
such contempt that his tongue refused to function. There
was nothing for him to do but sit silent. It was nearly five
o'clock in the morning. All Zoë's attempts to free herself,
to deceive or seduce him had not led to any result.

"It's all the same to me, somehow or other I'll get
word to the police."

"The hotel staff has been bought up, big money has
been paid."

"When there are more people in the street I'll break
a window and scream."

"That's also been taken care of. Even a doctor has
been engaged to certify that you are subject to nervous
fits. Madame, for the outside world you are, so to say,

in the position of a wife who is trying to deceive her husband. You are outlawed. Nobody will help you and nobody will believe you. Sit still and keep quiet."

She pulled at her fingers and said to him in Russian: "You're a swine, a filthy Pole, a lackey, and a boor."

Tyklinski began to bluster and his moustaches bristled. He had, however, been ordered not to start a slanging match with her.

"We know how women can curse when their boasted beauty fails to serve their ends," muttered Tyklinski. "I'm sorry for you, madame. Still you'll have to sit with me tête à tête for a day or two. You'd better lie down and soothe your nerves. Good night, madame."

To his astonishment Zoë obeyed him this time. She threw off her shoes, lay down, arranged her pillows, and closed her eyes.

Through her eyelashes she could see Tyklinski's fat, bad-tempered face watching her intently. She yawned once or twice and placed her hand under her cheek.

"I'm tired, I don't care what happens," she murmured and yawned again.

Tyklinski made himself more comfortable in his chair. Zoë's breathing was regular. In a short time he began to rub his eyes. He stood up, walked up and down the room, then leaned against the door frame. Apparently he had made up his mind to keep awake on his feet.

Tyklinski was a fool. Zoë had got out of him everything she wanted to know and now she was waiting until he dozed off. It was not easy for him to keep standing by the door. He looked at the lock and returned to his seat.

A minute later his heavy jaw dropped. Zoë immediately slipped off the bed. With a swift movement she took the key from his waistcoat pocket. She picked up her shoes and fitted the key in the door—the stiff lock suddenly squeaked.

Tyklinski cried out as though he had seen a nightmare, "Who's that? What?" He jumped out of his chair. Zoë, threw open the door. He seized her by the shoulders and she sank her teeth in his hand and bit through the skin with vicious pleasure.

"You bitch, *kurwa!*" he roared in Polish. He jabbed his knee into the small of her back and knocked her down. He kicked her back into the room and tried to lock the door. Something prevented him from doing so and Zoë saw his neck turn red under the strain.

"Who's there?" he asked hoarsely, heaving his shoulder, against the door.

His feet slid slowly back across the parquet floor and the door opened. He grabbed hurriedly at the revolver in his hip pocket but before he could use it was sent flying across the room.

Captain Jansen stood in the door. Wet clothes clung to his muscular body. For a second he looked straight into Tyklinski's eyes. His sudden forward rush was more like propulsion and the blow that had been intended for Rolling descended on the Pole: a double impact—a straight left with the full weight of the body behind it caught him on the bridge of the nose and a right hook to his chin. Tyklinski collapsed on the carpet without a sound, his face battered and a bloody mess.

Jansen's third move was to turn and face Madame Lamolle. All his muscles were in play.

"At your service, Madame Lamolle."

"Jansen, to the yacht, as quickly as possible."

"Aye, aye, madame."

She threw her arm round his neck as she had done earlier in the restaurant. She did not kiss him but brought her lips very close to his.

"The fight's only just beginning. The greatest danger lies ahead."

"Aye, aye, madame."

79

"Cabby, drive hell for leather to the quay. I'm listening, Madame Lamolle. While I was waiting in the smoking-room. . . ."

"I went to my room, removed my hat and cloak. . . ."

"I know. . . ."

"How?"

Jansen's hand trembled behind her back. Zoë responded with a caressing movement.

"I didn't notice that the cupboard in front of a door leading to an adjoining room had been moved. I hadn't had time to get as far as the mirror before the door opened and Rolling confronted me. I knew that yesterday he was still in Paris. I also knew that he's mortally afraid of air travel. . . . If he were here that meant that it was really a matter of life and death for him. Now I know what's in his mind but then I simply went mad. He had lured me into a trap. I called him all the names I could lay my tongue to. He stuck his fingers into his ears and ran out."

"He came down to the smoking-room and sent me back to the yacht. . . ."

"That's just it. What a fool I was. It's because of those dances and wine and other foolishness. . . . Yes, my friend, if you want to fight you've got to put all nonsense on one side. . . . Two or three minutes later he returned. I said we must talk it over. And then he told me in such rude tones as he had never dared use to me before that there was nothing to talk over and that I was to stay in that room until he released me. Then I slapped his face."

"You've got guts," said Jansen in admiration.

"My dear friend, that was my second mistake. But what a coward! He got his ears boxed four times and stood for it. He just stood there with his lips trembling. He tried to grab my hand but that cost him dearly, too. Then I made my third mistake: I cried."

"Oh, the scoundrel...."

"Wait a minute, Jansen. Rolling's a fool where tears are concerned, he is crushed by tears, he'd prefer to have his face slapped a dozen times. Then he called the Pole who had been standing behind the door and I saw that it had all been arranged beforehand. The Pole settled himself in an armchair. Rolling told me, 'As a last resort he's been ordered to shoot.' Then he went away. I got busy with the Pole. Within an hour I had all the details of Rolling's treacherous plan. Jansen, my dear friend, this is a question of my happiness. If you don't help me all is lost. Cabby, faster, faster...."

The cab drove swiftly along the water-front, deserted at that early hour before dawn, and stopped at the stone staircase at the foot of which a number of boats were tied up in the oily black water of the bay.

A little later Jansen, holding the precious Madame Lamolle in his arms, climbed noiselessly up a rope ladder thrown over the stern of the *Arizona*.

80

Rolling was awakened by the chill of the morning. The deck was wet, the masthead lights had grown pale; the bay and the town were still in shadows but the smoke over Vesuvius already had a rosy tinge.

Rolling glanced over shipping lights and outlines of vessels. He went up to the lookout and stood beside him. He gave a snort and then went on to the bridge. Jansen immediately came out of his cabin, fresh, clean, and well-groomed. He wished Rolling a good morning and Rolling answered with a snort just a little more polite than the one he gave to the lookout.

He stood for a long time in silence, twisting a button on his jacket. This was a bad habit that Zoë had once tried to break him of. Now it didn't matter. Apart from that, twisting buttons would probably be the fashion in Paris next year. Tailors would invent special buttons for twisting.

Suddenly he asked:

"Drowned people rise to the surface, don't they?"

"If you don't tie a weight to them," answered Jansen calmly.

"I'm not asking that: if a man is drowned at sea is that the end of it?"

"Yes, a man falls overboard, a wave sweeps him from the deck, or some other mishap—all that is classed as 'accidental death by drowning.' The authorities do not usually interfere."

Rolling shrugged his shoulders.

"That's all I wanted to know about drowning. I'm going to my cabin. If a boat comes up, I repeat, don't say that I'm on board. Receive the man and then report to me."

He went away. Jansen returned to his cabin where Zoë slept behind drawn blue curtains on his bunk.

81

Shortly after eight a boat pulled out to the *Arizona*. The ragamuffin rowing the boat shipped his oars and called out:

"Ahoy there.... Is that the *Arizona*?"

"Let's suppose it is," answered a Danish sailor leaning over the side.

"Is there anybody by the name of Rolling on board?"

"Let's suppose there is."

The ragamuffin exposed his magnificent teeth in a smile.

"Grab this."

Adroitly he threw a letter on to the deck, the sailor caught it, and the ragamuffin clicked his tongue.

"Hi, sailor, salt-eyes, give us a cigar."

While the Dane was looking round for something to throw at the ragamuffin the latter made off, dancing and grimacing in the boat, and from sheer joy of life on that hot sunny morning sang at the top of his voice.

The sailor picked up the letter and went to the captain with it (as he had been ordered to). Jansen pulled back the curtain and leaned over the sleeping Zoë. She opened eyes still heavy with sleep.

"Is he here?"

Jansen gave her the letter and she read it:

"I'm badly wounded. Have mercy on me. I fought like a lion in your interests but the impossible happened. Madame Zoë is at liberty. I fall to your. ...."

Zoë tore up the letter without finishing it.

"Now we can wait calmly for him. (She looked at Jansen and held out her hand to him.) Jansen, dear, we must come to an agreement. I like you. I need you. I suppose the inevitable must happen...."

She heaved a short sigh.

"I feel I'm going to have a lot of trouble with you. My dear friend, that's all so unnecessary in life—love, jealousy, faithfulness.... I know the meaning of infatuation. It's elemental. I'm just as free to give myself as you are to take me—remember that, Jansen. Let us come to terms: either I die or I'll have power over the whole world. (Jansen pressed his lips together, a movement that Zoë liked.) You will be the tool of my will. Forget that I'm a woman. I am fantasy itself. I'm an adventuress, d'you understand that? I want everything to be mine. (She described a circle with her arms.) The man, the one man who can give me everything, should soon arrive on the *Arizona*. I'm expecting him, so is Rolling. ...."

Jansen raised a finger and glanced round. Zoë pulled the curtains to. Jansen went to the bridge. There stood Rolling, his hands firmly gripping the rail. His face with its twisted and tightly closed mouth was distorted with fury. He was staring at the still hazy expanse of the bay.

"There he is," he muttered with difficulty; he stretched out his hand and his finger hung crooked over the blue sea, "in that boat over there."

The bandy-legged Rolling looked like a crab as he ran down the companion so fast that he frightened the crew. He disappeared into his own cabin, and from there he again confirmed his order by telephone, telling Jansen to take on board the man who was crossing the bay in a six-oared boat.

It had never before happened that Rolling had pulled a button off his jacket. Today he had twisted all three of them off. He stood in the middle of a luxurious cabin panelled in valuable woods and spread with carpets of Shiraz; he looked at the clock on the wall.

Having twisted off all his buttons he took to biting his nails. It was astonishing how quickly he had reverted to a primitive state. He heard the shout of the lookout and Garin's answer from the boat. His hands began to perspire at the sound of that voice.

The heavy boat bumped against the side of the yacht amidst the hearty curses of the sailors. Then came the creak of the gangway being lowered and footsteps. "Take hold of it ... careful. ... Right. ... Where to?" That was the boxes containing the hyperboloids coming aboard. Then all was quiet.

Garin had fallen into his trap. At last! Rolling held his nose between his cold, damp fingers and emitted hissing, coughing sounds. People who knew him maintained that he had never laughed in his life. It wasn't true. Rolling loved to laugh, alone and without witnesses, after some success; he laughed as he did now, almost soundlessly.

Then he took up the telephone receiver and called Jansen.

"Is he on board?"

"Yes, sir."

"Take him to the lower cabin and lock him in. Try to do it unobtrusively, without any noise."

"Aye, aye, sir," answered Jansen smartly. His answer came so smartly that it made Rolling suspicious.

"Hallo, Jansen."

"Yes, sir."

"The yacht must be in the open sea within an hour."

"Aye, aye, sir."

The crew began scurrying about the deck. The ship's engines started up. The anchor chain rattled. Streams of greenish water slipped past the portholes. The shore turned away. A damp wind blew into the cabin. A joyful sensation of speed could be felt throughout the *Arizona*'s graceful hull.

Rolling, of course, realized that he was acting like a fool. But he was no longer the former Rolling, the cool gambler, the invincible buffalo, the staunch church-goer who sat out the sermons every Sunday. His present actions were not dictated by gain—the torment of sleepless nights, his hatred for Garin, and his jealousy demanded that Garin be destroyed and Zoë returned.

Even that fantastic success, the destruction of the Aniline Company's works, was like a dream. Rolling did not even trouble to find out how many hundred millions the stock exchanges of the whole world had paid him on the morning of the twenty-ninth.

That day he had awaited Garin in Paris in accordance with their agreement but Garin had not come. It was a move Rolling had expected and he rushed to Naples by air.

Now that Zoë was safely out of the way nobody stood

between him and Garin. The settlement with Garin had been thought out to the last detail. Rolling lit a cigar. He deliberately lingered a few moments, then went out of his cabin into the corridor. He opened a door on the lower deck. There stood the boxes containing the hyperboloids. Two sailors, sitting on them, jumped up as he entered. He sent them away to the forecastle.

Closing the door on the lower deck he went slowly towards the opposite door, that of the chart-house. As he took hold of the doorhandle he noticed that the ash on his cigar was falling. Rolling smiled with self-satisfaction, his mind was clear, it was a long time since he had been so pleased with himself.

He threw open the door. In the chart-house, under the plate-glass skylight, sat Zoë, Garin, and Shelga, watching him as he entered. Rolling stepped back into the corridor. He choked, it seemed to him that somebody was stirring his brain with a spoon. Beads of perspiration stood out on his nose. And, strangest of all things, he smiled a foolish and sickly smile like a clerk who has been caught tampering with the firm's books (he had been caught himself like that some twenty-five years ago).

"Good morning, Rolling," said Garin, standing up. "Here I am, old man."

83

Horror of horrors! Rolling had made himself ridiculous.

What could he do? Grind his teeth, storm, shoot? Still worse, still more foolish. . . . Captain Jansen had betrayed him, that was obvious. The crew were not to be relied on and the yacht was in the open sea. By an effort of will (something gave way inside him) Rolling chased that damned smile away.

"Ah!" Rolling raised his hand and waved it in greeting. "Hallo, Garin. So you feel like a sea trip? I'll be glad to have you. We'll have a good time."

Said Zoë sharply:

"You're a rotten actor, Rolling. Stop trying to amuse the public. Come in and sit down. There are no strangers here—only your deadliest enemies. You've only yourself to blame for gathering such a jolly party for a Mediterranean cruise."

Rolling looked at her with leaden eyes.

"In big business, Madame Lamolle, there is no such thing as personal friendship or enmity."

He sat down at the table between Garin and Zoë as though he were taking his place on a royal throne. He placed his hands on the table. The silence that ensued lasted a full minute.

"Very well," he said, "I've lost. How much do I have to pay?"

Garin answered, his eyes flashing, a smile on his face as though he were ready at any moment to break into a hearty laugh:

"Exactly one half, old man, one half as we agreed at Fontainebleau. Here is the witness too." He jerked his beard in the direction of Shelga who was moodily drumming on the table with his fingers. "I don't intend to examine your books. At a rough estimate it will be a thousand million in dollars, as a final settlement, of course. The operation will be a painless one as far as you're concerned. You've scraped up a hell of a lot of money in Europe."

"It will be difficult to pay a thousand million at once," answered Rolling. "I'll think it over. O. K. I'll go to Paris today. I hope that by Friday, in Marseilles, say, I shall be able to pay you the greater part of the sum."

"Tut-tut-tut," exclaimed Garin, "but the point is, old man, that you will only be set free after the sum has been paid."

Shelga glanced swiftly at him but did not speak. Rolling frowned as he would at a foolishly tactless remark.

"Am I to understand that you intend to hold me on this vessel?"

"Yes, you are."

"I must remind you that I am a citizen of the United States of America and as such my person is inviolable. My liberty and my interests are protected by the entire United States navy."

"So much the better!" shouted Zoë, in a towering passion. "The sooner, the better! ..."

She stood up, stretched out her arms and clenched her fists so tightly that the knuckles showed white.

"Let all your fleet come against us, let the whole world rise up against us. So much the better!"

Her short skirt flew up from her swift movement. Her white sailor jacket with the gold buttons, her tiny head with its boyish bob and the fists in which she intended squeezing the fate of the whole world, her grey eyes, dark from passion, her excited face—the picture was at once both amusing and terrifying.

"I must have misunderstood you, madame." Rolling turned his whole body towards her. "You intend to fight against the United States navy? Is that what you wished to say?"

Shelga stopped drumming on the table. For the first time in a month he was in a jolly mood. He even stretched out his legs and leaned back as though in a theatre.

Zoë looked at Garin, her glance became even darker. "I have spoken, Pyotr Petrovich. Now it's your turn."

Garin put his hands in his pockets, stood up, and rocked to and fro on his heels, his bright red lips wreathed in a smile. He had a dandyish and far from serious look about him. Zoë alone guessed that behind it all was an iron will, a criminal will, bursting with energy.

212

"In the first place," said Garin, leaning forward on his toes, "we have no specific enmity towards the United States. We shall try to crush any fleet that attempts aggressive action against us. Secondly," he swayed back on his heels, "we do not insist on a fight. If the armed forces of Europe and America recognize our sacred right to the occupation of any territory that we need, our sovereign rights and so on, we shall leave them alone, at least in the military sense. If they adopt a contrary course we shall deal with the ground and naval forces of Europe and America, with their fortresses, bases, military supplies, general staffs, and so on, without mercy. The fate of the Aniline factories, I hope, should convince you that I don't throw words to the wind."

He tapped Rolling on the shoulder.

"To think there was a time, old man, when I asked you to be a partner in my enterprise. You didn't have enough imagination because you are not a man of culture. This business of taking the shirts off the stockbrokers' backs and buying up factories, that's all outdated. You missed your opportunity to work with a real man, with the real organizer of your crazy billions."

Rolling was beginning to look like a decomposing corpse. Forcing out the words with difficulty he hissed:

"You're an anarchist."

At that Shelga grasped his hair with his sound hand and burst out laughing so uproariously that Captain Jansen's startled face appeared at the skylight. Garin turned on his heels and again addressed Rolling:

"No, old man, there's a screw loose somewhere in that brain box of yours. I'm no anarchist. I'm that great organizer that people will be looking for with a lantern in daylight before much more time has passed. We'll discuss this when we have more time. Now write a cheque. And full speed ahead to Marseilles."

84

In the course of the next few days the following occurred: the *Arizona* dropped anchor in the outer roads at Marseilles, and Garin presented Rolling's cheque for twenty million pounds sterling at the *Crédit Lyonnais.* The director of that bank immediately left for Paris in a panic.

On board the *Arizona* it was announced that Rolling was ill. He was kept in his own cabin under lock and key and Zoë took ceaseless precautions to ensure his isolation. For three days the *Arizona* took on board liquid fuel, water, canned goods, wine, and so on. Sailors and idlers on the quay were greatly astonished when a lighter loaded with bags of sand put out to *"la belle cocotte,"* as they called her. It was said that the *Arizona* was going to the Solomon Islands and they were teeming with cannibals. Captain Jansen bought arms—twenty carbines, revolvers, and gas-masks.

On the appointed day Garin and Jansen again appeared at the bank. This time they were met by the Deputy Minister of Finance who had come specially from Paris. He was extremely polite and did not doubt that the cheque was genuine, nevertheless he would like to see Rolling himself. He was taken to the *Arizona.*

Rolling met him—a very sick man, with deep-sunken eyes. He could scarcely rise from his chair. He confirmed the fact that the cheque had been made out by him, that he was setting out on a long voyage and asked that the formalities be ended as soon as possible.

The Deputy Minister of Finance took hold of the back of a chair and delivered a speech, gesticulating like Camille Desmoulins on the great brotherhood of the nations, on the cultural treasures of France, and asked for more time to make the payment.

Rolling closed his tired eyes and shook his head. The matter ended with an agreement to pay a third of the sum in sterling and the remainder in francs at the current rate of exchange.

A naval cutter brought the money that evening. Later, when all visitors had gone, Garin and Jansen mounted the bridge.

"Pipe all hands on deck!"

The crew were drawn up on the quarter-deck and Jansen spoke to them in a firm, stern voice.

"The yacht *Arizona* is setting out on an extremely dangerous and risky voyage. I'm damned if I'll answer for anybody's life, for the lives of the owners or for the safety of the vessel. You know me, you sons of.... I'll double your wages and the usual bonuses will also be doubled. All who return home safely will be given a life pension. I give you until sunset to think things over. Those who do not wish to run the risk may take their traps ashore."

That evening eight men of the crew went ashore. The same night the crew was again made up to strength by eight desperadoes that Jansen picked up in the bars of Marseilles port.

Five days later the yacht lay in the Solent and Garin and Jansen presented a cheque on the Bank of England for twenty million pounds. (A timid question was put to the Prime Minister by the Labour Party leader in the House of Commons in this connection.) The money was paid. The newspapers raised a howl. There were working-class demonstrations in many cities. Journalists flew to Southampton. Rolling did not receive any visitors. The *Arizona* took oil on board and sailed away across the ocean.

Twelve days later the *Arizona* dropped anchor in the Panama Canal and sent a wireless message calling to the radio telephone MacLinney, the general director of Rolling Aniline. At the appointed hour Rolling, sitting in his cabin with a revolver at his head, ordered the director to pay one hundred million dollars to the bearer of his cheque, Mr. Garin. Garin left for New York and returned with the money and Mr. MacLinney. That was a blunder. Rolling talked with his director for exactly five minutes in the presence of Zoë, Garin, and Jansen. MacLinney went away firmly convinced that there was something fishy somewhere.

When all this business was over the *Arizona* left for a cruise in the deserted Caribbean Sea. Garin travelled the length and breadth of America, visited factories, chartered ships, purchased machinery, instruments, tools, steel, cement, and glass. His purchases were loaded on the chartered vessels in San Francisco. Garin's solicitor signed contracts with engineers, technicians, and workers. Another agent of his went to Europe and recruited five hundred men for police duty from amongst the remnants of the Russian White Army.

In this way a month passed. Rolling spoke to New York, Paris, and Berlin every day by wireless. His orders were harsh and implacable. After the destruction of the Aniline Company's works the European chemical industries ceased their resistance to Rolling Aniline. The new trade-mark appeared on all their produce, a yellow circle with three black bars, the words "Spans the Globe" above and "Rolling Aniline Company" below. It began to look as though every European would be branded with the yellow circle. In this way Rolling Aniline launched its offensive, advancing through the smoking ruins of the Aniline Company's factories in Germany.

A horrible odour of colonialism pervaded the whole of Europe; hopes were daunted, joy and happiness seemed to be gone for ever. Countless spiritual treasures rotted away in dusty libraries. The yellow sun with its three black bars cast its harsh light on vast cities, factory chimneys, and smoke clouds—advertisements, advertisements, ballyhoo that sucked the blood of the people, while in dirty brick-bound streets and narrow alleys, between shop-windows and advertisements, between the yellow circles, large and small, peered human faces, drawn and haggard from hunger, boredom, and despair.

National currencies dropped in value. Taxes skyrocketed. Debts increased. The yellow brand struck hard in the name of the sacred law that demanded respect for duty and justice. Pay up!

Money flowed in streams, rivulets, and rivers into the coffers of Rolling Aniline. Its directors interfered in the internal affairs of states and in international politics. They constituted a sort of Order of Secret Rulers.

Garin raced from one end of the United States to the other accompanied by two secretaries, a number of engineers, typists, and a host of messengers. He worked twenty hours a day, never questioned prices and did not bargain.

MacLinney followed his activities with alarm and surprise. He could not understand what all these purchases meant, why Rolling's millions were being so preposterously squandered. Garin's secretary, one of his typists, and two messengers were in MacLinney's pay. They sent him a detailed report to New York every day. Still it was difficult to make sense of that whirlwind of purchases, orders, and contracts.

At the beginning of September the *Arizona* again appeared in the Panama Canal, took Garin on board, steamed through to the Pacific Ocean, and disappeared in a south-westerly direction.

A fortnight later ten heavily loaded steamers set sail in the same direction under sealed orders.

85

The ocean was in a boisterous mood. The *Arizona* was under almost full sail with only her topsails furled. The sleek hull of the yacht, a frail egg-shell with a mass of wind-filled sail and humming rigging, would plunge into

217

the troughs between the rollers until she was hidden to her trucks by the waves, then she would rise again on the crest and shake off the spray.

The awning had been taken in and hatches battened down. The lifeboats had been secured to the decks. Bags of sand placed along both sides were fastened with wires to the deck. On the forecastle and the stern stood two pylons built of steel girders with a round, boiler-shaped dome on each of them, which gave the yacht the appearance of a semi-naval vessel.

Garin and Shelga stood on the bridge which only the spray reached. Both were in tarpaulins. Shelga's arm was now out of its plaster cast but was not yet strong enough for anything more than holding a box of matches or a fork at table.

"The ocean," said Garin, "and a tiny, fragile vessel ... a crystallized atom of human genius and will. ... We fly along, Comrade Shelga, and nothing can stop us. We struggle. ... And what waves. ... Look at them, like mountains."

A gigantic wave approached from the starboard. Its seething, foam-capped crest rose higher and higher. Below the crest the bottle-green water described an ever sharper curve until the wave collapsed into the sea. The *Arizona* heeled over to port. The wild wind sang through the sails and rigging, lifting the yacht out of the watery abyss; the vessel lay right over, exposing the red hull to the keel, climbed the curved surface of the wave, reached the crest, and disappeared in a shower of noisy foam. The decks, the boats, all disappeared under the water and the pylon on the forecastle was immersed up to the dome which surmounted it. Water seethed around the bridge.

"Glorious!" shouted Garin.

The *Arizona* regained her equilibrium, the water rushed from the deck and the trysails flapped as they lost the wind; the yacht plunged down again into the trough.

"Such is man, Comrade Shelga, such is man in the human ocean.... I've taken a great fancy to this little boat. Isn't it like me? We are both wind-borne.... Eh?..."

Shelga shrugged his shoulders but did not answer. It was no use arguing with this man whose self-admiration reached the point of ecstasy.... Let him go into raptures —the superman indeed! He and Rolling were bound to find each other on this earth: they were mortal enemies but one could not exist without the other. The Chemical King's loins had begotten this homunculus filled with feverish, criminal ideas who, in turn, fertilized the Rolling desert with his monstrous fantasy. They ought to hang together from the same bough!

It was difficult to understand why Rolling had not long ago been fed to the fishes. He had done what was required of him; true enough Garin had not got the thousand million he had demanded but he had received three hundred and it ought to be time to get rid of encumbrances. But no, something stronger bound these two men together.

Nor could Shelga understand why he had not been thrown overboard in the Pacific. In Naples Garin had needed him as a third person and as a witness. If Garin had appeared on board the *Arizona* alone unexpected difficulties might have arisen. It would have been much more difficult for Rolling to get rid of both of them at once. That was all obvious. Garin had won the game.

What did he want with Shelga now? While they had been cruising in the Caribbean there had been some restrictions. But now, out in the open sea, nobody paid any attention to Shelga and he did as he pleased. He watched and he listened, and he was beginning to get a hazy idea of some possible ways out of this foul situation.

The race across the ocean was more like a pleasure trip. Breakfast, lunch, and dinner were served luxuriously.

The company at table consisted of Garin, Madame Lamolle, Rolling, Captain Jansen, the first mate, Shelga, Garin's first assistant Čermak, a Czech engineer, an undersized and sickly man, with pale, staring eyes and a thin beard, and Garin's second assistant, Scheffer, a German chemist, a bony, shy young man that Garin had picked up in San Francisco dying of hunger.

In this strange company of mortal enemies, murderers, plunderers, adventurers, and starving scientists all decked out in full evening dress, Shelga, also in evening dress, ate and drank with pleasure, keeping quietly to himself.

On his right sat a man who had sent four bullets into him, on his left, a man who had murdered almost three thousand people, and opposite, a beautiful she-devil such as the world had never before known.

After dinner Scheffer played the piano and Zoë danced with Jansen. Rolling usually remained seated at the table and watched the dancers. The others retired to the smoking-room. Shelga smoked his pipe on deck. Nobody interfered with him, in fact, nobody noticed him. The days passed, each like the others. There was no end to that grim ocean. The waves rolled on as they had done for millions of years.

Today Garin, contrary to his usual custom, joined Shelga on the bridge and talked to him in friendly tones as though nothing untoward had happened since the day they were seated together on the Trade-Union Boulevard in Leningrad. This put Shelga on his guard immediately. Garin was in ecstasies over the yacht, himself, and the ocean but all the time he was obviously driving towards some goal.

Shaking the spray off his beard, he said with a laugh:

"I have a proposal to make, Shelga."

"Well?"

"Do you remember that we agreed to play a fair game?"

"Yes."

"By the way.... Tut-tut. Was that your man who fired at me out of the bushes? A hair's breadth from my skull."

"I don't know anything about it."

Garin told him what had happened at Stuffer's house. Shelga shook his head.

"I had nothing to do with that. But still, it's a pity he missed."

"It must be fate, eh?"

"Yes, fate."

"Shelga, I'm giving you your choice," Garin's eyes, cruel and implacable, came closer to him, his face took on an evil look, "either you stop playing the man of principle or I heave you overboard. D'you get me?"

"I get you all right."

"I need you. I need you for something big. We can come to an agreement. You're the only man I trust."

Before he could finish a huge wave, bigger than any of its predecessors, crashed over the yacht. Seething foam swirled round the bridge. Shelga was thrown against the rail, his staring eyes, open mouth, and a hand with the fingers spread disappeared under the water.... Garin dived into the maelstrom.

Afterwards Shelga often recalled that incident. At the risk of his own life Garin had seized him by the skirt of his tarpaulin coat and struggled against the waves until they had passed over the yacht leaving Shelga hanging over the bridge rail. His lungs were filled with water and he fell heavily to the deck. Sailors with great difficulty pumped the water out of him and carried him to his cabin.

Garin soon appeared. He had changed his clothes and was in a happy mood again. He ordered two glasses of grog, lit his pipe, and continued the interrupted conversation.

Shelga studied his mocking face, his agile body sprawled in a leather armchair. A strange, contradictory nature. A bandit, a scoundrel, a dastardly adventurer. . . . Despite all this, either from the grog or from the shake-up he had received, Shelga found it pleasant that Garin sat in front of him with one foot perched on the other knee and smoked and talked of various matters as though the *Arizona*'s sides were not creaking from the heavy blows of the waves, as though raging water was not streaming past the closed portholes and there was no pitching and tossing that sent first Shelga in his bunk and then Garin in his chair high up into the air.

Garin had changed greatly since the Leningrad days— he had become confident, cheerful, and friendly, such as only clever, confirmed egoists can be.

"Why did you let such a fine opportunity go?" Shelga asked him. "Or do you need my life so very badly? I don't understand you."

Garin threw back his head and laughed merrily.

"You're funny, Shelga. Why should I act logically? I'm not a mathematics master. What are things coming to? A simple act of humanity—and it's not understandable. What benefit do I get out of dragging a drowning man out of the water by his hair? None whatever. Just a feeling of friendship towards you. . . . Humanity. . . ."

"You weren't thinking of humanity when you blew up the Aniline factories, were you?"

"No, I wasn't," shouted Garin. "You're still buried under the wreckage of morality and can't get out into the open. Ah, Shelga, Shelga. . . . What are these little shelves you put everything on—this shelf's good and that shelf's bad. I can understand a winetaster: he tastes the wine, spits it out, and takes a crust of bread—this wine's good and that's bad. He is guided by his taste, by the

222

tiny follicles on his palate. That's reality. Where is you taster of moral values? What follicles does he use to test them?"

"Everything that leads towards the establishment of Soviet power throughout the world is good," said Shelga. "Everything that hinders it is bad."

"Superb, marvellous, I know. ... But what's all that to you? What binds you to the Soviet Republic? Are you economically dependent? Nonsense ... I offer you a salary of fifty thousand dollars a year. I'm talking quite seriously. Is it a go?"

"No," answered Shelga, calmly.

"That's just it, no. So you're not bound economically but ideologically, by bonds of honesty, the higher matter, in short. You are an inveterate moralist, which is what I wanted to prove to you. You want to turn the world upside down. You want to cleanse economic laws of the accumulated rubbish of millennia, to blow up the imperialist fortresses. All right, I also want to turn the world upside down, but in my own way. I'll turn it upside down by the strength of my genius."

"Oho!"

"In spite of everything, bear that in mind, Shelga. Listen to me: what is man, after all? Is he an insignificant microorganism clinging in indescribable terror of death to a ball of clay called the earth and flying through the icy darkness together with that ball? Or is he a Brain, a divine apparatus for the production of a special, mysterious form of matter called Thought—one micron of which matter can contain the whole universe? Well, what do you say?"

Garin settled deeper into his chair and pulled his feet up under him. His usually pale cheeks were flushed.

"I propose something different. Listen, my dear enemy. ... I shall acquire absolute power on earth. Not a single chimney will smoke unless I order it, not a single ship will leave harbour, not a single hammer will strike. Everything will be subordinated—up to and including the right to breathe—to the centre, and I am in the centre. Everything belongs to me. I shall engrave my profile on one side of little metal discs—with my beard and wearing a crown—and on the other side the profile of Madame Lamolle. Then I shall select the 'first thousand,' let us call them, although there will be something like two or three million pairs. They will be the patricians. They will devote themselves to the higher enjoyments and to creative activity. Taking an example from ancient Sparta we shall establish a special regime for them so that they do not degenerate into alcoholics and impotents. Then we shall determine the exact number of hands necessary to give full service to culture. In this case, too, we shall resort to selection. These we shall call, for the sake of politeness, the toilers...."

"That goes without saying."

"You may laugh, my friend, when we get to the end of this conversation.... They will not revolt, oh, no, my dear comrade. The possibility of revolution will be destroyed at the very roots. A minor operation will be carried out on every toiler after he has qualified at some skill and before he is issued a labour book. Quite an unnoticeable operation made under a casual anaesthetic.... Just a slight perforation of the skull. He will get a bit dizzy and when he wakes up he will be a slave. Lastly, there will be a special group that we shall isolate on a beautiful island for breeding purposes. All those left over we shall have to get rid of as useless. There you have the structure of the future mankind according to Pyotr Garin. The toilers will toil and serve uncomplainingly, like horses, for their food. They will no longer be people and they will have no worries except hunger. They will find happiness in the digestion of their food.

The élite, the patricians, they will be demigods. Although I despise people altogether, it is always pleasant to be in good company. I assure you, my friend, we shall enjoy the golden age the poets dream of. The impression of horror created by clearing the earth of its surplus population will soon be forgotten. On the other hand what opportunities for a genius! The earth will become a Garden of Eden. Births will be regulated. There will be selection of the fittest. There will be no struggle for existence, that will be lost in the haze of the barbaric past. A beautiful and refined race will develop, with new organs of thought and sensation. While communism is dragging all humanity behind it to the heights of culture I will do it in ten years.... What the devil! In less than ten years.... For a few only.... But, then, it is not a question of numbers."

"A fascist Utopia, rather curious," said Shelga. "Have you told Rolling anything about this?"

"It is not a Utopia, that's the funny part of it. I am only logical. Needless to say I've told Rolling nothing because he is simply a brute beast. Although Rolling and all the Rollings of this world are only doing blindly that which I shall integrate into a precise and finished programme. They are doing it barbarically, clumsily, and slowly. Tomorrow we shall reach the island, I believe. Then you will see that I am not joking."

"What are you going to begin with? Minting coins with your bearded mug on them?"

"Ugh, how that beard seems to get under your skin. No. I shall begin with defence. I shall fortify the island and simultaneously I shall start sinking a shaft through the Olivine Belt at feverish speed. My first threat to the world will be when I upset the gold standard. I shall be able to extract as much gold as I like. Then I shall launch my offensive. There will be a war more terrible than that of 1914. My victory is certain. Then will come the selection of whatever population is left after the war and the destruction of useless elements; my élite will begin to live like gods and the toilers will begin working conscientiously and will be as happy as the first people in paradise. Clever? Eh, you don't like it?"

Garin again burst out laughing. Shelga closed his eyes so as not to look at him. The game that had begun on the Trade-Union Boulevard was developing into a serious match. He lay back and thought. There remained only one very dangerous move that could lead to victory. In any case, at the moment it would obviously be wrong to refuse Garin point-blank. Shelga reached out for a cigarette. Garin watched him mockingly.

"Have you decided?"

"Yes, I have."

"Excellent. I'll put my cards on the table; I need you as much as a flint needs tinder. Shelga, I am surrounded by dumb brutes, people without any imagination. You and I are going to quarrel qu'te a lot but I'm going to make you work with me. At least during the first half of the game when we shall still be beating up the Rollings. By the way, let me warn you to beware of Rolling, if he's decided to kill you he'll do it."

"I've been wondering for a long time why you don't feed him to the fishes."

"I need a hostage. In any case he certainly won't be in the list of the 'first thousand.' "

Shelga paused for a short time and then asked:

"Have you ever had syphilis, Garin?"

"Believe it or not, but I haven't. I've often thought myself that there's something wrong in the top storey. I've even consulted a doctor. My reflexes are higher than normal, that's all. Come on, get dressed and we'll go in to dinner."

87

The grey storm-clouds had disappeared somewhere away to the north-east. The blue ocean had become delightfully caressing. The crests of the gentle waves glistened like glass. Dolphins swam in the wake of the yacht, chasing each other and leaping out of the water, oily and happy. Sea-birds soaring over the yacht's sails filled the air with raucous cries. In the far distance the outlines of a rocky island rose above the sea in a blue haze, like a mirage.

The lookout in the crow's nest shouted, "Land in sight." A shudder went through the people standing on deck. This land of the unknown future resembled a long cloud lying on the horizon towards which the *Arizona's* wind-filled sails carried them at top speed.

Barefooted sailors were swilling down the decks. A huge tousled sun blazed in the bottomless expanses of sky and sea. Garin, plucking at his beard, was trying to penetrate the haze of future events that enwrapped the island. Oh, if only he could know! ...

88

The autumn sunset was aflame behind the distant prospects of Vasilyevsky Island. The barges loaded with firewood, the tugs, the fishing boats, and the smoke swirling amongst the derricks in the shipyards were bathed in a sombre red glow. The windows of the empty palaces burned like fire.

A steamer approached along the blue-black water of the Neva out of the smoke in the west. Its siren howled, greeting Leningrad and marking the end of the voyage. The light from its portholes fell on the columns of the Mining Institute, the Naval School, and on the faces of people strolling on the embankment; the ship began tying up to the floating quay of the customs house, a red structure with white columns. The usual bustle of inspection began.

One of the first-class passengers, a dark-faced man with high cheek-bones, according to his passport a scientific worker from the Geographical Society of France, stood at the rail. He gazed at the town, wrapped in the evening haze. The rays of the departing sun still played on the dome of St. Isaac's, on the golden spires of the Admiralty and the Cathedral of SS. Peter and Paul. That cathedral spire seemed to have been designed by Peter the Great as a sword menacing all who approach Russia's seaboard frontier.

The high-cheekboned man stretched his neck to look at the cathedral spire. He seemed to be shaken and excited like a traveller who sees the roof of the house in which he was born after many years of absence. From the fortress across the dark waters of the Neva came the triumphant sound of bells; the setting sun played on the golden spire of the Cathedral of SS. Peter and Paul whose carillon was playing the *Internationale* over the graves of Russian past emperors.

The man gripped the rail hard, something like a growl came from his throat, and he turned his back to the fortress.

In the customs house he tendered a passport in the name of Arthur Levy and while his luggage was being examined he stood with bowed head so as not to betray the evil glint in his eyes.

Throwing a tartan plaid over his shoulder and with a small suitcase in his hand he went ashore on Vasilyevsky Island. Autumn stars filled the sky. He straightened his back and heaved the sigh that he had long withheld. Glancing at the sleeping houses, the steamer on which two lights burned at the mastheads and the dynamo was humming softly, he turned and walked towards the bridge.

A tall man in a canvas blouse was walking slowly towards him. As they passed the man looked into his face, whispered, "Good Lord" and suddenly called out after him:

"Volshin, Alexander Ivanovich?"

The man who had called himself Arthur Levy in the customs house stumbled but did not turn his head and hurried on towards the bridge.

89

Ivan Gusev lived with Tarashkin and was something half-way between a son and a younger brother to him. Tarashkin taught him to read and write and in other ways developed his mind.

The youngster proved so capable and industrious that he gladdened his tutor's heart. When they had finished their supper—tea, brown bread, and sausage—Tarashkin would fumble in his pockets for cigarettes, remember that he had promised his club colleagues not to smoke, would run his fingers through his hair and start a talk on something like the following lines:

"D'you know what capitalism is?"

"No, Vasily Ivanovich, I don't."

"I'll tell you as simply as I can. Nine men work, the tenth takes everything they make, they're hungry and he gets so fat he could burst. That's capitalism. Get it?"

"No, Vasily Ivanovich, I don't."

"What don't you understand?"

"Why they give him what they make."

"He makes 'em, he's the exploiter."

"How can he make 'em? He's only one and there are nine of them."

"He's armed and they're unarmed."

"You can always take arms away from anyone, Vasily Ivanovich. Your nine men must be fools."

Tarashkin stared in open-mouthed admiration at Ivan.

"You're right, old chap. You think like a Bolshevik. That's just what we did in Soviet Russia, we took away the arms, chased the exploiters away, and now all ten men work and all eat."

"We'll all get fat enough to burst."

"No, old chap, we don't have to get fat, we're not pigs, we're people. We have to turn our fat into mental energy."

"Meaning what?"

"Meaning that in the shortest possible time we have to become the cleverest and most educated people in the world. D'you get that? Good, now let's do some arithmetic."

"All right," answered Ivan, getting out a notebook and pencil.

"And you mustn't suck an indelible pencil, it's not nice. Get it?"

They kept hard at their studies all the evening until well past midnight when the eyes of both tutor and pupil refused to stay open any longer.

A well-dressed man with high cheek-bones stood at the club-house gate poking at the earth with his walking-stick. He raised his head and the strange look he gave Tarashkin and Ivan as they approached put Tarashkin immediately on his guard. Ivan clung to him.

"I've been waiting here since morning. Is that boy Ivan Gusev?" asked the stranger.

"What business is that of yours?" snorted Tarashkin.

"I beg your pardon, but let's be a little more polite, comrade. My name is Arthur Levy."

He took out a card, flashed it under Tarashkin's nose and added:

"I'm from the Soviet Embassy in Paris. Is that good enough for you?"

Tarashkin muttered something indefinite. From his pocket wallet Arthur Levy produced the photograph that Garin had taken from Shelga.

"Can you confirm the fact that the photograph was made from this boy?"

Tarashkin had to admit as much. Ivan would have slipped away but Arthur Levy gripped him by the shoulder.

"Shelga gave me this photo. I have secret instructions to take the boy to a certain address. In case of any resistance I have authority to arrest him. Are you going to submit?"

"What credentials have you?" asked Tarashkin.

Arthur Levy showed him credentials written on the letter heading of the Soviet Embassy in Paris and duly signed and sealed. Tarashkin studied the paper for a long time, sighed, and folded it in four.

"The devil knows what it's all about but it seems to be in order. Couldn't somebody else go in his place? The boy has to go to school...."

Arthur Levy's teeth flashed in a smile.

"Don't worry. The boy won't be badly off with me...."

91

Tarashkin had instructed Ivan to keep in touch with him during his journey. He was somewhat relieved when he got a postcard from Chelyabinsk:

"Dear Comrade Tarashkin,

"We're travelling all right. first class. The food's good
and I'm treated all right. In Moscow Arthur Levy bought
me a cap and a quilted coat and top-boots. The only
trouble is I'm lonesome. Arthur doesn't say a word all
day. By the way, in Samara I met a kid I used to know,
he's homeless, too. I gave him your address. I hope you
won't mind. I suppose he'll come so you can expect him."

92

Alexander Ivanovich Volshin came to the U.S.S.R. in
the name of Arthur Levy carrying papers from the Geographical Society of France. The papers were genuine
(and that had cost Garin a lot of trouble), although the
credentials and certificate of identification from the embassy were forged. The latter documents, however, Volshin
had shown to nobody but Tarashkin. Arthur Levy's official mission was the investigation of volcanic action in the
mountains (sopki, in the local vernacular) of Kamchatka.

Taking Ivan with him he left for Vladivostok in the
middle of September. Cases of instruments and other
equipment for the expedition had arrived in that port
from San Francisco at an earlier date. Arthur Levy was in
a hurry. In a few days he had mustered a party and on
the 28th of September left Vladivostok on board a Soviet
steamer bound for Petropavlovsk. The crossing was a bad
one. A north wind drove black clouds that scattered
grains of hard snow into the leaden waters of the Sea of
Okhotsk. The steamer creaked in all its seams as it plunged
its way through the grim watery waste. It took them eleven
days to reach Petropavlovsk. The horses, boxes, and stores
were unloaded and next day the expedition set out across
forests and mountains, following winding paths and river
beds through swamp and jungle.

Ivan led the expedition—the lad had an excellent memory and the sixth sense of a hunting dog. Arthur Levy was in a hurry: they set out in the early morning and marched till sundown without any halts. The horses were exhausted and the men grumbled, but Arthur Levy was implacable, he had pity on no man but he paid well.

The weather grew worse. The crowns of the cedars whined mournfully and at times they heard the crash of falling hundred-year-old giants or the rumble of avalanches of stones. Two horses were killed by falling boulders and two others disappeared into a bottomless quagmire.

Ivan usually went ahead of the column, clambering up hills and climbing trees to look for signs known to him alone. Perched on the swaying branch of a cedar-tree he shouted one day:

"There it is! There it is!"

On a vertical cliff hanging over the river they could see an ancient rock carving partially effaced by time, depicting a warrior in a cone-shaped cap holding a bow and arrow.

"Now we go due east from here, straight as an arrow, and we'll come to the Shaitan Rock and the camp's not far from there," shouted Ivan.

They made bivouac at this point. A huge fire was lit, the packs were remade and the tired men lay down to sleep. Through the darkness and the noise of the swaying cedars could be heard distant dull explosions and the earth shuddered. And when the fire died down there appeared a glow under the clouds in the east as though a giant smith were blowing up his coals in a forge between the mountains and their gloomy light flickered under the clouds. . . .

At daybreak, Arthur Levy, his hand on the holster of his Mauser, began kicking his men to wake them up. He did not allow them to light a fire and make tea. "Onward, onward. . . ." The exhausted men fought their way through a tangled jungle made worse by piled-up boulders barring their way. The trees were of tremendous height. Giant ferns hid the horses from view; the men's feet were torn and bleeding, another two horses had to be abandoned. Arthur Levy kept to the tail of the column, his hand on his pistol. It seemed that a few more steps forward and not a man would budge, even under threat of instant death.

Ivan's cheerful voice was carried back to them by the wind.

"There it is, comrades, the Shaitan Rock."

They saw ahead of them a huge rock shaped like a human head and wrapped in clouds of steam. At its foot a bubbling stream of hot water gushed out of the earth. From time immemorial travellers had bathed in that hot water to regain lost strength and had left their marks behind them on the rocks. This was the famous "living water" brought in legends by the Raven, water rich in radioactive salts.

93

All that day a north wind blew and heavy clouds rolled low over the forest. The tall pines moaned, the dark heads of the cedars were bowed, the larches shed their needles. Hard snow, mixed with a biting, icy rain, fell from the black clouds. The forest was deserted, for thousands of versts the conifers moaned over swampy ground and stone hills. Day by day it grew colder, the icy breath of the north under a completely overcast sky brought the terror of death.

No sound was to be expected in this wilderness except the howling of the wind and the noise made by the tree-tops. Birds had flown away, animals had migrated or were hibernating. And man could only come to such a place to die.

Nevertheless a man appeared. He was dressed in a torn russet fur coat belted low down with a rope and wearing high felt boots heavy and swollen from the rain. His face was hidden in a mass of tangled hair that had not been combed for years and grey locks fell on to his shoulders. Leaning on his gun for support he hobbled with difficulty around a hill, hiding from time to time behind tree-stumps. He stopped, bent down, and began to whistle:

"Whew, whew . . . Mashka, Mashka. . . . Whew. . . ."

Out of the dense grass appeared the head of a forest goat with the torn end of a rope dangling from a neck rubbed hairless. The man lifted his gun but the goat disappeared again into the undergrowth. The man growled and sank on to a boulder, the gun trembled between his knees, and his head drooped. He sat still for a long time and then stood up again.

"Mashka, Mashka. . . ."

His dull eyes peered through the undergrowth in search of his last hope, his tame goat: he would kill it with the last remaining shot, dry the meat, and thus keep alive for two or three months longer, perhaps even until spring.

Seven years before he had tried to find a use for his genius. He had been strong, healthy, and poor. Then came that fatal day when he had met Garin who had unfolded tremendous plans before his eyes; he had abandoned everything and come to this place, at the foot of a volcano. Seven years ago the forest had been cleared and a winter camp built with a laboratory, wireless station, and a tiny hydro-electric power station. The dilapidated turf roofs of the buildings with many holes in them could still be seen amongst the boulders that had at some distant time been cast up by the volcano; a dense wall of tall pines hemmed them in on all sides.

Some of the people who had come here with him had died, others had fled. The buildings had fallen to rack and ruin, the dam of the power station had been carried away by the spring floods. All the labours of seven years, all his astounding deductions, his investigation of the deeper layers of the earth—the Olivine Belt—would perish together with him because Mashka, that fool of a goat, would not come within gunshot no matter how much he called.

In former days he would have thought nothing of walking two hundred miles or so to the nearest human habitation. But now his legs and arms were stiff with rheumatism and scurvy had robbed him of his teeth. His last hope was the tame goat, Mashka; the old man had kept it for the winter, but the damned animal had rubbed through the rope that held it and escaped from its cage.

The old man took the gun and his last cartridge and went out to call the goat. Evening drew nigh, the piled-up clouds grew blacker, the wind grew more savage, bowing the huge pines. Winter was approaching and with it, death. His heart ached. . . . Could it be that he would never again look upon a human face, never again sit before a fire and breathe in the smell of bread, the smell of life? The old man sat and wept in silence.

A long time passed before he again called:
"Mashka, Mashka. . . ."

No, he would not kill it today. Groaning, the old man got up and plodded his way back to the camp. He stopped and lifted his head—the hard snow beat against his face, the wind ruffled his beard. He thought he heard. . . . No, no, it must have been the wind rubbing tree against tree. . . . Nevertheless the old man stood still for a long time, trying to calm his madly beating heart.

"Ee-ee-ee-ee . . ." came the sound of a human voice from the direction of the Shaitan Rock.

The old man gasped. Tears welled up in his eyes. Snow blew into his wide-open mouth. In the thickening dusk nothing could be seen in the open glade.

"Hi-i-i . . . Mantsev!" A resonant boyish voice drifted towards him down the wind. The goat's head appeared out of the undergrowth—Mashka walked up to the old man, raised its ears and also stood listening to those unexpected voices disturbing the wilderness. . . . They approached from right and left, calling to him.

"Hi, are you there, Mantsev? Are you still alive?"

The old man's beard trembled, his lips twitched, he spread out his arms and repeated soundlessly:

"Yes, I'm alive. I'm Mantsev. . . ."

Such magnificence had never before been seen by the smoke-blackened logs of the hut. A fire burned in a fireplace built of volcanic stone and pots of water were boiling. Mantsev's nostrils breathed in the long-forgotten smells of tea, bread, and bacon.

Loud-voiced men came in and out, bringing packs and unfastening them. A high-cheekboned individual gave him a mug of hot tea and a piece of bread. Bread! Mantsev shuddered as he hurriedly masticated it with his toothless gums. A boy squatted beside him watching in sympathy the way Mantsev took a bite of the bread and then hugged it against his beard as though he feared that this sudden noisy life that had burst into the half-ruined camp would dissolve like a dream.

"Don't you recognize me, Nikolai Khristoforovich?"

"No, I'm not used to people any more," muttered Mantsev, "I haven't eaten bread for a long time."

"But I'm Ivan Gusev. . . . Nikolai Khristoforovich, I've done everything you told me to. D'you remember how you threatened to knock my head off?"

Mantsev did not remember anything, he only blinked at strange faces lit up by the flames of the fire. Ivan began telling him how he had gone on foot through the taiga to Petropavlovsk, how he had hidden from the bears, had seen a red cat as big as a calf—he had been scared, but the cat, and three others following it, had gone past without touching him; how he had lived on cedar nuts he found in squirrels' holes; how in Petropavlovsk he had got a job on a steamer peeling potatoes; how he had reached Vladivostok safely and then hoboed his way under railway carriages for five thousand miles.

"I've kept my word, Nikolai Khristoforovich, I've brought people to you. Only you needn't have written that letter on my back with an indelible pencil. If you had asked me I would have given you my word and that would have been enough. But when you wrote on my back, it might have been something against Soviet power. You shouldn't have done it. You needn't count on me any more, I'm a Young Pioneer now."

Mantsev bent towards him and spoke in a hoarse whisper that contorted his lips.

"Who are these men?"

"A French scientific expedition, I tell you. They looked for me in Leningrad so I could bring them here to fetch you."

Mantsev seized him by the shoulder so hard that it hurt.

"Did you see Garin?"

"Nikolai Khristoforovich, don't try scaring me, I have Soviet power behind me now.... The right people got your letter.... What do I want with Garin?"

"Why are these people here? What do they want from me? I won't tell them anything. I won't show them anything."

Mantsev's face grew red as he stared round wildly. Arthur Levy sat down beside him on the bunk.

"Calm yourself, Nikolai Khristoforovich. Eat and rest. We have plenty of time, we shan't take you away from here before November."

Mantsev dropped down from the bunk, his hands were trembling.

"I want to speak with you alone."

He shuffled to the door, a structure of half-rotten,

unplaned boards. He pushed it open. The night wind tossed his grey locks. Arthur Levy followed him into the darkness and wet snow.

"I have the last cartridge in my gun. . . . I'll kill you! You've come here to rob me!" screamed Mantsev, trembling in fury.

"Come on, let's get out of the wind." Arthur Levy pulled him along and leaned him against the log wall. "Don't get so mad. Pyotr Petrovich Garin sent me for you."

Mantsev clutched Levy's arm frantically. His swollen face with its inflamed eyelids trembled and his toothless mouth sobbed:

"So Garin is alive? He hasn't forgotten me? We starved together and together we laid great plans. But that was all nonsense, delirium. What have I discovered here? I have delved into the earth's crust. I have confirmed all my theoretical postulates. I never expected such brilliant results. The olivine is here." Mantsev stamped his wet boots on the ground. "Mercury and gold can be obtained in unlimited quantities. . . . Listen, I used short waves to reach the core of the earth. There are devilish strange things going on there. I have turned all world science upside down. If Garin could lay his hands on a hundred thousand dollars, there's no limit to what we could do! . . ."

"Garin has thousands of millions at his disposal, the newspapers of the whole world are full of Garin," said Levy. "He has succeeded in building his hyperboloid, he has occupied an island in the Pacific Ocean and is making preparations for big things. He is only waiting for the results of your investigation of the earth's crust. He is sending an airship for you. If the weather doesn't prevent it we'll put up the mooring mast in a month from now."

Mantsev leaned against the wall, his head hanging, and for a long time did not speak.

"Garin, Garin," he repeated. There was pent-up anguish in his words of reproach. "I gave him the idea of the hyperboloid. I put the idea of the Olivine Belt into his head. The idea of an island in the Pacific was also mine. He stole my brain, he left my bones to rot in this accursed taiga. What is there left in life for me? A bed, a doctor, pap to eat. . . . Garin, Garin. . . . A thief who steals ideas from others! . . ."

Mantsev raised his face to the storm.

"Scurvy took away my teeth, ringworm has eaten away my skin, I'm almost blind, my brain has become dull. Too late, too late has Garin remembered me."

94

Garin sent a wireless telegram to the newspapers of the Old World and the New to the effect that he, Pierre Harry, had occupied an island in the Pacific Ocean, 130⁰ W. Long. and 24⁰ S. Lat., with an area of 21 square miles, together with all the adjacent islets and shallows, that he considered the island his exclusive domain and was prepared to defend his sovereign rights to the last drop of blood.

The general effect was one of hilarity. The little island in the southern Pacific was uninhabited and could boast of nothing but its scenery. There was even some confusion as to ownership: the U.S.A., Holland, and Spain all claimed it. There was no arguing with the Americans, so the others grumbled a bit and retreated from the dispute.

The island wasn't worth the cost of the coal necessary to get there but principles had to be upheld and so a light cruiser was dispatched from San Francisco to arrest Pierre Harry and erect on the island a steel mast with the star-spangled banner of the United States.

The cruiser left. The outcome of the absurd incident was the appearance of a foxtrot, *Poor Harry*, relating how poor Pierre Harry had fallen in love with a Creole maiden and wanted to make her a queen. He carted her off to an uninhabited island where they lived alone and danced foxtrots together, king and queen of the island. The queen said, "Poor Harry, I'm hungry, I want something to eat." In answer Harry only sighed and kept on dancing; alas, he had nothing to offer his queen except flowers and seashells. Then came a ship. The handsome captain offered the queen his arm and led her to a magnificent lunch. The queen laughed and ate. And so poor Harry was left to dance alone.... And so on.... In other words, it was all a good joke....

Ten days later a wireless message was received from the cruiser:

"Anchored in sight of island. No landing attempted, warned that island is fortified. Sent ultimatum to Pierre Harry who calls himself ruler of island. Gave him until seven o'clock tomorrow morning. When that time elapses going to send landing party."

It was all so amusing, poor Harry shaking his fist at six-inch guns. Neither on the next day, nor on the days that followed, however, was anything further heard of the cruiser.

No answer came to calls sent out. Certain people in the Navy Department began to frown worriedly.

The next thing was an interview given to the press by MacLinney. He maintained that Pierre Harry was the notorious Russian adventurer, Engineer Garin, with whose name a whole string of crimes were connected, amongst them the mysterious murders at Ville d'Avray, near Paris. MacLinney was the more astonished at the seizure of the island in view of the fact that on board the yacht that had taken Garin to the island was none other than Rolling himself, the administrative head of Rolling Aniline. Rolling's fortune had been used to make tremendous purchases in Europe and America and to charter vessels to transport them to the island. As long as everything was done in accordance with the law MacLinney had kept quiet, but now he insisted that one of the chief features of the Chemical King's character was his exceptional respect for the law. There was, therefore, no doubt that the impudent seizure of the island had taken place against Rolling's will and this was proof enough that the multimillionaire was being held prisoner for the sake of some preposterous blackmail.

This put an end to all the jokes. The Holy of Holies had been desecrated. Police agents gathered information concerning Garin's purchases during the month of August. The figures were stupendous. At the same time the Navy Department searched in vain for the cruiser—it had disappeared. To cap it all the newspapers published the story of the explosion at the Aniline Company's works in Germany as told by the Russian engineer Khlinov who had been an eye-witness.

The situation was scandalous. Under the very nose of the authorities, a common adventurer had made gigantic purchases of war materials, seized an island, and deprived the greatest of all American citizens of his liberty, and, what was more, this man was an amoral scoundrel, a mass murderer, the very spawn of hell.

The telegraph brought another amazing piece of news: a mysterious dirigible airship of the latest type had flown over the Hawaiian Islands, had stopped at the port of Hilo, taken in petrol and water, had flown over the Kurile Islands, descended again at Alexandrovsk on the Island of Sakhalin, and had then disappeared in a north-westerly direction. The letters P and G were seen on the metal flanks of the airship.

This made everything clear: Garin was an agent of Moscow. "Poor Harry" with a vengeance! Congress voted in favour of drastic measures. A flotilla of eight heavy cruisers was sent to "Blackguards' Island" as the American newspapers now called it.

That very same day all the world's wireless stations intercepted a short-wave message outrageous in its sheer impertinence and bad style:

"Hallo! Hallo! This is Golden Island, mistakenly called 'Blackguards' Island' by the uninitiated. Pierre Harry offers his sincere advice to the governments of all countries not to stick their noses into his internal affairs. Pierre Harry will defend himself. Every warship, or fleet of warships, that enters the waters of Golden Island will suffer the fate of the American light cruiser that went to the bottom in less than fifteen seconds. Pierre Harry sincerely advises the population of the world to forget politics and dance in care-free style the foxtrot written in his honour."

95

The dam in the gully close to the winter camp had been rebuilt and the power station started working. Daily, Arthur Levy received impatient messages from Golden Island asking whether the mooring mast was ready.

Electromagnetic waves, indifferent with regard to what had aroused them out of their cosmic repose, raced through the ether to enter the receiver and cry hoarsely into the earphones in Garin's frenzied voice: "If the mast is not ready in a week from now I'll send the airship with orders to shoot you, d'you hear me, Volshin?" and having said these words the electromagnetic waves returned through the earth to their original state of repose.

There was feverish activity in the camp at the foot of the volcano: a large area was cleared of undergrowth, the tall pines were felled, and an eighty-foot steel mast was erected on three legs dug deep into the ground.

Everybody toiled ceaselessly but Mantsev was busier and more excited than anybody else. By this time he had eaten his fill and had grown a little stronger although his mind was, apparently, permanently affected. There were days when he seemed to forget everything, would seize his shaggy head between his hands and sit motionless on his bunk, or else he would untie the goat Mashka and say to Ivan:

"If you like I'll show you something no other man has ever seen."

Holding Mashka by the rope (the goat helped the old man climb up the rocks), Mantsev, followed by Ivan, would begin his ascent of the crater.

The tall pines came to an end; higher up, amongst the boulders, there was only stunted scrub; still higher there was nothing but black stone covered with lichens and, in places, with snow.

The rim of the crater rose in crenellations like the half-ruined wall of some gigantic circus. Here, Mantsev knew every nook and cranny; groaning and taking frequent rests he would lead them zigzagging upwards from terrace to terrace. Only on one occasion, on a windless, sunny day, however, did they succeed in reaching the top. In the low sun the quaintly-shaped teeth of the surrounding rim cast long shadows on a copper-hued lake of molten lava covered with metallic cakes of the same material. Close to the western edge of the crater there was a conical eminence on the surface of the lava around which white smoke curled.

"Over there," said Mantsev, pointing a rheumatic finger at the smoking cone, "is a chimney, an abyss going down into the bowels of the earth such as no man has ever before peered into. I dropped slabs of guncotton down there and when the explosion flashed I started a stopwatch and calculated the depth by the time the sound took to reach me. I investigated the gases from there. I collected them in glass retorts, shone an electric light through them, and examined the rays in the prism of a spectroscope. In the spectrum of the volcanic gas I discovered the lines of antimony, mercury, gold, and many other heavy metals.... Do you understand all this, Ivan?"

"Yes, go on."

"Well, I suppose you do understand more than the goat Mashka. One day, when the volcano was particularly active, when it was coughing and belching from tremendous depths, at the risk of my life I managed to get a little gas in a retort. When I was on my way back to the camp the volcano began hurling ashes and stones as big as barrels up to the clouds. The earth trembled like the back of some awakening monster. But I paid no attention to such minor details; I rushed to the laboratory and examined the gas with the spectroscope.... Ivan, and you, Mashka, listen."

Mantsev's eyes flashed, his toothless mouth was twisted.

"I discovered traces of a heavy metal that is not to be found in the Mendeleyev Table. After a few hours in the retort the metal began to disintegrate, the retort shone with a yellow light, then blue and lastly bright red. I took the precaution of moving away—there was a deafening explosion, the retort and half my laboratory was blown to the devil. I called this mysterious metal 'M' because my name begins with M and so does the goat's. The honour of the discovery belongs to us both, the goat and me. Do you understand anything of what I'm telling you?"

"Go on, Nikolai Khristoforovich."

"Metal M lies in the lowest strata of the Olivine Belt. It disintegrates and liberates tremendous reserves of heat energy. I further maintain that the core or nucleus of the earth consists of metal M. As the average density of the nucleus is only eight units, approximately that of iron, while metal M is twice as heavy, the very centre of the earth must be an empty space."

Mantsev raised his finger, glanced at Ivan and the goat, and let out a wild laugh.

"Come on, let's take a look."

The three of them descended from the crenellated wall of the crater on to the metallic lake and, slipping and sliding over the cakes of metal, made their way to the smoking cone. Hot air escaped through cracks. The black openings of bottomless shafts gaped here and there underfoot.

"We must leave Mashka down below," said Mantsev, snapping his fingers at the goat's nose; followed by Ivan he made his way up the slope of the cone, clutching at the hot rubble that gave way under them.

"Lie on your belly and look."

They lay down on the edge of the cone to the windward of the smoking hole and hung their heads over it.

Inside the cone there was a depression with an oval hole about twenty-three feet in diameter in the middle. Heavy sighs emerged from this orifice and with them a distant rumbling as though, the devil alone knows how deep down, stones were rolling about.

After Ivan had been looking into the hole for some time he could distinguish a reddish light coming from an unimaginable depth. The light, at times dimming and then flashing up again, gradually grew brighter until it assumed a brilliant vermilion hue.... The earth sighed more deeply, the rumbling of the stones grew more menacing.

"It's beginning, we'll have to get away from here," said Mantsev. "That light comes from a depth of seven thousand metres. Metal M is disintegrating there and gold and mercury are boiling and evaporating."

He seized Ivan by his belt and dragged him down. The cone trembled, stones rolled down its sides, heavy clouds of smoke rolled out like steam from a bursting boiler, a brilliant crimson light streamed out of the depths, tinging the low clouds with its red hue....

Mantsev caught hold of the rope attached to the goat's neck.

"Run, run, boys!... It's going to spit stones!..."

Then came a heavy roar that was echoed throughout that stony amphitheatre and the volcano belched a huge block of stone into the air.... Mantsev and Ivan ran down, covering their heads with their hands; ahead of them galloped the goat, its rope dragging along the ground.

96

The mooring mast was ready. A message from Golden Island informed them that the dirigible had started out despite adverse barometric indications.

The last few days Arthur Levy had been trying to get Mantsev to speak frankly about his wonderful discoveries. They sat on a bunk as far as possible from the workers and Levy was pouring spirit into Mantsev's tea from his pocket flask.

The workers lay on the floor on beds of fir branches. From time to time one of them would get up and throw some cedar roots on the fire whose flames lit up the smoke-blackened log walls and the tired, bearded faces. The wind howled over the roof.

Arthur Levy tried to speak softly, caressingly, and soothingly. Mantsev, however, seemed to have gone quite out of his mind.

"Listen to me, Arthur Arthurovich, or whatever it is they call you. Drop your funny stuff. My papers, my formulas, my plans for deep drilling, my diaries are all soldered up in a tin box and hidden where no one will find them.... I will go with you in the airship and the papers will stay here, nobody will ever get them, not even Garin. I won't give them up, not even under torture."

"Calm yourself, Nikolai Khristoforovich, you're dealing with decent people."

"I'm not quite such a fool as you think. Garin needs my formulas.... I need my life. I want to bathe in a perfumed bath every day, smoke expensive tobacco, drink good wine.... I will get false teeth and eat truffles.... I, too, want fame, I've earned it! So to hell with all of you, including Garin."

"Nikolai Khristoforovich, on Golden Island you will live like a king."

"Cut it out, I tell you. I know Garin. He hates me because the whole of Garin is my invention. Without me he would have been a petty crook. You'll take my living brain on the airship with you but not the notebooks with my formulas."

Ivan Gusev, who kept his ears open, heard fragments of this conversation. On the night the mooring mast was ready he crawled over to Mantsev's bunk, found the latter lying with open eyes, and whispered in his ear:

"Nikolai Khristoforovich, give them all the go by. Better come with me to Leningrad. Tarashkin and I will look after you like a baby. We'll get you new teeth, we'll find you a good place to live—what d'you want to get mixed up with those bourgeois for?"

"No, Ivan, I'm done for, there are too many things I long for," answered Mantsev, looking up at the tufts of grimy moss that hung down from a crack in the smoke-blackened ceiling. "For seven years my fantasy has run wild under this damned roof.... I'm not going to wait another day."

For some time Ivan Gusev had known exactly what this "French expedition" was; he had been listening attentively, keeping his eyes skinned, and drawing his own conclusions.

He now followed Mantsev all the time, like a shadow; this last night he did not sleep at all and when his eyelids began to stick he tickled his nose with a feather or pinched himself where it hurt most.

At dawn Arthur Levy arose in a bad temper, put on his sheepskin coat, bound a scarf round his neck, and went out to the wireless station in a dugout near by. Ivan did not for a moment take his eyes off Mantsev. No sooner had Levy gone out than Mantsev took a good look round to make sure that everybody was asleep, slipped noiselessly from his bunk, crept over to a dark corner of the cabin, and raised his head. His eyes must have been too weak to see anything for he returned and threw some pine-knots on the fire. When they burst into flames he went back to the corner.

Ivan guessed what he was looking at: in the upper corner where the logs that formed the walls were jointed into each other there was a gap in the ceiling where the moss had been pulled out. This was what was bothering Mantsev. Standing on tiptoe he pulled a handful of smoke-begrimed moss from another part of the ceiling and with a groan stuffed it into the crack.

Ivan threw away the feather with which he had tickled his nose, pulled the blankets over his head and immediately dropped off to sleep.

The blizzard still raged on. For two days the huge dirigible had been hanging over the clearing, its nose tied to the mooring mast. The mast bent and creaked. From the ground the cigar-shaped body looked for all the world like the keel of a metal barge as it swung to and fro. Its crew had all their work cut out to keep it free of snow.

The captain, leaning out of the gondola, shouted to Artur Levy standing below:

"What the hell are we waiting for? We must cast off. The men are being worked to death."

Levy answered through his clenched teeth:

"I've spoken to the island again. The orders are to bring the boy at all costs."

"The mast won't hold."

Levy only shrugged his shoulders. It was not the boy that mattered, of course. During the night Ivan had disappeared. Nobody gave him a thought. They had been busy mooring the airship that had arrived at dawn and for a long time had circled round the clearing in clouds of snow. Then they had unloaded provisions for the camp. (The workers from Arthur Levy's expedition announced that unless they were given sufficient supplies and were well paid they would rip open the airship with a slab of guncotton.) When Levy first heard that the boy had disappeared he waved his hand and said that it didn't matter.

Things, however, turned out to be far more serious.

Mantsev was the first to enter the gondola of the airship. A minute later something seemed to worry him and he went back down the aluminium ladder and hobbled to the log cabin. Suddenly a scream of despair came from there. Mantsev appeared out of the snow cloud waving his arms like a madman.

"Where's my tin box? Who's stolen my papers? . . . You, you stole them, you crook!"

He seized Levy by the collar of his coat and shook him so energetically that his cap fell off.

It soon became obvious that the priceless papers for which the airship had come had been stolen by that damned boy.

"My papers! My formulas!" Mantsev shouted in a frenzy. "The human brain is not capable of reconstructing them! . . . What have I got to offer Garin? . . . I've forgotten everything! . . ."

Levy immediately sent a search party to hunt for the boy. The men grumbled, only a few of them agreed to go, and Mantsev led them off towards the Shaitan Rock. Levy remained standing by the gondola biting his nails. A long time passed. Two of the men from the search party returned.

"The blizzard's so bad you can't move out there."

"What've you done with Mantsev?"

"God knows. He dropped behind."

"Go and find Mantsev and find the boy. Ten thousand in gold for each of them."

The clouds grew darker as night drew on. The wind increased in strength. The commander of the dirigible again threatened to cut his mooring ropes and fly off.

At long last a tall man, in a long fur coat covered in snow, appeared from the direction of the Shaitan Rock carrying the boy in his arms. Levy rushed to meet him, took off a glove, and pushed his hand under the boy's coat. Ivan seemed to be asleep and his cold, stiff hands pressed a little tin box to his breast; this was the box with Mantsev's priceless formulas.

"He's still alive, a bit cold, though," said the tall man, a broad smile parting his snow-packed beard. "He'll come to. Shall I take him up?"

Without waiting for an answer he carried Ivan into the gondola.

"What now?" shouted the captain from above. "Can we cast off?"

There was indecision on Levy's face as he looked at him.

"Are you ready to take off?"

"We're ready," answered the captain.

Levy turned towards the Shaitan Rock hidden behind a solid curtain of whirling snow that fell from the black clouds. After all the main thing was on board, the box with the formulas.

"Let's go!" he said, jumping on to the aluminium ladder. "Cast off the ropes."

He opened a curved door and entered the gondola.

At the head of the mooring mast the crew began to hack through the hempen rope that held the airship. Roaring and back-firing, the engines started up; the propellers began to turn.

At this moment Mantsev, driven before the blizzard, appeared out of the whirling vortices of snow. Raised by the wind, his hair stood on end. His outstretched arms grasped at the disappearing outlines of the dirigible.

"Stop! Stop!" he shouted hoarsely. As the aluminium ladder of the gondola rose into the air and the bottom rung was about a yard off the ground he grabbed at it. Several of the bystanders caught him by his fur coat to hold him back but he kicked them away. The airship's metal belly swayed in the air, the engines hammered away, the airscrews roared, and the ship rose into the air amidst swirling clouds of snow.

Mantsev hung on to the lower rung like a leech. He was carried rapidly upward.... The people down below could see his straddled legs and the flapping skirts of his coat carried up into the sky.

How far he was carried off, at what height he lost his hold and fell, the watchers below did not see.

97

Leaning out of the porthole of the aluminium gondola Zoë looked through her binoculars. The airship seemed scarcely to move as it described a circle in the bright blue sky. Three thousand three hundred feet below stretched the boundless bluish-green waters of the ocean. The central point was a tiny island of irregular shape. Seen from above it looked like a model of the continent of Africa on a very small scale. Off the southern, eastern, and north-eastern shores surf-bound rocky islets and shallows looked like splashes in the sea. The western seaboard was open.

In a deep bay on the western side of the island the merchant vessels were moored close to the sandy littoral. Zoë counted them—twenty-four beetles resting on the surface of the water.

The island was intersected by ribbon-like roads converging in the rocky north-east where glass roofs gleamed in the sun. Workers were completing the building of a palace leading in three terraces to the sandy beach of a tiny cove.

At the southern end of the island stood a structure that from above looked like something a child had built with his Meccano set—a network of beams, girders, trusses, cranes, rails with trucks running along them. Dozens of wind motors were turning. Smoke came from the chimneys of power and pumping stations.

In the centre of these structures was the round black opening of a mine shaft. Wide steel conveyers ran from the shaft to the sea carrying away the extracted rock; the red pontoons of dredgers farther out to sea looked like red worms. A cloud of steam hung constantly over the mouth of the mine shaft.

Work went on in the mine day and night in six shifts: Garin was boring through the granite shield of the earth's crust. This man's daring bordered on madness. As Madame Lamolle looked at the cloud over the shaft the binoculars trembled in her hands tanned golden by the sun.

Regular rows of warehouses and dwelling-houses stretched along the low shores of the bay. Ant-like figures of people, toy cars, and motor-cycles moved along the roads. A lake gleamed blue in the centre of the island and from it a stream meandered to the south. Strips of farmland and vegetable gardens followed its banks. The whole eastern slope was an emerald green—here the herds were grazing in fields fenced off by hedges. Amongst the rocks in front of the palace at the north-eastern end of the island lay the brightly-coloured carpets of whimsically shaped flower-beds and plantations of trees.

Six months before the island had been a wilderness of coarse grass, stones, grey with seasalt, and anaemic bushes. Steamers had brought thousands of tons of chemical fertilizers to the island, artesian wells had been dug, plants and trees had been brought from over the sea.

From the height of her airship gondola Zoë looked at that tiny patch of bright and colourful, surf-washed land lost in the ocean, admiring it as a woman would a jewel held in her hand.

There had once been Seven Wonders in the world. Three of them have been preserved only in legend—the Temple of Diana at Ephesus, the Hanging Gardens of Semiramis, and the bronze Colossus of Rhodes. As Zoë was wont to repeat daily, the mine on Golden Island must be considered the Eighth Wonder of the World. At dinner in the recently completed hall of the palace, with its huge windows open to the ocean breeze, Zoë raised her glass to drink a toast:

"Let us drink to the miracle, to genius and daring!"

The entire select society of the island rose and greeted Zoë and Garin. All of them were enthralled by feverish activity and fantastic plans. Let people on the continents howl about the contravention of rights. They weren't worth worrying about. Here, day and night, the shaft gave forth its subterranean roar, the scoops of the elevators crashed as they delved deeper and deeper towards inexhaustible supplies of gold. The Siberian goldfields, the canyons of California, the snowy wastes of Klondike were nothing but old-fashioned, amateurish diggings. There was gold here underfoot, in any place, it was only necessary to bore through the granite and pass the upper layers of the boiling Olivine Belt.

Garin found the following entry in the unfortunate Mantsev's diaries:

"In the present era, the one immediately following the Fourth Ice Age and characterized by the extremely rapid development of one genus of vertebrates devoid of a hirsute covering, capable of moving erect on its hind legs, and furnished with an aptly designed oral mechanism enabling it to produce varied sounds, Earth presents the following picture.

"Earth's outer covering consists of solidified granites and diorites varying in thickness from three to sixteen miles. The outside of this crust is covered with marine deposits and the remains of extinct vegetable (coal) and animal life (oil). Under this crust is the second envelope of the globe, the Olivine Belt, a layer of molten metals.

"In some places, in certain parts of the Pacific Ocean, for example, the Olivine Belt is close to Earth's surface, lying at a depth of but some three miles.

"The depth of this belt is, at the present time, over sixty miles and increases at the rate of half a mile every hundred thousand years.

"In the molten Olivine Belt three strata are to be distinguished: the upper, lying closest to the earth's surface, consists of ash and lava thrown up by volcanic action; the second layer is olivine, iron and nickel, that is, the component elements of the meteorites that fall to Earth on autumn nights; the third and last layer consists of gold, platinum, zirconium, lead, mercury.

"These three strata of the Olivine Belt repose on a cushion of helium gas condensed to a liquid state, the product of atomic disintegration.

"Lastly, under this cushion of liquid helium lies Earth's nucleus. It is solid and metallic, its temperature is that of outer space—273⁰ below zero centigrade.

"Earth's nucleus consists of heavy radioactive metals. Two of them, uranium and thorium, standing at the end of Mendeleyev's tables, are known to us. They themselves, however, are the products of the disintegration of a basic super-heavy metal until now not known to man.

"I found traces of this metal in volcanic gases. This is the metal M. It is 11 times heavier than platinum and has tremendous radioactivity. If one kilogram of this metal could be brought to the surface every living thing within a radius of several miles would be killed, every object covered by its emanations would become luminous.

"The fact that Earth's core has a specific gravity of only 8 units (the specific gravity of iron) has always led to the erroneous assumption that the core is iron and since metal M cannot possibly be in a porous state under a pressure of a million atmospheres there is only one conclusion to be drawn:

"Earth's nucleus is a hollow sphere or bomb composed of metal M and filled with helium crystallized by the gigantic pressure.

"The following is a cross-section of Earth:

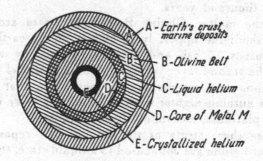

A - *Earth's crust, marine deposits*

B - *Olivine Belt*

C - *Liquid helium*

D - *Core of Metal M*

E - *Crystallized helium*

"Metal M, of which Earth's core or nucleus is composed, is constantly disintegrating into other, lighter metals, thus liberating huge quantities of heat energy. The core of Earth is growing warmer. In thousands of millions of years' time Earth will become hot all through and will burst like a bomb forming a sphere of gas the size of the orbit described by the moon; it will glow like a tiny star, will again begin to cool down, and shrink to the present size of our planet. Again life will appear on Earth, thousands of millions of years later man will appear, the tempestuous progress of mankind and a struggle for a higher social order will begin all over again.

"Once more Earth will warm up unceasingly from atomic disintegration in order to again burst as a tiny star.

"Such is the cycle of terrestrial life. There has been an infinite number of these cycles and an infinite number of them is yet to come. There is no death. There is only eternal renewal. ...."

This is what Garin read in Mantsev's diary.

99

The upper edges of the shaft were clothed in armour plating. As the shaft grew deeper massive cylinders of high-grade steel were lowered to line its walls. This lining ended at the point where the temperature changed suddenly to three hundred degrees. This had occurred at a depth of three miles from the surface with the loss of a whole shift of workers and two hyperboloids.

Garin was not satisfied with the progress made. The lowering and riveting of the cylinders had hampered the work. Now that the walls of the shaft attained red heat they were kept cool by compressed air forming a reliable sheath of armour. These walls were strengthened by diagonal trusses.

The shaft was not very wide, only sixty feet in diameter. Its interior was an intricate system of air pipelines, return pipes, beams and trusses, wires, duralumin wells within which ran the scoops of the elevators, platforms for transfer from elevator to elevator, and other platforms for the hyperboloids and machines producing liquid air.

The whole was set in motion by electricity—lifts, elevators, and machinery. Caves were dug in the sides of the shaft to house machinery and rest-rooms for the workers.

A second parallel shaft was sunk to unload the main shaft; this smaller shaft, nineteen feet in diameter, connected the caves by electric lifts that travelled at terrific speed.

The most important work, that of boring, was conducted by the co-ordinated action of hyperboloid rays, liquid air cooling systems, and elevators that removed the rock. Twelve specially constructed hyperboloids that derived their energy from electric arcs with shamonite electrodes cut into the rock and melted it; it was immediately cooled with a stream of liquid air, disintegrated into tiny particles and scooped up by the elevators. The steam and gases produced by combustion were removed by suction fans.

100

The palace at the north-east end of the island had been built to Zoë's fantastic designs.

It was a huge structure of steel, glass, dark red stone, and marble containing five hundred halls and other rooms. The façade with two wide marble staircases rose up directly from the sea. Waves broke on the lower steps and on pedestals surmounted by four latticed bronze towers carrying bronze spheres that contained loaded hyperboloids guarding the approaches from the sea.

The staircases led to an open terrace on which were two deep porches supported by square columns leading into the interior of the building. The whole stone façade, slightly out of the vertical after the manner of ancient Egyptian structures, modestly decorated, with high narrow windows and a flat roof, presented a severe and even gloomy appearance. The other façade, on the contrary, the one facing an inner courtyard laid out as a garden with rambler roses, verbenas, orchids, lilac in bloom, almonds and tree lilies, was decorated in exuberant, even coquettish style.

Bronze double gates opened into the central part of the island. This was a *château*, both house and fortress. On a high rock near by stood a five-hundred-foot tower communicating with Garin's bedroom by an underground passage. Powerfull hyperboloids stood on a platform on the tower. An armoured lift would take Garin from the earth to the platform in a few seconds. Everybody, even Zoë, had been forbidden to approach the base of the tower on pain of death. This was the first law of Golden Island.

Zoë's apartments were situated in the left wing of the palace, Garin's and Rolling's in the right wing. Nobody else lived there. The building was reserved for the time when it would be the greatest good fortune for any mortal to receive an invitation to Golden Island to look upon the resplendent face of the ruler of the world.

Zoë was preparing herself for this role. What with one thing and another she had her hands full. Conventions had to be elaborated for her rising in the morning, her appearance in the palace, small and grand receptions, lunches, dinners, masquerades, and entertainments. Her artistic temperament found every opportunity for expression. She loved to repeat that she had been born for the world stage. The maintenance of court etiquette was in the hands of a Russian émigré, a famous ballet producer. A contract had been concluded with him in Europe and he had been awarded the Order of the Divine Zoë (gold and diamonds on a white ribbon) and the ancient Russian title of *postelnichi* (Gentleman of the Bedchamber).

Apart from these internal, palace laws she and Garin drew up the *Commandments of the Golden Age*, the future laws for all mankind. This was more in the nature of a general draft and basic ideas that had to be put into legal form by jurists. As Garin was feverishly busy she had to find time for him whenever he was available. In her study there were always two stenographers, day and night.

Garin came direct from the mine, worn out, dirty, and smelling of earth and machine oil. He ate hurriedly, lay down on the satin sofa with his boots on, and was soon enveloped in a cloud of pipe smoke (he was placed above all etiquette, his manners were sacred and their imitation was taboo). Zoë strode up and down the carpet picking over the huge pearls of her necklace with her delicate fingers and trying to get Garin to talk. He needed a few minutes of death-like repose before his brain could resume its feverish activity. In his plans there was neither evil nor good, neither cruelty nor mercy. He was amused only by the clever solution of a problem. This "coolness" made Zoë indignant. Her big eyes grew dark, a tiny shiver ran down her nervous spine and she spoke in a low voice full of hate (in Russian so that the stenographers would not understand):

"You're a poseur. You're a terrible man, Garin. I understand wanting to skin you alive and watch how you suffer for the first time in your life. Don't you really hate anybody or love anybody?"

"Nobody but you," answered Garin with a grin, "but your pretty head is full of crazy nonsense. I have but a few seconds to spare. I'll wait until your ambition has been satisfied to the full. Still, you're right in one thing, my love: I am too academic. Ideas evaporate if they are not permeated with the spice of life. And the spice of life is passion. You have a superfluity of it."

He glanced sideways at Zoë—she stood before him, pale and motionless.

"Passion and blood. An old recipe. But why on earth should you skin me? You can skin somebody else. It seems that for the sake of your health you simply must wet your handkerchief in that crimson fluid."

"There are many things I can't forgive people for."

"The short men with the hairy fingers, for example?"

"Yes. Why do you bring that up?"

"You can't forgive yourself.... For five hundred francs they called you by phone, didn't they? You darned your silk stockings in a hurry, bit off the thread with those divine little teeth when you hurried away to a restaurant. And the sleepless nights when you had two sous in your bag and the horror of what might happen next day... the horror of falling still lower.... And Rolling's pug nose is also worth something."

With a crooked smile Zoë looked him straight in the eyes and then said:

"I shan't forget this conversation to my dying day, either."

"My God! And only a minute ago you were accusing me of being academic."

"If I have my way I'll hang you from the hyperboloid tower."

Garin jumped up, seized Zoë by the elbows, pulled her on to his knees, and kissed her upturned face and tightly pressed lips. The two stenographers, fair-haired, marcelled, as indifferent as dolls, turned away.

"You funny, foolish woman, understand me, it's only like that that I love you.... The only being on this earth.... If you hadn't been twenty times within an inch of death in lousy railway trucks, if you hadn't been bought like a harlot, could you possibly have understood the full measure of human daring? Could you have walked across this carpet like a queen? Would I have thrown myself at your feet?"

Zoë freed herself in silence, adjusted her dress with a movement of her shoulders, went away into the middle of the room and from there still looked wildly at Garin.

"Well, where did we stop?" asked Garin.

The stenographers took down the thoughts he formulated. During the night they were transcribed and were handed to Madame Lamolle next morning in bed.

Rolling was sometimes invited as an expert on certain

questions. He lived in magnificent apartments, not yet quite finished. He left his rooms only at meal times. His will power and his pride had been broken. He had changed considerably during the past six months. Garin he feared, and he tried to avoid being alone with Zoë. Nobody knew or cared what he did all day. He had never read a book in his life. Apparently he did not keep notes. It was said that he had acquired a passion for collecting pipes. Looking out of the window one evening Zoë saw him sitting by the water on the last step but one of the marble staircase, looking sadly at the ocean out of which, a hundred million years ago, his ancestor had crawled in the form of an anthropoid lizard. This was all that was left of the great Chemical King.

The loss of three hundred million dollars, imprisonment on Golden Island or even Zoë's faithlessness would not have broken him. Twenty-five years before that he had sold shoe polish on the streets. He liked fighting and knew how to fight. How much effort, talent, and will power had been applied to compel people to pay him, Rolling, those little discs of gold. The war and subsequent impoverishment of Europe—these were the forces aroused to bring gold flowing into the vaults of Rolling Aniline.

And now this gold, the equivalent of power and happiness, would be scooped out of a mine by dredgers *in unlimited quantities* like clay or mud. It was here that Rolling felt the ground slipping from under his feet, and ceased to feel himself the lord of nature, *homo sapiens*.

Daily, on Garin's insistence, he still dictated his will by wireless to the directors of Rolling Aniline. Their answers were vague. It was becoming clear that the directors did not believe in Rolling's voluntary seclusion on Golden Island.

"What shall we do to ensure your return to the continent?" they asked him.

"The course of treatment for my nerves is proving effective," answered Rolling.

Another five million pounds sterling was obtained by his orders. When he ordered a similar sum to be paid out a fortnight later, Garin's agents, who tendered Rolling's cheque, were arrested. This was the first sign of the continent's offensive against Golden Island. A fleet of eight ships of the line was cruising in the Pacific Ocean in the vicinity of 22⁰ S. Lat. and 130⁰ W. Long., awaiting orders to attack the island.

101

The six thousand employees of Golden Island had been gathered from all corners of the earth. Garin's first assistant, Engineer Čermak, holder of the title of governor, settled his workers by nationalities in fifteen camps divided from each other by barbed wire fences.

The barracks and churches built in each camp were as far as possible national in character. Canned goods, biscuits, jam, barrels of sauerkraut, rice, pickled jellyfish, salted herring, sausages, etc., etc., had also been ordered (from American factories) labelled in the appropriate languages.

Twice a month working clothes cut in national style and once every six months national holiday costumes were issued—*poddevki* and *svitki* for the Slavs, cotton blouses for the Chinese, frock-coats and top-hats for the Germans, silk shirts and patent-leather shoes for the Italians, loin-cloths decorated with crocodile teeth and beads for the Negroes, etc.

A staff of *provocateurs* was organized by Čermak to justify the barbed wire in the eyes of the people. There were fifteen of them and their job was to excite national hatred: moderately on working days but on holidays up to and including fisticuffs.

The island police, recruited from amongst Wrangel's ex-officers, wore the uniform of the Order of Zoë—a short jacket of white wool with gold facings and tight-fitting canary-yellow trousers; they maintained order and did not permit the various nationalities to annihilate each other.

The workers were paid very high wages as compared with those on the continent. Some sent the money home on the first steamer, others banked it on the island. There was nowhere to spend money except on holidays when bars and a Luna Park were opened in a deserted canyon in the south-eastern part of the island. In the same place there were fifteen brothels, also maintained in national style.

The workers knew the purpose of the huge shaft they were digging into the heart of the earth. Garin had announced that when they were paid off he would allow everybody to take as much gold with him as he could carry on his back. There wasn't a man on the island who could look without excitement at the steel conveyers carrying rock from the bowels of the earth well out to sea, who was not intoxicated by the yellowish smoke hovering over the mouth of the shaft.

102

"Gentlemen, we have come to the most perilous moment in our work. I had expected it and prepared for it, but that, of course, does not lessen the danger. We are blockaded. A wireless message has been received: two of our vessels, loaded with girders for the strengthening of the shaft, canned goods, and frozen mutton have been seized by an American cruiser and declared prizes of war.

This means that the war has begun. From hour to hour we must expect an official declaration. One of my immediate aims is war. It is beginning, however, earlier than I want it to. They are getting too nervous on the continent. I foresee their plan, they are afraid of us and hope to force us into submission by hunger. For your information, the food on the island is sufficient for a fortnight, not counting live cattle. Before those fourteen days are over we must break the blockade and bring in food. It is a difficult but quite feasible task. In addition to this my agents were arrested when they presented Rolling's cheque. We have no cash in hand. Three hundred and fifty million dollars have been expended to the last cent. A week from now we must pay wages and if we pay by cheque the workers will riot and stop the hyperboloids working. From this it follows that we must get money within seven days."

The conference was held in the twilight of Garin's still unfinished office. Present were Čermak, Engineer Scheffer, Zoë, Shelga, and Rolling. Garin, as was usual with him in moments of danger or of great mental strain, stood with his hands in his pockets, rocking back and forth on his heels and speaking mockingly. Zoë, a little hammer in her hand, was in the chair. Čermak, diminutive and nervous, with bloodshot eyes, coughed and said:

"The Second Law of Golden Island reads: nobody must attempt to discover the secret of the hyperboloid. Anybody who touches even the outer housing of the hyperboloid is liable to the death penalty."

"Such," confirmed Garin, "is the law."

"In order the ensure a successful outcome for the enterprises you have mentioned at least three hyperboloids will be required: one to obtain money, a second to break the blockade, and the third for the defence of the island. You will have to make an exception to the law for two of your assistants."

Silence followed this speech. The men studied the smoke of their cigars. Rolling sniffed at his pipe in deep concentration. Zoë turned her head towards Garin.

"All right," he said with a careless movement of the hand. "Publish the decree. Exempted from the Second Law are two people on the island, Madame Lamolle and...."

He leaned across the table and slapped Shelga heartily on the shoulder.

"The second person to whom I trust the secret of the apparatus is Shelga."

"That's where you make a mistake, comrade," said Shelga, removing Garin's hand from his shoulder. "I refuse."

"On what grounds?"

"I'm not obliged to explain. Think for yourself and you'll understand."

"I'll trust you with the destruction of the American fleet."

"A nice job and no mistake. I can't."

"Why the hell can't you?"

"What do you mean, why? It's a slippery business."

"Look out, Shelga."

"I'm looking."

Garin's beard stuck out, his teeth flashed. He restrained himself and asked softly:

"What have you got in mind?"

"My line, Pyotr Petrovich, is quite obvious. I hide nothing."

This short conversation was in Russian so that nobody except Zoë could understand it. Shelga returned to his doodling on the paper in front of him.

"Very well," said Garin, "I'll appoint only one person as my assistant with the hyperboloid, Madame Lamolle. If you agree, madame, the *Arizona* is at your disposal, you set sail tomorrow morning."

"What am I supposed to do out at sea?"

"Plunder every vessel that comes your way on the Trans-Pacific route. In a week from now we must pay the workers."

103

At 23:00 hours, an unknown object flying over the Southern Cross was reported from the flagship of a squadron of the North American fleet.

The bluish rays of searchlights, like the tails of comets, swung across the starlit sky and came to rest on that unknown object. It stood out in a bright patch of light. Hundreds of binoculars examined its metal gondola, the transparent discs of whirling propellers and the letters P and G on the flanks of the airship.

Morse lamps winked from ship to ship. Four seaplanes took off from the flagship and roared their way upwards to the stars. The squadron, sailing in line ahead, increased its speed.

The roar of the aircraft grew weak and indistinct. Suddenly the airship towards which they were racing disappeared. Everywhere handkerchiefs came out to wipe the lenses of binoculars but no matter how the searchlights tried to find it the airship was nowhere to be seen in the dark, night sky.

At last the rattle of machine-guns could be heard: the aircraft had found their target. The machine-guns stopped suddenly. An incandescent fly twirled round in the sky and then dropped down. The people watching through their binoculars gasped—a seaplane had fallen and plunged into the black waters. What had happened?

Again came the rattle of machine-guns, only to break off just as suddenly while one after the other three remaining aircraft plunged headlong through the rays of the searchlights and corkscrewed into the sea. Morse lamps flickered on the flagship and there were answering flashes up to the very horizon. What had happened?

The next thing they saw was a ragged black cloud moving against the wind, quite close to them and at right angles to the line of ships. The airship, hidden by a smoke screen, was losing altitude. " 'Ware gas," was the order flashed from the flagship. Anti-aircraft guns barked. Simultaneously gas-bombs fell on the deck, the bridge, and the armoured gun turrets.

The first victim was the admiral, a handsome twenty-eight-year-old officer, who was too proud to don a gas-mask: his hands tore at his throat as he fell with a swollen, blue face. The gas-masks proved ineffective and in a few seconds all those on deck were dead. The flagship had been attacked with an unknown gas.

The vice-admiral took over the command. The cruisers went on to a starboard tack and opened fire from their anti-aircraft guns. Three flashes of fire from the guns turned the sea blood red. Three swarms of screaming steel devils were carried nobody knew where; their bursts lit up the starry sky.

Following the three volleys, six seaplanes, their crews in gas-masks, took off from the vessels of the squadron. It was now apparent that the first four aircraft had perished in the gas-filled smoke screen around the airship. The honour of the American navy was at stake. Lights were extinguished on the vessels, the only light came from the stars. Waves breaking against the steel flanks of the warships and the song of the aircraft engines were the only sounds that broke the silence of night.

At last! Rat-a-tat-tat. The music of the machine-guns came out of the silver mist of the Milky Way. Then it sounded as though bottles were being opened there—the aircraft were bombing their target. The brownish-black cloud in the sky grew lighter and a huge metal cigar, its blunt nose pointed downwards, slipped out of it. All along its metal back tongues of flame were dancing. It slanted downwards leaving a tail of fire behind it and disappeared in flames over the horizon.

Half an hour later it was reported from one of the seaplanes that had swept down over the burning airship and machine-gunned every living thing on or near it.

The victory had cost the American squadron dear: four seaplanes with their crews had been lost, twenty-eight officers, including the admiral, and a hundred and thirty-two naval ratings had been killed by poison gas. It was not only a matter of losses, but of the humiliation of magnificent cruisers armed with heavy artillery proving as helpless as wingless penguins: the enemy had bombed them with an unknown gas just as he pleased. They must have their revenge, they must have an opportunity to show the real might of naval artillery.

This was the spirit of the dispatch which the vice-admiral sent to Washington that night reporting the details of the battle. He insisted on the bombardment of Blackguards' Island.

The Naval Secretary's reply came a day later: to proceed to the island and level it with the sea.

104

"Well?" asked Garin in a challenging voice as he placed the wireless earphones on the table. (The conference continued with the same participants, except Madame Lamolle, who had left.) "Well, gentlemen, I can congratulate you. The blockade has been lifted. The American fleet has been ordered to bombard the island."

Rolling shuddered and rose from his chair, his pipe fell from his mouth, his blue lips were twisted as though he wanted to say something but could not.

"What's wrong, old chap?" asked Garin. "Are you so

worried about the approach of your own country's war-ships? You're in a hurry to hang me from the yard-arm? Or are you scared of the bombardment? Of course it would be a foolish end for you to be blown to little wet pieces by American guns. Perhaps your conscience is troubling you? Look at it whichever way you like, it's your money we're using to fight with."

Garin laughed shortly and turned away from the old man. Rolling did not, after all, manage to say a single word; he dropped back into his seat and covered his earthy-hued face with his trembling hands.

"No, gentlemen.... Without risk you can only earn three cents on the dollar. We are going to take an enormous risk now. Our reconnaissance airship has done a splendid job. Let us stand to honour the memory of the twelve members of the crew, including its commander, Alexander Ivanovich Volshin. The airship managed to inform us in detail of the strength of the squadron. There are eight heavy cruisers of the latest type, each with four three-gun turrets. After the battle they must have at least twelve seaplanes left. In addition to this there are light cruisers, destroyers, and submarines. If we count the force of each shell as a hundred-and-fifty-million-pound impact, a volley fired by the entire squadron would mean an impact of roughly two thousand million pounds on the island."

"So much the better," whispered Rolling at last.

"Stop whining, grandad, you ought to be ashamed of yourself.... I forgot, gentlemen, we have to thank Mr. Rolling for having been so kind as to place at our disposal a new and still secret invention, a gas known as 'Black Cross.' Using this gas our airmen brought down four seaplanes and put the flagship out of action...."

"No, Mr. Garin, I was not so kind as to place 'Black Cross' at your disposal," shouted Rolling hoarsely. "With a revolver at my head you forced me to give an order to send containers of 'Black Cross' to the island."

He choked and staggered out of the room. Garin began to unfold his plan for the defence of the island. The attack was to be expected in three days.

105

The *Arizona* had raised the pirate flag.

This does not mean that she carried the romantic skull and crossbones of the buccaneers. Such horrors would only be found on bottles of poison nowadays.

In fact no flag at all had been raised on the *Arizona*. The two latticed turrets carrying the hyperboloids distinguished her from all other ships in the world. The vessel was commanded by Jansen, under Madame Lamolle's orders.

Zoë's magnificent apartment—bedroom, bathroom, dressing-room and drawing-room—was locked up. Zoë had her quarters in the captain's deck cabin together with Jansen. The former luxury, the blue silk awning, the carpets, cushions, armchairs, had all been removed. The crew, taken on in Marseilles, were armed with Colt revolvers and short carbines. The object of the voyage had been announced to them and they had been promised prize-money from every ship captured.

All available space on the yacht was occupied by cans of petrol and fresh water. With a good wind and under full sail, aided by her powerful Rolls Royce engines, the *Arizona* sped like an albatross from crest to crest of the ocean waves.

106

"The wind is approaching a gale, sir."
"Take in the tops'ls."
"Aye, aye, sir."

"Change the watch every hour. Keep a man in the crow's nest."

"Aye, aye, sir."

"If lights are seen wake me."

With screwed up eyes Jansen peered into the endless waste of the ocean. The moon had not yet risen. The stars were hidden in a haze. For the five days they had sailed to the north-west the feeling of nervous exultation had not left him. Had not his ancestors lived by piracy? With a nod he wished his first mate good night and entered his cabin.

As he entered the cabin all the muscles of his body experienced a familiar shattering sensation, a toxic that robbed him of his strength. He stood still under the frosted hemisphere of the ceiling light. The low, comfortably furnished cabin, all leather and polished wood, the stern habitation of a lonely sailor, was filled with the presence of a young woman.

Most prominent of all was the perfume. A thousand devils! ... The pirate chieftainess used perfume that would have excited a corpse. Her flannel skirt and golden sweater were flung carelessly over the back of a chair. Stockings and garters lay where they had been thrown on the carpet and one of the stockings seemed to have retained the shape of her leg.

Zoë was asleep on his bunk. (Jansen had not undressed all those five days and had slept on the sofa.) She lay on her side, her lips partly open. Her face, tanned by the sea breezes, seemed calm and innocent. A bare arm was thrown over her head. A Pirate Queen!

Zoë's militant decision to occupy the cabin together with him had been a severe test for Jansen. From the standpoint of fighting tactics it was, of course, a right decision. They were on a voyage of piracy that might well end in death. In any case if they were caught they would hang together from the same yard-arm. That did not worry him, it was, if anything, an inspiration. He was Madame Lamolle's subordinate, a subject of the Queen of Golden Island. He loved her.

However much it is explained, love is still a strange thing. Jansen had had experiences with girls in the bars of seaports and with splendid lady passengers who had surrendered themselves to his nautical embraces out of boredom or curiosity. Some of them he forgot like the empty pages of an empty book, others he liked to remember during a quiet night watch as he paced the bridge in the starlight.

That affair in Naples, when Jansen was awaiting Madame Lamolle's telephone call, had had much in common with former adventures. But that which should have followed the dinner and dances had not happened.

And now, six months later, he could scarcely believe that he had actually danced with his hand on Madame Lamolle's back. Could it be that only a few minutes, a half-smoked cigarette, was all that had separated him from unbelievable happiness. Today, when he heard her voice from the other end of the yacht he shuddered as though in warning of the storm arising within him. When he saw the Queen of Golden Island sitting in her wicker armchair on deck and scanning the horizon, something inside him, way beyond the threshold of reason, sang and sorrowed of love and devotion.

Perhaps he owed it all to the vikings, his pirate forefathers, who had sailed the seas in their red dragon boat with its high poop and a cock's head prow, a square sail and shields hanging over the side. Standing by the mast, Jansen's ancestor sang of blue waves, of storm-clouds and of a flaxen-haired maiden who stood by the distant shore gazing out to sea awaiting him—the years pass and her eyes are like the blue seas and like the black storm-clouds. And it was from this distant past that fits of dreaminess descended on poor Jansen.

As he stood in the cabin that smelt of leather and perfume he gazed in despair and admiration at the sweet face he loved. He was afraid she would awaken. Silently he went to the sofa and lay down. He closed his eyes. He heard the noise of the waves breaking against the yacht's hull, the noise of the ocean. His ancestor sang an ancient song of a beautiful maid. Jansen put his arm under his head and sleep and happiness overtook him.

107

"Captain! (A knock at the door.) Captain!"

"Jansen!" the note of alarm in Madame Lamolle's voice penetrated his brain like a needle. Captain Jansen jumped up, with wildly staring eyes dragging himself out of his dream. Madame Lamolle hurriedly pulled on her stockings. Her shirt had slipped down leaving one shoulder bare.

"Alarm," said Madame Lamolle, "and you're asleep."

There came another knock on the door and the mate's voice said:

"Captain! Lights on the port bow."

Jansen opened the door. The damp breeze filled his lungs. He coughed and went on to the bridge. It was a pitch-black night through which two lights rocked up and down by the waves could be seen far away to port.

Without taking his eyes off the lights Jansen felt at his breast for his pipe. He sounded a note and was answered by the boatswains.

"Pipe all hands on deck! Take in all sail!"

Pipes sounded and orders were given. Sailors appeared from the forecastle and lower deck. They swarmed the masts like monkeys, swaying with the spars. Halyards screamed through the blocks. Raising his head, the boatswain swore by all the saints there are, as the sails were taken in.

Jansen gave his orders:

"Hard a-port! Full speed ahead! Lights out!"

Depending now entirely on her engines the *Arizona* made a sharp turn to starboard. As she turned a huge wave rose against her hull and swept across the deck. All lights were extinguished. The hull of the yacht trembled as she raced on at full speed in complete darkness.

The lights seen by the lookout rose speedily from beyond the horizon to be followed by the dark silhouette of a smoky two-funneled passenger boat.

Madame Lamolle came on to the bridge. She was wearing a knitted cap with a pompon, a fluffy scarf wound round her neck and hanging down her back. Jansen handed her his binoculars. She raised them to her eyes but the yacht was tossing so badly that she had to place her hand on Jansen's shoulder to steady them. He could feel her heart beating under her warm sweater.

"We'll attack!" she said, looking him straight in the eyes, her face close to his.

The passenger steamer noticed the *Arizona* when she was some five hundred yards away. A lantern was waved from the bridge and a siren moaned its low note. The *Arizona*, without lights, did not answer the signals, but continued to bear down on the fully lighted ship. The steamer slowed down and began to turn to avoid a collision....

Here is how the incident was described a week later by a correspondent of the *New York Herald*.

"... It was a quarter to five when we were awakened by the howl of the siren. The passengers tumbled out on to the deck. After the lighted cabins the night seemed as black as ink. We noticed that there was alarm on the bridge and searched the dark sea with our binoculars. Nobody knew exactly what had happened. Our steamer slowed down. Suddenly we saw it ... some unknown type of ship was bearing down on us at full speed. It was a long, narrow vessel with three tall masts, her lines like those of a fast-sailing clipper; fore and aft rose two strange latticed towers. Somebody shouted jokingly that it was the Flying Dutchman. For a moment everybody was in a panic. A hundred yards away the strange vessel hove to and somebody shouted through a megaphone in English:

" 'Stop your engines. Put out your fires.'

"Our captain answered:

" 'Before I obey your orders I want to know who is giving them.'

" 'The order is given by the Queen of Golden Island,' came the answer from the vessel.

"We were dumbfounded: was this a joke? Another piece of impertinence on the part of Pierre Harry?

" 'I can offer the Queen a vacant cabin and a hearty breakfast if she's hungry,' shouted the captain in answer.

"These words came from the foxtrot *Poor Harry*; they were greeted with a hearty laugh on deck. Immediately a ray appeared from the fore tower of the mysterious vessel. It was as thin as a knitting needle, blindingly white, and came from the dome on the tower without spreading. At that moment nobody dreamed that before their eyes was the most terrible weapon ever devised by the human brain. We were in a jolly mood.

"The ray described a loop in the air and then descended on the bows of our ship. We heard a horrible hissing sound and saw a greenish flame made by steel being cut. A sailor standing in the bows screamed wildly. The whole bow of the ship, above the water-line, collapsed into the sea. The ray was lifted, trembled for a moment in the air, and then passed over us parallel to the deck. The tops of the two masts fell to the deck with a crash. In a panic passengers rushed for the gangways. The captain was injured by a piece of the wreckage.

"The rest of the story is known. The pirates, armed with short carbines, approached in a boat, came on board, and demanded money. They collected ten million dollars from the mail-bags and the passengers' pockets. When the boat with the loot returned the pirate ship's decks were flooded with light. We saw a tall, slim woman in a knitted cap come down from the latticed tower and hurry to the bridge. She took up a megaphone, leaned back and called to us:

" 'Now you may go your ways in peace.'

"The pirate ship turned about and at a tremendous speed disappeared over the horizon."

108

The events of the past few days—the attack made on the American squadron by the airship P.G. and the order given to the squadron to bombard the island—excited the whole population of Golden Island.

The office was inundated with applications to leave work. Deposits were withdrawn from the savings bank. Workers conferred with each other behind the barbed wire, paying no attention to the yellow and white policemen pacing the intersecting lanes with gloomy and determined faces. The whole settlement was like a disturbed beehive. In vain were trumpets blown and kettle-drums banged in front of the brothels in the canyon. Luna Park and the bars were empty. In vain did the fifteen *provocateurs* make inhuman efforts to divert the bad mood of the workers into national squabbles. In those days nobody wanted to bash somebody else's face in just because he lived behind a different barbed-wire fence.

Engineer Čermak pasted up government bulletins all over the island. Martial law was declared, meetings and gatherings were prohibited and nobody was allowed to ask for discharge until further orders. The population was cautioned against criticism of the government. The work in the shaft must continue day and night. "Those who do their utmost to support Garin in these days," said the bulletin, "will be rewarded with fabulous riches. We ourselves will drive cowards from the island. Remember, we are fighting against those who bar our road to wealth."

Despite the decisive tone of this bulletin, on the morning of the day before the attack was expected, the mineworkers announced that they would stop the hyperboloids and the liquid-air plants if wages were not paid by midday (it was the usual pay-day) and if a message were not sent to the American government announcing their peaceful intentions and the cessation of hostilities.

If the liquid-air machines were stopped the shaft would burst which might lead to the eruption of molten magma. The threat was a very real one. Engineer Čermak, forgetting himself in his excitement, threatened to shoot the workers. The yellow and white police gathered at the mouth of the mine. Then a hundred workers went down the shaft to the side caves and from there telephoned to the office:

"We see no other way out but death, at four o'clock we shall blow ourselves up together with the island."

That, at least, was a four-hour respite. Čermak removed his guard from the mine and hurried to the palace on a motor-cycle. There he found Garin and Shelga talking, both of them excited and red in the face. Garin jumped up like a madman when he saw Čermak.

"Who did you learn your administrative idiocy from?"

"But...."

"Shut up! You're dismissed. Go to the laboratory or to hell or wherever else you like.... You're a fool!"

Garin threw open the door and pushed Čermak out.

He returned to the table on the corner of which Shelga sat with a cigar between his teeth.

"Shelga, the hour which I foresaw has come, only you can get this movement under control and save the situation.... This business on the island is more serious than ten American navies."

"Aha," said Shelga, "it's time you understood...."

"To hell with your lessons in politics.... I appoint you governor of the island with special powers.... Just you try to refuse," screamed Garin excitedly, his voice rising to the highest note. He jumped towards the table, opened a drawer and took out a revolver. "In short, if you refuse I'll shoot you. Yes or no?"

"No," said Shelga with a side-glance at the revolver.

Garin fired and Shelga raised the hand that held the cigar to his temple.

"You filthy swine."

"So you do agree?"

"Put that thing down."

"O. K." Garin threw the revolver back in the drawer.

"What do you want? That the workers should not blow up the mine? All right, they won't. There are some conditions, though...."

"I agree in advance."

"That I remain a private individual on this island such as I have been up to now. I'm neither your servant nor a mercenary. That's the first. All national boundaries are to be removed today and all the wire taken away. That's the second."

"I agree."

"Your gang of *provocateurs*...."

"I have no *provocateurs*," answered Garin promptly.

"That's a lie."

"All right, it's a lie. What shall I do with them? Drown them?"

"This very night."

"All right, consider them drowned." (Garin made some rapid notes on his writing-pad.)

"The last condition is: no interference in my relations with the workers."

"Is that so? (Shelga frowned and started getting down from the table. Garin seized him by the arm.) All right, I agree. The time will come when I shall break you, anyway. What else?"

Shelga squinted as he lit his cigar and his wind-tanned face with its little blond moustache, snub nose, and sly smile could not be seen through the curtain of smoke. Just then the telephone rang. Garin picked up the handset.

"Yes, Garin speaking. What? Wireless message?"

He threw down the telephone handset and picked up the earphones of the wireless receiver. As he listened he bit his nails. His lips twisted into a smile.

"You may calm the workers. We shall pay tomorrow. Madame Lamolle has got hold of ten million dollars. I'll send an excursion dirigible immediately. The *Arizona* is only about four hundred miles away to the north-west."

"That makes things easier," said Shelga. With his hands in his pockets, he went out of the room.

109

Hanging from the ceiling straps so that his feet did not touch the floor and shutting his eyes, Shelga held his breath for a second as he flew down in the steel box of the lift.

The parallel shaft was unevenly cooled and the lift had to fly from cave to cave through belts of heat so that only the speed of the descent kept it from burning up.

Shelga watched the red needle on the meter and at a depth of twenty-five thousand feet switched on the rheostat to stop the lift. He got out at cave number thirty-seven. A thousand feet lower down was the bottom of the shaft where hyperboloids were working; from there came sharp, incessant bursts as the white-hot rock was cracked by the stream of liquid air. The scoops of the elevators carrying the rock to the surface rasped and clattered.

The inside of cave number thirty-seven, like all the others, was a riveted steel cube. Liquid air evaporated outside its walls to cool the surrounding granite. The belt of boiling magma was, apparently, not very far, nearer than had been expected from the data obtained by electro-magnetic and seismographic prospecting. The granite was heated to a temperature of 500^0 C. If the machines supplying liquid air for cooling were stopped for a few minutes everything would be burned to ash.

Inside the steel cube there were beds, benches, and buckets of water. A four-hour shift reduced the workers to such a state of exhaustion that they had to be laid out on the beds half-dead to recover before being sent to the surface. Ventilator fans and air-supply pipes hummed loudly. The lamp hanging from the riveted ceiling cast a bright light on the gloomy, unhealthy, puffy faces of twenty-five men. Seventy-five other workers were in the caves above and could communicate by telephone.

Shelga came out of the lift. Some of the men turned towards him in silence, giving him no greeting. They seemed to be firm in their decision to blow up the shaft.

"I want an interpreter. I'm going to speak Russian," said Shelga, sitting down at the table and pushing aside with his elbow tins of jam and Epsom salts and unfinished glasses of wine. (All of this was generously supplied to the workers by the management.)

A round-shouldered, bony Jew, with a bluish pale face under the stubble of his beard, came up to the table.

"I'm the interpreter."

Shelga began to speak:

"Garin and his enterprise is nothing more than the extreme development of capitalist consciousness. Farther than Garin nobody can go—the forcible conversion of the working section of mankind into beasts of burden by an operation of the brain, the selection of the 'lords of life,' the élite, the checking of the further progress of civilization. The bourgeoisie has not yet understood Garin and he's in no hurry to make them understand. They consider him a bandit and land-grabber. In the end they will realize that Garin's system is the logical end of imperialism. Comrades, we must prevent the most dangerous thing of all—we must stop Garin from coming to terms with them. You'll be having a tough time if he does, comrades. You people in this box have decided to die so that Garin won't quarrel with the American Government. Just you think it over. If Garin wins it'll be bad, if the capitalists win it won't be any better. If Garin comes to terms with them that will be the worst of all. You still don't appreciate your own worth, comrades, strength is on our side. In a month's time, when the elevator scoops start carrying gold to the surface, it won't be for the benefit of Garin but your benefit, for the benefit of that cause which we must fight for all over the world. If you trust me, really trust me, to the end, savagely, then I'll be your leader. Elect me unanimously. If you don't trust me. . . ."

Shelga stopped, looked round at the gloomy faces of the workers who were staring at him with unwinking eyes, and scratched the back of his head with some force.

"If you don't trust me, I'll talk some more."

A broad-shouldered youth, naked to the waist and grimy from soot, walked over to the table. He bent down and his blue eyes stared into Shelga's face. Hitching up his trousers he turned to his mates.

"I trust him."

"We trust you," said the others. Those words were repeated by telephone through thousands of feet of granite: "We trust you."

"If you trust me, all right," said Shelga. "Now for

the other points: the national boundaries will be removed by this evening. Your wages will be paid tomorrow. The police can guard the palace—we can manage without them. The fifteen *provocateurs* we'll chuck into the sea, that was one of the first conditions I made with Garin. The next thing is to get to the gold as quickly as possible. Right, comrades?"

110

That night the wandering beams of searchlights were observed to the north-west. Sirens sounded the alarm in the harbour. At dawn, when the sea still lay in shadow, the first heralds of the approaching squadron appeared: aircraft circled over the island, gleaming in the rosy light of dawn.

The police opened fire from their carbines but soon gave it up. The inhabitants of the island assembled in groups. Smoke continued to swirl over the mine. Ship's bells rang out the hours. A crane lifted huge bales tied with crossed ropes from a big steamer and brought them ashore.

The ocean lay calm, covered by a light mist. Aircraft propellers hummed in the sky.

The sun rose in a hazy ball. It was then that they all saw the smoke clouds on the horizon. They stretched out like a long, flat thunder-cloud towards the south-east. Death was drawing nigh.

Everything was quiet on the island, even the birds brought from the continent had stopped singing. At one place a bunch of people rushed to the boats in the harbour and crowded into them; the overloaded boats put out hurriedly into the open sea. There were, however, but few boats and the island was open on all sides, not a scrap of cover anywhere. The people stood about in silence as

though they had been struck dumb. Some lay face downwards on the sand.

No movement was to be observed in the palace. The
bronze gates were closed. Guards in high, wide-brimmed
hats and white, gold-trimmed tunics, carbines slung
across their backs, marched up and down under the sloping red walls. To one side rose the high, latticed tower
of the big hyperboloid. The rising blanket of mist hid its
summit from view. There were few people, however, who
had any faith in this defence: the brownish-black cloud
on the horizon was too substantial and menacing.

Suddenly many heads were turned fearfully towards
the shaft. At the mine the siren had sounded for the third
shift. What a time to work! Curse the gold! Then the
clock on the palace tower struck eight. At that moment
the heavy roar of thunder rolled across the ocean. The
squadron had fired its first volley. The seconds of waiting
seemed to spread into space, into the whine of the
approaching shells.

111

When the squadron fired its volley Rolling was standing on the terrace above the staircase leading to the sea.
He removed his pipe from his mouth and listened to the
whine of the approaching shells; no less than ninety steel
devils packed with melonite and explosive gas were flying
towards the island aimed directly at Rolling's brain. Their
sound was a roar of victory. It seemed that his heart would
burst at the noise. Rolling beat a hasty retreat towards a
door in the granite wall. (He had long since prepared for
himself a shelter in the cellar to be used in case of
bombardment.) With a roar the shells burst in the sea,
sending up columns of water. The range was short.

Then Rolling looked towards the top of the latticed
tower. Garin had been sitting there since the evening

before. The dome was revolving, as he could see by the movement of the vertical loopholes. Rolling put on his pince-nez and lifted his head. The dome turned very quickly right and left. As it moved to the right he could see the gleaming barrel of the hyperboloid moving up and down the loophole.

The most terrible of all was the speed with which Garin worked the hyperboloid. And the silence—there was not a sound on the island.

A dull, expanding sound came from the sea, like a bubble bursting in the sky. Rolling adjusted the pince-nez on his perspiring nose and looked towards the squadron. There floated three mushrooms of yellowish-white smoke. To the left of them ragged clouds welled up, turned blood red and grew into a fourth mushroom. The fourth peal of thunder rolled towards the island.

The pince-nez would not stay in place on Rolling's nose; nevertheless, he stood there manfully and watched the mushrooms grow on the horizon as one after the other the eight warships of the American squadron were blown into the air.

Again there was silence on the island, on the sea, and in the air. The lift descended quickly inside the latticed tower. Doors slammed inside the house and Garin ran out whistling a dance melody out of tune. His face was tired and worn out and his hair stuck out in all directions.

He did not notice Rolling and began to undress. He went down the stairs to the edge of the sea and there removed his silk shirt and salmon-pink underpants. Looking out to sea where smoke still hung over the spot where the squadron had been destroyed, Garin scratched himself under his arm-pits. His body was as white and plump as a woman's and there was something shameful and disgusting in his nakedness.

He tried the water with his foot, squatted like a woman

to meet an incoming wave, swam a little, and immediately came out; it was only then that he saw Rolling.

"Hallo," he drawled. "Do you want to take a dip, too? It's hellish cold."

He gave a giggling little laugh, picked up his clothes, and went back to the house in all his nakedness, swinging his underpants in his hand and making no effort to cover himself. Rolling had never experienced such humiliation in all his life. His heart chilled from hatred and loathing. He was unarmed and defenceless. In that moment of weakness he felt the whole weight of his past upon him, the weight of strength expended, the buffalo-like struggle for the first place in life ... and to think that it should all end with this obscene scoundrel, the conqueror, marching triumphantly past.

As he opened the huge bronze doors Garin turned round.

"Come in to breakfast, grandad," he said, "we'll share a bottle of champagne."

112

The strangest thing in Rolling's behaviour was the obedient way in which he plodded in to breakfast. At table there was only one other guest, Madame Lamolle, pale and untalkative after her recent shattering experiences. When she raised her glass to her lips it rattled against her even, dazzlingly white teeth.

Rolling seemed to be afraid of losing his equilibrium and stared all the time at one point, the gold foil of a champagne cork made in the shape of that accursed apparatus that had destroyed, in the course of a few minutes, all Rolling's former conceptions of might and power.

Garin, his wet hair uncombed, without a collar and still wearing a crumpled scorched jacket, kept up a nonsensical stream of chatter, swallowed oysters, and drank several glasses of wine one after another.

"Only now I realize how hungry I was."

"You've worked hard, my friend," said Zoë, softly.

"Yes. I admit that there was a moment when I grew afraid, when the horizon was hidden in the smoke of gunfire.... They got in first.... The devils.... If they'd increased the range by a cable's length nothing would have been left of this house, or of the island, for that matter...."

He drank another glass of wine and, although he had said he was hungry, elbowed the liveried waiter away when he offered him another dish.

"Well, grandad?" He turned suddenly towards Rolling and stared straight at him, this time without a trace of a smile. "It's time we had a serious talk. Or are you waiting for more staggering effects?"

Without a sound Rolling placed his fork on his plate and lowered his eyes.

"Speak, I'm listening."

"And about time.... Twice already I've offered you a partnership. I hope you remember. I don't blame you, though: you're not a thinker, you belong to the buffalo genus. I'm repeating my offer. You're surprised, eh? I'll explain. I'm an organizer. I'm going to reconstruct the whole of your top-heavy capitalist system with all its foolish prejudices. Do you get that? If I don't do it the Communists will eat you up with a pinch of salt and smack their chops in delight. Communism is the only thing in life that I really hate.... Why? Because it will destroy me, Pyotr Garin, and a whole universe of plans in my brain.... You may ask what I need you for, Rolling, when I have inexhaustible supplies of gold under my feet."

"Yes, I do ask that," muttered Rolling, hoarsely.

"Take a glass of gin with cayenne pepper, old man, that will clear your brain for you. Do you imagine for one moment that I intend to turn gold into dung? I shall certainly arrange a few warm days for all mankind. I will lead people to the very brink of a fearful precipice when they will hold in their hands a pound of gold that costs two cents."

Rolling suddenly raised his head and his dull eyes showed a youthful sparkle and his mouth twisted into a crooked smile.

"Aha," he croaked.

"Just that—aha! You're beginning to understand at long last? In those days of wholesale panic we, that is, I and you and three hundred other buffaloes, or universal gangsters, or kings of finance—choose whichever name you like best—will seize the world by the throat. We'll buy up all enterprises, all factories, all railways, all air and sea fleets. . . . Everything that we need or that is likely to be useful to us will be ours. Then we'll blow up this island, mine and all, and announce that the world's supply of gold is limited, that the gold is in our hands and will return to its former function as the only measure of values."

Rolling listened, leaning back in his chair, his mouth full of gold teeth opened like that of a shark and his face turned red.

Thus he sat motionless, his tiny eyes gleaming. For a moment Madame Lamolle even thought that the old man would have a stroke.

"Aha," he croaked again. "It's a bold idea. There are chances of success. But you haven't taken into consideration the danger of strikes, rebellions. . . ."

"That was my first consideration," said Garin abruptly. "We'll begin by building huge concentration camps. All those who are not satisfied with our regime will go behind the barbed wire. Then we'll introduce the law on mental castration. And so, my friend, do you elect me your leader? . . . Ha!" (He suddenly winked and that was almost terrifying.)

Rolling lowered his head and frowned. He had been asked and had to think before answering.

"Do you compel me to take this step, Mr. Garin?"

"What do you think, old man? Do you want me to beg you on my knees? I'll compel you if you don't realize yourself that for a long time you've been awaiting me as a saviour."

"Very good," said Rolling through his clenched teeth and he stretched out his rough, bluish hand to Garin across the table.

"Very good," repeated Garin. "Events are developing at high speed. On the continent the three hundred kings must have their minds prepared. You will write them a letter on the imbecility of a government that sends a squadron of warships to bombard my island. You will prepare them for the 'gold panic.' (He snapped his fingers; a liveried lackey approached.) Pour out some more champagne. Rolling, we'll drink to the great and historic coup d'état. Think of it, pal, Mussolini's just a puppy compared to us. . . ."

And so Pyotr Garin came to an agreement with Mr. Rolling. History had been given the spur, history went galloping forward, its golden-shod hoofs clattering over the skulls of fools.

113

The reverberations in America and Europe that followed the destruction of the Pacific Squadron were terrific and unprecedented. The United States of America had been dealt a blow that resounded throughout the world. The governments of Germany, France, Britain, and Italy all at once and with unhealthy nervousness took heart: they wondered whether this year (or perhaps any other year) they might be able to default in paying interest to an America already glutted with gold. "The colossus, it seems, has feet of clay," said the newspapers, "it is not so easy to conquer the world. . . ."

At the same time the news of the *Arizona*'s piracy caused a hold-up in sea trade. Steamship-owners refused to load cargoes, steamer captains were afraid to cross the ocean, insurance companies raised their premiums, there was chaos in the banking world, bills of exchange were protested, a number of commercial houses went bankrupt, and Japan began hurriedly dumping her cheap goods on the American colonial markets.

The disastrous sea battle had cost America a large sum of money. Her prestige, or "national pride," as it was called, had suffered severely. Industrialists demanded the mobilization of all sea and air fleets—war to the victorious end, cost what it might. American newspapers threatened to remain in mourning (the names of the newspapers were printed in a black frame—this produced an effect on many people and did not cost much) until Pierre Harry was brought to New York in an iron cage and executed on the electric chair. Terrifying rumours of Garin's agents, armed with pocket infra-red ray machines, circulated amongst the population of the country. There were cases of unknown people being beaten up and of momentary panics on the streets, in cinemas and in restaurants. The Washington government thundered forth weighty words but actually was in a state of utter confusion. The only vessel of the whole squadron to escape, a destroyer, brought news of the battle so ghastly in its details that the ministry was afraid to publish it. Seventeen-inch guns were powerless against the light-ray tower on Blackguards' Island.

These disconcerting facts led the Government of the United States to call a conference in Washington. The watchword of this conference was: "All men are children of the same God, let us think of the peaceful prosperity of mankind."

When the date of the conference was announced newspaper offices and the wireless stations of all countries received information to the effect that Engineer Garin would be present in person at the opening of the conference.

114

Garin, Čermak, and Scheffer descended in the lift into the depths of the main shaft. Endless rows of pipes, cables, trusses, elevator wells, platforms, and iron doors flashed past the mica windows.

They passed through eighteen strata in the earth's crust, eighteen layers that marked eras in the planet's history like the rings in the trunk show the age of a tree. Organic life began in the fourth stratum "from the fire," the stratum formed by the Paleozoic ocean. The virgin waters of this ocean were saturated with some life force unknown to us. They contained radioactive salts and large quantities of carbonic acid. This was the "water of life."

At the dawn of the next era, the Mesozoic, gigantic monsters came out of the water. For millions of years they made the earth tremble with their cries of hunger and lust. Still higher up in the shaft they found the remains of birds and, higher still, mammals. This latter stratum was close to the ice age, the grim dawn of mankind.

The lift was passing through the nineteenth and last stratum, created out of the flames and chaos of volcanic action. This was the earth of the Archaean Era, a solid mass of dark-red, small-grain granite.

Garin bit his nails in impatience. None of the three spoke. It was hard to breathe and each of them carried an oxygen apparatus over his back. They could hear the roar of the hyperboloids and the explosions.

The lift entered a belt of bright light cast by electric lamps and came to a stop over a huge cowl collecting gases. Garin and Scheffer donned round rubber helmets, like a diver's, and climbed through one of the manholes of the cowl on to a metal ladder that led straight down for a distance equal to the height of a five-storey house. They climbed down to where the ladder ended on a round platform. On this platform several workers, naked to the waist, wearing masks and carrying oxygen containers over their backs, crouched over the housings of the hyperboloids. The workers stared into the roaring pit, regulating and directing the rays.

Similar vertical ladders with round steel rungs led from this platform to the lower one. There stood the liquid-air cooling apparatus. Workers on this lower platform, dressed in rubberized felt clothing and wearing oxygen masks, controlled the work of the coolers and the elevator scoops. This was the most dangerous place to work in. Any awkward movement would bring a man under the seething ray of the hyperboloid. Down below white-hot rocks burst and exploded in the stream of liquid air. Fragments of rock and clouds of gas came from below.

The elevators removed up to fifty tons of rock an hour. The work was going well. As the elevator scoops dug deeper the whole system was lowered—the "iron mole," constructed according to Mantsev's drawings, consisting of the circular platforms with the hyperboloids and the cowl of the gas collector. The strengthening of the shaft began above the "mole" system.

Scheffer snatched a handful of grey dust from one of the scoops as it flew past. Garin rubbed it between his fingers. He wrote a few words on a cigarette box.

"Heavy slag. Lava."

Scheffer nodded his round bespectacled helmet. Moving carefully along the edge of the circular platform they stopped under instruments hanging on steel hawsers from the monolithic wall of the shaft and moving downwards together with the whole "iron mole" system. These included barometers, seismographs compasses, pendulums recording the degree of acceleration of the force of gravity at a given depth, and electromagnetic measuring instruments.

Scheffer pointed to a pendulum, took the cigarette box from Garin, and wrote on it slowly in his meticulous German handwriting:

"Acceleration of the force of gravity has risen by nine-hundredths since yesterday morning. At this depth acceleration should drop to 0.98, instead it rose by 1.07. . . ."

"Magnets?" wrote Garin.

Scheffer answered:

"Today all magnetic instruments have stood at zero since morning. We are below the magnetic field."

Resting his hands on his knees Garin stood for a long time looking down into the black pit that narrowed to an almost imperceptible point where the "iron mole" roared as it bit its way deeper into the earth. That morning the shaft had begun to penetrate the Olivine Belt.

115

"How do you feel, Ivan?"

Shelga stroked the boy's head. The boy was sitting with him at the window of a little seaside house looking at the ocean. The house was built from coastal rock plastered with light-yellow clay. Outside, waves raced the blue ocean, white with surf where they beat against the reefs and the sandy beach of the tiny isolated cove where Shelga lived.

Ivan had been brought to the island on the airship half-dead. Shelga had brought him round with the greatest difficulty. If he had not had a friend on the island it is scarcely probable that Ivan would have lived. He was badly frost-bitten, he had a cold and, worst of all, he was morally depressed: he had trusted people, had made every possible effort, and what had happened?

"There's no going back to Soviet Russia for me, Comrade Shelga. I'll be arrested."

"Don't be a fool. It's not your fault."

Whether Ivan sat on a rock on the beach, caught crabs or wandered about amidst the marvels of the island, amidst strange people and bustling activity, his eyes, with an expression of nostalgia, would constantly turn to the west where the flaming ball of the sun set and where, far beyond the sun, lay the Land of Soviets.

"It's night now," he said in a quiet voice, "but in Leningrad it's morning. Comrade Tarashkin has had his breakfast and gone to work. At the club-house they're caulking the boats now, the flag will be raised in a fortnight."

As Ivan grew better Shelga began cautiously explaining to him the situation on the island and soon discovered, as Tarashkin had done, that the boy was quick to get the hang of things and that his attitude was irreconcilably Soviet. If he had not whimpered so much about Leningrad he would have been a wonderful boy.

"Ivan," said Shelga one day, cheerfully, "I'm going to send you home soon."

"Thank you, Vasily Vitalyevich."

"But there's one little job you've got to do first."

"I'll do it."

"Are you any good at climbing?"

"In Siberia I climbed hundred-and-fifty-foot cedars to get the cones, I climbed so high I couldn't see the ground."

"When the time comes I'll tell you what to do. But don't wander about the island too much. You better take a line and fish for sea urchins."

116

Garin now went forward confidently with his work in accordance with a plan found amongst Mantsev's notes and diaries.

The scoops had passed through the thick stratum of magma. At the bottom of the shaft the roar of the subterranean ocean could be heard all the time. The walls of the shaft, frozen to a depth of one hundred feet, formed an indestructible cylinder; nevertheless the shaft vibrated and there were such jolts that they had to concentrate on freezing operations. The elevators were now bringing to the surface crystallized iron, nickel, and olivine.

Strange phenomena were observed. A fluorescent glow appeared in the sea where the pontoons and conveyer belts deposited the extracted rock. For several days the glow increased in intensity until a huge mass of water and sand together with the pontoons and conveyers flew into the air. The explosion was so terrific that workers' baracks were blown down by the hurricane blast and the wave that swept over the island almost flooded the shafts.

They had to load the rock straight on to barges and take it well out to sea; there the glow and the explosions never ceased. This was explained by some still unknown phenomena connected with the atomic disintegration of metal M.

What was happening at the bottom of the shaft was no less strange. It began with the magnetic instruments that shortly before had stood at zero suddenly revealing a magnetic field of tremendous strength. The needles swung over to the limit of their indicating power. A trembling bluish light appeared in the shaft. The very air underwent a change. Nitrogen and oxygen atoms, bombarded by myriads of alpha particles, disintegrated into helium and hydrogen.

Part of the liberated hydrogen burned in the hyperboloid rays, flames swept through the shaft accompanied by little pistol-like explosions. The workers' clothing caught fire. The shafts were shaken by the ebb and flow of the magma ocean. It was noticed that the steel scoops and iron parts of the elevators acquired an earthy-red coating. The rapid atomic disintegration of the machinery had begun. Many of the workers were burned by invisible rays. Still the "iron mole" continued biting its way through the Olivine Belt with all its former persistence.

Garin scarcely ever left the shaft. It was only now that he realized to the ful the madness of his undertaking. Nobody could say exactly how deep the seething subterranean ocean lay, or how many thousand feet he would have to continue through molten olivine. Only one thing was certain—the instruments showed the presence of a solid magnetic core of extremely low temperature in the centre of the earth.

There was a danger that the frozen cylinder of the shaft, denser than the molten mass which surrounded it, would be torn off and pulled to the centre by the force of gravity. Dangerous cracks appeared in the walls of the shafts and gases surged, hissing, through them. The diameter of the shafts had to be reduced to a half and extra-strong vertical props were put in.

A lot of time was taken by the erection of a new "iron mole" half the diameter of the former one. The only comforting news came from the *Arizona*. The yacht was again sailing under the pirate flag; it had burst into Melbourne harbour at night, set fire to warehouses filled with copra to announce its presence, and demanded five million pounds. (As a warning the Marine Esplanade had been wrecked with the hyperboloid ray.) Within a few hours the city was empty and the money was paid out by the banks. As the *Arizona* left the harbour she was fired on by a British warship and was holed above the waterline by a six-inch shell; the yacht then attacked and cut the warship into pieces. The battle was commanded by Madame Lamolle from the height of the hyperboloid tower.

The report of this action put Garin in a good mood. He had fallen victim to dismal thoughts during the past few days. Suppose Mantsev had been mistaken in his calculations? As in the deserted house in the Petrograd District a year before, his brain began to seek ways of salvation in the event of the shaft proving a failure.

On 25th April, standing on the circular platform inside the "mole" system, Garin was the witness of an unusual phenomenon. From the cowl of the gas collector above him came a shower of mercury. The hyperboloids had to be stopped and the refrigeration at the base of the shaft was lessened. The scoops had passed the olivine and were now bringing up pure mercury. In the Mendeleyev tables mercury was followed by the metal thallium. Gold (atomic weight 197.2 and number 79) was higher than mercury in the tables.

Only Garin and Scheffer knew that a catastrophe had occured and there had been no gold in the strata of metals lying in the order of their atomic weights. It was a real catastrophe! That damned Mantsev had made a mistake!

Garin's head dropped. He had expected all sorts of things but not such a pitiful end as this.... Scheffer absent-mindedly held out his hand to catch the drops of mercury that fell from above. Suddenly he seized Garin by the elbow and dragged him to the vertical ladder. When they had got to the top, entered the lift and taken off their masks. Scheffer stamped on the floor with his heavy boots. His bony face, with all its childish simplicity, was radiant with joy.

"It's gold!" he shouted, roaring with laughter. "We're just sheep's heads.... Gold and mercury boil side by side. What happens? Mercurial gold!... Look!" He opened a hand on which lay a few drops of mercury. "There's a sheen of gold in the mercury. This is ninety per cent red gold!"

117

Gold poured out of the ground of its own accord like oil. Work on the deepening of the shaft was stopped. The "iron mole" was dismantled and taken out. The temporary trusses were removed and replaced by massive steel cylinders in the thickness of whose walls refrigerator pipes were laid.

The mercurial gold was forced upwards by superheated steam, and it was only necessary to regulate the temperature to get it at any level of the shaft. Garin's calculations showed that when the steel cylinders had been lowered to the bottom of the shaft it would be possible to force the gold to the top of the shaft and then scoop it up on the surface.

A mercury pipe-line was hastily built from the shaft to the north-east. Furnaces with ceramic crucibles to extract gold from the mercury were erected in the left wing of the palace under the hyperboloid tower.

To begin with Garin proposed bringing gold production up to ten thousand poods a day, that is, one hundred million dollars' worth.

An order was sent for the *Arizona* to return to the island. Madame Lamolle answered by congratulating them and sent out a radio message to the whole world saying that she had ceased pirate operations in the Pacific.

118

Shortly before the opening of the Washington Conference five ocean-going steamers entered the harbour of San Francisco. They raised the Dutch flag and tied up peacefully amongst a thousand other merchant vessels in the expansive, smoky bay, bathed in summer sunshine.

The captains went ashore. Everything was in order. The sailors' washing was hung up to dry on the vessels, the decks were being swilled down. It was the cargo of the five vessels sailing under the Dutch flag that astonished the customs officials more than a little. They were informed, however, that the ingots of yellow metal were genuine gold brought here for sale.

The customs men laughed at a good joke.

"How much do you sell your gold for, eh?"

"At cost price," answered the first mates. (Exactly the same conversation, word for word, took place on all five vessels.)

"And how much is that?"

"A dollar twenty a pound!"

"You don't seem to value your gold very high."

"We're selling it cheap—we've got plenty," answered the mates, sucking their pipes.

And so the customs officials wrote into their records: "Cargo, ingots of yellow metal, described as gold." They laughed and went their way. Actually, however, it was no laughing matter.

Two days later in the advertisement columns of the San Francisco morning newspapers, on yellow and white posters on the hoardings or simply chalked on the pavements, appeared the following notice:

"Engineer Pyotr Garin, considering the war for the independence of Golden Island to be concluded and profoundly regretting the losses suffered by his opponents, respectfully offers the people of the United States five shiploads of gold as a beginning of peaceful commercial relations. Ten-pound ingots of gold are offered at a dollar twenty a pound. Those interested may obtain them at tobacconists, oil shops and dairies, at newspaper and shoe-shine stands, etc. I ask you to convince yourselves of the genuineness of the gold of which I have unlimited supplies. With my respects, Garin."

It goes without saying that nobody believed this ridiculous advertisement. The majority of the agents hid their gold ingots. Nevertheless the name was on everybody's tongue, Pyotr Garin, the pirate and legendary scoundrel who was again disturbing honest people. The evening newspapers called for the lynching of Garin. At about six in the evening crowds of idlers made for the harbour where, at spontaneous meetings, they passed a resolution to sink Garin's ships and hang their crews from lamp-posts. The police had difficulty in holding back the crowd.

In the meantime the port authorities were making investigations. The papers of all five steamers were in order, the vessels themselves were not subject to sequester since they belonged to a well-known Dutch steamship company. Nevertheless the authorities demanded that the sale of the ingots that caused so much excitement amongst the populace be prohibited. Not one of the officials could resist the temptation, however, when two gold ingots found their way into his trouser pockets. Test them as you like for colour, weight or by biting—it was real gold, believe it or not. The question of their sale was left open, tacitly ignored for the time being.

Then some taciturn sailors carried sacks of the mysterious ingots in the editorial offices of thirty-two daily newspapers. "A present," were the only words they said. The editors were indignant. A terrible hubbub occurred in each of the thirty-two offices. Jewellers were sent for. Bloodthirsty measures were proposed to avenge the impertinence of Pierre Harry. But still the ingots disappeared, nobody knew how, from the offices of all thirty-two papers.

During the night gold ingots were scattered on the pavements. By nine o'clock notices were hung up in all the barber's and tobacconist's shops: "Red Gold Sold Here at $ 1.20 per lb."

The people of the city succumbed.

The worst of it all was that nobody knew why gold was being sold at a dollar twenty a pound. Only a fool, however, would have missed the chance. Crowds milled and surged in the streets. Thousands of people crowded the water-front where the steamers were moored, and howled for ingots. Gold was sold directly from the gang-ways of the vessels. That day the trams and underground railway stopped working. There was chaos in private and government offices: instead of working the clerks made the rounds of the tobacconist's shops asking for ingots. Shops and warehouses were closed, the assistants had left —thieves and burglars were at large in the city.

A rumour spread that the gold had been brought in limited quantites and that no more shiploads of gold would arrive.

On the third day a gold rush began all over America. West-bound trains carried excited, puzzled, doubtful, and disturbed fortune-hunters. People fought for places in the trains. There was terrible confusion in this wave of human idiocy.

Late, as usual, a government instruction arrived from Washington: "Place a police cordon around the vessels laden with the so-called gold, arrest the officers and crews, and seal the vessels." The instruction was put into effect.

The infuriated crowds of people that had come from other parts of the country, leaving their businesses or their jobs to swarm on the hot, sunny San Francisco water-front, where everything edible and been consumed as though by locusts—these swarms of savages broke through the police cordon, fought like madmen with revolvers, knives, and even teeth, threw many of the policemen into the bay, released the crews of Garin's steamers, and organized an armed queue for gold!

Another three steamers arrived from Golden Island. They used derricks to unload bundles of ingots directly on to the water-front where they stacked them in huge piles. There was something unbearably horrible in all this. People in the queues trembled as they looked at the treasure that lay glittering on the roadway.

By this time Garin's agents had completed the erection of street loudspeakers in all big cities. On Saturday, when work in office and factory was over and the townspeople filled the streets, a loud voice, speaking with a barbaric accent, but with extraordinary confidence, rang out all over America.

"Americans! This is Engineer Garin talking to you, the man who has been outlawed, whose name is used to frighten children. Americans, I have committed many crimes, but all of them lead to one goal, to the happiness of mankind. I have occupied a piece of land, an insignificant island, in order to bring a gigantic and unprecedented enterprise to a successful conclusion. I decided to penetrate into the bowels of the earth to reach virgin deposits of gold. At a depth of 25,000 feet the shaft reached a deep stratum of molten gold. Americans, everybody sells whatever he's got. I am offering you my ware—gold. When I sell it at a dollar twenty a pound I earn ten cents on the dollar. That's a modest profit. Why am I forbidden to sell my goods? Where is your free trade? Your government is trampling underfoot the sacred principles of liberty and progress. I am prepared to pay war indemnities. I am prepared to return to the state, to companies, and to private individuals all the money that was requisitioned by the *Arizona* from ships and banks in accordance with the customs of war. I ask only one thing—give me freedom to sell my gold. Your government forbids it and has placed my ships under arrest. I put myself under the protection of the people of the United States."

That same night the loudspeakers were destroyed by

the police. The government appealed to the reason of the population:

". . . Suppose the notorious bandit, who has come here from Soviet Russia, Engineer Garin, is telling the truth, then it is all the more necessary to fill in the shaft on Golden Island and prevent any possibility of there being unlimited supplies of gold. What will happen to the equivalent of labour, happiness, and life if gold can be dug up like clay? Man must inevitably return to his primitive state, to barter, savagery, and chaos. The whole economic system will be wrecked, industry and commerce will decay. There will be no incentive for people to strive for higher spiritual values. The big cities will perish. The railways will be overgrown with grass. The lights will go out in the cinemas and pleasure grounds. Man will again hunt for his living with a flint spear. Engineer Garin is the greatest of all *provocateurs*, a servant of the devil. His object is to devaluate the dollar. In this he will not succeed. . . ."

The government drew a pitiful picture of what would happen if the gold standard were abolished. There were, however, few reasonable people to be found. The whole country went mad. Life came to a standstill in all cities as in San Francisco. Trains and millions of cars raced to the west. The nearer they got to the Pacific coast the more expensive became foodstuffs. There was no means of transport available to carry food. Hungry fortune-hunters broke into the food shops. A pound of ham cost a hundred dollars. In San Francisco people died in the streets. Others went mad from hunger, thirst, and the intense heat.

At railway junctions and along the tracks lay the bodies of those who had been killed storming the trains. Along roads and lanes, across mountains and through forests groups of the fortunate ones made their way back east with sacks of gold ingots on their backs. Those who fell behind were murdered by the local inhabitants and gangs of bandits.

The hunt for the "gold-bearers" began—they were even attacked from aeroplanes.

At last the government took extreme measures. . . . Congress passed a law mobilizing all men between the ages of seventeen and forty-five, all failing to comply to be tried by court-martial. In the poorer districts of New York several hundred people were shot. Armed soldiers appeared on all railway stations. Some people were seized, some were pulled off trains and the soldiers fired into the air and at the people. Still the trains left crowded with passengers. The privately-owned railways found it more profitable to ignore government instructions.

Another five of Garin's steamships arrived in San Francisco, and in the open roads, in view of the whole bay, stood the beautiful *Arizona*, "the menace of the seas." Under cover of her two hyperboloid towers gold was unloaded from the steamers.

Such was the situation when the opening day of the Washington Conference came. A month before America had owned one half of the world's supply of gold. Today America's gold fund had been reduced in value to one two hundred and fiftieth part of what it had been. At the cost of inhuman effort, with terrific losses and the spilling of much blood this could have been overcome. But suppose that mad scoundrel Garin should decide to sell his gold for fifty or for ten cents a pound. Elderly Senators and Congressmen strode up and down the lobbies, their faces white with horror. The industrial and financial kings let their hands fall despondently.

"It is a world catastrophe, worse than a collision with a comet."

"Who is this Engineer Garin?" they asked. "What does he really want? To ruin the country? Rot. Incomprehensible. What is he trying to achieve? Does he want to be a dictator? Let him, if he's the richest man in the world. After all we ourselves are as fed up with this democracy business as we are with margarine. There are riots, disorders, lawlessness in the country, it really would be much better if a dictator were to rule, a leader with the grip of a bulldog."

When it became known that Garin himself would appear at the conference so many people gathered in the hall that they hung from columns and crowded the windows. The chairman appeared. They sat in silence and waited. At last the chairman opened his mouth and all those in the hall turned towards the high white and gold door. It opened. In walked a man of average height, unusually pale, with a dark pointed beard and dark eyes framed in black rings. He was dressed in an ordinary grey suit, a red bow tie, brown shoes on thick soles and in his left hand a pair of new gloves.

He stopped and took a deep breath. He nodded his head briefly and walked briskly up the steps of the rostrum. He stretched to his full height. His beard stuck out in front. He moved the carafe of water to the edge of the rostrum. It was so quiet in the hall that the splash of the water could be heard. In a high-pitched voice and with a barbaric accent he said:

"Gentlemen, I'm Garin. I bring the world gold. ..."

The hall thundered with applause. The whole audience stood like one man and shouted in a single voice:

"Long live Mr. Garin! Long live the dictator!"

Outside the hall a crowd a million strong roared, beating time with their feet:

"Ingots! ... Ingots! ... Ingots! ..."

119

The *Arizona* had just returned to the harbour of Golden Island. Jansen, reporting to Madame Lamolle, informed her of the situation on the mainland. Zoë received him in bed amidst her lace pillows (the minor morning reception). The half-dark bedroom was filled with the pungent smell of flowers that came drifting through the open windows. A manicurist was working on her right hand. In her left she held a mirror and looked at her image with dissatisfaction as she talked.

"But, my friend, Garin's going out of his mind," she said to Jansen. "He's devaluating gold. He wants to be the dictator of the poor."

Jansen took a side-glance at the magnificence of the recently decorated bedchamber. He answered, holding his cap on his knees:

"When I met Garin he said that you were not to worry, Madame Lamolle. He will not depart one iota from the programme laid down. By knocking the bottom out of gold he has won a battle. Next week the Senate will declare him dictator. Then he will raise the value of gold."

"How? I don't understand."

"He will issue a decree prohibiting the import and sale of gold. In a month it will rise to its former price. We haven't sold so very much. There was more noise than trade."

"And the mine?"

"The mine will be destroyed."

Madame Lamolle frowned and lit a cigarette.

"I understand absolutely nothing."

"It is essential to limit the amount of gold available or it will lose its odour of human sweat. Needless to say, before the mine is destroyed sufficient gold will be extracted to ensure that Garin is in possession of more than fifty per cent of the world's gold supply. So if the value does drop, it can only be a few cents on the dollar."

"Excellent ... but how much will they assign me for my court, for my fantasies? I need a terribly big sum."

"Garin asks you to draw up an estimate. You will be assigned by law just as much as you need."

"How do I know how much I need? That's all so silly! Firstly, in place of the workers' quarters, warehouses, and workshops I shall build theatres, hotels, and circuses. That will be a city of wonders. Bridges like those in the old Chinese pictures will link the island with the surrounding islets and reefs. There I will build bathing pavilions and pavilions for games, harbours for yachts and airships. At the southern end of the island there will be an enormous building visible for many miles: 'The Resting Place of Genius.' I'll plunder all the museums of Europe. I'll gather together everything that mankind has created. My dear, my head aches with all these plans. In my dreams I see marble staircases leading up to the clouds, festivals, carnivals...."

Jansen sat up in his gilded chair.

"Madame Lamolle...."

"Wait," she said impatiently, "in three weeks' time my court will arrive. The whole gang will have to be fed, entertained, and kept in order. I want to invite two or three real kings from Europe and a dozen princes of the blood. We'll bring the Pope from Rome on an airship. I want to be anointed and crowned in proper form so that no more vulgar songs should be composed about me."

"Madame Lamolle," said Jansen in imploring tones, "I haven't seen you for a whole month. So far you are still free. Let's put out to sea. The *Arizona* has been reconditioned. I want to stand beside you again, on the bridge under the stars."

Zoë looked at him, her face grew tender. Smiling she stretched out her hand to him. He pressed his lips to it and stood bent over it for a long time.

"I don't know, Jansen, I don't know," she said, touching his hair with her other hand, "sometimes it seems to me that happiness is only in the striving for happiness.... And in memories.... But that's in moments of weari-

ness. . . . Sometime I'll come back to you, Jansen. I know
you'll wait patiently for me. Do you remember? . . . The
Mediterranean Sea, the glorious day when I appointed
you Commander of the Order of the Divine Zoë. (She
laughed and squeezed the back of his head between her
fingers.) And if I don't come back, Jansen, your dreams
and your longing for me—are not they also happiness?
Oh, my friend, nobody knows that Golden Island is a dream
that I once saw in the Mediterranean Sea; I was dozing on
deck and saw staircases and palaces, more and more palaces,
each more beautiful than the others rising in terraces out
of the sea. And there were many beautiful people, my people,
my own, you understand me? No, I shan't rest until I've
built my dream city. I know, my faithful friend, you offer
me yourself, the captain's bridge and the wastes of the
ocean in place of my mad delirium. You don't know
women, Jansen. We're frivolous and wasteful. I threw
aside Rolling's billions like an old glove because they
could not save me from old age, from decay. I followed
Garin, a beggar. My head was turned by a crazy dream.
Still, I loved him only one night. Since that night I cannot
love again like you want me to. My dear, dear Jansen, tell
me what I am to do with myself? I must fly away into
dizzy fantasies until my heart stops beating. (He rose
from his chair and she suddenly seized him by the hand.)
I know, there's only one man in the world who loves me.
You, you, Jansen. Can I ever be sure that I shan't come
running to you and say, 'Jansen, save me from myself. . . .' "

120

In the little yellow house in the cove on a distant
part of Golden Island, heated discussions went on all
night. Shelga read a hastily drawn-up proclamation:

"Workers of the World! You know the extent and results of the panic that swept the United States when Garin's gold ships entered San Francisco harbour.

"Capitalism is tottering: gold is losing its value, currencies are tumbling, the capitalists have nothing with which to pay their mercenaries—police, punitive troops, *provocateurs*, and traitors from amongst the working-class leaders. The spectre of proletarian revolution has risen to its full height.

"Although it was Engineer Garin who dealt capitalism this terrific blow, there is nothing he wants less than revolution.

"Garin wants power. On his way to power he is crushing the resistance of the capitalists who have not yet learned that Garin is a new weapon in the struggle against the proletarian revolution.

"Garin will soon come to terms with the biggest capitalists.

"They will declare him dictator and their leader. He will keep in his possession half of the world's supply of gold and will then order the mine on Golden Island to be filled in so that the amount of available gold will be limited.

"Together with a gang of the biggest capitalists he will plunder all mankind and make slaves of the people.

"Workers of the World! The hour of decisive struggle has arrived. This announcement is made by the Revolutionary Committee of Golden Island. The Committee announces that Golden Island, the mine, and the hyperboloids are placed at the disposal of the revolutionary workers of the whole world. Unlimited supplies of gold will now be in the hands of the working people.

"Garin and his gang will defend themselves desperately. The sooner we take the offensive the surer will be our victory."

Not all members of the Revolutionary Committee approved the proclamation, some of them wavered, afraid of its boldness: would they be able to arouse the workers so quickly? Would they be able to get weapons? The capitalists had their navies and powerful armies, they had police armed with gas and machine-guns. ... Would it not be better to wait or, if they must act, then begin with a general strike? ...

Shelga spoke to the waverers with suppressed fury.

"Revolution is the higher strategy. Strategy is the science of victory. He wins who takes the initiative into his hands, he who has courage. You can weigh things up quietly after our victory, when you're thinking of writing the history of that victory for future generations. We shall be able to organize an uprising if we devote all our energy to it. We'll get weapons in the course of battle. The victory is certain because all toiling mankind is determined to win and we are the vanguard. That's how the Bolsheviks talk and the Bolsheviks know no defeats."

When these words had been said a big blue-eyed young miner, who had remained silent the whole time, took his pipe out of his mouth.

"That's enough," he said in a deep bass. "That's enough talk. Let's get busy."

121

The tall, grey-headed valet, in livery jacket and stockings, entered the bedchamber noiselessly, placed a cup of chocolate and biscuits on the bedside table, and with a faint rustle opened the blinds on the windows. Garin opened his eyes.

"Cigarette!"

He had been unable to cure himself of that Russian habit of smoking before breakfast although he knew that American high society, who followed his every move and word, regarded smoking on an empty stomach as something in the nature of immorality.

Daily feuilletons in the American press had completely whitewashed Garin's past. In the past he had only drunk wine when he had been compelled to, in actual fact he was an enemy of alcoholic liquors; his relations with Madame Lamolle were those of brother and sister, based on a community of spirit; it turned out that their favourite amusement, when he and Madame Lamolle had time to rest together, was the reading aloud of the most loved chapters of the Bible; some of his more desperate exploits (the Ville d'Avray business, the explosion at the chemical works, the sinking of the American squadron, etc.) were just fatal accidents, others were due to the careless handling of the hyperboloid, in any case the great man showed sincere and profound penitence and was ready to enter the church in order finally to wash away his involuntary sins (a struggle for Pyotr Garin had already begun between the Catholic and Protestant Churches), and, lastly, he was credited with having been interested from childhood in at least ten different forms of sport.

Garin smoked his cigarette and then squinted at the chocolate. Formerly, when he was still considered a blackguard and bandit, he would have asked for a brandy and soda as a morning pick-me-up—but for the dictator of half the world to start the day on brandy! Such immorality would have alienated the whole of the sound, reliable bourgeoisie that had mustered around his throne like Napoleon's Old Guard.

With a scowl he sipped the chocolate. The valet, standing at the door in a sort of sad solemnity, asked in a low voice:

"Will Your Excellency permit his private secretary to enter?"

Garin sat up lazily in bed and put on a silk dressing-gown. "Send him in."

The secretary entered, bowed with dignity three times, once at the door, once in the middle of the room, and once at the bedside. He wished Garin a good morning and cast a scarcely perceptible glance at the chair.

"Sit down," said Garin, yawning so that his jaws cracked.

The private secretary sat down. He was a bony middle-aged individual with a wrinkled brow and sunken cheeks, dressed in dark clothes. His eyelids were permanently half-closed. He was considered the most elegant gentleman in the New World and had, as Pyotr Petrovich thought, been planted on him by the big financiers as a spy.

"What's new?" asked Garin. "Any change in the price of gold?"

"It's rising."

"But slowly, eh?"

The secretary raised his eyelids with a melancholy look.

"Yes, feebly, very feebly."

"Damn them!"

Garin pushed his bare feet into brocade slippers and began pacing the white carpet of his bedchamber.

"Damn them! Sons of bitches! Idiots!"

Involuntarily his left hand crept behind his back, the thumb of his right hand he stuck in his pyjama cord and so he strode back and forth with a lock of hair falling over his forehead. The secretary apparently thought this an historical moment: he sat bolt upright on his chair with his neck craned out of his starched collar—it seemed to him that he was listening to the march of history.

"Damn them!" said Garin for the last time. "I regard the slow rise in the market price of gold as lack of confidence in me. In me! You understand? I will issue a decree prohibiting the free sale of gold ingots on pain of death. Write this...."

He stood still, glanced sternly at the abundant rosy bottom of Aurora flying across the ceiling amidst clouds and cupids, and began to dictate:

"The Senate decrees that from today's date...."

When this business was finished he lit a second cigarette. He threw the butt into his unfinished cup of chocolate and asked:

"What else is there? Have any attempts on my life been discovered?"

The secretary's long fingers with long polished nails extracted a sheet of paper from his brief-case; he read it to himself, turned it over, and then turned it back again.

"The police have uncovered another two attempts on your life, sir, one yesterday evening and one at half past six this morning."

"Aha, very good. Publish it in the press. Who were they? I hope the crowd dealt with the scoundrels? What?"

"Yesterday evening a young man, apparently of the working class, was discovered in the palace park with two iron nuts in his pocket, each weighing a pound. Unfortunately it was late, and there were not many people in the park, only a few passers-by who, learning that the villain wanted to attempt the life of their adored dictator, succeeded in striking him. He has been detained."

"Were those passers-by private individuals or agents?"

The secretary's eyelids fluttered and he gave a slight smile with the corners of his mouth, an inimitable smile, the only one of its kind in North America.

"It goes without saying, sir, they were private individuals, honest traders who are devoted to you, sir."

"Find out the names of the traders and give them my heartiest thanks through the press. Let the arrested man be tried with the full severity of the law. After he has been sentenced I will pardon him."

"The second attempt was also made in the park," continued the secretary. "A lady was observed looking up at the windows of your bedchamber, sir. The lady was found to be in possession of a small revolver."

"Was she young?"

"Fifty-three. An old maid."

"What did the crowd do?"

"The actions of the crowd were confined to tearing off her hat, breaking her umbrella, and trampling on her handbag. Such mild measures are to be explained by the early hour and the pitiful picture presented by the lady herself who immediately fell into a swoon at the sight of the enraged crowd."

"Give the old crow a passport and send her out of the United States immediately. Treat this incident very hazily in the press. What else?"

At five to nine Garin took a shower and then surrendered himself to the attentions of the barber and his four assistants. He sat in a special chair, like those dentists use, covered in a linen sheet in front of a triple mirror. His face was given a steam bath, and at the same time files, scissors, and chamois leather pads wielded by two blondes fluttered over the fingers of both hands while the nails of his toes were attended to by two skilled mulatto girls. His head was washed in several toilet waters and essences, given a slight touch with the curling-tongs, and arranged so that the bald patch did not show. The barber had been awarded the title of baronet for his exceptional artistry; he shaved Pyotr Petrovich, powdered him, and scented his face and head with several different perfumes—rose for the neck, lily of the valley behind the ears, *bouquet Vernet* for the temples, apple-blossom around the lips, and the most delicate of perfumes, "Twilight," for the beard.

After these manipulations the dictator might well have been wrapped in cellophane, placed in a box and sent to an exhibition. Garin could scarcely tolerate this procedure to the end; he was subjected to it every morning, and the newspapers wrote about his "quarter of an hour after the bath." And so he had to put up with it.

314

He then went to the dressing-room where he was awaited by two lackeys and the valet holding shirts, socks, shoes, and so on. For today he had selected a speckled brown suit. Those pigs of reporters had written that one of the most astounding talents of the dictator was his ability to select a tie. He had to submit and watch his step. Garin selected a peacock-blue tie. Cursing under his breath in Russian he tied it himself.

As he walked to the dining-room, decorated in medieval style, he thought to himself:

"I can't stand this for long, it's a hell of a regime they've foisted on me."

During breakfast (again not a drop of alcohol) the dictator was supposed to examine his correspondence. About three hundred letters lay on a tray of Sèvres china. Munching fried smoked fish, tasteless ham, and oatmeal porridge boiled in unsalted water (the morning meal of sportsmen and people of high morals), Garin picked out the crackling envelopes at random. Opening them with a dirty fork he read hurriedly:

"My heart beats wildly, I am so excited my hand is scarcely able to pen these lines. What would you think of me? Oh, God, I love you. I have loved you from the moment I saw your photo in the newspaper (name of paper). I am young. I am the daughter of respectable parents. I am burning up with the desire to become a wife and mother...."

Such love letters from different parts of America were usually accompanied by a photograph. The pictures of these pretty faces (tens of thousands of them had accumulated in the course of a month) with their fluffy hair, innocent eyes, and silly noses were horribly, deadly boring. To make that crazy journey from Krestovsky Island to Washington, from the unheated room in the deserted house in the Petrograd District where Garin had dashed from corner to corner with clenched fists seeking the almost non-existent way out (flight on the *Bibigonda*) to the president's gilded chair in the Senate where he had to go twenty minutes later ... to horrify the whole world, to become master of the subterranean ocean of gold, to achieve power over the world—all this only to be trapped into the most boring Philistine life.

"To hell with it all!"

Garin threw down his napkin and drummed on the table with his fingers. He was cornered. He had reached the summit and there was nothing else to strive for. He was dictator. Should he demand the title of Emperor? If he did they would worry him to death. Flee? Where to? And what for? To Zoë? Ah, Zoë! That important relation that had come into being on a damp, warm night in the old hotel at Ville d'Avray, had been broken. The whole fantasy of Garin's adventure had been born that night, to the rustle of leaves outside the window, amidst tormenting caresses. He had been filled with the exultation of the forthcoming struggle, and it had been easy to say, "I place the world at your feet." But now Garin was the victor. The world was at his feet. And Zoë?—Zoë was far from him, a stranger, Madame Lamolle, the Queen of Golden Island. Somebody else's head was turned dizzy by the perfume of her hair and the steady gaze of her cold, dreamy eyes. He, Garin, the world conqueror, had to eat unsalted porridge, and yawn as he looked at the foolish physiognomies sent him. The fantastic dream of Ville d'Avray had drifted away from him. Issue decrees, ape the great man, be respectable on all occasions. Oh, hell. A drop of brandy wouldn't do any harm.

He turned towards the footmen who stood like stuffed dummies near the doors. Two of them stepped forward immediately, one bowed in his direction in an attitude of interrogation and the other said in a sexless voice:

"Your Excellency's car is ready."

The dictator entered the Senate banging his heels defiantly on the floor. He took his place in the gilded chair and in a metallic voice pronounced the formula opening the session. His brows were knitted and his face expressed energy and determination. Dozens of cameras and cinecameras photographed him at that moment. Hundreds of beautiful women in the boxes reserved for the public cast adoring and voluptuous glances at him.

On this day the Senate had the honour of offering him new titles: Lord of Lower Wales, Duke of Naples, Comte de Charleroi, Baron Mühlhausen and Co-Emperor of All Russia; the United States of America, being a democratic power with no titles to offer, had given him the rank of "God's Businessman."

Garin tendered his thanks. He would have found great pleasure in spitting on those fat and respectable bald heads that sat in front of him in the amphitheatre of the world senate. He realized, however, that he would do nothing of the sort but would stand up and thank them.

"Just wait, you bastards," he thought as he stood up (pale, small in stature, and with a pointed beard) before the applauding amphitheatre, "until I bring you a draft decree on racial purity and the selection of the first thousand. . . ." Still he felt bound hand and foot and that as the bearer of such titles as Lord, Duke, Comte, and God's Businessman he would not do anything so drastic. Now he must leave the Senate Hall for a banquet. . . .

In the streets the dictator's car was greeted with shouts of welcome. If one looked closer one could see that the shouts came exclusively from hefty young men who looked like plain-clothes policemen. Garin bowed and waved a hand clad in a lemon-coloured glove. If he had not been born in Russia and had not lived through a revolution, that journey through the city, amidst cheering crowds expressing their loyalty by shouts of "Hip, hip, hurrah!" and throwing flowers at him, would have given him great pleasure. Garin, however, was a man whose mind had been poisoned. He was angry: "Cheap, cheap, shut your mouths, you oxen, there's nothing to shout about." At the entrance to the City Hall he got out of the car and dozens of ladies' hands (the daughters of kerosene, railway, canned goods, and other kings) showered him with flowers.

As he ran up the stairs he blew kisses right and left. In the banqueting hall music was played in honour of God's Businessman. He took his seat and everybody sat down. The snow-white tables, arranged in the form of the letter "U," were a mass of bright flowers and glittering cut-glass. Beside each plate lay eleven silver knives and as many forks of different shapes and sizes, to say nothing of spoons, large and small. He dare not make a mistake in taking the right knife and fork to eat.

Garin gritted his teeth in exasperation: aristocrats! Out of the two hundred people at the banquet a good hundred and a half had sold fish in the streets, and now they did not find it decent to eat with less than eleven forks! But all eyes were fixed on the dictator and on this occasion, too, he submitted to the pressure of public opinion and his behaviour was exemplary.

After turtle soup the speeches began. Garin listened to them standing, a glass of champagne in his hand. "I'll get drunk!" was an idea that zigzagged through his head. But even that was out of the question.

He assured his two pretty, talkative neighbours that he really did read the Bible every evening.

Between dessert and coffee he answered the speeches:

"Ladies and gentlemen, I regard the power with which you have endowed me as the finger of God, and it is the sacred duty of my conscience to employ this power, unprecedented in world history, for the extension of our markets, for the prosperity of our industry and commerce, and for the suppression of the immoral attempts of the mob to overthrow the existing order of things. . . ." And so on.

The speech made a delightful impression. It is true that at the end of it the dictator added, as though to himself, three very energetic words, but they were said in an unknown tongue, presumably Russian, and passed unnoticed. Then Garin bowed on all sides and left the hall to the music of trumpets, the roll of kettle-drums, and shouts of joy. He drove home.

In the vestibule of the palace he threw his hat and stick on the floor (panic amongst the footmen who rushed to pick them up), plunged his hands deeply into his trouser pockets and, thrusting his beard out angrily, marched up the thick carpet of the stairs. His private secretary awaited him in his study.

"There will be a dinner in honour of the dictator at seven o'clock in the Pacific Club; a symphony orchestra will play."

"I see," answered Garin and again added those three incomprehensible Russian words. "What else?"

"At eleven o'clock in the White Hall of the Indiana Hotel there will be a ball in honour of. . . ."

"Telephone to both places that I'm ill, that I ate too much crab at the City Hall."

"I make bold to suggest that a pretended illness may only give rise to greater trouble: the whole city will immediately come here to express sympathy. Apart from that there are the newspaper reporters—they would even climb down the chimneys."

"You're right. I'll go." Garin rang the bell. "Bath. Get evening dress ready with all orders and regalia." For some time he walked or rather ran up and down the carpet. "What else?"

319

"In the reception-room some ladies are awaiting an audience."

"I won't receive them."

"They have been waiting since midday."

"I don't want them. Turn them out!"

"It's too difficult to combat them. I make bold to say: these are ladies from the highest society. There are three famous women writers, two cinema stars, one who is world-famous for her travels in a car and another famous for her philanthropy."

"All right, send one in. It doesn't matter which."

Garin sat down at his desk (on the left, a radio receiver, on the right, the telephones, in front, the mouth-piece of a dictaphone). He took a clean sheet of paper, dipped a pen in the inkwell, and then stopped to think.

"Zoë," he began to write in Russian, in a firm, round hand, "my friend, you are the only one who will understand what a fool I've made of myself...."

"Sh-sh-sh..." came from behind his back.

Garin turned sharply in the chair. The secretary was already slipping out of the side door—in the middle of the room stood a lady in light green. She gave a weak little scream and clenched her hands. Her face wore the appropriate expression for one standing before the greatest man in history. Garin looked at her for a second and shrugged his shoulders.

"Get undressed!" he ordered brusquely, turned in his chair and continued writing.

At a quarter to eight Garin hurried to his desk. He was in evening dress with all his stars and regalia and a sash across his waistcoat. There were abrupt signals coming from the wireless receiver which was always tuned to the wavelength of the Golden Island station. Garin put

320

on the earphones. Zoë's voice, clear but toneless, like a voice from another planet, kept repeating in Russian:

"Garin, we're done for.... Garin, we re done for.... There's an insurrection on the island. The big hyperboloid has been seized. Jansen's with me. If we can we'll escape on the *Arizona*."

The voice broke off. Garin stood at the desk but did not remove the earphones. His private secretary, with Garin's silk hat and walking-stick in his hands, was waiting at the door. The receiver again began to emit signals. This time it was a man's voice, sharp and gruff, speaking in English:

"Workers of the World. You know the extent and results of the panic that swept the United States...."

He listened to Shelga's proclamation to the end and then removed the earphones. Without any haste, with a crooked smile, he lit a cigar. Out of the drawer of his desk he took a bundle of hundred-dollar notes and a small nickel apparatus shaped like a revolver: this was his latest invention, the pocket hyperboloid. With a motion of his eyebrows he called the secretary.

"Order the touring car to be ready immediately."

For the first time since he had been in Garin's service the secretary raised his eyelids and his reddish eyes registered surprise.

"But, Your Excellency...."

"Shut up. Give an immediate order to the General in Command of the army, the city governor, and the civil authorities that martial law is introduced as from seven o'clock. Riots to be suppressed by shooting."

The secretary immediately disappeared through the door.

Garin walked over to the triple mirror. His face was pale and he looked like a little wax figure in his orders and regalia. He looked at himself for a long time and suddenly one of his eyes winked mockingly of its own accord. "Take to your heels, Pierre Harry, take to your heels as quickly as you can," he said to himself in a whisper.

122

Towards evening on 23rd June things began to move on Golden Island. The whole day the ocean had been stormy. Heavy black clouds came up from the south-west and fiery zigzags tore the sky asunder. The island was covered in a haze of fine spray.

Towards evening the storm drew farther off, the lightning flashed far away on the horizon but the wind continued with unabated fury; it bowed trees to the ground, bent the tall lamp-posts, tore the roofs from the barracks in formless sheets, and whistled and howled in every corner of the island with such Satanic fury that every living thing sought shelter. Ships strained at their hawsers in the harbour, several barges were carried out to sea; in a small bay opposite the palace the *Arizona* bobbed up and down like a fisherman's float.

The population of the island had been considerably reduced in recent times. Work in the mine had been stopped. Zoë's tremendous building programme had not been commenced. Only about five hundred of the six thousand workers still remained on the island. The others had left, loaded with gold. The empty barracks, Luna Park, and the brothels had been removed and the ground levelled for the future structures.

There was absolutely nothing for the police guard to do on that peaceful patch of land. The time had gone when the yellow and white policemen had stood with their rifles on rocks like watch-dogs, or marched up and down the barbed-wire alleys, significantly rattling their rifle bolts. The policemen began to drink. They longed for big cities, for smart restaurants, for jolly women. They asked for leave, they threatened to revolt. There was, however, a strict order from Garin to the effect that nobody was to be granted leave or discharged. The police barracks were kept under the constant menace of the muzzle of the big hyperboloid.

There was heavy gambling in the barracks. Losses were paid in promissory notes since everybody was fed up with the sight of the gold that lay around in heaps of ingots. They staked their mistresses, their weapons, their well-smoked pipes, a bottle of old brandy, or just played for "a smack across the muzzle." By evening the whole police force was dead drunk. General Subbotin found it difficult to maintain—well, not discipline, that would be expecting too much, but just ordinary common decency.

"Gentlemen officers, you ought to be ashamed of yourselves," General Subbotin's voice could be heard every day in the officers' club, "you have sunk to the very bottom. you vomit on the floor, and the place stinks like a brothel. You hang around in your underpants because you've gambled away your trousers. It grieves me that I am unfortunate enough to have to command such a herd of swine."

No measures proved effective. Still, there had never before been such drunkenness as on the day of the storm, 23rd June. The howling wind brought with it a terrible nostalgia. it brought up distant memories and old wounds were opened. The spray beat at the window like rain. Celestial artillery roared time and again in a hurricane of fire. The walls trembled, glasses rattled on the tables. The police guards sat with their elbows on long tables, their dashing heads in their cupped hands, unwashed, uncombed; they were singing a song that belonged to their enemies: "Oh, where are you rolling, little apple...." This song, carried to a tiny island lost in the wastes of the ocean, the devil alone knew from what remote life, was like a breath from their distant homeland. Drunken heads nodded and tears rolled down their cheeks. General Subbotin had become hoarse in his efforts to check the debauchery; finally he sent them all to the devil and got drunk himself.

The Revolutionary Committee's reconnaissance (in the person of Ivan Gusev) reported on the deplorable situation at the police barracks. Shortly after six in the evening Shelga, accompanied by five hefty miners, went to the guard-room and started a quarrel with two tipsy sentries who stood guard over the arms racks. The sentries, carried away by the colourful Russian colloquialisms, were easily distracted and were soon knocked off their feet, disarmed and bound hand and foot. Shelga obtained a hundred rifles. These were immediately distributed amongst the workers who came running from lamp-post to lamp-post, from tree to tree and crawling across the open spaces.

A hundred men burst into the police barracks. There was a tremendous commotion and the police met the attackers with bottles and stools, retreated, took up positions, and opened fire from their revolvers. On the staircases, in the corridors and in the dormitories the battle raged. Drunken and sober men fought in a hand-to-hand struggle. Savage howls escaped through the broken windows. The attackers were few in number, one to five, but they used their callused hands like flails against the flabby yellow-white policemen. Reinforcements arrived and the police began jumping out of the windows. Fire broke out in several places and the barracks were soon hidden in smoke.

123

Jansen ran through the empty, unlighted rooms of the palace. Surf seethed and thundered on the verandah. The wind howled, rattling the window-frames. Jansen called to Madame Lamolle, and listened with growing alarm.

He ran downstairs to Garin's apartments, taking the stairs in giant strides. Below he could hear shots and odd shouts. He looked into the inner garden—it was deserted, not a soul was to be seen. On the opposite side, under an ivy-clad arch, people outside were trying to break down the gates. How could he have slept so soundly that only a bullet which broke the window had awakened him? Had Madame Lamolle escaped? Could she have been killed?

He opened the first door he came to and went in. Four bluish spheres and a fifth, hanging from the mosaic ceiling, lit up tables covered with all sorts of apparatus, marble panels with measuring instruments, varnished boxes and cupboards with electronic lamps, the driving belt of a dynamo, and a writing-desk littered with drawings. This was Garin's workroom. On the floor lay a crumpled handkerchief. Jansen picked it up, it smelled of Madame Lamolle's perfume. Then he remembered that a subterranean passage led from this room to the lift of the hyperboloid tower and that there must be a hidden door somewhere. Madame Lamolle had, of course, hurried to the tower as soon as the first shots were fired. Why hadn't he thought of that before!

He searched for the hidden door. Then came the sound of breaking glass, the trample of feet, and voices calling hurriedly to each other on the other side of the wall. They had broken into the palace. Why was Madame Lamolle so slow? He jumped to the carved double doors and locked them; he took out his revolver. It seemed that the whole palace was filled with the trampling of feet and shouting voices.

"Jansen!"

Before him stood Madame Lamolle. Her bloodless lips were moving but he did not hear what she said. He stared at her, breathing heavily.

"We're done for, Jansen, we're done for!..." she repeated.

She was wearing a black dress, her thin, clenched hands were pressed to her breast. Her eyes were as troubled as a blue storm.

"The lift of the big hyperboloid is not working," said Madame Lamolle, "it has been raised to the top. Somebody is sitting in the tower. He climbed up the outside, up the lattice-work. I'm sure it's that boy, Gusev. . . ."

She glanced at the carved doors and her clenched fingers cracked. Her brows were knitted in a frown. Behind the doors dozens of feet were stamping madly. From outside came a savage howl followed by some bustling and then hurried shots. Madame Lamolle sat down swiftly at the desk and closed a switch; the dynamo began to hum softly and the pear-shaped valves gave off a bluish glow. She tapped with the key sending out call signals.

"Garin, we're done for. . . . Garin, we're done for . . ." she said, bending over the microphone.

A minute later the carved doors cracked under blows from fists and feet.

"Open the door! Open! . . ."

Madame Lamolle took Jansen by the hand, dragged him towards the wall, and with her foot pressed on a whorl in the carved ornament near the floor. A cloth-covered panel between two half-columns slid back noiselessly. Madame Lamolle and Jansen slipped through the secret opening into the underground passage and the panel returned to its original place.

After the storm the stars winked and burned brighter than ever over the troubled ocean. The wind was strong enough to carry them off their feet and the surf thundered against the rocky shore. Through the noise of the ocean shots could be heard. Hiding behind bushes and rocks, Madame Lamolle and Jansen ran to the North Bay where a motor-boat was always kept. On the right the black outlines of the palace towered above them, on the left were the white-capped waves, and in the distance the dancing lights of the *Arizona*. Behind them was the latticed silhouette of the hyperboloid tower reaching up into the sky; at the very summit there was a light.

"Look," cried Madame Lamolle, turning back as she ran and waving her hand in the direction of the tower, "there's a light up there. That's death!"

They went down a steep slope to a bay protected from the waves. Here a little motor-boat bobbed up and down; it was moored to a small landing-stage at the foot of the staircase leading to the palace verandah. She jumped into the boat, ran to the stern, and with trembling hands pressed the starter.

"Quicker, Jansen, hurry up!"

The motor-boat was locked to a chain. Jansen thrust the barrel of his revolver into the hasp and tried to break the lock. Doors on the verandah opened with a crash and armed men appeared. Jansen threw down his revolver and seized the chain near the staple. His muscles cracked, his neck swelled, and the hook on his tunic collar broke. Suddenly the engine began to splutter. The men on the terrace were already running down the staircase waving their rifles and shouting to them to stop.

Mustering every ounce of strength Jansen tore out the chain and pushed the spluttering boat far out into the water; on his hands and knees he crawled along the deck towards the tiller.

Describing a small arc the motor-boat raced towards the narrow outlet of the bay followed by shots from the shore.

"Lower the storm ladder, you devils," roared Jansen from the motor-boat that was dancing on the waves beside the *Arizona*. "Where's the first mate? Sleeping? I'll hang him!"

"Here I am, sir."

"Cast off the anchor chains, start up the engines. Full speed ahead! Lights out!"

"Aye, aye, sir."

Madame Lamolle was the first to mount the ladder. She leaned over the rail and saw Jansen try to stand up, fall on his side, and try in vain to catch a rope that had been thrown to him. A wave covered him together with the boat and then again his face appeared, spitting out salt water and distorted with pain.

"What's the matter, Jansen?"

"I'm wounded."

Four sailors jumped into the boat, seized Jansen and carried him on board. On deck he fell again, his hands pressed to his side, and lost consciousness. He was carried into his cabin.

At full speed, cutting through the waves, the *Arizona* drew away from the island. The first mate took command. Madame Lamolle stood beside him on the bridge, her hands gripping the rail. Water poured off her, her dress clung to her body. She watched the distant glow grow brighter (the police barracks burning) and saw clouds of smoke, pierced with spiral tongues of flame, cover the island. Suddenly she seemed to notice something for she seized the officer by the sleeve.

"Change your course to the south-west."

"There are reefs there, Madame."

"That's not your business. Sail through there keeping the island on the portside."

She ran to the latticed tower of the stern hyperboloid. A sheet of water racing from the bows along the deck swept her off her feet. A sailor picked her up, wet and mad with rage. She tore herself away from him and climbed up the tower.

On the island, high above the smoke of the conflagration, a star shone blindingly bright—that was the big hyperboloid working, searching for the *Arizona*.

Madame Lamolle had decided to fight since there was no possibility of getting away from a death ray with a radius of many miles from its high tower. The ray at first darted about amongst the stars along the horizon, describing a circle of two hundred and fifty miles in a few minutes. Now it was persistently searching the western sector of the ocean raising heavy clouds of steam where it touched the crests of the waves.

The *Arizona* was moving at full speed some seven miles off-shore. She dived up to the masthead in the troughs of the waves and then rose again on the crests. It was at such moments that Madame Lamolle hit back at the island with her ray from the stern tower. Already wooden buildings here and there had caught fire. Showers of sparks were thrown high into the air as though the fire were being blown by some giant bellows. The red glow cast its reflection over the whole of the black, troubled ocean. When the *Arizona* rose on the crest of a wave her silhouette was observed from the island and the incandescent white needle of the ray danced round her, darting up and down in zigzags, striking the waves quite close to her, at first near the bows and then just astern.

It seemed to Zoë that the blinding star was flashing straight in her eyes, while she herself tried to aim the muzzle of her hyperboloid direct at the star on the distant tower. The *Arizona*'s screws raced madly in the air as she nosed down into the trough of a high wave. That was the moment when the ray found its target, rose, flickered, as though measuring the distance, and then dropped straight on to the profile of the yacht. Zoë closed her eyes. The hearts of all those on board the vessel who watched that duel must have stood still.

When Zoë opened her eyes there was a wall of water in front of her—the *Arizona* had dived into an abyss. "This isn't death yet," thought Zoë. She took her hands off the hyperboloid and they hung helpless by her sides.

When they were again lifted by a wave they saw why death had given them a miss. Huge clouds of smoke covered the island and the hyperboloid tower—the oil tanks must have blown up. The *Arizona* could now get away quietly behind the smoke screen.

Zoë did not know whether she had managed to smash the big hyperboloid or whether its star was only hidden by the smoke. What did it matter now.... With difficulty she climbed down from the tower and made her way, holding on to the rigging, to the cabin where Jansen lay breathing heavily behind the blue curtains. She dropped into an armchair, struck a wax vesta, and lit a cigarette.

The *Arizona*'s course was north-west. The wind had abated somewhat but the sea was still boisterous. Many times a day the yacht sent out prearranged signals, trying to get in touch with Garin, and hundreds of thousands of wireless receivers all over the world heard Zoë's voice: "What are we to do? Where are we to go? Our latitude and longitude are such and such. We await orders."

Ocean-going steamers that picked up the message hurried away from the terrifying spot where the *Arizona*, the "menace of the seas," had again appeared.

124

Golden Island was wrapped in a cloud of burning oil. A calm had set in after the hurricane and the black cloud rose straight up to the clear sky casting a huge shadow for several miles over the ocean.

The island seemed dead, the only sign of life being the rattle of the elevator scoops at the mine.

The silence was broken by the music of a slow, solemn march. Through the smoky gloom some two hundred people could be seen: they were marching with their heads raised, their faces set and determined. At the head of the column four men carried something wrapped in a red banner. They made their way up the rocky eminence where the hyperboloid tower stood; at the foot of the tower they laid down their burden.

It was the body of Ivan Gusev. He had been killed the day before during the battle with the *Arizona*. Climbing the lattice-work sides of the tower like a cat he had switched on the hyperboloid and searched for the *Arizona* amongst the huge waves.

The fiery ray from the *Arizona* danced over the island, setting fire to buildings, cutting lamp-posts and trees down. "The bitch," whispered Ivan, turning the muzzle of his apparatus and helping himself with his tongue as he had done during Tarashkin's lessons.

He caught the *Arizona* in his sights and struck with the ray close to her bows and stern, gradually shortening the angle. The smoke from the burning oil reservoirs hampered him. Suddenly the *Arizona*'s ray turned into a blazing star that struck right into Ivan's eyes. Cut through by the ray he fell on to the housing of the hyperboloid.

"Rest in peace, Ivan, you died a hero," said Shelga. He dropped on to his knees beside Ivan's body, turned back the corner of the red banner, and kissed the boy's forehead.

Trumpets sounded and the voices of two hundred men sang the *Internationale*.

Shortly after this a powerful twin-engined aeroplane rose out of the cloud of smoke. Gaining altitude, it turned off to the west....

125

"All your instructions have been carried out, sir."

Garin locked the door, went over to a flat bookcase, and passed his hand over the right side of it.

"The knob of the secret door is on the left," said the secretary with an ironic smile.

Garin cast a swift, strange glance at him. He pressed the button and the bookcase moved silently away, revealing a narrow entrance into the secret rooms of the palace.

"You first, please," said Garin, making way for the secretary. The secretary turned pale while Garin, with icy politeness, raised the muzzle of the ray revolver to the level of his head. "It would be more sensible to obey, Mr. Secretary...."

126

The doors of the captain's cabin were wide open. Jansen lay on his bunk.

The yacht was scarcely moving; in the silence the waves could be heard splashing against the hull of the ship.

Jansen's wish had come true—once again he was at sea alone with Madame Lamolle. He knew that he was dying. For several days he had struggled against death— he had a penetrating wound of the stomach—but at last he gave up. He gazed at the stars through the open door whence came the breath of eternity. He felt neither desire nor fear, nothing but the importance of the transition to eternal peace.

Madame Lamolle entered the cabin, a shadow against the background of the stars. She bent over him and asked in a whisper how he felt. He answered with a movement of his eyelids and she understood that to mean: "I'm happy because you're with me." Then his chest heaved several times spasmodically, gasping for breath; Zoë sat beside the bunk without a movement. Sorrowful thoughts must have filled her head.

"My friend, my only friend," she said in quiet despair, "you are the only one on earth who loved me. To you alone I was dear. You are going.... How cold, how cold...."

Jansen did not answer although a movement of his eyelids seemed to confirm the approaching coldness. She saw that his nose had grown sharper and that his mouth formed a weak smile. A short time before his cheeks had been flushed with fever, now they were waxen. She waited many minutes more, then touched his hand with her lips. He was still alive. Slowly he opened his eyes and his lips parted. Zoë thought he was trying to say, "Good."

Then his face changed. She turned away and drew the blue curtains with care.

127

The secretary, the most elegant man in the United States, was lying face downwards, his cold fingers clutching at the carpet; he had died instantaneously, without a sound. Garin bit his trembling lips and slowly returned the ray revolver to his jacket pocket. Then he went to a low steel door, selected a combination on the disc known to him alone, and the door opened. He entered a ferro-concrete, windowless room.

This was the dictator's private safe. In place of gold or securities there was something of immeasurably greater value to Garin in the safe: it was Garin's third double, Baron Korf, a Russian émigré who had sold himself for a huge sum of money, had been brought from Europe and kept in secret, at first on Golden Island and then in the secret rooms of the palace.

He sat in a leather armchair, his feet on a low, gilded table on which stood vases with fruits and sweets (he was forbidden to drink). Books—English detective stories— were lying on the floor. From sheer boredom Baron Korf was spitting cherry stones at the screen of the television set that stood about three yards from his chair.

"At last," he said turning lazily towards Garin as he came in. "Where the hell have you been? Listen, do you intend to keep me in this hole much longer? By God, I'd rather starve in Paris...."

Instead of answering Garin took off his sash and threw down the dress jacket with orders and regalia.

"Get undressed."

"What for?" asked Baron Korf, with a flicker of curiosity.

"Give me your clothes."

"What's it all about?"

"And your passport, all your papers.... Where's your razor?"

Garin sat down at the dressing table. His face screwed up in pain as he scraped off his beard and moustache without lathering his skin.

"Incidentally, there's a man lying in the next room. Remember, he's your private secretary. When he's asked for, you may say that you've sent him on a secret mission.... Do you get that?"

"But what's it all about, I'm asking you?" shouted Baron Korf, grabbing Garin's trousers as they flew across the room.

"I'm going to leave here by a secret door leading to the park and my car. Hide the secretary in the fireplace and go into my study. Immediately call Rolling on the telephone. I hope you have thoroughly memorized all the workings of my dictatorship. I come first, then my first deputy, the Chief of the Secret Police, then my second deputy, the Chief of the Propaganda Department, then my third deputy, the Chief of the Department of Provocation. Next comes the Secret Council of the Three Hundred, headed by Rolling. If you have not become an absolute idiot you should know all this by heart. Take off your trousers, damn you. You'll tell Rolling by phone that you, that is, Pierre Garin, will take over command of the army and the police. You're in for a tough fight, pal."

"One minute, suppose Rolling should guess from my voice that it's not you but me. . . ."

"What the hell does it matter to them? . . . As long as there's a dictator. . . ."

"Does that mean that from this minute I'm to be turned into Pyotr Petrovich Garin?"

"I wish you success. May you enjoy your power to the full. All the instructions are on my writing-desk. I'm disappearing. . . ."

Garin winked at his double as he had done recently at the mirror and disappeared through the door.

128

No sooner was Garin driving alone in a closed car through the central streets of the city than all doubt left him, he realized that he had taken his departure only just in time. The working-class districts and the suburbs were noisy with hundreds of thousands of people crowding in the streets. Here and there the flags of the revolution waved over their heads. Barricades were hastily erected across the streets; overturned omnibuses, furniture thrown out of windows, doors, lamp-posts, and iron railings provided the material.

Garin's experienced eye told him that the workers were well armed. Lorries that forced their way through the crowds carried machine-guns, hand-grenades, rifles. This was without doubt the work of Shelga.

A few hours before Garin would not have hesitated to hurl his troops against the insurrectionists. Now, however, he only pressed his foot more nervously on the accelerator as he raced along amidst curses and shouts: "Down with the Dictator! Down with the Council of the Three Hundred!"

The hyperboloid was in Shelga's hands. The insurrectionists knew this and shouted about it. Shelga would carry the revolution through in the same way as a conductor plays an heroic symphony.

The loudspeakers, set up on Garin's orders during the gold sale, were now being used against him—they carried news of widespread insurrection.

Garin's double, contrary to Pyotr Petrovich's expectations, had begun by determined action and not without some success. His picked troops stormed the barricades. The police dropped gas-bombs from aircraft. Cavalry sabred their way through crowds at crossroads. Special squads smashed open doors, broke into working-class homes and destroyed every living thing.

Nevertheless the insurrectionists held out stubbornly. In other cities, in the bigger industrial centres, they took the offensive with great determination. By midday the flames of insurrection had spread over the whole country.

Garin got every ounce of speed he could out of the sixteen-cylinder engine of his car. Like a hurricane he swept through the streets of provincial towns, knocking pigs and dogs out of his way, killing chickens. Before pedestrians had time to look round, the huge, black, dusty car of the dictator, roaring and rapidly diminishing in size, disappeared round a bend.

He stopped only for a few moments to refill the tank and top up the radiator. He raced on all through the night.

By next morning the dictator's power had still not been overthrown. The capital was in flames, fired by incendiary bombs, something like fifty thousand dead lay in the streets. "Good old Baron!" laughed Garin, when the loudspeaker at a street corner told him the news.

At five o'clock the next day his car was fired on.

At seven o'clock, driving through some provincial town he saw revolutionary banners and crowds of singing people.

The whole of the second night he drove on westwards—on to the Pacific Ocean. At last, as he was filling up with petrol at dawn on the third day he heard Shelga's well-known voice in the loudspeaker:

"Victory, victory.... Comrades, the terrible weapon of the revolution, the hyperboloid, is in my hands...."

Garin gritted his teeth, did not listen to the end, but hurried on. At ten o'clock in the morning he saw the first placard at the roadside; in huge letters the following was written on a hoarding:

"Comrades.... The Dictator was taken alive but proved to be Garin's double, left in his place. Pyotr Garin has escaped. He is fleeing westwards. Comrades, be vigilant, stop the dictator's car. (Here followed a description.) Garin must not escape revolutionary justice."

At midday Garin noticed a motor-cycle following him. He did not hear the shots but a bullet-hole surrounded by cracks appeared on the windscreen a few inches from his head. The back of his head went cold. He squeezed all he could out of the engine, raced over a hill, and made for some wooded mountains. An hour later he entered a canyon. The engine began back-firing and then choked. Garin jumped out, twisted the wheel and sent the machine flying down a precipice; stretching his cramped legs with difficulty he clambered up a steep slope to a pine wood.

From above he saw three motor-cycles tear along the highway. The last of the three stopped. An armed man, naked to the waist, jumped off and bent over the precipice where the dictator's car was lying.

In the wood Pyotr Petrovich threw away all his clothes except his trousers and a singlet, cut the leather of his shoes, and set out on foot to the nearest railway station.

On the fourth day he reached a lonely farm on the seacoast near Los Angeles where, as usual, his dirigible stood in a hangar ready for immediate flight.

129

Dawn broke in a cloudless sky; a rosy haze lay over the ocean. Leaning out of the porthole of the gondola Garin, with great difficulty, discovered with the aid of binoculars the tiny shell of the yacht far down below. The vessel lay dozing on the smooth water, sparkling through the light haze.

The dirigible began to lose altitude. Its body gleamed brightly in the morning sun. As the gondola touched the water a boat put off from the yacht, Zoë at the tiller. Garin could scarcely recognize her so drawn was her face. He jumped into the boat with a smile as though nothing had happened, sat down beside Zoë, and patted her hand.

"I'm so glad to see you. Don't worry, baby. It didn't come off, but what does it matter. We'll start something else going. What are you pulling this long face for?"

Zoë frowned and turned away so as not to look at his face.

"I have just buried Jansen. I'm tired. And now nothing at all matters."

The sun appeared from beyond the horizon, the huge ball sped across the empty blue space, and the haze melted like a phantom.

A broad path of sunlight with bright oily speckles lay across the sea and against it the *Arizona*'s three sloping masts and hyperboloid towers cast a black silhouette.

"A bath, breakfast, and bed," said Garin.

130

The *Arizona* turned back to Golden Island. Garin had decided to strike a blow at the very heart of the insurrection—to capture the big hyperboloid and the mine.

The yacht's masts were chopped down and the hyperboloid towers were masked with boards and sails to change the ship's lines and enable her to approach Golden Island unobserved.

Garin had confidence in himself, he was determined and cheerful—his good mood had returned.

Next morning the captain (Jansen's first mate) pointed to some feathery clouds in alarm. They rose rapidly from over the horizon and covered the whole sky at the tremendous height of some thirty thousand feet. A storm was approaching, perhaps the dreaded typhoon.

Garin was busy with his own plans and told the captain he could go to hell.

"Typhoon? Don't talk rot. Full speed ahead!"

The captain looked gloomily from the bridge at the quickly gathering clouds and ordered the crew to secure the boats and everything that might be washed away and to batten down the hatches.

The sea grew dark. The wind came in squalls, its ominous howl warning the sailors of impending catastrophe. The heralds of the storm, the high cirrus clouds, gave way to low black masses crawling over the sea. The wind began to churn up the sea and the heavy rollers were flecked with white foam.

From the east a dense black cloud with a leaden lining came rolling towards the yacht. The squalls increased in fury. Giant waves crashed over the vessel's decks. Soon there were no foam-flecked crests, the fury of the wind tore them from the waves and spread them in a blanket of fine spray.

"Go below," said the captain to Zoë and Garin. "In a quarter of an hour we shall be in the centre of the whirlwind and the engines won't save us."

The typhoon struck the *Arizona* in all its fury. The yacht rolled from side to side until her keel was out of the water, she no longer answered rudder or engines but raced round in rapidly diminishing circles to the centre of the typhoon, the "hole," as the sailor call it.

The centre of the typhoon is a "hole" often as much as three miles in diameter; winds of hurricane strength surge in all directions from this centre in their effort to restore equilibrium on the periphery.

It was into such a maelstrom that the frail shell of the *Arizona* was carried.

The black clouds were so low that they reached the deck. It was as black as night. The yacht's hull creaked and groaned, the people on deck hung on to any fixed object to save themselves from being blown or washed away. The captain ordered the sailors to lash him to the rail of the bridge.

The *Arizona* was lifted mountain-high on a wave, rolled over on her side, and slid down into the depths. Suddenly they came into a patch of brilliant sunlight, where there was no wind and transparent green water like molten glass rose in waves as high as a ten-storey house that crashed into each other with a terrific splash as though Neptune, the Lord of the Depths, was slapping his hands on the water in anger.

This was the centre of the typhoon, the most dangerous spot. Here the stream of air drove vertically upwards carrying the fine spray to a height of thirty thousand feet where it spread in the form of cirrus clouds, the heralds of the typhoon.

Everything had been swept from the decks of the *Arizona*, boats, hyperboloid towers, the funnel, and the bridge together with the captain.

The typhoon, surrounded by darkness and whirling winds, raced on across the ocean carrying with it on the tops of gigantic waves the yacht *Arizona*.

The engines had burned out, the rudder had been torn off.

"It can't stand it any longer," groaned Zoë.

"It must end some time. Oh, hell!" answered Garin, hoarsely.

They were battered and bleeding from being hurled against the walls and the furniture of the cabin. Garin had a bad cut on his head. Zoë lay on the floor holding on to the leg of the bunk. Together with the two people, suitcases, books that had fallen out of the bookcase, sofa cushions, life-belts, oranges, and broken crockery rolled about the floor.

"Garin, I can't stand it, throw me in the sea."

A terrific jolt tore Zoë from the bunk and sent her rolling. Garin tumbled across her and was brought up against the door.

Then came a crash and rending sounds—the thunder of falling water—human wails. The cabin fell apart and a gigantic torrent of water caught up the two people and hurled them into the seething, cold green depths.

When Garin opened his eyes, some four inches from his nose a tiny hermit crab, that had crawled half-way into a mother-of-pearl shell, stared at him and wiggled its whiskers in astonishment. Garin tried hard to understand: "Yes, I'm alive...." For a long time, however, he had not strength enough to get up. He lay on his side on the sand with his right arm injured. His face racked with pain, he made an effort to pull up his legs and sat up.

Near by stood a palm-tree, the wind bending its slim trunk and rustling its leaves. Garin got to his feet and staggered along the beach. All round, as far as the eye could see, were blue-green sunlit waves that broke with a crash on the low seashore. A few dozen palms spread their wide, fan-like leaves to the wind. Here and there on the beach lay fragments of wood, boxes, rags, ropes—all that was left of the *Arizona* that had gone down on the outer reef of a coral island together with her crew.

Limping painfully, Garin made his way to the interior of the island where there was high ground covered in low bushes and bright green grass. There Zoë lay on her back with her arms outspread. Garin bent over her, afraid to touch her body lest he should feel the coldness of death. Zoë, however, was alive, her eyelids quivered, her parched lips opened.

There was a tiny lake of rain water on the coral island, it was bitter to the taste but fit to drink. In the shallows there were several kinds of shellfish, polyps and prawns, all of which had once served as food for primitive man. Palm leaves could serve as clothes to keep off the heat of the midday sun.

Two naked people cast up on the naked earth could manage to live somehow. And they began living on that island lost in the watery wastes of the Pacific Ocean. There was not even the hope that some passing ship might see them and take them off.

Garin collected shellfish or caught fish with his shirt in the fresh-water lake. In one of the boxes thrown up from the wreck of the *Arizona* Zoë found fifty copies of a luxuriously printed edition of projects for the palaces and pavilions of Golden Island. In the same book were the laws and rules of court etiquette "drawn up by Madame Lamolle, ruler of the world...."

For days on end Zoë would lie in the shade of their palm-leaf tent turning over the pages of the book created by her insatiable fantasy. The other forty-nine copies, bound in gold-embossed morocco leather, Garin used to build a wind-break.

Garin and Zoë did not talk. Why should they? What was there to talk about? They had been isolated individuals all their lives and now they had the most perfect isolation.

They lost count of the days and at last stopped trying to count them. When storms raged over the island the tiny lake filled with rain water, but there were long months when the sun burned fiercely in the cloudless sky and then they were forced to drink brackish water....

Maybe Garin and Zoë are to this day still gathering shellfish on that islet. Having eaten her fill Zoë sits down to turn the pages of the book with plans of marvellous palaces, where her beautiful statue stands amidst marble columns and gorgeous flower-beds while Garin, his nose buried in the sand, his back covered with his rotting jacket, relives the past in his dreams.